T0155090

THE COLLECTED FICTION
OF KENNETH KOCH

THE COLLECTED FICTION
OF KENNETH KOCH

Introduction by Jordan Davis

COFFEE HOUSE PRESS

MINNEAPOLIS

2005

COPYRIGHT © 2005 by the Kenneth Koch Literary Estate
BOOK DESIGN Coffee House Press
COVER ART *Luna Park,* 1960 © Alex Katz

Coffee House Press books are available to the trade through our primary distributor, Consortium Book Sales & Distribution, 1045 Westgate Drive, Saint Paul, MN 55114. For personal orders, catalogs, or other information, write to: Coffee House Press, 27 North Fourth Street, Suite 400, Minneapolis, MN 55401.

Coffee House Press is a nonprofit literary publishing house. Support from private foundations, corporate giving programs, government programs, and generous individuals help make the publication of our books possible. We gratefully acknowledge their support in detail in the back of this book.

Good books are brewing at coffeehousepress.org

LIBRARY OF CONGRESS CATALOGING-IN-PUBLICATION DATA

Koch, Kenneth, 1925–2002
[Selections. 2005]
The collected fiction of Kenneth Koch / introduction by Jordan Davis.
p. cm.
ISBN-13: 978-1-56689-180-6 (hardcover : alk. paper)
ISBN-10: 1-56689-180-9 (hardcover : alk. paper)
ISBN-13: 978-1-56689-176-9 (pbk : alk. paper)
ISBN-10: 1-56689-176-0 (pbk : alk. paper)
I. Title.
PS3521.O27A6 2005
813'.54—dc22
2005012570

FIRST EDITION | FIRST PRINTING

1 3 5 7 9 8 6 4 2

Printed in Canada

CONTENTS

INTRODUCTION

by Jordan Davis

Love poetry, epic poetry, drama, opera, film, art, parody, criticism, pedagogy, comics, fiction: while it has long been clear that Kenneth Koch was an adventurous explorer of literary modes and genres, the extent of the territory he annexed is only now coming into view. This book includes an important part of that territory, all the fiction Koch considered complete for publication—two early stories, the novel *The Red Robins,* the collection *Hotel Lambosa,* and eight later stories—work that runs from exuberantly witty to startlingly clear, from brutal to tender, from self-critical to imperviously innocent. As for adventure some of the formal innovations in Koch's fiction can be appreciated instantly, while others are more challenging.

In 1975, not long after the release of his best-selling teaching guide *Rose, Where Did You Get That Red?,* he published both the popular and notorious poetry collection *The Art of Love* and the novel *The Red Robins.* Everything about the book, down to the rough paper, stood out from the literary fiction then on the market. Other Vintage paperbacks were designed to fit on lazy susan racks in drugstores and sell at drugstore prices, using seductively intellectual marketing copy on the back to close the deal. *The Red Robins,* on the other hand, appeared in the large format of smaller presses' paperbacks. At $5.95 its list price was three times the going rate for a paperback. And as for the cover copy:

> This is Kenneth Koch's first novel. It concerns a group of young aviators called the Red Robins who lead a strange existence going from place to place in Asia.

Full of comedy, mystery, suspense, *The Red Robins* brings into the realm of the novel certain remarkable qualities of Kenneth Koch's other work. It is a surprising and original book.

Indeed. Koch once said that what he liked in novels was "the excitement of love and the excitement of being alive, all the excitements next to each other . . . something enormously lacking in American and British novels. What's my favorite 19th-century English novel? Without thinking I'd say *Middlemarch*. But even that is lacking this sensuousness."* Partly an homage to the wide-eyed style of "boys' book" writers such as H. L. Sayler ("The Airship Boys" series), partly an attempt to fuse, as he put it, "feeling, thought, sensation, past, present, future, nonsense, sense, real-time, speeded up time, slowed down time," *The Red Robins* was from its first paragraph sufficiently unlike other fiction to startle all but the most intrepid reader:

> Jill ran her fingers down the tough golden beard of history. It was fine being there, but she wished there had been boards on the floor. Professor Flint was late; it was already three o'clock. "Chow down!" shouted the corporal, and all the men ran into the eating quarters. "Very tropical weather, Sergeant," said "Dutch," an unusual man who had been hanging around the camp a lot recently. The cord snapped, having suddenly come undone, and the hawsers slipped out onto the blue, frothy waters of Lake Superior.

Hawsers are ropes used to moor ships; the word recurs throughout the book, usually just in time to signal that a story you may have thought would turn out to be the real action of the novel is in fact slipping away. There are at least three distinct scenes in this first

---

*I interviewed Koch over several months in 1995. Part of that interview was published in the *American Poetry Review*; this quotation and all others attributed to Koch here are from the other, unpublished part.

paragraph alone, four if Professor Flint is late to meet someone besides either Jill or the corporal. It would be a mistake to see these scenes as being in an ironic relation to each other, but neither can they rightly be called absurd. What is truer to the dazzling effect of these semi-related actions—presented without pause for six pages—is that this "slipping away" feeling *is* the real action. Koch explained how he assembled the first chapter:

> I tried to make it so I got a surprising sensation out of every sentence and it was constantly changing directions. I tried to supervise it in such a way that all these changing directions were like some kind of town. . . . All the sentences were like the last sentences of novels or the first sentences of short stories. . . . I tried to get together twenty or thirty sentences like this.

While no later chapter brings about this rapid dazzlement and dislocation with every new sentence, the abrupt changes from chapter to chapter can be just as disorienting. With a love of digression to rival that of *Tristram Shandy*, *The Red Robins* shifts from prose to verse to drama, from love story to comic travelogue to a battle between the forces of the equally villainous "Santa Claus" and "Easter Bunny," consistently thwarting the expectation that it will offer any conventional narrative satisfactions at all. What Koch gives instead is an atmosphere of continuous tension, desire, and partial comprehension, across which bright, savage, and unusual characters zoom.

About the supervillains named after the secular icons of Christian holidays, perhaps little needs to be added to Koch's observation that "they're full of power and pleasure, full of joy." They stand with early Kochean inventions such as Dog Boss, the tortured zillionaire whose obsession with dogs propels the action of the epic poem *Ko, or a Season on Earth*, and of the character Bertha (of the play of the same name), the mad queen of Norway who orders her army to give up the country so she might conquer it again. The Robins, by contrast, are the mortals in this epic—though just as ruled by the need for delight as their godlike leader, they inhabit a world of possibilities and predicaments they only sometimes understand. To emphasize their semi-instinctual behavior, Koch sometimes "tried to think of the main characters as though they were really birds. It gave [them] a certain oddness."

In its mixture of comedy, exoticism, and virtuosity, *The Red Robins* is recognizably by the author responsible for both the rollicking cartoon scroll of events in *Ko* and the non-syntactical long poem *When the Sun Tries to Go On*. The novel's acute psychological insights and sudden poignant turns, however, are characteristic of the reflective mood that transforms Koch's work beginning with the 1975 poem "The Circus." Although he came to enjoy writing about his methods and subjects, Koch chose not to clarify what prompted the change in tone that saw his restless inventiveness mix with careful observation and reminiscence, fantasy opening onto autobiography.

Fifteen years passed before he wrote fiction again. Between *The Red Robins* and *Hotel Lambosa*, Koch published two collections of short poems and two of long poems, as well as a book of very short plays. He also survived prostate cancer. Koch disclosed in a 1995 interview that after the operation to remove the cancer, he was (irrationally) afraid that, since he was aware that the inspiration for his work had always seemed to be sexual, he might not be able to write anymore.

Unconsciously, Koch was living out a story told to him by the Argentine poet and fiction writer Jorge Luis Borges, who had been a visiting professor at Columbia University in the 1960s:

> Borges told me that the way to become a short story writer was as follows. He had been a poet and he had been in a very bad automobile accident. He had hurt his skull and there was a very great possibility that there was damage to his brain, and he was afraid to write poems because he was afraid it would show there was damage. So he wrote out Pierre Menard. He sent it out as a piece of true literary criticism to the greatest magazine of Argentina, *Sur*. . . . He wrote stories as criticism to prove he hadn't lost his mind . . .

And without remembering what Borges had said I began to write stories.

(Coincidentally, Borges also features in the history of Koch's first extended story, "The Postcard Collection." Seated next to Borges at a dinner party, Koch mentioned this story, alternately a minutely observed record of incunabula and a plaintive love song, written before Koch was aware of Borges's *ficciones*. Borges replied, "Thank you for being influenced by me without having read me.")

Elliptical and brief, the stories in *Hotel Lambosa* recall Borges's elegant contraptions much less than they evoke Hemingway's Nick Adams stories and Yasunari Kawabata's Palm of the Hand stories. The stories' emphasis on yearning and tension provides some thematic overlap with the novel; Koch's attitude toward closure and resolution has changed dramatically, though, as has his regard for the seriousness and beauty not only of incidental details, but also for the heroics and failings of ordinary personages. "People who would have been of no importance in the time of Louis the Fourteenth are now the object of attention. Even their slightest feelings are the objects of attention, of the most intense and serious kind," he writes in "An Adventure of the Fifth Sense."

As if straight out of Stendhal, these sentences provide a rationale for Koch's interest in and method of autobiography: he wishes to disclose the complete truth without making the reader feel as though he is making a confession. (In a series of "rules" Koch suggests poets apply to their work before releasing it to the public, he states clearly that the answer to "Does it reveal something about me I never want anyone to know?" should be *no*.)

Some of the stories in *Hotel Lambosa* refract intimate experiences addressed at length in poems from 1975 and after, such as "To Marina" and "With Janice," while others expand on casually mentioned details. For example, 'Libretto' follows the lead of a single line in "The Circus." (Koch took this experiment in genre translation a step further, adapting *Hotel Lambosa* for the stage, as he had done earlier with *The Red Robins*; both plays can be found in his last drama collection, *The Gold Standard*.)

In "The Villino," "Artemis," "Antonellos," "Negative Blood," and other stories, however, Koch begins to provide information missing from his earlier autobiographical works. His parents, mainly absent from his work until now, make an awkward appearance at the start of the book—while traveling *en famille,* his father is propositioned by a hustler and his mother "encourages the local 'artists-for-tourists' by purchasing samples of their work." Koch's first marriage, which could previously have been described as an object of the author's mystery and remorse, is depicted here as rather more of a collaboration:

> She wanted something, too, she told me, from our making love. "I want to experience evil," she said. "I've never done this before."

One could also compare the fragmented autobiography of *Hotel Lambosa* with the thematic treatment Koch goes on to give his life in his collection of poems, *New Addresses* (2000). As with these poems, many of which take on such crucial yet set-aside subjects as carelessness, insults, and orgasms, Koch's stories are not exclusively autobiographical: characters more of Koch's imagination than his everyday life include rabbits, Egyptian deities, and Oaxacan calaveras. Readers who favor Koch's comic side will want to turn directly to the stories set in Oaxaca, particularly "A Miracle of Saint Brasos" and "A Man of the Cloth," skipping from there to the previously uncollected "The Soviet Room," a straight-faced update of socialist realism, and "The New Orleans Stories," a gangster parlor comedy serial.

The first and earliest piece in this book, "The Beverly Boys' Summer Vacation," is a prime example of Koch's finding joy in the naïve enthusiasm of certain children's stories. By isolating and magnifying that joy for an audience unsure whether to take it seriously, he hoped to make out of something familiar or forgotten a new kind of excitement, a desire that runs throughout all of Kenneth Koch's fiction.

THE COLLECTED FICTION
OF KENNETH KOCH

THE BEVERLY BOYS' SUMMER VACATION

1958

CHAPTER 1.
THE BEVERLY BOYS AT TOWN HUT

One year, Bobby, Bill, Jim, and Aunt Bertha Beverly were all installed at Town Hut, where the Boys spend their vacation, on the shores of the lake, every summer. Then they received a letter from Mr. Beverly's lawyer in the city, telling them that Town Hut had been sold, and that the Boys could not spend the summer there. The letter said that there was another hut, Roundup Hut, in the interior of the woods, where they could go and stay instead, and where they would be sure to have a good time. Aunt Bertha Beverly read the letter to the boys. At first they were sad, but then they became very interested in the new hut. Aunt Bertha Beverly cooked a big steaming hot dinner, and after dinner everyone went to bed.

CHAPTER 2.
A LAST WINK

The Beverly Boys knew it was their last night at Town Hut, where they had had so much fun in previous summers. In the morning Bobby didn't want to get up right away because it made him so sad to leave the summer home. Aunt Bertha let him stay in bed an extra five minutes, so as to have a last wink of sleep at Town Hut.

CHAPTER 3.
JIM BEVERLY SEES A SNAKE

Just as the wagon was about to set off for the new hut, Jim Beverly saw something slithering in the leaves. "Look out, Bobby!" Jim called, and Bobby jumped away from the place where there was the slithering. When Aunt Bertha said, "What is it?" Bobby told her, and Aunt Bertha said that it was probably only a harmless garter snake, but that Jim was right to have called Bobby about it because there are some snakes which distill a deadly poison.

CHAPTER 4.
JIM BEVERLY'S STORY

While the wagon was heading for Roundup Hut, Jim Beverly told the other Beverly boys and Aunt Bertha a story. It was about a king and a queen who lived in a big castle. Everyone liked the story, and it made the trip a lot more fun. When the story was over, Bobby asked Jim to tell another story about a king and a queen, but Aunt Bertha began to sing a railroad song, and so the boys all joined in and sang as they went along.

CHAPTER 5.
THE OLD TIMERS AT ROUNDUP HUT

The Beverly Boys felt like Old Timers in the woods by the time they got to Roundup Hut. They had come over so many trails, and seen so many different kinds of trees! Roundup Hut was not as fixed-up as Town Hut had been, and when the wagon came to rest outside it maybe there was a little disappointment. But not for long! "Here we are!" said Aunt Bertha, and all got out of the wagon and went inside.

CHAPTER 6.
A SIMPLE COTTAGE

Jim and Bobby and Bill looked around at their new home. "I like it," said Bobby. "So do we," said Jim and Bill. "I do too," said Aunt Bertha, "though it is only a simple cottage. We like it because we are all here together and to us it is as wonderful as a castle. Now we must all get ready for dinner!"

CHAPTER 7.
CRUEL WAVES

One day Aunt Bertha and Bobby were out searching for fuel. Dry sticks and leaves were very hard to find because it had been raining. While Bobby was looking for some sticks near the stream, he heard a tiny noise. He looked down and saw a baby robin on the ground at his feet. Across the stream was a tree with a nest in it. "The little fellow must have fallen out of its nest during the night," said Aunt Bertha when Bobby showed her the fallen bird, "and then the stream, which has been swollen by the rain, must have washed him away from his home. We will have to do something about that," said Aunt Bertha.

CHAPTER 8.
AUNT BERTHA BEVERLY TO THE RESCUE

Aunt Bertha Beverly picked up the little baby robin in her hand, stepped across the stream and gently placed it back in the nest with the other little robins and the eggs. "I hope its mother will come back soon," said Aunt Bertha. Then she and Bobby went back to the camp.

CHAPTER 9.
THE PHANTOM WOODSMAN

That night there was a great thrashing of the trees. Aunt Bertha told the boys next morning that there had been a big storm in the forest, but a woodchopper who had stopped there then to get a drink of water said that the trees had been thrashing because the phantom woodsman was abroad in the forest, and that the trees made a great noise like that every year on the same night.

CHAPTER 10.
BILL BEVERLY SEES A LIZARD

One morning Bill Beverly was walking through the woods carrying water for Aunt Bertha. Suddenly he heard a loud splash! He looked down at the bucket he was carrying, and saw that a little green lizard had jumped into it. Bill set the bucket down and put a stick into the water so that the lizard would crawl on it. When it did Bill took the lizard out of the bucket and placed it on the ground. Then he watched it dart into the underbrush.

CHAPTER 11.
TIME FOR LUNCH

"Time for lunch!" called Aunt Bertha Beverly. What a fine meal! There were tomatoes and sausages and bacon and baked potatoes and apples and oranges and walnuts, along with plenty of cold milk!

CHAPTER 12.
THE MISSING BREAD BASKET

Everyone was very hungry. "I would like some bread," said Jim. "Where is the bread basket?" They all looked and looked, but they could not find it. Then Aunt Bertha remembered that she had covered it up with leaves to keep the biscuits warm. "Biscuits!" the boys exclaimed in unison. Aunt Bertha sent Bobby to fetch the bread basket where she had left it, and to shake the leaves off. Then the boys ate the biscuits greedily. "We have had such a good lunch that it makes me sad," said Bobby after they were done eating, "and I will now tell you why."

CHAPTER 13.
BOBBY BEVERLY'S TALE

"When we were at the lake," Bobby Beverly began, "I met a boy there. He lived on a tugboat with his father. One night the tugboat crashed against a rock and the boy's father was killed. The boy did not have any money and did not have anything to eat. His name was Tugboat Ted, and he was as old as I am, with red hair."

CHAPTER 14.
TUGBOAT TED

Just as Bobby Beverly was finishing his story, everyone heard a loud CRASH! "Why, the top of the kettle as gone and fallen off!" exclaimed Aunt Bertha. "How did that ever happen?" "I am sorry, ma'am, it was I who knocked it off," said a clear, boyish voice, "while I was drawing nearer to hear the story about me." Everyone turned to see a sturdy, redhaired little boy dressed in rags, and with a piece of wood from a ship in his hand. "Why, it's Tugboat Ted himself!" exclaimed Bobby, and all gathered around to meet the new boy. Aunt Bertha invited him to stay at the camp, and that night cooked up a big hot meal to feed the hungry waif.

CHAPTER 15.
A CAROUSING OF LANDLUBBERS

What good times the boys had with their new friend! They went everywhere in the wood and played many games. Ted called them "landlubbers," and they asked him what it meant. He said that it was a name given by people who live on the sea to those who live on the land. Then the boys called themselves "The Landlubbers," and played many games with this new name.

CHAPTER 16.
AUNT BERTHA'S "FRIENDS"

One day a raccoon, a badger and a chipmunk came and sat in the clearing where the boys were eating breakfast. Aunt Bertha saw them and gave them some little pieces of bread and bacon rind. The animals ate greedily. Then every day they would come and sit in the same place, and Aunt Bertha would give them something. Jim Beverly said that they were Aunt Bertha's "friends."

CHAPTER 17.
BOBBY BEVERLY AT TOP-NOTCH PEAK

"Before our vacation is over," thought Bobby Beverly one fine morning, "I am going to see what is up on top of Top-Notch Peak." That day, at breakfast, Aunt Bertha announced that the wagon would leave at two o'clock in the afternoon. Bobby quickly packed all his things and put them in the wagon. Then he began to climb up to Top-Notch Peak. The sun was very hot. When he came down, Bill Beverly asked him where he had been. "I climbed up to Top-Notch Peak," Bobby answered. "But it was so hot that I did not want to stay there very long." Then Bobby climbed into the wagon.

CHAPTER 18.
A DRINK OF WATER

Just before the wagon was about to leave, Bobby Beverly became very thirsty. "Gee, I'd like a drink of water," he said. Tugboat Ted, who had not yet climbed on, went over to the well and brought Bobby back a cup of clear, sparkling water. Bobby thanked him. Then Ted climbed on, and the wagon began.

CHAPTER 19.
GREEN ARE THE TREES

On the ride back everyone noticed how green the trees were. "It is September already," said Aunt Bertha smilingly, "and yet the leaves have not yet begun to turn. Maybe the trees are like us, and want to remember and enjoy as long as possible the fun they have had during the summer."

CHAPTER 20.
THE BEVERLY BOYS BACK HOME

Jim couldn't believe his eyes when he saw the old brick chimney and the yellowish, dusty drive. "We're back home!" he gaily cried. "Back home!" After the brothers' excitement had calmed down a little, they all helped Aunt Bertha out of the wagon with her things. A big hot meal was waiting for the boys inside. They ate greedily. "Oh, that was good!" said Bobby. "I'm sleepy," said Bill. The boys were very tired indeed, and all were soon asleep. And the most comfortable bed in the house was given to Tugboat Ted. "The poor little motherless darling," said Aunt Bertha, as she looked at the sleeping boy. "And now I must get on to bed myself, for I too am tired."

CHAPTER 21.
MEMORIES OF A VACATION

Next day at breakfast, Bobby Beverly turned to Tugboat Ted. His eyes were bright with enjoyment. "We certainly had a good time at Roundup Hut, didn't we, Ted?" Bobby asked. "You bet we did!" Bill Beverly added. "And, just think, if it weren't for our vacation this summer we'd never have met Tugboat Ted!"

THE END

THE POSTCARD COLLECTION

1964

On the first card, which seemed to be a French one from around 1928, which had already been sent through the mails and had writing on the back, was a picture of an old woman in a yellowish-pink dress holding a watering can and bending over some flowers; the blossoms were red, blue, and purple, one of them yellow; most of the background of the card was yellowish-pink, though with a little more grey intermixed than in the old woman's dress. However, in the upper left hand corner was a splash of green shaped more or less like a leaf-mint, and over this green was inscribed in printed writing the word "Auvergne." The handwriting on the back of the card was slanted and thin, in dark blue ink. The words it contained were not all legible because someone had apparently spilled liquid (most likely water) on some of them and this had washed away certain parts of their letters, here the angle of a K, there the tall blue stem of a T. The message was written in French; what could be read of it was, roughly, as follows (translated into English): "Theo, my dear—The Auvergne is as beautiful as you have always . . ." (said? told me? No, not "told me" because then the objective pronoun "m" would have been visible before the "have," the "avez"). After this point the writing on the card was largely blurred. There was some clarity again toward the end: ". . . a large one" (masculine gender): "un grand"—or possibly, "a great man" (no, in that case "grand" would be, necessarily, followed by "homme," which it was not); perhaps, "a big one." But a big or great what? A kiss, perhaps, or a hug; maybe a drink—perhaps the writer was explaining that someone had given her (him?) a big glass (not cup, which is feminine) of delicious local Auvergne wine to drink; if the latter explanation is true, then the sentence could be reconstructed as follows: "We just wanted a sip of the local wine, and we asked the man for it, wanting a small glass, but he gave us a big one." On the whole, however, this sentence seems rather clumsy and long. If one accepts it as a more or less accurate reconstruction of the meaning, however, then one is forced to suppose that the writing on the card which precedes it and follows the words "Theo, my dear—the Auvergne is as beautiful as you have always (said?)," that the words in the middle say something like "Or at least so it seems. Though it is rather hard for me to tell, I am so tipsy just now. Gerard and I just had a rather too-refreshing moment at the Caves Gibicault; I'm sure you know them, the ones outside of town. Well, you have told me how generous are the people here!" It is possible, of course, that the main body of the card is concerned with something entirely different; the sentence ending with "un grand" could very well be some such thing as "He has a little shoe and I have a big one." It is possible, too—and this would defeat all but the most painstaking and even inspired efforts—that in the blotted-out sentences the writer of the card was merely indulging in the free association of images or words; or even in the half- or super-conscious ordering of such free-flowing associations, which constitutes poetry.

Turning the card over again, it is possible to examine the picture with a view to discovering just what it is about it that has made us suppose, half-unconsciously, it's true, that it was written by a woman in her middle years, perhaps beyond, though most likely between the ages of 40 and 50. One notices on second perusal that the scene pictured on the card is not entirely the product of human imagination (ramifications of this problem suggest themselves at once but had better be resolved later); more simply, the scene is not entirely painted but is, aside from the green leaf-mint splash signifying "Auvergne," the lettering, and the coloration of the background, woman's face and gown, and flowers, a photograph—perhaps photo-montage would be a more exact description since one easily detects a sort of incongruity between the old woman in her bending position (she looks more as though she were stooping to water vegetables which grow very close to the ground) and the flowers, as well as, of course, and this phenomenon is common to so many words, suggesting as it does the limits, after a certain point necessary ones, of the skill and knowledge of the artist or perhaps indeed of his aesthetic intentions, between the woman-flowers cluster and the background, which has a generalized quality not present in the aforementioned. We have in some way (perhaps correctly) unconsciously identified the woman pictured on the card with the author of the message on its other side. This identification was partial, however, since we had supposed in the writer a greater degree of culture and urban sophistication than seems present in the old woman; in fact it's this "urban sophistication" in a rather naive form which is what appeals to us so little in the message we have figured out for the back. One gets the feeling that the writer might have led a happier life, full of more real satisfactions, if she had been more like the pictured old woman, whom she no doubt felt superior to when she purchased the card. Perhaps not; but that would suggest a sweetness and a calm in her one could not help but admire. We should in that case have to change our estimate of the contents of the message on the back; for the one we have constructed would never spring from a truly sophisticated yet serene and loving soul.

Yet again, the last hypothesis—that the card was written from deep wells of sunlight and contentment—seems contradicted by the scene that is pictured on the card. That scene is, as we have already noticed, naive and even simpleminded. Then was the card sent to amuse the recipient? This possibility is rendered unlikely by the first and almost completely legible sentence on the back (see above).

Or was there a confusion in intention, a striking difference between the impulse to purchase that particular card and the emotion and cross-currents active in the purchaser at the time of writing the message? Was one meant to correct the other? How much of reality, of what we see, is born of that sort of connection, of that kind of need for the amendment of initial impulses—or is what I am talking about rather the working out of concealed realities by the use of half-understood contradictions?

Was the writer first moved by naive enthusiasm, then embarrassed by the simplicity of the card? If so, we have to suppose something ironic in the message, such as (after the Dear Theo sentence) "though it's nothing like this card, which has given me, a newcomer here, a little laugh, but which will probably give you a big one!" Or was it quite the reverse? and was the writer, actually liking the Auvergne and liking the recipient "Theo," yet moved by a self-destructive impulse only thinly veiled as an outwardly directed one, since it was always in truth directed at her warmest and most spontaneous emotions (perhaps this arose from a shame deeply felt in infancy or childhood), subtly (perhaps for "Theo" quite obviously) attacking, by the naive imbecility of the card, the presence of this spontaneous enthusiasm in herself. A fear, then, of being naive, or perhaps even a far deeper problem, a mistrust of all one's emotions—perhaps more accurately this: one great emotional scar, one terrible wound inflicted by and on one's feelings at some time in one's life—then, forever after, every emotion strongly or spontaneously felt, every feeling which seems to shadow these painful and primal ones, these huge feelings which did not work out, to shadow them as the light yellow-green of the front of the postcard in question might shadow the sunlight on the fields of the Auvergne, every such emotion then recalling the large painful ones, thus every access of joy immediately corrected by pained remembrance, by pain.

If all this is true, picture and card may be reconstructed to read *secretly* somewhat like this: "Theo, my dear—how happy I am and yet how miserable! Is the Auvergne a reality? If, at a moment, I find it such, it then seems to me the most beautiful poetry there is, for just as for most persons poetry, or beauty, is an adornment, an extension of reality, of life, for me it is the peering through, that is, of the black cloak of death and fog which my unfortunate character at once pulls down to cover, to suffocate everything. So the very falseness of this card, the sentimental idiocy of flower-watering peasantry, the too-bright, too-colorful, too-improbable flowers, are but a mirror of the falseness, for me, of any duration of an individual joy, of joy of any kind. I do not know if this overhanging gloom of mine, this extended inner voice which whispers always of death and dissatisfaction is an unfortunate product of experiences particular to me, or if it is a generalized problem of man. Yours, in the hope of some solution during this life, Magda."

But here I think we may leave this hypothesis, for the moment at least. For, given the "Theo my dear, etc." actually legible on the back of the card, the hypothesis has to be somewhat modified.

On the basis of this sentence one would guess the writer not to have been an intellectual capable of the subtlety of expression contained in the hypothesized "secret message." However, does it matter? With what are we really concerned? Doesn't there exist such an intellectual somewhere inside every human being, an "inward intellectual" who can be brought into the light, from whom we can be freed only by what he is continually urging us to: the fullest exercise of our intellectual and above all our imaginative powers?

Is there not, inside every one of us,
An "intellectual," who, when the bus
Is ready to depart, says "Do I really
Want to get on?" and makes us miss it nearly?
And is not such a one at work in all
The choices we make dressing for a ball
Or walking down the quais to pick a card
To send to someone? Though we try quite hard
To sublimate him he is always there,
Like the hair cell that underlies the hair.
True, great and passionate experience
Can so inundate every human sense
With fire and glory that the "intellect-
Ual" gets deader than one might expect;
But once the passion's gone, then he arises.

And thus great art with its so great surprises
Like passion that endures is all that can
(If even it can) change one to a man
Or woman of whom the surface is as thrilling
As Italy, and far more warm and willing
To move about; and yet not constantly
Is such great pleasure possible to me,
So I regard these postcards, these half-arts,
In nervous patience till the glory starts.

Were I to put the card in a novel, I should have imagined its message as follows: "Thank you for the kiss. It is true, perhaps, that in the middle of the Auvergne I should not have noticed you, or rather *recognized,* had you not, just before kissing me, slightly tilted your straw hat to the left, then let me feel the warmth of your lips. Ann."

But this happy version would have come about because the intellectual inside of me has direct connections, and constantly, with the surface, and will not allow any nonsense. If you are attached to the sensual life, he would say to me, with its sun-scorched hat-tilting, write it out, put it in, perhaps it will come true. We never know.

As if the evidence of any one thing we had seen were not totally damning!

The second card, which featured on its picture side the various kinds of French currency circa 1908 implanted on a heady blue, white, and green background of scenes from the Bois de Boulogne, had written on its back merely "Hi" in English, and after that "A toi" in French ("to you," or more properly "to thee"), and was signed very clearly in the purplish red ink that had written the rest, "Mary." This address is easy to make out: Mr. Alfred LaFont, 3836 Retreat Street, St. Paul, Minnesota, USA. There is no return address save for the words (a name) "Mary Ryan." Oh yes. Underneath it in very blurred writing is "Hôtel de l'Universe, rue Monsieur-le-Prince, Paris."

And who are (or were, for death strikes everywhere: and the date on the postmark is 1909) these two, Mary and Alfred, and how were they related to one another? I should like to look some more at the front of the card.

On one of the coins, which is colored silver and like all the rest somehow made into a kind of paper bas relief actually on the post-card, is pictured a woman whose long full dress seems to belie her youthful walk, her slim form, her clear cheek (her face is not visible save for the left cheek). Her hair is voluminous and youthful-looking too, and is gathered behind her head into a fat "pony-tail" type of hairdo. Her silver gown is slightly raised up over her tiny left shoulder, probably chiefly to suggest the fullness of the material, to add to the sense of richness one seems meant to feel about this woman all round. Her little right arm is extended to the side as well as slightly behind her, as though its activity could scarcely keep up with the pace of her stride; for the coin scene catches the woman in a moment of movement and activity. Furthermore her right arm is slightly bent at the elbow, the two sections of her arm thus creating an angle of about 130°. Another angle is created by her hand and wrist, which are tilted at from 95-100° away from the forearm. About 1 ½ times the length of the forearm away from the lowest (the highest on the arm) point of the wrist, one eighth of an inch below, though with its straight silver rays passing apparently under the arms and wrist without really touching them, which presumably would burn them, because it is a sun, is about 1/20 of a round object that seems to be the sun; aside from sending out rays of its own, it is intercepted by a straight line crosswise, which is thinner and has less body than the rays. This interpretation, however, does not merely pass under or beyond the sun as its rays pass beyond the woman's arm and hand—on the contrary, it effectively cuts it off: there is no more sun beneath the line. This same line, however, does not cut off the woman, but, like the sun-rays, seems to pass under her or beyond her, at about an inch or two (according to scale—actually as pictured it is a distance more like 1/1000 of an inch) above her knees, or rather, where one assumes her knees are beneath the folds of her dress. There is thus a suggestion, of a purely mechanical origin, of the superiority of the figure of the woman to the other elements in the composition: everything passes beneath or beyond her; and, perhaps most strikingly of all, her body is the largest element in the composition and the one that is by far the most raised up; her silver figure triumphs in uninterruptibility, size, and volume. She is the highest, silveriest, and then she is moving too, which always catches the eye; or rather she is sculpted as if in movement. Her left arm is extended straight down and forward, creating an angle of about 40° with the perpendicular line of her body. Its hand is holding something slightly larger than her head, something polygonal in shape, which at first view seems to be a small shield and even perhaps to be stuck to her arm in some way rather than to be clasped by her fingers. Further observation, however, coupled with intellectual reminiscences of what this scene is probably supposed to represent, leads one to speculate that the held object is probably a sack of some kind, most likely a repository (if true, this would explain the position of the right arm and even the nature of the woman's movement across the coin) for grain or seed. The woman's right knee is slightly bent, yet the foot is flat on the ground; the left leg, on the other hand, is bent slightly from the hip and again abruptly from the knee, in such a way that the bottom of the foot (shoe) makes an angle of 60° with the flat horizontal (in this case the bottom and top of the card). Around the circumference of the coin, at varying short distances from the moving woman, are letters which spell out "RÉPUBLIQUE FRANÇAISE."

I love you. It is ridiculous to try to hide this from you by going over the collection. When I see the blue on the card I see your eyes; they float into my vision and there is no more work possible for that day. Or if yes, if there still is work possible it is not longer work of the same kind, for all my clear observation is disturbed by an overwhelming desire to tell a truth which is not, so to speak, "in the cards." I want to say "I love you" over and over again, as if that somehow had a meaning which could sustain us. "Sustain us? no, that is overdramatic; we are not falling. But we are deliberately exposing ourselves to the dangers of the air.

And to say that "is not in the cards" is perhaps wrong too. For isn't this card, with its complex and beautiful surface (of which I have described only the tiniest part), its loveable red-and-purplish ink, as well as the air of freshness about the spacing of the message, and that message itself, in its simplicity, its directness, its nearly John Donne-like force (what more "metaphysical" and direct can one say—Hi! A toi, America, France, you, I, the world, our love) evidence entirely to the contrary? Are we not, in fact, in the presence of one of the sweetest moments in the world, the conscious and unconscious moving together, in a single dance, or perhaps merely a striding along, which expresses in its mingling of absence and presence the irresistible nature of life's minutest failures?

For this I have to thank France. And I shall thank you too. And what of the manufacturers of postcards! far from my coin, to the right, and above the grand lac of the Bois de Boulogne, that cornucopia exuding pink and blue bank notes of fifty, one hundred, five hundred, and one thousand francs!

When you're free of indigestion
Follow this divine suggestion:
Let the richness of
The earth enslave your love.
I mean 'engage your love'
But it is all no matter;
Life is shapeless as a glove
Yet a formal matter.
Inside this five-fingered
Easily-splayable form
Poets who have lingered
Find this to keep warm:
"Always let variety
Substantiate your feeling
And love's sweet society
Will pay you richly when the springtime's dealing,
Otherwise
Avoid horrible disease that flies

About.
Sit down sometimes. When you feel like it, shout.
And most of all
Do the impossible. Call
Sleep being awake,
And zero all you want to take."

Advice that's hard to understand,
But on the other hand
Come to me while I am sleeping
Dear zero in my keeping.

After a night of intensely various and gentle visions I return to the collection.

A floral decoration in blue, a decoration which is festooned around the outside of a blank white rectangle inside which is imprinted a poem, in French, entitled (in Latin) "Ultima Verba." The poem, which is printed in a sort of rounded type with the little arabesques of branching ink between some of the letters, has twelve lines, and reads (translated loosely into English, that is, reading and translating one word at a time, as each word comes along, and not surveying and studying the whole in the attempt to make a perfect poem) as follows:

Beneath your eyes O adored woman
I've assembled all these materials
Which piled up encumbered on my table
Bearing the name "Little Floral Games"!

Metrical lines, prose sweet and pretty,
Lofty sonnets, or modest quatrains,
Words where wit and grace are joined—
All has more or less passed through your hands.

If, listening to you, lovable sovereign,
I had been able to award to the competitors

Gold and silver flowers, like a real Mycenas,
One would have seen me giving them handfuls.

Unfortunately, perhaps, the message is completely blotted off the back of this card; there is nothing but a small smear of red ink. It is doubtful that it was ever sent through the mails. There seems to be a certain amount of redness faded onto the poem-side of the card too, as though the card had perhaps been kept for a long time in juxtaposition with something red—a shirt pocket, a red velvet vest, hose, flower petals, a red-covered book. Perhaps there had never been any intention of sending it; perhaps there had. In any case, about this there is no evidence.

Printed in the bottom right-hand part of the card, and in slightly larger type than in which even the title of Ultima Verba is printed, are the words (in French) "Little Floral Games."

The poem, which is signed (I forgot to mention this) in printed handwriting "Alfred Saurel," seems to me extremely bad, defective in technique as well as in thought; I have the impression that the author is saying something very banal, which he is trying to dress up with a selection of literary clichés from various epochs (such as calling his wife "aimable souveraine"). And what he seems to be saying is that he has gathered together a lot of material for a magazine or anthology and that he has not paid the contributors; he rather hopes, too, one would gather, that these unpaid poets and authors will be happy to accept instead of money the assurance that the editor's wife liked their works so much that she would have prevailed upon her editor husband to pay them if he had any money.

A further study of the blank side of the card reveals that it was printed in 1888.

It is difficult to tell whether it was stupidity, technical ineptitude, or a mind enfeebled by old age or disease that could result in such a poem as this one—perhaps all three. It is possible too that Saurel wrote very quickly, in great bursts of enthusiasm, sometimes badly, sometimes well, and had not the critical sense or the patience to know when the products of his creative spasms were worth preserving. However, the badness and flatness of this poem are so remarkable as to suggest limits beyond which this poet's genius could not go.

There is another poetic card like the last, an encircled and decorated poem covering the outward face of the card; red and blue and green flowers are intertwined about its rectangular topside, falling down in gentle sweeping lines which considerately never touch the poem's words. This poem too is one of the Petits Jeux Floraux de Marseilles Series. The message on the back—and how old this one is too! the postmark is 1888—is written in brown ink, very hard to decipher, but says this (in French): "Dear Hal, The winter has come and gone. xxxxxxxxxxx umbrella. xxxxxx not at all by the sea xxxxxx Raspail xxxxxx will not xxxx sun xxxxx Gambetta xxx (signed) xx olphe." It is addressed to "M. Alphonse de la Roche, boulevard du Temple, xxxxxxx France." (Undoubtedly Paris) Here is the poem (translated by the usual method):

When your beautiful eyes mount, O young girl!
Toward the blue firmament sown with pearls of gold
What dream you? Tell me? Your lip so gentille
For this world of a day does she still murmur?

Is it the butterfly whose wing so weightless
Shoots out in twirling, on the evening breeze,
Or the ravishing echo of a voice which to you is dear,
Which is it that makes your eye gleam with a ray of hope?

One would say that your breast palpitated at every murmur
And that the crazy breeze and its enchanting breath
Even up to the slightest shudder of immense nature
Found something like an echo in the depths of your heart.

Ah! If along the sounds which strike your ear
There is one which dies and revives alternately,
One which in the distance at each instant awakens
Beautiful angel, it is a sigh of love from my heart.

One turns this postcard over in amazement. Why did someone named Adolphe send this card to someone named Alphonse de la Roche? Is it, perhaps, within the possibilities of French names that Adolphe was a woman and not a man? But even supposing Adolphe to be a woman, is it hard to understand why she would send this card bearing a poem obviously addressed by a man to a young girl, to a man, to Alphonse de la Roche. If, on the other hand, Adolphe is a man, the selection of the verse-card is, if understandable, some-what reprehensible. Well, at the least unusual. But somehow from the contents of the card (what is written on the backside of the poem), one does not get the impression that there is any sexual meaning intended in the sending of this card (except, of course, the usual: impelling an object forcibly toward another who may be expectant but is by the nature of the situation passive; as what I am writing, beautiful and responsive reader, is intended to enter into your soul—and after?). One does not get this impression for the simple reason that the message written on the card (for all its gaps) seems very straightforward, newsy, and factual—though it is possi-ble, of course that one may miss, seventy-some-odd years after the fact, a long time for words and their associations to change, a certain esprit or double-entendre. However, I am not satisfied with what I now know, and I think some further research is necessary. Of course, the card could have been merely chosen at random, with the sender not noticing what was printed on the face, or observing merely that it was a poem and thinking "Oh, Alphonse (is Alphonse perhaps a woman too? No, there is the "M.") likes poetry! I'll send him this." In fact, there is one possibility which may save me a trip to the library if it turns out to be tenable—that is, that Alphonse was a child; in this case, if he were a child who liked poetry, and if the card were from a grown-up friend, member of family or no, man or woman, it seems in no way extraordinary that such a grown-up friend would be likely to send Alphonse a card with a poem on it—perhaps to correct his taste (as if to say, "Here's what your aunt Eliane thinks poetry is, not that beastly gutter-talk of Verlaine and Corbière which you are so fond of"), perhaps out of kindness and in ignorance of what his taste in poetry was, or again perhaps it was sent by a person with equal or superior critical standards who naively, but correctly, or else somewhat smilingly, and either tongue-in-cheek or tenderly, perhaps both, having discerned what little Alphonse's literary preferences were, had decided to satisfy him, come what may, with this pretty card.

This whole child hypothesis seems to me vitiated, however, by the discernible contents of the message written on the card's back: why, I should wonder, the reference to Gambetta? But it strikes me now that my objection is not very well-founded. For if Alphonse was an intelligent adolescent he probably had political views as well as poetical ones, and it may have been that the same aunt (or uncle—in fact, if this is true it seems more like an uncle) who was satisfying his literary taste (either correctly or incorrectly, and either kindly or ironically) was at the same time twitting the boy about his political "heroes." "Well, what do you think, now," the card might have said before it faded, "of your Mr. Gambetta?" There is also the possibility, of course, a light one but still made somewhat greater by the presence of another street name— "Raspail"—on the card, that the writer was referring not to the politician but to the street named after him, the Cours Gambetta. Then the chief content of the message might be the writer's eagerness to return to Paris.

What I am led more and more to believe, however, on the basis of this and the previous card, was that "Little Floral Games" was something more than an anthology or magazine and represented a kind of literary "movement." In this case, it must have had its zealots, and perhaps the person who sent this card was one, perhaps the person who received it was another; or perhaps it was only Alphonse who was a Petits Jeux Florauxiste (as they may have called themselves). In this case, the content of the poem on the card would be considered of much less importance than the fact that the poem there imprinted was a little floral game, *qu'il faisait partie du mouvement p.j.f.* The sender of the card, then, would not have selected or sent the card with the intention of its recipient seeing his (the sender's) thoughts and feelings projected into the actual lines of the poem, but merely with the idea of showing the poem's existence, as if to say "We (or you) (or I) have triumphed again. Here is Hern's (the poem in question having been written by Ludovic Hern) poem in print!" or "Alphonse, my dear, ah! what do you think of our movement now!?" Of course the possibility immediately suggests itself, too, that this card may have been sent, and the one preceding it bought, out of the same complicated and ultimately self-defeating motivations that prompted the sending of the first card, the woman-farmer-of-Auvergne. Certainly, though Hern's poem has a kind of delicacy and consistency within its own genre that was completely absent from the poem of his editor Jaurel, it is easy to conceive of the person who sent it feeling scornful of its rather sticky sentimentality, its too frequent platitudes, and, as well, its complete emptiness of any content that would interest a grown man except at certain very rare and half-conscious moments. In this case, then we would imagine an Adolphe not a part of the Petits Jeux Floraux movement, if indeed there was one, and who had sent this card as a mere joke to a friend whose literary tastes were as sophisticated as his own, perhaps however with the same secret complex of reactions that we imagined may have motivated the sending of the Auvergne card. Was Adolphe secretly attracted, as it is indeed not difficult to be, by the somewhat sleepy beauty of the poem, for all its limitations, and then, scornful of himself for being so attracted, impelled to send, as a result of self-destructive impulse, the card bearing the poem to Alphonse de la Roche? If one imagines a vicious relationship between the two, the self-destructive complex which then would have motivated the sending of this delicately tender and utterly sexless love poem seems even more apparent.

Perhaps the message read

Dear Hal, The winter has come and gone. (So
I fear has your) umbrella (and the wits of the
poet of the verse on the verso ((The writing would
have had to get very small here to accommodate
itself to the space available))

small here. Not at all by the sea, (a stone's
throw, really, from) Raspail, (do I miss you? I)
will not (say so in the) sun, (by Saint) Gambetta.
(Viciously, Ad)olphe.

This message is especially obscure toward the end. What, for example, is the meaning of, "Do I miss you? I will not say so in the sun, by Saint Gambetta"? Unless some very private allusions are being made, the sentence is nonsense. Perhaps, in fact, it should read (which would fit in just as well with the available evidence— i.e. the remaining words and blank spaces): "do I miss you? I need not, will not say—you are my moon, my sun, my Jules Ferry, my Gambetta!" In the event our latter hypothesized version of the sentence is correct (oh your beautiful lips, your eyes, your clear cheek, I cannot resist them much longer, my imagination is already on the prowl, leaving behind the cards as an eagle leaves the sun when he is struck by dark necessity; help! back!), then there need be no dubiety whatsoever about the complex and self-destructive impulses that motivated this card's sending—card which as we have it now shows a double desire to be direct and tender (in the poem and in the message), and a desire both times mocked by the desirer, for the inanity of the poem as applied to a mature and guilty passion is not greater, surely, than the impropriety of evoking, in the name of such a love, of any love, the presences of Gambetta and Jules Ferry, bewhiskered politicians who, no matter how effective their governmental policies might be, were not of a sort to set a lover's pulses spinning, universal wheels in motion, spots darting from one flower to another, of the sun, as if glass bees, not they, not at least on the basis of their names on the grey austerity of a card.

But another aspect of the situation has to be considered, an aspect which could not have been treated quite so clearly at the time of the woman-from-Auvergne postcard. That aspect is simply this: given the apparently necessarily defensive nature of the adult psyche (a defensiveness which may be no more protective, say, than a linen suit; but think, even there, how much a linen suit does keep off—such damaging sun ((one could die for the lack of one's suit)), chilling rain ((only keeps off a little, then can become damaging itself in being rain-chill retentive)), fragments of dust continually hurled at us like postcards through the mails, but faster and with what motive? a mystery of nature), given the defensive nature of the soul, shall we not assume also that it is on its guard against whatever is too obviously directed against it with an aim of penetration? and will it not be actually pierced most easily by the disguised, by the oblique? and does not, furthermore, each soul have at least an unconscious awareness of this proclivity and weakness in other souls and, therefore, select, when it wishes to effect a penetration, some weapon so subtle or self-mocking as to pass unnoticed through those fibers which, no matter how closely woven, are made of mortality and are thus bound to be open to death and thus to love, desire, hopefulness, hopelessness? Brief, is not the disguised self-mocking avowal of such a card as this perhaps the most effective means of communication, I will not say between people, but between souls? It is true that about 95% of the card's effectiveness would be cast off as follows by a sensitive recipient: "Ha! irony, self-mockery; affection, yes, but inferiority, uncertainty of deepest feelings, or shame about them, shall I never escape from this monkey cage, my deepest feeling is not mockery, beyond this there is something, ha, hollow . . ." etc. The possible penetration of the other 5% is difficult to gauge, but its chances may appear in a clearer light if we imagine the chances of anything penetrating from an absolutely serious and soulfully loving card:

> I love you, darling. Do not let them torment you, mislead you. I am coming back. The great sun and the moon are witness that you are my only love, my apple, my Eden, my God, if you desire. Until that happy moment when, brimming with tears, these two poor eyes that stare at the empty you-less grey of this card will once again be fastened upon those eyes and other features for which they were created. Thine. Adolphe.

The thought of Adolphe writing this to a man is absurd but is the thought of his writing it to a woman any less repellent? In any case this message does not fit in with the words which actually remain on the back of the card.

The least one can say is that there are a great many human relationships and a great many situations inside other relationships in which there is no communication without disguise and self-mockery. Probably most of this disguise and self-mockery are so *built-in* to the situation and relationships, so *usual*, that they are rarely, except at the heights of hysteria or inspiration, recognized as such. For example, coming to call for you in an automobile is one, my dearest (which I can barely wait to do), or "talking to you" on the telephone.

From this built-in disguise and mockery, what way out? Because one feels all the same (remembering the pleasure of past occurrences) the superiority of absolute openness, lack of disguise (a kind of movement one is always trying to achieve in the ocean by throwing out one's arms, but waves cannot perfectly accomplish what only comes from the inside as prompted by another human being). Naturally it is very dangerous (*dit-on*); but given its absolute superiority, who could care? It is questionable that the way out could be found by means of a postcard, I mean by sending one, even by sending a great many. By sending enough though, I suppose, an aesthetic pattern could be set up which might, if assembled in the atmosphere of right emotions, liberate the recipient from absolutely everything except—except what? But postcards themselves are a self-mockery and a disguise; so is all art; and so, for that matter, is talking through the vocal chords, the trachia, and the epiglottis.

Away! I am returning to my hypothesis that this postcard was sent by one member of the Petits Jeux Floraux Movement to another. In order to check up on this hypothesis I am going to the Bibliothèque de l'Arsenal (to its Provençal et littérature du sud la France collection) to see if the name "Alphonse de la Roche" appears on any of the P.J.F. posters. If it does, then that I will take as sufficient evidence my hypothesis is correct. I sense I feel a certain need to be saved from the billowing abstractions and uncertainties which my previous hypothesis got me into. I also feel, in general, a kind of illness of having been too long away from the object of my research, the postcard itself, a condition which makes me aware that if I stay away from a specific object long enough I am bound to be carried away and then practically swallowed up by the same billowy clouds which begin by appearing as appealing abstractions which can take me away from a too dumb attachment to the dung on the cement (if that is what I happen to be looking at) but which end by drowning me in the dung and the essence of dung, with no sidewalk there at all, and no lamppost to lean on, no café at the corner, no one to call on for help. Abstract ideas are really horrible seducers leading me away from the part of the neighborhood I know, like parents with their arms outstretched who keep moving backwards and then down the stairs. What I always end up in a real heap of, when I am so separated from the real, is self-hatred and disgust, and precisely that feeling that I am out of contact with "reality." All of which makes me wonder if there is not mirrored that fear, too, on all of these postcards, in either a conscious or an unconscious way—that is, a fear that one is not part of a world that is real, and, coupled with this fear, a desperate attempt to project oneself into such a world, a world which had recognizable objects in it, and above all recognizable traits, intellectual, emotional, a world in which it is actually possible for one to "go somewhere," to have definite feelings about this going, and even be liked, hated, or loved a little more or less for these feelings and for one's expression of them. Of course, this "secret" message need not be any more conscious in the writer's mind than the "secret message" of pain and fear we discussed in relation to the postcard woman-from-Auvergne.

> *Inside each person is a doubt*
> *A child comes out*
> *Of mother;*
> *Maybe fear of smother*
> *Causes this,*
> *But whatever it is*
> *The inscription on paper*
> *Of messages, like dots of pepper,*

Reassures, if only for a moment, that solace and doubt;
Then later moment death comes turns the lights out.

Dear genuineness, I love you!
So come with me
Along these Jackie wastes
And the Billy sea
Until each from another
One and two
Baby out of mother
Five make three
Dear Calm: I am here, I really am.

Dear, I love you
Of this I have no doubt
Except as of everything
Flower leaf man
And among the every
Noise you hear
As if attuned to them what about a string of butterfly
Twirling in the evening air
Among them there, one you hear
Is the sound of me writing this card,
Am writing you this message
In the Gaston air.

. . . . .

Every card, then, according to my new theory,
Would be an expression of self-hate and a doubting of reality.
It will be a relief, such a relief to go to the Library,
To the Library across the river, and find out something with certainty!

. . . . .

But before I do this I must acknowledge that I have left certain matters up in the air. Because I suggested that obliqueness, self-mocking, self-hating, even, were the most effective attitudes for penetrating another human soul, but I did not prove it, I talked around it, and then I ran away from it into another major subject, which I can't help feeling I got to somewhat slyly and not by a direct path at all, really, that subject being of course the above, the subject of the doubting of reality as being a major factor in all choices of communication, in all communication, and yet I did not treat this subject completely either but merely "jumped" into it and tried to get off with its essence, whereas ideally I should explain it and, not only that, show its connection with the mockery and anti-self motivations that also enter into almost every human action, such as the choice and sending of a postcard. As to what motivates the manufacturers of postcards, that is another subject, whose complexity makes me weak to think of it.

Revenons en arrière! the day is beautiful, the sun is shining, and the glossiest cards glint strangely in the falling light of autumn; soon everything is dusky brown, then green again, a sweet inter-mingling of colors: these distinctions between one thing and another actually make you present to me physically, they change what I do, the works of my blood and hands, into a mist of poems.

And what about the maker of this book? But I wish to return to unreality and self-denial. I cannot imagine why I am describing these cards instead of sending them, unless there is a self-mockery, a self-denial in art that is less obvious than that in a blatantly senti-mental, stupid card sent off by a sophisticated hand. Art's self-mockery then would be no less real than the other but, if that is possible, ever more real for being a part of the very structure of what is said, for being "built-in," as the motor is built into the auto-mobile, and as the epiglottis is built into the body. As far as postcards go, their real absurdity, their built-in self-denial, is the very fact of their existence. Once one accepts the fact that they do exist, then anything one writes on them or anything one intends to commu-nicate by the poem or picture they bear on their front is based on a solidly built-in absurdity but exists above it, as a city exists above its sidewalks and streets and yet cannot exist without them; but in art, ideally, the writer or painter can throw himself into the process at precisely the moment when it becomes arbitrary, becomes absurd, and can thus try to make his houses of the same cement with which he is making the sidewalks, and also the air. When one is confronted with the city of Paris on a photo-postcard, what does one feel? Whatever it is, one is at second remove from the self-destructive and the absurd, which is why it is also sometimes so poignant, like an awareness of tenderness or pain from a great distance. The distance here is psychological. There are moments, however, when these cards, through some secret and exact adjustments of their own, enter into reality with a flash and even a flame. The times I have thought of destroying the collection have been numerous, but the recollection of even one of these wonderful moments has always been enough to convince me that I should save it.

As for the doubting of my reality, to the point of doubting one's own existence, which I said I wanted to connect with the self-hatred and self-mockery implicit in communication, I now think the connection is perfectly obvious. Because these feelings are precisely what one needs to convince oneself that one is really alive and there. It is true, however, that the final product is almost always (one can hope that some day one of them will not be!) a disappointment, more! it is a mere piece of paper, canvas, or cardboard, with something scrawled on its face—who has time to look at it or read it? Everyone is walking up and down the streets, with warm thighs pushing upward and outward through pantaloons and dress, faces moving, and the air, the air hovering expectantly over all. What do you want to do to us, air? eat us? Is air a vulture? Is it just waiting until we die? Is it that stink, from that one simple sacrifice alone, that satisfies her? O Messaline Air, or is it love you are thinking of making with us mortals? Now that, for example, that invocation, is doomed to be lost forever, rolled up and left inside some shuddering flute of time.

"It is very bad for me to be left in here"—so says every message on every card and in every poem in the world. But what way is there to set them loose like swallows?

Again, this is getting too metaphysical, too far away from the cards, though with a reason, and I hope a good one—they always do this to me, and to everyone who interests himself in the collection: there is a liberation, a billowing out and up, resulting in a greater inclusiveness (even love becomes included in the direct postcard argument itself, is no longer a separate thing the cards reinforce or deny, becomes "intellectual" or nearly so in the Platonic sense) which would however have been impossible without minute attention to the cards' particulars. It is as in a garden that spreads out until it covers a city; staring hard at the plants one finally turns one's head and finds out one is everywhere and obliged to solve everything. But my ambitions for the moment are more modest. At any rate, let us return to the point that all these communications, represented by the poems and the cards, are disappointments—they do not "equal" the body, or even a headache, effort must be expended to regard them and to read them. Yet somehow one can use their solace, so one continues to write and to send them (ah, how the flower boxes are appearing in the windows)

(and a window box) Left punch, right jab
(is appearing in the flowers)!

Excellency, let God appear to us sometime today
         (Max Jacob)

Bong! The drums
                    Easter cheer
sister swallow |And so
there is a
black face appearing in the flowers

. . . However, it is necessarily true, that after even a limited experience with poetry, with postcards, one begins to know in advance, at least with a part of one's consciousness, that the results will not be satisfying, even though many other benefits may indeed arrive ("accidental aspects")—positions, appointments, the love of beautiful women, all things falling off the shoulder like a shawl made of ice. So that, by the time one is mature (I mean capable of communicating any-thing beyond a simple desire, though perhaps I have this all reversed), there is, in each communication one tries or decides to make, a built-in compensation for the foreknown fact that the communication cannot possibly have the desired effect. Therefore a little "death" is put into poems, and even into some cards, which can act as an inoculation and make them in effect "deathless." Still unsatisfying, but deathless nevertheless, existing to go on taunting and teasing mankind until all are in a common grave. The essential quality of all these immortal works is that they have annealed inside them "death, time hopelessness, all present and accounted for, Sir." Who? are you calling me "Sir," lovely poem? "Yes, Sir, we have ever treated you with respect, we great poems, but you shall die all the same. May I make your bed?" No, will you just keep handing me those postcards, please; there's a good poem. As William Blake said, "Enough! or Too Much."

In any case now it should be obvious that this built-in sense of or allowance for failure is intimately connected with, if not exactly the same thing as the built-in self-hatred and self-mockery spoken of before. I.e.—dealing with particulars, describing them, touching them, paying for them, sending them, all these things done to reas-sure one of his existence and of the reality of his feelings and of other things—this effort itself secret, and secretly investing every action (and perhaps most obviously acts of communication) with a kind of death, a mockery, a self- (and on the highest level too, the level involving existence itself, a sort of twisted form of the meta-physical dissatisfaction expressed by all art—naturally, there, in the midst of praises) despising. Most of the cards, of course, exhibit a far cruder version of these phenomena than do the great works of art I have been using as the secret basis of this discussion.

To return to one or two matters:

I. Is the communication which includes self-mockery and a built-in failure and death the most effective means for the penetra-tion of souls? The question is impossible to answer because in a cer-tain sense there is no other possible kind of communication. It is true that one can, sometimes with a minimum of built-in failure or death, "strike it lucky" both for one's own and someone else's emotional state and for a moment communicate as directly as a bee attacking a white throat. But the soul filled with death is always waiting below the bee and the throat to have its revenge in dreams and in a thousand postcards (thoughts), very many of them sweet as the smell of raw shellfish on a November night.

II. Does the second (i.e. the silver sowing girl) postcard now seem as perfect and sublime as it did before? How can it? The kind of enthusiasm it inspired was obviously an enthusiasm of the moment. If it were really capable of inspiring any other kind (*the* kind, I would say), there would be no point in my continuing this description of the collection. See above. It was not too unlike the "bee sting."

III. In what light now do you view the gyrations of thought which led to the suppositions (that now seem rather naive) about the pain and self-doubt implicit in the writing and sending of the Auvergne postcard? I view them as having been necessary preparation for the state of illumination. At the same time, I would not renounce them for what they are in themselves, for, dear, they are part of a process, and how can I be sure the flowers will continue to turn and to glow in this now dusty greying air were I to cut off a piece of their stems, not to say anything of their roots.

I will stand up now and cross the Seine.

(Later) There is no Alphonse de la Roche listed in any connection whatsoever with the Mouvement Petits Jeux Floraux de Marseille. If he did not have a pen name (a possibility that just occurred to me, but on which it will be hard to check up), then we are in the midst of a problem again, though fortunately (or unfortunately) by now it is a problem which has begun to seem of less and less importance to me, almost to the point, I mean to say, of fading back into the vast anonymity from which all these postcards, in fact all these words, as the result of a puzzling—if by now, I hope, self-described—and very considerable effort and desire, have been momentarily brought into being.

THE RED ROBINS

1975

To Emily

CONTENTS

CHAPTER 1
THE RING OF DESTINY

Jill ran her fingers down the tough golden beard of history. It was fine being there, but she wished there had been boards on the floor. Professor Flint was late; it was already three o'clock. "Chow down!" shouted the corporal, and all the men ran into the eating quarters. "Very tropical weather, Sergeant," said "Dutch," an unusual man who had been hanging around the camp a lot recently. The cord snapped, having suddenly come undone, and the hawsers slipped out onto the blue, frothy waters of Lake Superior.

Joycie was swimming, as usual, without any clothes on. A big bird passed over the tub which had been covered with black tar by a recent accident. The planes sped by. Jules hugged Bonny, but Bonny wasn't very responsive and so Jules finally shrugged his trembling yellow shoulders and went back into the little hut where he began pulling apart the whitefish. "So this is Alaska," said Uncle Mutt—"quite a layout you've got yourself here!" Lyn was afraid he would try to sleep with her because she didn't have any clothes on.

"Santa Claus" mounted the big black sweating horse panting with energy; "Santa Claus" was the nickname of this big criminal who rode off into the West. The little blue bottle had been lost for two weeks; on it was engraved the name Sarah F. Johnston, Townsfoot, Illinois, and looked as if it had been etched on by a screw. Thalia took all her clothes off and looked at the big monkey who was swinging around, apparently vaguely in search of oranges and lemons. "It's a shame Jules is illiterate," Bud said; "we could have gotten him a job with the service; now, though, every chance of that is dead."

This time the country began to deliberate quite a lot about the hawsers. Some said the distance Mole had walked was not being reported right. John worked up a temper and then went to see Pete. His bicycle was missing a bumper. In Kenya the old woman in delirium imagined that she saw snow. "I don't know how I have been alive all this time without knowing what life was all about!" Early said. "Imagine—that I just met Orange last year! we were both at a dance, a local, native affair, and, I suppose, quite naturally, being the only White Europeans there we were thrown together. I think, though in spite of the role of chance and similarity, there was something more—we were 'right' for each other in a way I can't totally understand." "I wish I could have an experience like that!" "You will!" said Early, and patted him on the head as if he were a plane. They took off at dawn looking for the rest of us, but though we signaled at them all day they just kept flying over and flying over until finally our leader suggested that we send the locket back to Mrs. J., and the girls slipped into a sweater although it was very hot.

The motors idled. "Santa Claus" stepped up and swatted a fly. We ate supper motionlessly, waiting for the signal of splashing paddles on the river. When it came we entered our drivers' kit and sped northward for two hundred miles. Then, noticing that it was following us, we got out, filled out a report to the Plague Committee, and sat down there on the ground, waiting for it to come and do its worst. The ennui became almost unbearable. Forests shook. Lyn took off her sweater and performed "semi-nude" imitations of all the Japanese prints of Hokusai.

It was midnight before supper was served to the whole bunch. By the time we got to bed it was dawn. A yellow cloud emerged from the trader's cigarette. The little Japanese children were sweating profusely and not one whit ashamed of it either. Doctor Hubson began stabbing them in the arm one by one. "Now these boys will never get cholera or typhoid fever," he said. The last jab shook the whole bunch. Nat had been unwinding the film; Joyce had taken off her garments in order to go swimming in the beautiful, poisonous little river; "Don't drink the water!" Nat had yelled. But the Colonel's car bumped along the road. A green cloud of essence of cholera came steaming into Mount Fujiyama.

The cards were bolted to the table—a kind of card trick. But the gust of wind emerging from "Santa Claus's" eye was quite a serious matter. Jill took over the steering controls because she saw a pink cloud of cheese down below, and she slipped, hup, out of her blouse, and tup, out of her brassiere, so she could handle every control mechanism securely. Bob watched the varicolored little birds pop around among the trees. "I wish that you'd been my professor really," Lyn said.

"The caresses on shoulders are not properly applied to knees," Kanna said; "oh darling, hold me tight"; but he spilled her out; and the next day the plane came with its bold tips. "The hair of this jungle would steam water out of a rose," Balcony said, sliding down the twisty white rope to a berth in the frog pond; "wow! Jesus!" The Shaman looked at the situation coolly, but you could tell that though he was silent his silence was an intense silence; it all boded ill for the "Red Robins." Finally, though, he spoke, and, as he did so, he lowered his immense and swaying body humbly to one knee: "Only teach me," he begged, "only teach me to play 'Stardust' on the harmonica, and you can do anything to my people that you want."

Jules plucked a trembling leaf from the season's last red branch. Joyce stammered and spilled things on Bob's knees; he took her on his knees then and closed her gentle, protesting lips with a kiss. The Hindus were all naked to the waist. It was a nice day in Ceylon. The canaries were waiting cautiously; they had had experience with white men before; but Carl was too smart for them: he had woven his big net out of canary feathers! Fred said, "We had some bad luck; you can just leave it at that," but the Indians weren't satisfied and said they were going to have some white men's scalps in the affair though it was the last thing they ever did, which, as it so happened, it turned out that it was, because when they began organizing into their scalping expedition, their canoes already partly launched onto Lake Superior, a tremendous storm came, which killed them almost all. Planes were able to pick up a few lemons from their local depots, but rust had destroyed by far the greater part of the crop, at which sugar interests were violently disturbed, from flower-capped Honolulu to white-wavelet-ringed Tahiti, beneath the immortal stars.

The gas did not come in time, so as a result the war had to be fought chiefly by the "Pelicans." Old Mrs. Meyerhazy was dying, her immense white body sprouting everywhere in hairs and sweat. "Oh God," said the child doctor, "I would so surely like to eat a lemon!" After ransacking the doorways of Honolulu they still came after. Now a cloud was blue. Sumner said he saw a star formation two nights previously which had been an almost exact replica of Jill's body stripped of everything but her brassiere.

Brutes! The plane arrived, filled with children's-sized white shoes. Ernie put a tag on each of the attractive women. Three days later he died of a virulent attack of poison ivy. Sylvia smiled. She took out the tiny bottle and poured its contents over the food. There was a tremendous explosion.

CHAPTER 2
AN EVENING WITH THE KOYAMI
REPERTORY COMPANY

That night, after the plane had been parked in the middle of the field, a troupe of Japanese Noh players came out and performed the following drama:

The Dream of a Ruki-Fai-An

An old priest enters and seats himself comfortably beneath a tree, after having thrice turned around, and having shown by his gestures that he is very tired, has been traveling a long while, still has a long way to go, but feels, at least, that he has now done enough for this one day. His name is Ruki-Fai-An. Almost immediately upon sitting down beneath the tree the old man falls asleep. Three young girls enter (all played by old men, as is customary in Noh theatre): They are the dream of Ruki-Fai-An. After they have danced and made various traditional Japanese gestures associated with girlishness, accompanied by sounds, groans, grunts, and bits of language incomprehensible to our Western ear, they creep, one by one, up to the sleeping priest and kiss him gently on the cheek and lips. Then, after a final short choral dance and song, they go off. Ruki-Fai-An awakes, obviously immensely refreshed, and prepares to continue his journey.

One of the oldest of the Noh players, who could speak a little German, told us that this play had been given regularly on this night for over one thousand years. The crickets (or the Japanese equivalent of them) were chirping vivaciously in the bushes, and there was exceedingly bright starlight. Every one of us was in high spirits, and Lyn really had practically to be restrained from throwing herself, half nude as she was, around the neck of one of the old men who had played the part of a young girl in the play. "He's cute!" she said—rather she cried out—"he's just adorable! I could eat him up! Oh I want to hug and kiss him!" But we restrained her, especially Bob, who is very jealous anyway, and besides would never want anything untoward to happen to any of the girls in the party since he had made a solemn pledge to their mothers that no harm should befall them. It was after midnight now, so the old Noh leader thanked us and left. We watched them trudging off through the weeds, in the starlight, some forty dollars richer for their evening's prank, and Don said, "I wonder if they are not, in their own way, far happier than we! After all. they have, every night, their art, these Noh plays of which we have just seen a wonderful example (and I want to tell you that I really enjoyed it, no matter what anyone else thought!)"—Don was famed for his "independence"—"and they seem, also, to live close to nature in a way which is practically incomprehensible to us, much less possible." "It's precisely our superior civilization and knowledge that allow us to 'see' this," Bill pointed out; "think what they would give to be able for one moment to regard things from the height WE do!" We all felt that this had summed up the question. Jane thought she heard a tiger in the brush, but soon all were fast asleep.

CHAPTER 3
THE TIGER HUNT

There are no tigers any more. No tigers. There is a tiger with me now. He is a useful tiger. My tiger, I call him, and, for me, he eats up everything that is around me that I don't like. Which is some days almost everything except the air; and on other days includes that foul stinking air. My tiger would eat ME up, which would be to my delight, but for a paradox which reason cannot resolve. He is my creation, my tiger, and the weather cannot, except in a symbolic sense, destroy the day.

Everything is being gotten ready for the tiger hunt. My tiger stands about idly, watching them play. He knows where the tigers are—i.e. in human hearts. But their preparations go on and on. There are sounds of rifles oiled, locks slipped, horses' feet, and there is the shine of sunlight on flintlock, the red glow of expectation and gleam of sweat on human faces, a warm hint of even hotter summer weather in the trees. It is now 120 in the shade. I do not think I will be able to stand it, but I fasten on my hat and go with them.

Sensing Bud morose and depressed, in other words more than usually sad and introspective, Lyn leaned forward so he could see inside her brassiere and said, "Darling! soon they are going to get the tiger! Isn't that exciting!" "I don't see why we came on this beastly hunt!" Bob said. "Good heavens! if you agree with me—" an astonished Bud could only murmur, "then why—?" Finding herself, at this moment, a bit "out of it," Lyn hastily pulled a big red magnolia blossom from a nearby branch and stuffed it into her bosom, as if to show that to get and do that had been the main reason why she had leaned over that way and shown (by accident, she now wanted the men to believe) her lithe, curvaceous, and extremely unmasculine charms. If Bud was fooled, it was only because he was paying very close attention to something else. "Help!" Lyn called out. A little worm had been on the red magnolia blossom and now it had slipped down between her breasts, biting her or doing something that felt very much like that. Bob reached down immediately and got the devil out. Then, his hand and wrist as though paralyzed by soft white snow, and his whole body electrified like the throat of a caroling Neap-Auk, he suddenly realized what he had done. Lyn, flushed with Bud could not tell whether it was pleasure or embarrassment, leaped off her mount and darted into the surrounding brush. Almost at once she gave a shrill scream. She had discovered the tiger!

Noises of ropes. A noise of lifting up. A noise of ropes. A noise of lifting down. Hawser-like sounds with bulky clearness. When will I return to Lake Superior? The teachings of Buddhism. The smell of jasmine in their temples. None is so miserable as I.

ROAR!

"Jill, have you finished sketching the tiger?" (They were back in the hotel.) "When you finish your sketch, would you show it to Miss Finney? She said she was very interested in your artwork, and I think it might get you somewhere if you showed it to her." "Darling, where could it possibly get me? Here I am, after all, already, in Juoad-Puhr!" And the sleek sound of servants rolling the heavy blue tumblers toward their mistress who sits drinking with a man in a white coat in the hotel garden. "The palace is yours, Missus, if only you would sign these days."

A bird of blue buckwheat floats in with the smell of salt from the sea.

•

The tiger's skin has now been fastened to the top of the "Line-up."

CHAPTER 4
RIVER TRANSPORTATION

Twisting to the right, twisting to the left, a river craft, said Marco Polo, or some such famous name, and many a one after him, is what you make of it—or, as some seafaring men prefer to call any boat, "her." Now, I am an inland seafaring man myself, since this is my first trip, and we after all crossed the ocean in our plane, which in itself scarcely allows a man to qualify himself a sailor. Well, I am an inland sailor now; a type despised perhaps by those who sail the "higher" seas, but a classification which will do for me, and with little discomfort either, for I have had, and scarcely think this situation will change in the future, little to do with that tough and mucky lot who trade their bedrooms for cabin bunks, their porkchops for biscuits, and their pretty lasses for bloody screeching parrots for the space of six twistings of the fathomlessly gorgeous moon. Aye, aye, boys, there she is up there, shining for us inland sailor boys as well as for you, and we shall enjoy her charms on dry land a lot sooner as well, though you may pretend such charms as we claim exist on dry land be only phantoms of a dry, spiritless, and sterile imagination. Why, think you God created the moonlight only so she could shine on the sea? It would have been a great waste, that, and all unlike the mellifluous and mysterious Master of us all in his deep and remarkable ways. Why would he have it shine on land, then? If you can answer me that, I shall come and join you, trade in my comfortably fleeting bark, with just a faint breath of papayas in the night wind sighing through the trees (never far away from us, but far enough!), from my comfortable blanket beneath the stars, I will come and trade it all for your famous feathery stench of parakeet and the dry taste of biscuit that sticks in a man's throat like that powdered nutshell the baggy-trousered Arabs believe will put new life in an old man's body, if he but swallow enough of it, and make a young girl able to conceive. Bejesus if I think it have that effect on you, for you are from what I hear the most sterile and most promiscuous lot of promenading skeletons that ever used God's green-feathered earth as a jumping-off place to be always squeezing together, like frightened sheep, in your wooden- or steel-walled coffin, to go sailing away, and all around in it too. And so proud that it is clean!

But, all that argument to one side, if I were to be told that I had but seventy or less years to spend on this planet, spend them how I would, I should certainly decide to spend at least three on a river. A river is the cussedest kind of transportation that you ever did see, but that doesn't mean it's not the cleanest, safest, finest, most manlike, and most all-out man-satisfying way of seeing anything, of getting on with it, of running away or going home, or doing anything else you can dream up that folks usually do when they can't stand one place and rightly think things might be a little better in some other. Now, I know a lot of people think highly of a road or the air, but a river has three advantages over both of them (and probably too over any other means of transportation of folks or materials they can think up): In the first place, it's clean, which a road aint, and the air aint always, either, what with all them dust and other particles always floatin UP, like books says, and I figure it must be a mighty cloud of dust and such-like things to move through up there. Now, a road you can't keep clean when you have horses on it or no matter what else that's alive and breathin, except perhaps maybe only man, and then again about him you caint be too sure neither, especially if they aint nobody lookin. A river, though, keeps washin itself away, like a bath when there aint no plug but the water keeps rushin in. Why, we even go INto water to git clean, anybody knows that. And we wouldn't hardly go there to GIT something that the thing we was supposedly to git it from didn't have it itself, now would we? A river, you might say, is just about the cleanest thing there could be, because it's always givin ITSELF a bath, washin itself away, down to the sea, and us, when we are fortunate enough to have a craft and to be out upon it, along with it. Now, the other thing that puts a river up over road or air is that it's soggy. When you really get down into it, no matter what river it is, the bottom and sides of it are always soft black mush. This won't seem no advantage to nobody who's never been throwed on his head onto the hard earth by a colt or to nobody who's never thought what it would be like to be dropped onto same from the sky (I guess they aint none of them livin that has actually done it and so could tell us about how it feels, but if we got anything to separate us from the dumb beasts it surely aint the nice way we treat one another but the power we got to imagine things we aint actually done.) Well, like I said, to them as hasn't BEEN thrown or imagined fallin, then that sogginess won't seem like somethin that sets a river up, so it's either agree or not agree and I can't see arguin it no more than that. The third thing that puts a river up is that she won't let you sink, but will keep you afloat, and take you along and land you somewheres while she's doin it, at that. You see, her current is stronger than her downward pull, and so naturally no body that aint big enough to counteract that pull by the force of its own gravity aint never going to sink but instead is goin to be moved right along—no critter smaller than a elephant has anything to be afraid of from fallin in a river. A *ocean*, yes; or a road, which will just leave you there, till somethin steps on you, or rides right over you; and the air, well, we already talked about that, there aint no way to keep afloat up there unless you got wings, which I aint, and so that part don't properly interest me nohow. Them as has wings and hasn't never been throwed from a horse or stubborn old jackass and hasn't never wondered what it was like to be dropped from the sky, they probably aint readin this anyway as they are most likely pluckin their wings and combin them out and all that and gettin them all nice for the next county fair where they're going to be the big attraction, you can't have no doubts about that, or else if they aint got wings and are just the ones who never wondered, why then them are them that wouldn't go around readin no book anyway, and if they *are* readin this one I can just say, "It's HARD, that's what anything but a river bottom is when you fall onto it from the sky—whether you, dumb old Luke Fairwether and Jimmy Swartling, ever thought about it or not. You hadn't better be *tryin* it, neither!"

So that, I'd say, is what puts a river up over all other modes of transportation: it's clean, it's soft, and it won't let you sink, but will float you on down to some pleasant bank, and all free of charge.

We have been floating through the Burma jungle for nine days and there is still no sign of a change. Some tubers have left small, wet marks on the upper caulking spins of the poops, but Don assures us there is no cause for worry. Last night we saw our first indication that there might be human life somewhere about (and, along with that life, some means of attaining our desperately needed food and water)—an arrowhead, or perhaps the tip of a small spear, and in the distance a puff of smoke. Today, however, once more, there was nothing.

The Chieftain receives the banana leaves, folded into the shape of a pipe. "Bring me the music of the most glistening girls," he whispers to his competitor, "that I may smoke." And he throws the broken arrow piece into the air. "If it land by water, our pact is broken. Great steam shall unfold from the East."

CHAPTER 5
SNOW!

The first thing I noticed was the snow. It seemed to come up like a whole lot of larvae. We were ready for just about anything, but not snow. It surprised us and scared us, and what's more it kept on falling. We've kept on up the coast now anyway, but Bob wants us to go back. He says it isn't safe, he promised to keep the Robins together, etc. I wonder how much he understands of what we are all doing here. Marvin has already panicked, says he *will* reach Pai-Kuht, doesn't give a damn if anyone else does, either. So much for him. There are still quite a few of us left, however . . .

Because I do not hope to return again,
Little ballad, to Tuscany,
Take then some news of these to all those interested
Because I do not hope
Because my summation has been disabled
And water rats
Because I do not hope, Tuscany
Lies next to the Marches still
And some day
When I have turned into a puff
Of air, a blaze
Of island smoke
Ah but
I revere you
Returning on the boat

I saw your red hair on your overcoat
Sleeve . . .

Jill said, "Listen, I have been to the Agora of Athens, and to all
the famous seragli of the East, and here you have come to me with
your mouth open, begging that I see a piddling sight like snow for
the first time in a Tropic Zone. Ah, shall you never leave me the
'peace of great experience,' all of you? Is my loneliness doomed
always to be the sole bastion of itself?"

Bob naturally had long ago, seeing that the snow was keeping
on falling, and that there seemed to be about to be other unusual
and possibly dangerous happenings as well, Bob, I say, had naturally long ago begun to try to arrange transportation for the voyage home. The planes, of course, could not take off in that blizzard,
and so he went around to each shipping office in the district, saying
"Ehreng Za-Do," which means Do you have any tickets, and they
always answered him, "Woolp-klo," which means, No, I am sorry,
sir, we do not.

No, if I take a drink you will never let me leave Pai-Kuht! No, I
shall not take another one. Hah! your promises, your promises!
You promised me in the first place that we would never stay in this
hotel! And then you swore we would have separate rooms! and
then—no! I do not want "a cup of tea!" I tell you I am leaving! You
swore that even though you slept in the same rooms with me we
would have separate beds, and then, that since there was only one
bed, you would sleep at my side, on the floor. No, no! go from me!
I do not want another drink here in Pai-Kuht! You disgust me! . . .
And then when you did worm your way into the bed, your promise to lie quietly . . . Hah! no! I will not "speak with you" about it.
There is nothing to say! And then, when you did what you had so
solemnly promised me you would not do, then you swore you
would not move, but leave—and you did leave, but after . . . Well,
now it is I who am leaving! Leaving!

Why do you seek me, god of the sickly wail and uneuphonious song? Is it that I and my kind have offended you in the temples of hillocks? of pillows? For under this stillness I shall never wash the feet of that Illyrian idol whose mother dropped her baby, ao Zagreus, into the pool from which a shy perfume ceaselessly pulses. Dragons! and a store marked "Singing," another, "Clouds." It is too late for us to give over entirely our drifted sensitivity. Yet I would change it all for a paper marker, if you would consent to puff on it, that it be carried, and I also, among the columns of your divine keep.

CHAPTER 6
CARL—AND OTHERS

He was a man with dreams, and Carl called him "High Octane"; they met him when they were in the East. The hotel tables were piled high with every type of commodity; you actually had to fight your way through them. "Santa Claus" was seated at one of the tables, looking like the greedy dog he was. There wasn't another person there with the courage to sit *down* at one of the tables, except Lyn, and she was a girl, perched on the edge of a table top speaking in low tones with Frank. Then Jill and Barbara appeared, and everyone paled. "Tubber" was wearing raincoat and rainboots, and he stood under the hotel porch chatting with "High Octane." When they got up to the proper altitude, Jill tried to take over the controls, but Bob suddenly spanked her so hard that out she flew into the blue, blue sky.

Snow reappeared, like a small shop. It was kept up very well. No one got typhus, though a few people died of dropsy. Ann kept the American flag in the back room. Sometimes an octopus would come in and they would "rain the chute"—that is to say, the octopus would get on top of Ann and she would feel happy. Sometimes it would want to stay there too long and she would not let it. She would give it *beqja* and fish to eat. Then, sometimes, as a special treat, she would let it look at the flag. They had a little house there, called a "hut-boat." Actually, it could float, too. That's why they called it a boat. Bob thought it was humdrum to have a madman's fate, but he used to keep his tusks there nonetheless. He was not the kind of person who could ever have gone back to the States.

Joycie knew that, so she gave him all the sand he wanted, and all the spittle. They had a little hut you could catch octopus in. It had a net on it, and the octopus would lift up the net to get the little imitation fish they would place inside. Above the net was a knife. It had a kind of spring attachment, like a guillotine. When the octopus would put his arm in to get the fish, they would push the spring. The knife would come down and chop off his arm. Then he would put in another one. Up went the knife, and that one would be chopped off too. They had a whole shed there filled with octopus arms. They called it the "Armory." Jake thought that was funny, but Ann said she would kill him if he ever hurt an octopus again. They still kept swimming up in droves because on that part of the coast there are a lot of them.

The White House Secretary hesitated before the Chieftain's door. Had it all been a terrible blunder? At least we can boast of a substantial improvement in our apple crop. Jasmine kissed him, then began to bite, bit him on the lower lip and wouldn't let him go. The airplane instructor fortunately was an experienced "snow pilot," and so he built the house right away.

"Yes, why don't you bring a number of them around to the pool. There I can taste them, and read to my heart's delight. On this night, this night, this night in which the world shall have taken on a new cleanliness, whiter than dust. And I be a successful man in my own age. A veritable tower, who does not need exile for his swill. Bring them to the pool." A thousand servants. And the tracery of sharks. Suddenly in this silence.

Bugs stood out on the caterpillar plants making a round place where they would later leave holes. Alvin pinched Lyn's breast. He was new in our bunch. The snow covering up the caterpillar-tree worms made them look like the grey beards of tiny old men. There was a reddish-black flash to the south. Where is Flint? And also Jill is absent. "I am yours," Lyn said; but the boys wanted to go even further.

"They shall come, but fly so high that we shall never see them again, ever."

Neal made it on a "flash flight" back to the States, but Philipps refused to believe this incredible tale. "Why, you will have to find someone else to believe that!" the jolly-hearted old-timer scoffed. "I will take it as high as the White House," Earl said. And he went there. They set him down on a pink-and-red upholstered Empire couch and let him wait there, holding the three-pointed light-yellow crown in his hands for what seemed to him an interminable period of time. Then Lyn came out and washed her stockings. "Aren't they ever going to let me in there?" the monarch replied, believing, in his delirium, that he still owned all those countries. Sarah looked down at the red moss pityingly. "To think that that too," the Captain said, "is a form of life!" "If that is true, why then—" the President excitedly said. "Yes, that's right, Sir," shouted Bob, suddenly turning round from him, on a hunch.

CHAPTER 7
ALUHA-NE-HA

Mona, sweating as she had never been since she came to Tahiti, knew that the end was near.

A man in a white gown stood staring silently at the "Bianca Madonna."

The mood of the island was now definitely "Pro-Native," "Anti-Interference."

But she had done nothing but try to be happy.

That sow near the edge of the grass fence was her own.

A little boy who has been asleep wakes up and calls, "Anneh-ha!" "Anneh-ha! Anneh-ha! Anneh-ha!" he calls. In the blue air a pink bird grows quiet to silence his shout.

In the pharmaceutical hut a beetle is beginning to be born. In the life process everywhere such passion and such ecstasy!

The "Christ-Man" walks over to Mona-ha.

"We are going pagan now," he says. Seemed a million years since she had seen Lyn or Bob.

The "band" rattled at another station.

"Listen," Bud said, "we must think of her!" Playing on his xylophone.

"Didn't you hear the child calling you?" he said.

She cried. "My name is not Anneh-ha, but Aluha in your language—Mona in my own."

"From now own," the man in the white coat said, "your name shall be none at all."

"I am—" She smiled—"I am Mona. I am Aluha-Ne-Ha," she said.

"But we shall not grant it her . . ." So many years away, the wet sail crossing the distance.

Like waving corn. Meanwhile from a distance Ben was tinkering with the engine.

He came near where Mona was but then crossed over.

She heard the shrill voices of the loons.

"Dad" sitting in Panama hat still working on his "Chrestomathy."

He crossed over until she came along.

CHAPTER 8
THE PRESIDENTIAL BRIEF

 The presidential brief treated these matters as follows—

Subject: German-American Tourism in Polynesia and the Far East, Specifically As It Regards the Correct Retinue and Behavior of Such Private Individuals Who Choose to Leave This Fair Land, and, Even More Specifically, of Groups, Such As the Red Robins, Who, by Their Conduct Abroad, No Doubt Invite Reflection on the Manner of Life Led Here in These United States; Along with Several Recommendations to Such Americans As May Chance to Visit Foreign Shores; plus (perhaps) a Brief History of the Red Robins (or else a Selection from the Hinduism Index) and a Description of Official Feeling about the International Criminal Santa Claus.

Of all the Red Robins, Lyn is the most beautiful, Bob is the best talker, Louis the most serious, Sam the happiest, Jill the quietest, Neal the most wholehearted in everything he does, and Bud the all-around most considerate of other people's feelings. When such people tour, they are bound to give a certain impression of our national life and standards. Therefore:

1) It is highly desirable that the young women show the "line of points" and "baboon's teeth" on the breast and the inner thigh.

2) Young and middle-aged alike should show a knowledge of the "Sixty-Four Points." Private discussion with alien individuals will be in this way abetted. In the Malay States, especially, where prelates

are few and far between, it has been thought desirable to eliminate the potentially criminal element in favor of the sexual—to stress, in a word, the essentially civilized refinements on one's animal nature in the presence of savages who, having, surely, that in common with us, will be reassured and not find us (as was sometimes the case, according to reports, during the last great International Exposition) too unlike themselves and therefore of a species that it cannot be a serious crime to kill.

3) When foreigners talk to you, try to speak to them in a normal, equable tone. Do not become frenziedly excited if you can possibly avoid it.

4) The monkey is a sacred animal in many countries. Keep such facts in mind, and beware of your conduct toward most of the animals that you will meet. A cow may be sacred here, a swordfish there.

5) Keep your planes as quiet as possible during night and early morning hours. Remember that people in other countries need sleep just as much as we do, and that they are likely to find it difficult to sleep if there is a loud sound of motors.

6) The same sun shines on American and stranger alike. All men are equal. Treat them as such.

7) "Indecent" exposure by young women is held under a mortal taboo in some countries beyond the Pacific, whereas in others it is considered perfectly natural. In metropolitan China the young women cover their breasts, even though it is there perhaps that one most wishes they would not. A small guide to correct behavior in regard to dress may be obtained from the Foreign Office or from any U.S. consulate abroad.

8) The general rule for our own women to follow is that they should wear the minimum amount of clothes permitted, so that the marks can be as visible as possible.

9) When lying down with a young woman of another country, a citizen should first inquire of her knowledge of the "Sixty-Four Points," so as to be able to deem what is considered fit and proper by her own people. For example: although the anal or "lower" congress is held in high esteem by the Persians, it was little practiced in India and points east before the introduction of sodomy by the Musulmen early in the twelfth century. Mouth congress is considered improper feminine behavior by some Orientals; the greater part of them will practice it gladly, however, if the subject is introduced in the proper fashion.

10) I earnestly wish that the Robins would come back to the United States; however, this is not an order.

11) And as for Santa Claus, that fiendish crook who's stolen the name of the bravest laddie in all Christendom, I wish him the unholy fires of Hades to burn his brave face. May he be speared, as men spear the suction-footed frog the Malay call the "octopus," and may the Mountains of Hell cover him for all the wrong he has done. And may my darling come to me, burning with dark desires. May I be man enough to fulfill them. May I lose the name "Oven Face." May I have the agreement of you all in wishing the Red Robins a thoroughly wonderful trip?

Appended to the Brief were these notes from the Hinduism Index, presumably to help with international communication.

Ee-Plath-Ha. The breasts and sides of a woman.
Mag-h. The woman's smile, seen from the side and from the back, when she turns to look at a man for the first time.
Je-the. Light reflected in the woman's eyes during the act of love.
Hochomak. A man who looks like an ape and is favored only by certain types of women.
Mok-t. Woman white as a polar bear. An abnormality in most Hindoo regions, though not a repellent one. The word is not used for those afflicted with leprotic whiteness—such a woman is called "A-ga-tho-nan."

Jeraydeh. The first mild evening after the beginning of a love relationship. When it occurs to great and famous persons it is gen-
erally regarded as a sign of peace.

Ir-doh-ta. A woman's eyes.

Alaquatah. The man's wrist, at the moment he is picking up the
wedge, or "ooldoothah."

Tin-dra. A moment of the day in which a man sees more than two
seductive women. These moments are highly esteemed and
often recorded in notebooks by the Hindoos.

Soomh. The soft lower portion of a young girl's belly, a favorite target for "Rikk-hi," or love arrows.

Shehr-at. A rapid and indifferent pelvic movement.

El-umh. The shirt of a duck (idiomatic expression for "fair weath-
ered friend").

Cao-duhvb. Carved lemon blossom (a highly esteemed Hindoo dish).

Flao-oot. Braved breast—that is, the girl's breast after one has dared
to touch and caress it. Forever after, it is said to have a different
feeling to the hand of the lover.

Shem-raht. A Jewish book used for Hindoo holy purposes. The book
is not recognized as sacred by the Jewish religion.

Vi-o-go'h. Literally, "the loveliest blossoms of the field." In its idiomatic
religious use, however, it refers to the vision of the softened breasts,
abdomen, thighs, and knees of the beloved woman which the
lover possesses after the act of possession when he is viewing her
from above and looking from the head down. The opposite view is
called *Vogh'* or *flax,* when the lover regards the gratified beloved
from the pelvis up. A good deal of the most striking Hindoo poetry
is concerned with these two "visions" or "moments." Much that
seems obscure in the lyric and even in the allegoric literature of the
land is made clearer by an awareness of the frequency of, and an
understanding of the various conventional elements of this theme,
the *Vi-o-go'h-the* or "love-moment-of-vision."

CHAPTER 9
AN ARM AND A LEG

"So at last you have come back to me, my pet," said Mr. Broadhurst with a twinkle in his lustful eyes (a twinkle that, it must be confessed, barely shaded the expression of total and bestial lust which dominated his every feature). Lyn sat down and made herself comfortable. "I have come to talk to you about Jill," she said. "You remember that time after . . ." "That will do, that will do," said Mr. Broadhurst; "if I want to talk about Jill I can talk to her myself. Now that you are here let us talk about you." "Me? there is nothing to say about me," Lyn said modestly, searching around the room for the picture of Bud which she had come to get. "Why don't we have a 'Bourbon Cocktail,' " cried Mr. Broadhurst. "All right," she said, and he ran out into the kitchen on little egg feet. When he was once safely out of the room my intrepid aviatrix went at once to his safe and placed four sticks of dynamite there; lighting a match she took a deep breath but just then she heard the booming voice of Albert Broadhurst from behind her. "Drop that flame," he cried, and she turned, bewildered, to his primrose kiss . . . When Albert awakened it was already light, and the tiger hunt began. Luc and Lyn were safely ensconced in the "hutment" which was the most attractive feature of the mud and grass river boat which Louis had given to Luc. Had his experience all been in vain? Albert scanned the Asian coast disconsolately. He decided that, having nothing else to do, he would go to the octopus market and have a look. Now, you must know that the octopus market in Ytek is one of the wonders of the world. Men have traveled thousands of miles to see it, and women, faint souls, have passed away at the very thought of its bloody and grisly horrors. Once the French poet Margève visiting in these parts happened to come upon the thing by accident, and left a record of his experience (the last thing, by the by, that he ever wrote) which begins

Si le bon dieu a commencé
Par donner tout ce qu'il fallait
A Adam et à Eve—
Cheval, chat, chien, tout utile—
Ce que je me demande, Seigneur,
Est simplement cela—comment
As-Tu jamais créé le Poulpe
Qu'on voit ici saigner . . .

For my own part, it is less the bloody and horrible aspects of the market that attract my interest than it is the human ones. What a symphony of chatter! of buy and sell! of how much this! and how high that! of cut his legs off for me will you and those are not legs those are arms, what matter?! And what feed for a novelist, for a teller of tales! Who is that man there selling only the eyes? how did he awake this morning? and where does he go to pluck them? how, my laddies, and this is your novelist's great dilemma, does the earth seem to him this morning? the same, think you, as it seems to you as you sit in your well-kept room overlooking the garden, with the fresh bare paper before you and the maids in white starched dresses awaiting your command in the pantry—? And who will tell me the story of that old woman in an octopus-hide coat, who is huddled in converse with a bearded stranger over there across the way?

Jill uncrossed her legs coolly. Her whole body was blasted with love. So are you set upon going away? she said. Yes he said. She smiled up at him a little sadly. He took the blue skull and cross-bones into his hands and kissed it. The gigantic airplane slowly settled down on the white mountain. The bridge had hair on it. Luc said it was a "sacred horse." When Louis returned to the monastery he found another gift from Ellen. That time it had been flowers;

this time it was a human head. But already they were moving about him, "blasting the incense." She crossed the little garden quietly and bumped into the white wall. Don lay there bleeding. The Moslem women picked it up and "garnished" it. Neal started up the plane, but both of them had already almost certainly lost the use of their left legs.

October. Albert was sad. He took down the book of Noh Plays and began to read. The plays were good. He laughed. It was fun reading them. They had many different plots. But there was always a priest. Albert called Bob, but Bob was gone. Albert called Bill. In came Bill. Albert said to Bill, "Ha ha. In each Noh play there is a priest." "Ha ha," Bill said. "Ha ha ha ha," Albert said. Bill laughed again too. Then both men laughed a long time. Then they went to bed. Albert laughed again. He was already in bed. He called in to Bill. "There is a priest in each play!" Bill laughed and both were in bed. "Ha ha." Albert felt better. "Ha ha ha ha." *But he remembered that moment long ago when Lyn destroyed the ring.*

CHAPTER 10
BARE KNEES

With our skirts drawn up around our thighs, and then dry out, the storm beginning to seep through the bamboo slats, all the same, we began to talk about some of our more noteworthy experiences. It was a generation of *things* we discussed in the frogs' air there, as the dryness traditionally associated with intense lightning splattered us on this blue occasion into, not out of, the sheets of our truth. It was a high time for vigor, and some, as the flashes grew yellow and blue, spoke in tall, proud voices of exiles beyond the vishnu tree in the harbor, of a place where women's tails were dusted daily by young foodless Francophiles, and where the matter-of-factness we all associated with Tahiti and with the springtime Marianas could have been seen for the solemn pink hoax that it was. In any case, impossible to go up in the planes, even for purposes of reconnaisance, with such flashing, and so we kept sitting, standing, staying, like bunched-up straw more wet than dry, with our skirts (when we were girls) drawn up around the thigh, and watching to see if there was any change. Eventually it came. To some, the lightning seemed like a mirror trick, and they went outside.

Beyond the horizon
When the evening is blue
If you are flying
We fly there too
Just call us

And we'll respond
Good evening to you all
The picnic tables are stacked
And bugs are beginning
To scuttle over tables all
Rolling up their food in ball
But we won't eat those insects
Because we're human
We're oh so human
We'd like to meet you some night
In that evening sky
To discuss our adventures
And listen to yours
And now for the moment farewell!

Then:

Judy, far off in the Stati Uniti
How I miss you, miss you, Judy
You are my ideal girl!

The raging black Hawaiian sea thenceforth drowned out all noises.
And a traveler, coming over the Ka-Zeeh Pass of Mount Kor-Nisha,
would swear that he had seen nothing more than the raving and
buzzing of the summer flies. He would perhaps have been surprised by their pinkness, even their redness, had he viewed them
up close, or, if he had been especially attentive, by the long steely
sound of mechanical humming, which was a strange noise to be
coming from insect jaws. Kah-ze-bah! Gongzah Gahng-tai!

They made for mount Taisho and then across the Great Asian
Divide to Kujiki, down over the Baijaki Pass, then to follow the
Cirrhonean Wetlands as far as Mochaigin, where one Hoo-Long
map says the magic country begins.

CHAPTER 11
AMONG THE ISLANDS

Far away, in Modeste, Arizona, a gasoline pump was being filled with fuel. You could smell it in the faraway. Everyone nodded and sang. It was a big day for the "Cold Bachelors." Organized originally as a sub-group for a group of working auctioneers in Southern California, the "Milers a Minute" had been delighted at joining the "Home-Runners" for the purpose of forming the new "Cold Bachelors Heading-for-the-Eastern-Sun Movement."

The "Cold Bachelors" were organized along the lines of a primarily "service" organization. Chet Byers (also called "Rebo") was in charge. Taken under advisement by the simplest and most trusting of doves, the Bachelor management would henceforth have nothing to fear unless they decided to leave U.S. shores and embark for the Far East, which, with what was to become their characteristically bad luck, they did. They came out to help the Shards. Well, the Shards, they, at least were somehow powerful. But the Bachelors at first were nothing. The Bluebirds came later, and they were a mighty group, but the Bachelors were attempting to cope with fundamentals at a time when civilization had long ago passed them by. Neither in Canton nor at any point in the snowy East, nor on the sun-spotted mountains of Tai-Chong could the Bachelors overcome their essential dilemmas. At Easter Island they landed first and made obeisance there. But soon the world had blown them down. This was before they actually joined the Shards. The Shards were run by the Easter Bunny and hated the Red Robins. The trouble with the Cold Bachelors was that they did not know how to fly.

If the white men brought religion, still the Admiralties were pale and gold, stifling in the summer heat, mere bits of earth and grass and stone, not anywhere near what Baudelaire called "a forest of symbols." But there were also many little bits of shell; and one day the Robins built an airship out of sea shells, and the tiny black and white birds of the Islands were to see them no more.

"Compare me to an intense rose," Lyn said, leaning back out of the cockpit, with her nose tilted upwards, and the clouds above her. "Quick! we have to get back for the fishing expedition. I hear the Shards are after us again." "They'll never get us," Lyn said, laughing. She was wearing a taboo-looking blouse. "Santa Claus is too good a fighter. And besides," she added, her white teeth glistening like the Hawaiian Isles, a regular string of pearls, "we have a brand-new density of war-scope with the revived and monastery-liberated Louis!" "Right," said Early, "right as a bamboo bathtub!" They all laughed and, getting out of the dumpy little rowboats, began the long swim to San Marc.

Meanwhile the Shards were just coasting along, the Easter Bunny was standing at the masthead, they were singing a couple of songs, when suddenly they saw the forms of Lyn and some of the others in the water. "The enemy is right in our power," they said. "We cannot let this occasion pass! Let us kill them if we can!"

One of the Shard songs—
Death to all who challenge our mad Bunny!
Death and torture to any who dismay
His regal presence!
We are loyal to the end.
Whatever he wishes, we will do it!
We care nothing for the consequences
We hold him in such awe
To do what he says is all we ever wish!

There are actually such creatures in the Southern Pacific, I can assure you. And they are not just the products of an imagination's leap. The totalitarian impulse of some and the others' wish to be totally submissive to them are facts which can be verified on most any sunny day. Go out and try it. Or rather do not. Let the Robins go for you. And above all beware of the fate that is going to befall the Sad Bachelors. For they will, eventually, I think, be covered over by the sea.

CHAPTER 12
SUNSET OVER ASIA

Sunset over Asia! And the clouds over Tufu, perfect and golden. Jill threw her pajamas into a bag. She was going home! Mom and Dad had been sitting on the steps of the Bengal Coluhdson for the major part of five or six days, waiting for their pretty little baggage, and now she came, with one leg after the other, a sexy girl. "You jujube, you teenager!" said the ape, and devoured her. Jill woke up. Bob said, "Jill, wake up!" She said, "I'm already awake." He said, "There's a big fire in the jungle. Look at it. How could all those wet things burn?" Jim came in. "They dried out the jungle and then they set fire to it." "What nonsense," Santa Claus says. Big Bill Tanerlane comes in and plays a drum. "Doo de doo dee doodee," chanted all the kids. Santa Claus walked over to the gaily decorated table on which Master Chung was sitting. "What are your thoughts for the day, sir?" Bob said. Master Chung eyed him sideways. "Give to the needy," he said. Pat and Lyn and Bob and Jill went out in the hot summery jungle. The fire was almost completely died down. Chung eyed her. "I'd better be getting over to Mom and Dad," she said. "They want me to go home."

How many mothers and fathers had waited for sons or daughters at that hotel! How many unhappy cries, how many sad, slow realizations! None of their children would ever come back or go home! There was a graveyard for parents there, full of sculptured Chinese angels. Parents would pass it on the way to the Coluhdson, not knowing what it was. "Soon," they would think,

"Jill or Bob, or whoever my child is, will be in my arms and then come home with me." They wished to marry, to bear children, to go into business. They didn't seem to know what the President had done to the country, what insects had done to our lives. Mother sat in her chiffon dress, waiting. Father raffled his cuffs. "Surely she will be here soon," he sighed, "for the sun is now high in the Bengal heavens for the fifth day!" "She will never come," said the mother. But now she was there, all legs of her. "Mom and Father, I am not going home. I just—can't," Jill said, twirling about and showing them the candy-looking Cantonese ruffles underneath her skirt. "I just can't now. I don't know why. I don't suppose I ever will really."

Wet sails smacked in the distance by harmony's waves sent cool steely breezes against the motionless hides of ten elephants waiting in Bombay for a no-good ship which would never take them, as Don had heard and someone had ordered, to the elephant skidrow for death. More likely a hide market would evade their fleas! And now the huge Dutch custom liner sailed by as well. A smell of lavender soap was in the breeze, presaging nine o'clock, when Miss Poulton would come out of her store, close the gate, and be a shimmering waving presence in the eyes and mind. Santa Claus glanced around. He thought he knew how her father felt. Would those two meet? "Jill, I want you to come home," her father said. But she had vanished into a kind of womanliness in which both he and her mother had lost their belief.

"Father," she said, "what if I did come back?" But by this time she knew that there was no hope, the mother, and so she restrained her husband's arm by touching his wrist with her pale hand. He turned on her, his eyes were shining. "Let me try more, Mother," he said. She said, "No, Jill will never come home."

"But what, daughter, have you here? The dark blue clouds will find you floating, a dismayed and fatherless Robin, with nothing of your own you cannot hide." "No, Mother," Jill said. "No, that's not the way it is."

A tender strain of violin music came floating to them on the steps of the Coluhdson as they sat there in the middle of the day and Jill suddenly remembered it was spring. She remembered a May evening filled with frost-white butterflies and tulip-and-rose-bearing sticks.

"One of us—Louis—has found a way of religion over here," Jill said. "Bob has found tigers. And I have found something else." "What is it, dear?" her mother said. "You can bring it back to the States." "It's, it's a way of feeling," Jill explained. "I—I also think I've fallen in love." "What is his name?" asked her father. "Santa Claus," Jill said, "but of course not the real one, I mean the one in stories, but someone else." "Let him be brought before me." "Father, he will not come." "Why cannot I meet the man my daughter loves?" "Perhaps you can, but not here, but not now." "Why?" "Well, all right, well, then, yes, perhaps you can. At least I'll try. You want to see him now?" "Maybe we do not," said the mother. "Will it make us unhappy?" "No," her daughter said, "but you must promise to be kind. He is a rather unusual kind of man. He might be—violent." "Then so might I," said the father. "Oh my God," cried the mother and she almost sank, fainting, to the steps, which were as snowy white as any leper's cheek and brow, though these were hard, like shoulders.

Santa Claus said he would meet them at five o'clock. Jill was trembling as she led him there. A twittering canary called its headless mother in a voice cemetery beyond the sea. Five kinds of apricot were poisoned by mail—a special sort of process. Jill's father affably smiled. "We are happy to meet a friend of our daughter," he said. Jill's mother was dressed in frills of white. "Jill has told us wonderful things about you," she murmured. Santa Claus began discussing the recent Bengali political campaign with Jill's father, who ended up saying, "Well, I must say he's a pretty nice guy!" Jill's mother was charmed by Santa's attentiveness to the few, rather feeble, bird-like attempts she made to enter the conversation. "Well," said the father over breakfast the next day, "we may stay here and become Robins ourselves!" Jill was happy it had sort of worked out. "He's a fine man, to care for her," the father said. "Though she doesn't need him," said the mother, "being such a strong, fine, independent girl herself."

After lunching with Jill and Santa Claus at the Coluhdson "Harbour Club" next day, the middle-aged couple flew away, much happier, all in all, than most parents who have come to Asia to try to make their children come home.

THE MENU
Shrimp Cocktail
Assorted Hors d'oeuvre, Sydney Style
Harengs refroidis
Filets of Sole, Sydney
Roasted Fox
Pilot's Salad
Mousse Tour Eiffel
Fruit Canopy
Demitasse

CHAPTER 13
AN AFTERNOON WITH THE
COMÉDIE FRANÇAISE

"It is interesting," Jim said, "to think about the heart of an animal. We, according to the customs of travel we have, we have the habit of looking at them almost every week if not every day or even every hour—I mean to say we look at animals—I don't say that we are wise enough to know the animal heart."

"We can try," said Lyn.

A dog spoke: "I am an 'animal,' though civilized and domestic. And I am not known. When the wind blows, that great hot and ferocious wind which comes, they say, from Rhodes and the Alsatian Sea, I have in my heart that which is very unknown to man.

"Ah, Man! with his machines, his tools, his odd customs! and who does not know at all the generous manners of the animal, for all his Aeneid and his Dostoievsky. Not even the most ordinary things. Should I not say that we are unknown countries? And if we now ask you for help, it is that we have intention to bring you Nobility—simplicity in your movements, and the blood of the great lands and their oceans in your heart.

"What makes our largenesses and our nobilities is our relation to nature and the fact that we are WITHOUT HOPE.

"I love Man—but what if it were my destiny TO BE?"

The profound influence of a gun on him (the dog). Oh sure. And next day Bob hopped a ride to Hawaii on the *Aphrodite*. "To drink myself the hell out of here," Bob said. And Jill took the airmail roseleaves along. They were apes in bed together then.

"I did not want to bother Man. Ah, but. Suddenly all at once I was able to speak. And what would I be now amidst the jungle of other dogs . . . ?"

CHAPTER 14
JIM BEGINS TO WRITE

Jim began writing poetry chiefly to please Jill, who at one point felt bored by our travels, feeling that just coursing about the way we did was "shallow," so she started to write. Jill's poems weren't very good (a few were interesting, but not really original); Jim's, on the other hand, were good from the start, even though he had very little technical skill. They were good because, while rather strange, they had the ring of honesty about them, they seemed to treat of experiences which to Jim in one way or another were urgent and real. Now, sometimes, he finds a letter, in a small Chinese hotel, from an admirer who had hoped he would stop there and had written, "Master, I hope you receive this. It seemed to me that during your travels you might stop at this little town, in this hotel. . . ." Jim pretends to be surprised, but I think that by now he has a strong sense of his literary power and that he feels assured of his new vocation as an artist.

He began to write in Shanghai.

SITTING IN SHANGHAI AND LOVING YOU

The hawser out the window
Is black and green and white;
Into the motionless mittens
Of Shanghai comes a sound of duskiness.
It is frigid above the heads
Of believers in their twelfth selves—

To believe in one self is to be near you
But of this, being near you is the condition.

BLAME

I have traveled over twenty thousand miles
Seeking for happiness
And the sparkle of crystalline seas.
What I've found instead is a penchant for whales,
A neat tornado of tea leaves,
And the burning license-plate of your head.
Am I to blame for this
Or is the pure snow of your vision? my vision? vision?
Say yes or no—
Then kiss me again, Jill darling, and I'll go.

Since Jim had been writing for so short a time, one couldn't say
that his style had changed very much. What there was in these early
poems was an ever-varying freshness. Here is one written in Pai-Kuht:

THE TREETOPS

Seeing along the tops of trees,
Jill, can we go
Where no one dares
But towers?
Each has an insect's face,
Their perfume is bright and green.
Love stands atop these valleys
With a palace of swords.
Outside the tops,
Impeccable,
Outside their arms,
The road uncoils before us like a ribbon—
And day has as many leaves
As light may face.

Here is another, written on the road to Fu-chu-foo:

POPULARITY AND FOUNTAINS

They say that popularity, like fountains,
Is very big, and that mountains, like a heartbreaker
Are cold. But my weeping, like champions,
Is strong against whatever
Your smiles, like a daze, are for—
As a rose, these combs are meant for you forever.

The poem accompanied the gift of some combs at the time we were spilled from our car. Louis, flying overhead, had to rescue us That was one of our most difficult trips, the one to Fu-chu-foo. Jim wrote only one poem while we were there:

THE BLACK

The black
Horror of a visage
Where the forest
Suddenly curdles
To slat boats, comets of disease,
Scarlet hedges
Mentioned one time
Only
By the clocks of a dame
Corset
Arrested disease clouds elephant death vulneragality
Is
Antlered.

Another poem, untitled:

She is standing on my eyelids
As I walk through Shanghai levels

And the sea
Boisterously calls me—
Though shark and barricuda play
At Tomaguchi Beach
My heart is stricken
By the thought of one person, Jill, undressed,
She is standing there
Naked
She is standing there
Our hands touch—crustaceans, Villiers.

Another:

Love is my medicine
No other can cure
This aching, this striving
Which here
In fair Ragh-Puht
Drives me to insensate despair!

Once, on the way back to Shanghai, our car broke down, and
Jim wrote this poem:

It is the time of the breaking down of bits of gears;
I for one will be happy when we return to the planes;
I could fly about in the Indian or China sky for fifty years
And never tire of it, O never tiring.

Come, my yellow rosebud, come, my Jill,
Though changed by time let me not to the marriage of
True minds admit impediment: your eyes,
Though colors break, have other eternity than parts of cars.

To love a broken gear, what is that? But to love someone,
Eye faded, skin gone slack—not that we are threatened with that
As yet—is good, as is to love winter, autumn . . .

Radiant the human colors affection gives:
Thus from this breakdown may we learn
Of love, what ours may be, and is.

Most thought, at the time, that this was Jim's greatest moment as a lyric poet, and it is true that here, in a way, he expressed his highest human feelings in a form more classical and succinct than any of us were even able to imagine as being possible. However, as time tracked him down, through another autumn, summer season, spring and winter, Jim began to bear down in a different way: he tried to hear words individually, words and their sounds, in trying to find not the highest kind of comments *about,* but the actual felt and shifting pathways of things. First he expressed, in Ben-Ghai, his desire to do it·

AND

You, O tiger of peripheral thought,
Not. I walking, the ambulant ocean seeing,
A blue wavecap here and there. Jungle hot.
And between them the people, individual as a blue wasp—
Santa Claus, Arthur, and Jill
Or sometimes even the stones—everything
Like a sweet blackness
Deadened by a similarity that makes them gay
To cross into that, like a chicken emerging
And the blue asphalt of thought.

There were so many blue wasps that summer! so many young girls dancing in frocks at the hotel! so much orange! so many teetertotters left abandoned in the public square! The railroad train stopped. It looked like a smokestack. Then green spots started to appear all over its wheels and sides.
Jim wrote:

It has a green exzema
Which protracted its foolishness

Poor foolish smoke-last train
 Sweet locomotive, dead poor selfish thing,
"Ped-ped" over the landscape, oh have you
 Seen it they called that train
"The Monarch Engine"?

 Another:

 Oh in the precinct of whales
 What mouth shall spout, which?
'Tis not mouth which spout
 But vent-in-flesh, hooray hooray.
 Combray can I flash you American this one?
 They back and forth.
 I wonder how he who why they
 And always the same dull "But thyself"
 At age twenty
 She appeared
 Slimmer than a shield
 I understand your metaphysical spout
 Danced together
"Americanized by this time"
 Or nearly so, the steam clouds from an engine
 As on an April day the smoke from a train.

CHAPTER 15
THE APES OF BANZONA

Sing, Muse, the war between the Apes of Banzona
And the good people, who had come from far over the sea
To hunt tigers, to have adventures, and in general
Escape from the terrible humdrum which they feared
Their lives would have if they remained in America,
Deutschland, Italy, Peru, and France!
Sing of the war's cause, the threat posed by haughty Banzonino
Who promised the Robins extinction if they did not leave at once,
Unreasonable threat! not just one island but Asia and the earth as
   a whole,
Whereat the Red Robins took counsel, and Santa Claus was foremost
Among the elect assemblage. "Children," he said, "we will never be
   frightened away!"
"Not ever," Bud laughed, and he imagined the insides of ships
Filled with machinery and pipes, all usable as weapons
With which the enraged Robins could crush the enemy Banzona
And he laughed at the thought that they would ever surrender
And a large white captain emerged from the island underbrush
And addressed them in these words: "I am a marauding captain
Long have I lived on this island, I know these apes;
I warn you, begone; for nothing can withstand them."
Jill laughed in silly apprehension; she accosts the wanderer,
"Why do you say, wanderer, that they are invincible?
Do you not know who we are?" "Aye, you are the Bold Bluebirds
   and I have heard much of you."

"No, we are the Red Robins, and none can withstand us."
"Why, ye look to me like a band of silly adolescents
With one old man to guide ye or else be guided
By your juvenile fears and lusts—well, I want no part of ye.
Remember the captain who warned against the terrors of Banzona
For ye shall not prevail, but rather be smashed into grit and mica!"
And they watched him stamping off into the brilliant dust
Of the island-carrying dawn, and Bob said, "Wait!" when they
    wished to at once resume the counsel,
"There is something I want to see"—he lifted a gold-filed telescope
To his burning eyes. "It is as I thought," he said,
And he told what he had seen: two hundred yards in the distance
The captain had shed his costume, becoming the Ape
That he truly was in an instant; and, filling the jungle
With gestures suggestive of cursing and threats, he had gone on his
    way.
"That gives us hope," Jill said, "for surely those apes must fear us,
As we are more intelligent than they—that they send an agent
To dissuade us from battle argues they do not wish to battle us,"
And Santa agreed and then he turned from them, his eyes brim-
    ming with tears:
"Once," he said, "I hoped to be a man of peace, to embody in my
    person
The hopes and dreams of all mankind; but I became a criminal
Out of bitterness, reacting against a cruel and bitter world;
Then, in Asia, one morning, surprised in my fears
By the tender sunshine of Raguht, and in the fair persons
Of you, Bob, Lyn, and Jill, at the time of the Slimy Green Things,
I had the wish to reform, to change, to be once again the good great
    Will
Of Kindness, and now these Ape-men force me again to damage;
I do not wish war, but by God if they oppose us with the bitter weapons
We shall destroy them." Then Louis stood straightforward in
    Santa's place
And addressed the wet-eyed assemblage, for they had broken at
    Santa's tears

Into a general moisture, which the hot island sun was not drying
Because they continued to flow, the tears of the people. "You have
    heard what Santa
Has said; now hear me, Lord of the Bluebirds and Strangers!"
Whereat they were all quiet; you could not hear one of them chirp-
    ing or quarreling, as sparrows sometimes do above an East Side
    apartment
When there has been celebration the night before, and Madam is
    sleepy
And she calls to her maid in distress, "Joyce, quiet those sparrows,
I must sleep," yet she knows she cannot do it, there was no such
    piping
After Louis had commanded silence; instead, they waited for his
    words.
"My counsel is to go and attempt to make peace;
Let them know we do not fear them but that we do not wish to visit
    disaster
Upon their hair-boned heads." At this there was general laughter
And some surprise among the Robins, who were ready for war.
"No! let us tear them into shreds and pieces," shouted Bud, now
    standing forth, now demanding the attention
Of the brilliant flyers: "they have no right to attack us;
They have no cause to emit us from all the land. Now let this coward,
Let him go and tell them of our intentions;
Then we shall see if he is brave enough to stand and fight."
Then Bud sat down. But Louis rose and challenged him to single
    combat
In the air; each, Louis said, would rise up five hundred yards
And there combat, with roop-darts and bastions. But Santa inter-
    posed, pointing a red-gloved finger
In the direction where the captain had gone: "That way lies our
    enemy, not here!"
Tell, Muse, then, how each of the Red Robins prepared for battle
Against Banzona, and yet how the counsel of Louis
In spite of their fearless readiness, sank into each skull and pre-
    vailed.

For when they saw themselves attired for the combat,
Thinking of the bodies of their friends beneath the padding and
    helmets,
The bodies so simple, wanting nurture, sweet gentle repose, and
    love,
The bodies which might be ruined by the weapons of Banzona,
Seeing this thing, and thinking too of the young of Banzona
And the helpless old, and the wives of warriors, thinking these
    things even Bud relented,
But it was not so simple. For the Apes at that very instant
Came charging toward them screaming. And so Louis went forth
Speedily, in his airplane gloves, smashing a light bulb on a rock,
    whereat the apes, startled,
Stopped short in complete silence. "Listen," Louis said, "men and
    apes do not need
War, they need peace, friendship. We have done no harm to your
    island
Nor shall we do any. And we shall depart this day. Only make us
    gift offerings
And we shall respond the same." "You must leave here by death,"
    brash Banzonino replied,
"We came not to make treaties but to destroy irreverent strangers;
Now make ready for battle, for soon your hapless bodies shall be
    hung from these monkey-loved trees
Until they rot; they shall be as a sign, too, to others
To stay in their own place, or die!" But another, older-looking ape
    stood forward and said,
"Come, let these not-unfriendly-seeming strangers depart in
    peace!"
"God bless you," Jill said, moving toward the peace-favoring gorilla,
With a white handkerchief in her hand, and, suddenly, all the apes
    applauded,
Showing that they wished for peace. And Banzonino, seeing the
    tide turned against him,
Ran to the high cliff, Eng-gho-fee in Banzonanian language, Head-
    Seat in ours,

So called because it is so high, resting amid pink clouds at sunrise
and sunset, white clouds at noon,
That it is said to be the Banzonanian deity's head rest, he half octo-
pus and half ape
The hero of long old stories in which the people still believe,
To this place Banzonino went, and, threatening vengeance
In a time to come, when he would be united with other violent
powers,
He vanished into the rays of the sun—it seemed so, but actually he
dove into the sea
And swam to eastward, with huge limbs churning. The apes now
all were for peace, and they gave the good people
Breadfruit and wooden carvings, which they said were images of
their gods.
And the Red Robins gave them each a ride in a plane, along with
ear-phones, goggles,
Muffs, and other flying equipment. There was much merrymaking
that night.
At dawn the Red Robins departed, when the shore was golden,
And Santa Claus rose, a representative of his people,
To say last words: "We have given, I hope, by our friendship
And peaceful resolution, a shining example. Now, God bless you,
and farewell!"
Then the Red Robins entered their airplanes and rose into the sky.
They called again, Farewell!
And the Apes of Banzona gathered up the driftwood on the beach
And built great smoky fires, sacrificing to their gods
Coconut and plantain root, asking that peace be theirs always,
from that day forward.

CHAPTER 16
THE RIVAL

The Easter Rabbit sat on Terranfazer Plaza, sipping his drink, which was a concoction of vodka and cranberry juice which Emna, the bartender's girl, had fetched him from the plaza owner's home. Everyone around him was drinking ale. Everywhere around me is the blue sky. She wrote home that the birds were bothering her. But in fact I had not seen Cyrus since the days of the big flotilla against the snails. Hello, Irene said, crowding her narrow body against a wall. She smiled at her in return, by the banana leaves, where a tiny insect was running back and forth. Mr. Terranfazer himself was soon to lift up his heavy body and come to where the Rabbit was. Why did he hate the Robins so much? The slimy green things were one example; the drooping parachutes were another. And that time he enlisted the help of the "Human Barricudas."

Po Cho sat staring at the fading colors. Soon they were replaced by others. It was morning! He ran to get the okeh from the great white fur chief to start activities of the day. Yes, go ahead. That they may begin. And Allen? Gin? Dorothy? Will you all get ready? Can you all be ready by three? For we're going to take a sweet cruise and sail against those dastard Red Robins! Will we wipe them out this time? I hope so, love. Oh darlings, come now and pray and prepare with me. Young octopus stood up. The tiger smiled. I won't go!

Cranberry Juice Island remained coal red in the blueprints of dawn. Here and there a solitary screechbird called out "Hi! A farthing!" Then all would be still.

Then, Mother, what happened? The old, gray-haired quiet lady closed up the prayerbook with a smile. "We can only wait and see," she said.

Dracula had been watching the Red Robins closely all this time, and when he saw Jill slip, he tapped the Easter Bunny on the back. Here's our chance, he said. Dracula and the Easter Bunny swooped down. Their only aim was to kill them at one fell swoop. The Easter Bunny fell hard on Jim, Bob, and Rusty. Dracula, on the other hand, was caught at the edge of a machine gun and immediately burst into flame.

The Easter Bunny popped his big fat body into a rowboat and set out rowing fast as he could over the waves, singing "Sweet Mawinnih" and other violeted lilaced lyrical island songs, for which the sweet yellow clouds dropped him many a penny; and the Robins, too exhausted now to move on, merely watched him hail off with glad relief. At another time they would have pursued him. Magnified was his name. Santa Claus distracted by the burning.

Finally, easily now, the boat bursts in the sea. But I continue, by magic powers, to move so easily. So sang the Easter Bunny as his frail craft disintegrated into the wash and he was propelled as if by the warm light breeze of a magic current swiftly over the Western wave. Soon the orange of another day shall ennoble me, and make me strong. Then—death to the Robins!

Jill called Santa Claus over to look at the matting on the floor of her plane. The white duck light was flooding the morning with palenesses of yellow. "It looks like very sound matting to me," Santa Claus said, and he grasped her hand, then pulled her to him and held her in his arms—and as they stood there it all seemed worth it to them, no matter what was going to happen to them after that.

CHAPTER 17
MIKE

My name is Mike, and I am a man-eating tiger. My kind stems from up around Kuannon, which is an old Indian word for "ring-face," and I guess that region must have gotten its name from us tigers who wear upon our brownish-red faces one and sometimes two or three medium-sized white rings. Sometimes, when the harvest is good and the sheep are fat, I like to pounce down into the valley and carry off some plump little lambs to my den and eat them. But whether the harvest is good or not, my favorite food is men. Men have a *je ne sais quoi*, I guess you could almost say it was an "intellectual" flavor, that kind of flavor you can only develop after you have spent a few years engaged in speculative thought. It's like the patina on some of the beautiful Chinese jars that some of these men have made. It's an "extra." As we tigers say, "Man is the only animal who is his own sauce." I don't blame them for trying to kill us! How would you like to have somebody after *you* who wanted to eat you?

I am a tropical plant. My name, for you, is Jim. I have a more complicated name in plant language, a language which is completely unnoticed not to say undeciphered and which, even if it were discovered, would make the decipherment of Linear-B seem like child's play. At any rate, to continue. Now, I like tigers because tigers don't like plants. There are two ways of liking, obviously enough. I don't like to eat tigers, or really, to do anything with them, but I like the fact that they don't want to do anything to me.

Do you like me? If so, which way do you like me of the two ways I have named?

I am a gland, a part of a red bird's body. Without me the bird would not function normally but would flap wildly around on one wing, screaming its head off. In fact, it is doing that now, because I am not "doing my part" but am, instead, talking to you. My name is Pyotor (in gland language), I live in the jungle inside this bird, and I am the organ which gives him his sense of balance and his ability to control his actions.

My name is Roughie and I am a stone. You have walked over me many times and not noticed me. I don't blame you at all. But when you need a stone, to crush a rattlesnake or an asp, then, then you run through the jungle shouting, "Where is Roughie? Oh where is a stone? I'd give anything to find a stone!" Why don't you stop to appreciate me now?

My name is Elia. I am a possibility which has not yet been discovered by mankind or by animals. I am ignorant. I don't even know whether I am a solid, a liquid, or a gas, an idea or an emotion. I am motionless. The rattlesnake moves right through me, and the Tibetan monkey-bear. Yes, you are right, I do know about other things, but I know nothing about myself. Please find me. I will love you if you do—if I am capable of that.

Lyn, you have had a bad dream and that is all. Imagine your getting upset! But in his hands he had nothing but a small piece of white shell.

In the distance the waves raised their huge blue viewpoint down into the square coats of all the ungovernable emotion fragments in the invisible universe.

CHAPTER 18
PHOTOGRAPHS ON LEAVES

Where they had been before was now a frozen pool covered with autumn leaves. On each autumn leaf was the color photograph of a particular person. Here was one of Mahatma Gandhi, wearing his wrap-around hip-cloth and white turban. He seemed to have a sad and permanent meaningful look in his eyes. Over on the other side of the pond was a leaf photograph of Pandit Nehru. He had on a tall white hat and was smiling grimly at the viewer—in this case Jill, who had gotten up early and was examining the leaves. And here was one of India's Prime Minister Shastri too. He had a sad and almost childish but meaningful and almost mystical expression around his face and eyes. He wore a white turban and a greyish tan Indian cloth coat. Future rulers of India also seemed to be pictured on the leaves, but Jill wasn't able to figure out who they were. One leaf showed a woman wearing golden beads, with a heavy bosom covered by a white cloth smock; she had black hair, which was brushed back somewhat stiffly from her eyes. She was not smiling. Another leaf pictured an East Indian man in a tall Western-type high hat and carrying grey gloves and a cane. He had moist dark eyes which were quite large and which stared sternly at the viewer. There seemed to be hundreds of pictures of Indian heads of state, and Jill, intrigued by finding them, began to look to try to find something else.

CHAPTER 19
LYN'S LIFE, PRECEDED BY THE INDICTMENT OF AMERICAN SOCIETY

Betsy Bunch arrived before the rest of the girls for the big special meal for abandoned pilots at the once luxurious Coluhdson. Small round tables covered with gay crepe paper of all sorts and colors were scattered over its immense porch, and to the rear of same, given the special occasion, had been installed gun racks and places to plop off heavy equipment—pipes, goggles, etc. It was a good time to be happy, Molly thought. And then the other guests began arriving too. Such an odd bunch. Seemingly every foreigner in the entire Shanghai zone, many of them chattering gaily, others obviously depressed. Lou, whom Sarah had known on Lake Superior, was of course the big surprise of her day, and as the blue clouds scudded across the sky that day they sat over a "blubber cocktail," chattering in the warm, soft weather to their hearts' content. It was evening before any of them noticed that the Imam had twisted the country into the shape of a large bird and that the establishment known as the "hotel" had long ago ceased to exist! They were lying (or seated) among rocks and stubble.

After a while they began to understand a few expressions, such as "Large Red Bird" and "Big Icicle with Which White Man Punctures the Bridal Coat of the Sky."

Lyn put down her pen and Bud read the manuscript. "Why, Lyn, it's anti-American!" he said. A white wave of foam rubber suddenly appeared in the midst of San Francisco's V.E. Day celebration, causing a great deal of trouble until it was carried away. A psychoanalyst was shot to the moon. Bud rose, still holding the ms. in his hand: "Lyn, you are anti-U.S.!"

"Not at all!" Lyn tried to explain. Blue numbers racing across a blackboard in a childhood's oblivion of speeding evasions. "How white you are, cupcake," Charles said, and then the arrow struck him. "Surely the wrong man!" wailed his baleful new grass-clothed wife. And she was right.

I have taken all the old pencils off the shelf to bring you new ones, archaic and beautiful, it was a fine Hawaiian day and the necromancer perhaps was going to determine the paths of the robin. You must come to me now or lose this. Come to me now.

The midsummer sun broke spindles in Saudi Arabia. And in the glass houses on Crete, babies were crying, till their kindly mommies in yellow frock gowns came spinning to attend to them. And the sea whistles, calling for blue, more blue, ever bluer than blue. In Ankhor Vat a child is crying too, but its delirious mommy lies broken at the bottom of a wall made of shell, and white ears point over her, a page is turned of life's enormous book.

"Let us build a chapel to the old earth," said Bud, inspired. "No," said Mona (a very different girl from the one we had seen before), "all she cares about is food." "Let us give her an octopus, then," Bob said, and they sacrificed one on the ground.

A blue day and sky. Beneath the red linen coat, white linen trousers. And a thin pink in the upper left-hand part of the eye. "Like a good child, yes, but without either father or mother—an orphan, a growing candlestick of wood—"

Lyn's Life, preceded by the Indictment of American Society, intended to supplement and in a way supplant all other such indictments, from Melville to Khrushchev. In Stockholm the old civics professor sat reading. Jim honored the Oldsmobile by opening its hood. Herb's mother was a psychoanalyst. Birds sang in the swamps, hopeful over the eggs. The arrow, which failed to reach its target, was nevertheless captured in a painting, which hangs in Schoolbury. Now the indictment:

1) American schools should open later and close early. In Tahiti the climate is beautiful and maybe in America it would be seen to

be beautiful too if the schoolchildren were given a proper amount of time to enjoy it.

2) There is not enough "team spirit." Make the actions of each individual count toward the whole.

3) There is not enough of an incentive to the average individual to make something bright, savage, and unusual out of himself. He, like all his fellows, tends to fall back into the humdrum of everyday routine.

4) Each person should specialize in one of the fine arts from earliest childhood.

5) In a culture where success is esteemed and where there are, more than anywhere else, real and feasible means of accomplishing success, you are likely to end up with a society which is little more than a nightmare vision of that success. Society needs "depth"—of artistic interest, of esthetic interest, of a personal interest in the farthest and most distant pleadings and problems of every human being everywhere.

"Mr. Mackintosh, will you wake me at five? Yes, I want to be awakened at five. Something important is happening then. Yes, at the docks. A ship is arriving. Oh may it be given me now to find him, may that be my good fortune! Thank you, Mr. Mackintosh, yes, at five."

Toilets of silence! and the marzipan ring! all the old places he had used to go! Now they jabbed quietly at the still-quivering body of the gigantic airman. Lake Huron looked up hotly at the hovering silver eagle. "I shall take my bath with me, like a river. I shall see them, no matter how high they fly." Jabbing softly in the hot, quiet air. Sssssss-zing! sssssss-zing! They motioned dumbly to their leader, who suddenly spoke with a sweet and native English voice. The tin corpse was carried in free of charge and studied with impetuous detail. It had turned out to be a very bad day for "gambling in silence."

The abandoned pilots were all able to get away. Some of them smiled at what Lyn wrote; many more were interested in her. She said, "It's what I believe," and waved goodbye to many, there in the wavy summer heat. On the rocks she wrote some more: What is available to us at any given time is bound to be affected by the attitudes we bring to it from outside. Therefore a threatening view of life is not the best one to have. My own life—she stopped for a moment to think—well, you see what that has been like.

It was a strange dream, and Mr. Uterus gave Santa Claus the five dollars for Lyn's body just before Lake Huron smashed them away. On the pebbles, a Greek bandleader, excited by the thought of going still higher, forced Christ to strew sand on Kerkyra so that there would be nice beaches there for indented feet. Such is the power of sand over the human mind.

CHAPTER 20
THE SLIMY GREEN THINGS

"The Priest" is an exposed pier, or wharf, which reaches into downtown Shanghai from the sea. By the time Bud and I had gotten to it, we noted, to our horror, that it was now covered with tiny green hard-shelled creatures who seemed to be exuding a sort of emeraldine slime over everything that touched them. The people of Shanghai—shopkeepers, travelers, and the like—were naturally keeping their distance from the unusual-appearing wharf, and I can't blame them for it either!

Bud said he had told Lyn and Jill he would meet them there, and he was afraid that they might come there anyway and not notice the creatures before they got there. A huge fat-looking man was standing closest to the thing, and I don't know whether I felt more delight or fear when he recognized us and said hello. Behind him we could see the towers of the city, and at his feet we saw the creatures (I realized now that they were a special breed of clams) crawling and crawling, and bleeding and bleeding—or perhaps "breeding" would be a better word for what they were doing—who knows?

We were unable to find a hotel room for that night. This was because the city, as we were to find out, was in a sort of state of panic over the "Appearance," as it was called, of the green creatures, who, for all we knew, might have held some place in the local mythology. At any rate, this panic meant that the hotel rooms were full. For many people stayed in that part of the city that they happened to be in before the clams appeared, rather than take the chance of crossing their path. As for ourselves retiring from the city that night, the way to the airport was crowded, even jammed, with vehicles of every kind, vehicles filled with hysterical and superstitious passengers who did not wish to risk a moment in the "city of the green clams."

One might imagine that this hasty exodus would have more than made up for the shortage of hotel rooms caused by those who had chosen to remain in one part of the city or the other, but such was not the case. Practically no one, one might say, in the whole of China that night was sleeping in his own bed; and I reflected, as I folded Lyn into my arms, that we were not either—but then we never did, committed to wandering as we were, although on this particular night we felt more than a modicum of fear, since we were lodged, thanks to the graciousness of his kind suggestion proffered to us at "The Priest" pier, at the home of Moon, the brother of Santa Claus, for he was the white, huge stranger—a man who, though he was now being kind to us, remained for all that an international criminal of high degree and a person, perhaps one might even say a monster, of completely unknown powers. It comforted me to hear friends in the adjoining room; and, sure enough, when we awoke safe and sound in the morning, the creatures were gone! "The Priest" was just as white and board-like and shining as it had ever been. Lyn says it was all only a nightmare, and, as much as I would like to believe her, I am still able to see something in the distances of her eyes which reveals to me that she does not wholly believe this to be true.

CHAPTER 21
CHATTING WITH A CHINESE PHILOSOPHER

"Comparatively—comparatively," announced Ni-Shu, "the poetry of Keats and Shelley can scarcely be compared. However, since I am one of the few critics (I think!) who very clearly prefer the work of Shelley to that of mountain Keats, I must blue birds begin with rotten straphangers as the Yugoslavian boat 'sinks'; it dives into the ocean, and when it reemerges, Nineveh is on deck, by copulation submerged."

Go on with your criticism, said Santa, it seems to me you are getting lost in that part.

Yes, said Chen-yu.

Ni-Shu said, It is all a part of that. It is a new kind of a criticism.

Santa: Well, so . . .

"Keats sees a flower. What does he do? He smells it, perhaps tastes it even, stares at it, sees its purples and its reds, and even hears its motion in the light, close-to-the-ground breeze. Thus in this poems we FEEL like a flower—or so it would seem. But the impression is false. A flower does not know how it smells and tastes, or even how it looks. Can you say you know the same about yourself? Shelley comes upon a flower and it is mere radiance, mere language; there is no intention whatsoever that we be made to feel exactly how the flower feels and smells: what it IS to be a flower. And thus by not trying this he accomplishes it, Shelley does. There is this radiance, this piece of word, this language fragment floating around, I am sure it is exactly how a flower feels. It's how I feel."

I think he is right, said Jill. How nice to get a Chinese viewpoint on our own literature.

Are you English? asked Ni-Shu.

No, American, said Jill, as are a number of us here; but we consider that a part of "our" literature anyway.

"Actually it is very far from being so," said Ni-Shu; "there is probably a greater likeness between any two literatures of the world than there is between that of America and England. This is because the surface similarities are so great that the writer in either country (perhaps more particularly in the United States) is not driven to express himself *peculiarly* in what amounts to a totally radical fashion. That is to say, the writer does not need to find the exact words for every thing, kind of person, and action and then fit them all together to make a whole and coherent truth. Already given a language that had partly done this (for its past, at least, for it is a process which must be continually re-done) the American writer, in being able to dispense with the central, nay crucial nub of the creative process, has created a literature unrivaled anywhere for its weirdness and for the apparently helter-skelter triviality of its concerns. It is like the sort of bread that might be baked by a baker who had already been given the crusts. Very much like that. So not only the content but even the *surface* of American books is utterly mystifying! But these books, to return to my main point, do come to bear certain (perhaps accidental) resemblances to the literatures of such out-of-the-way places as Africa and the Far East, but they will never resemble any English work until they have fled full circle, perhaps all the way around the globe: through Irish, Finnish, Hindustani, Turkish, Melanesian, Afghan, Japanese, and so forth. For English is what the American 'language' or literature is being created FROM, therefore of necessity by very definition fleeing from. Much American snobbery consists in trying to be English, but the snob would be spending his time far better if he would begin being Finn or Afghan, for it is only through that path, in that direction, that he shall ever succeed in his goal of becoming English."

Do you think that our travels are making us more English? asked Jill.

I don't know, said the Chinese philosopher. Do you want to be?

I don't know, Jill said. But not all of us are American. Bud is German, and we're all of very varied descent.

Yes, all you Americans are, said Ni-Shu. Well, now I must be going. Come, Chen-yu. Santa Claus, it has been a great pleasure to hear the opinions of your young people.

It has been OUR great pleasure to listen to you, Master, said Santa Claus. And he very politely took them to the door, where the President was waiting for them in a big snowy plane with deep-blue upholstered seats.

Goodbye, Santa, said Ni-Shu, climbing into the cockpit beside the President; and "Goodbye" sang Chen-yu. "Don't forget us at Christmas time, Santy," laughed the President, and the plane sped away.

My God I'm bored, said Lyn.

Lyn! Jill looked at her a little sternly. Jill, that's not fair! I thought it was loads of fun and very interesting.

There is something in what she says, Bud said in a husky German accent.

It reminded me somewhat of the message we derived out of the Japanese Noh players, Bob said, staring out sleepily now at the misty white elephant tusks which symbolized that the dawn was once again to be difficult and bloody. But we had better be getting a little sleep. There is difficult work to be done for the raid of tomorrow. Full of thought, we turned in.

CHAPTER 22
ACE

Ace was someone who was hard to find, but when the chips were down he would always be close around. He hadn't come over with us in the first place, but joined us, we didn't mind, it just seemed natural to have him around. He was fun to have around, good for a joke, not so serious as Bud and Bob. Bud of course is German and that explains it but Bob I wonder sometimes why he takes everything so seriously—of course he is very heroic. Last night when he took me in his arms and began to read aloud from *Bagavadghita*, I thought I was going to cry. He is, in his seriousness, somewhat like a spider.

Ace, though, you can always count on for a big laugh and the rough tenderness of people who love the air. His face is lined with tiny blue dots, and through every line on his face you can see the sky. Under his left eye is that gorgeous blue stretch of sky near Pekin, matted with blue and white clouds. One flies there with trepidation and joy. And here under his right eye is the blue-black sky above Russia, its Siberian wastes. There it is always December, and the grey lumber of the clouds is little consolation to the freezing pilot who wishes to build a log-fire of his own deceit—anything, to make him warm! And here beneath his left cheek is the blank warm clear sky over the central plains of Magwahn—one gazes down and can practically see into anyone's fireplace and home. The air is so clear here that one associates it with the earth and with the things of the earth, so that one has properly speaking no absolute conception of it as "air" at all. And here beneath his cheekbone's bump is much high unclotted blue air over the islands—Tahiti and Machabru! There the air suggests what's down below, or else is identified with it so much in the pilot's mind, that when he comes to those cold mute lovely spaces he feels a relief such as one should feel at the islands them-selves—that air-space seems to him calm and deep, and protected. Even though he go through it quickly, he will remember it ever, like (do I dare say it?) a hasty kiss, stolen between doorway and hall-light in the freeze of winter. Chartres, Bois de Boulogne, Forêt de Fontainebleau, all are mirrored in the "feelable" atmosphere of cloud spaces, air. A huge highway runs toward the sea, Johnny, and it is dripping with red blood. "Ace" has cut himself shaving. "Are you a good pilot, Ace?" "I'm better at it than I am at shaving," he mod-estly says. I place his hand over mine, and soon we are ready to go. Downtown Pai-Kuht has never seemed so beautiful, even though it is freezing cold. After our shopping is over, Ace and I relax on an escarpment and I can gaze once more into his face. And there is the Chinese sky! My God! The clear space over Tin Fan we have been seeking for so long. Ace—! But now it is gone. He turns in another direction. "Jill, what really is your interest in me," he asks.

Oh Ace! I really like him, so what should I say? I like your shoul-ders and your arms, your gun, the way you handle yourself at the wheel and the controls. I admire you as a person and as a pilot, and I like very much to look at you—it makes me feel . . .

He turns to me the vast, ignorant hollow of his face. I see the sky above Naples (potted like palms) and the oceanic sky of Biarritz. He smiles. He calls me "apples" and "plums." Then we make ready for the 100,000 mile flight home. Already Alaska is splatting green fire beneath us. Aleutian steam ignites the teleview. And here is Russia, "pastured like the sea." And here is "Apples," myself, our destination, and many another Red Robin out to greet us, who ask "Was it grand?" Ace goes sloshing along in his splinters. "Confidentially," I whisper to Gin, "I think Ace is the best pilot who has ever flown in the sky!" "What?" says Bobby Bud. He repels me—I don't like his calling me "Surprises." I wish he would just go lie down in the mud, and that an ape would bite him—or that the tin bathtub would cut his hand!

CHAPTER 23
A BIZARRE OCCURRENCE

Once you have gotten off your fanny and really looked around it, an Oriental city can be a blindingly beautiful sight. So we found Pai-Kuht, at any rate, or, rather, so we are finding it. We left Tin Fan Road and came out here to see what we could see. We've had some complications of a personal nature—Jack and Milly have had a fight—so we no sooner came close to finally achieving a kind of unity, when here we are, quite definitely on the verge of losing it. Yet the food is good, the walks (those out of town, if one does not get out too far, into "tiger country") are delicious, and the city itself, as I suggested above, is of an incredible beauty. Lyn and I are together all the time. I can't even imagine what time was like before I met her, before I knew her, before we found this "square road and the title to a lifetime of happiness." We have decided to do a lot of things together. She wants to help the lepers, with medicine, nursing, and such. I can help out delivering food, piloting the plane, etc. Pai-Kuht! whoever thought I could find happiness within your maxim-covered walls?

. . . Alas—disaster! It seems we are trapped indeed. Pai-Kuht seems much less beautiful today than it did yesterday when I still thought we would be able to leave when we liked. Hear the Mariner ring his bell? He is ringing it to herald the most unlooked-for and strange event that has ever come to this part of the world or to Pai-Kuht. A raging, violent snowstorm has suddenly begun—the only snowstorm ever to afflict this area—and has already, in the space of six short hours, cut off all means both of communication and of transportation. We struggled out to the airfield and tried to manage our planes, but it was hopeless. The snow was already six feet deep on the wings, and the engines were frozen tight, the gasoline useless inside them. No local mechanic will work in the storm, and we have neither clothing nor equipment that would enable us to withstand the really insupportable and ugly cold. Lyn contracted a terrible chill, waiting for me while I fooled with the planes. The gloves I had to wear were so awkwardly thick that my hands inside them were useless. Lyn began shaking all over, then started to scream. She screamed nonsensical things, as though the cold had actually made her temporarily lose her mind. I left my useless work at the planes at once. No longer a question now of our helping the lepers—it is we who need lepers to help us!

My immediate job was to get Lyn home, into our, unfortunately, vast, glacial hotel room and bring her back to her self and her senses by keeping her warm. I got into bed with her and stayed there. My God she was cold! I stayed there, hugging her in my arms and legs, absolutely wrapped around her—not allowing myself to go to sleep, either, since that might have relaxed my hold—for more than seventeen hours. The hotel was freezing—actually far below: all day and all night one could hear the boards "snapping their warp." At the end of those many hours she was suddenly herself again and rose like a gorgeous white lily from our bed of (by now, considerable) pain. She helped me then to relax my own now tortuously twisted limbs, covered me over with all the sheets and blankets she could find, and told me I must rest, which I did, gasping with relieved anxiety and falling into a deep sleep of twenty hours.

I am recording this in the early morning, some days since the beginning of the storm. It's still far below freezing, but we have brought Bung-Ko burners into the rooms, and it is at least possible to get out of bed without screaming in pain—the cold in the first few days bit into our bodies in an extraordinary way. And now we get into our airplane gear and brave it out into the elements—still terribly cold. But there is at last some hope that we can depart.

CHAPTER 24
SNOWY LIPS OF COUSIN

"First snow of the year, Fai-Guhst—oh Santa, my dear, dear man! If you think I am going to be silent—!"

The tough blue figure stirred quietly next to the window. "Although you can't see them too much . . ."

Lyn was standing in the aviary. "Hello, Bob," she said.

"I . . ."

The smell of soap filled the universe. Five o'clock in the morning. "Lyn . . ."

In the morning, after the boop and gloop, a separation of tens from fives. The black morning drifts idly. "Was your—?"

"I could have loved her but she was only sixteen." In that fresh morning they standing there say it, to say it. "I could have loved her." "Did you or didn't you?" "Time splashed in my way."

"Oh, ridiculous!"

A car pulled up and the sun gets out! Dr. Sleeveless In the hospitals of time, Jill's "wounded knee." The burns over the tiger skin. "Could time rush—?" It was springtime in Honolulu. Pink blossoms brushed the streets with faraway fantasies of a captain's eyes. He has lived long on the boards of his boat, a boast bearer for an era. Now peonies steam into renewed vigor as monks and clouds—"You know," said Jill, "a peony-covered evening." The symphony concert was still. Only here and there the wing of a butterfly, tenderly and mothily white, would recall the waves hitting Venice to a retired summer poetaster who, his garterless socks gathered far below his knees, tieless and shoeless, sits dreaming at the furthest border of the Lanakai, far from the choruses of village girls, seemingly.

Seemingly! Lyn paused over the delicious fleshily moody-seeming half-eaten mango. Seemingly! So many washes at the hotel, so many masquerades, Venices of American (or Asian) wretchedness! Introduce me to your sister! I won't! I will! She is a bee-sized octopus! Oh you joke, madman, come on, around the corner, where the Avenue of Blossoms becomes clear!

Hooray! The cry went up when she first appeared on the street, beneath the barriers of the Lanakai Hotel, with her young arms like plum blossoms and her hair light green-blue—amazing! No, it's blonde, what's the matter with you? Sunshine, quick as a dachshund, nails everybody's ears.

"The difference between me and you—" "Who cares, Santa?" It was time for the opera. In the beds we were lost and asleep. Caliban arrived at four p.m.

"Will you introduce me to your cousin . . . ?"

"No!"

"I remember her large breasts, her evenings. I remember her breasts had wings those evenings. South of there, pretending an interest in the hockshop of her kisses . . . And the news praised me—"

"Take us away!" she said.

Kisses.

Santa: "Or—?"

"Or the blue universe of your hair will go cracking into the sabres. That's all! A thousand mornings, each with its own ice of time! . . ."

Bears came out those mornings, filled with engines; railings went toward the sea. "Cousin," in what curving way can you be hump to me again?

"Wait . . . !"

Her torn shirt. On the dais, with a long blue dictionary . . . Wrote, "Oh, my dearest Jill . . ."

"I don't care—"

"Oh, introduce me—please! . . ."

CHAPTER 25
MARIAN AND DOCTOR PEP

"Well, Marian, so you turned out to be nothing but a filthy little whore!" said Dr. Pep, staring down the Azhakansee where the first sleepy glimmers of dawn were just getting busy removing the damp yellow cobwebs of night from the purply coiffured trees which were staring down with impunity on the naked form of a seven-year-old boy who was vainly trying to make the *Queen Mary* start. "Here's news!" barked Caliban, riding up. "We've been invited to a party! I see through the torn envelope above the paper that this is an invitation to Dr. Santa Claus's big Red Robins Ball. I hope we are all going to be able to go," he said with fear, seeing the expression on Marian's face and sensing that she had once again gotten into trouble with Dr. Pep and would not be allowed to go to it. That might mean that he, Dr. Pep, would not go either, if he were feeling so cross, and especially if he were feeling jealous of Marian, and in that case of course the whole Azhakansee River group, including Caliban himself, would have to stay home. So, immediately on seeing this, he tried, in his clumsy way, to patch things up. "Hey, I'll bet Marian will look beautiful in a dress!" he said but then quickly regretted what he had uttered. Dr. Pep gave him a fierce look. "Hand me that at once and get out of here!" shrieked Dr. Pep. And "What the hell do you mean, reading my mail? If you ever try that again, I will kill you!" The Indian fled, through the scattered trees. Meanwhile Marian had turned away weeping. "I no do bad to Doctor Sweetheart," she stated brokenly; "I no make big fat hand with man—he merely show me motor—to how *Queen Mary* work. Me want to go to party with sweet Doctor man." Pep's heart was softened, as it always was by the pretty girl's explanations. Besides, this one had seemed particularly convincing. "All right," he said, "go and get yourself ready. Meet me here at six o'clock. And don't go walking around that way, in the deepest part of ships, ever in the future!" Marian danced delightedly over the lawns, but not before having given the ancient, three-foot-high, orange-speckled man a gay and refreshing kiss, just smack on his beak-shaped mouth. "You make big darling, Doctor Pape!" she cried; and away she went. The doctor stood his ground thoughtfully. A party! It had been years since he had been to one. "I wonder who will be there? Will I still be able to dance? And Marian—will she make me jealous? Will I feel odd because of my strange appearance? Do they know that when I am not Dr. Pep I am Varsails of Michigan? That so much would not have happened without me? I guess they do, or else why would I be invited? Well, then, that's settled: I'll go. But Caliban must stay behind and look after the farm. Cal-i-BA-AN!"

Caliban was bitterly disappointed. "It did no turn out the way I think," he groaned. Moonlight cloaked the Azhakansee in its bitter haze. By the time Dr. Pep and Marian had arrived at the dance, Caliban, drunk and lying with the pigs, had already gone to sleep.

"Greetings!" said Santa Claus to Dr. Pep when they arrived. "I haven't seen you in a month of black Sundays!" "You jest, evil stealer of the purple Himalayas," retorted Pep, sizing up Santa Claus immediately as the person who had made his country flat. "Nothing you say will change the resolution I have to kill you!" And he pulled out a thirty-foot blade. But Santa Claus grounded him. "Take him to the hotel and wrap him up till he is better," Santa Claus said—to Marian; "I didn't want there to be any trouble at the party. Besides, er, what on earth did he mean? Well, we shall see, when—and if—he wakes up."

Almost everyone was dancing, and the scene which presented itself to poor Marian after she had dutifully bound up Dr. Pep in linens at the hotel was such as might have turned the heart even of a girl much more accustomed to comfort and luxury than she!

What was there ever, in the company of Dr. Pep, but the killing of geese and the eating of them? the walks along the river? the jealous fits? All of these, I think, Marian appreciated at their proper value. She was not a selfish girl, or a silly girl, or a foolish one, either. But she was a girl to whom life had so far denied a great many things, and it seemed to her now that she saw them all, flittering like the dancers, before her. "Yes, I will be glad dance," she said, surrendering her pink-clad body to Bob—and she was swept off.

A coat of hair
I'd love to get and have
A coat of hair
Whether it be goat hair
Or old-time octopus and lovely float hair . . .
Oh if it e'er should be
That you two go there
Address it well for me
The Market of Human Hair
Tell it I love her
As when the first night I and she
Met she said Are
You going to rape me
It was on a great bed
Beside the sea
I was free of care . . .

Fred Mace is arriving at the party! He comes up riding a buffalo, and the smell of real buffalo sweat and grey tiny buffalo whiskers all of this is making his arrival quite an event indeed. He has with him on his saddle a lovely young girl dressed in orange, named Ice Queen, whom he hands down amid the loving strokes of violins, and she begins to dance. "I cannot do 'spaghetti,' but I can do perfect climate when I am with you!" The band steams on. Jill reposed her drowsy head on Santa's frosted red bosom. Santa stole a look at the clock which had fallen off the hotel. "I think we had better be getting into the planes," he said.

A man with opera glasses, Tornado Town, interrupted Bill in his parley with Dr. Rustin, saying he expected trouble with the stranger (Dr. Pep) whom Santa Claus had sent off to the rooming house. He ran over to the place where Pep had been put, only to be interrupted in his course by an extremely animated quarrel between three young girls dressed in red and two young men wearing yellow coats spotted with brown which seemed to be hide-of-giraffe. "Where is our messenger?" Bill pointed out past the trees. The young fireman had a broken arm. Pep had gone, no one knew how; and Marian was to pass, from that time forward, many a sleepless night.

She knew she'd felt imprisoned by the odd little man. What could she do now? Going back to Caliban and the animals seemed strange to her, but that is what she did.

CHAPTER 26
ROBINS IN MALAYA—ACE IN
AUSTRALIA

Rounding the bend, the boat hit gusts of white water without sound, and a covey of light-blue ducks flew out of the covert. And then it crashed against the rocks. We have been two days now rebuilding it. Meanwhile much else has gone on. Jim has the youngest girls lined up against a group of trees. The edge of this coastline is shaped like a scissors. Quiet people worked in the banks, and they came out to watch the gulls fly on Saturday and Sunday. There were two bays just barely surrounded by beach, and then a long tong- or beak-like stroke of silver shore jutting into the sea. Ace was in Australia at this time.

"What they said about the Blood Market," Jim was saying, "is true. There's an old man there whose beard is tangled and grizzled with blood. It's really been nice talking to you. Don't be afraid of the blood or anything. I have a feeling you don't understand me. Luc, come talk to the girls a little in French. Tell them they don't have to stay lined up." Luc came over. They stopped standing in a line then and formed a large circle. They were very pretty girls, all right, and Jim and Luc and Bud too all wanted to stay there a while and have a good time, but we had to be moving on. We never saw those particular girls again.

Santa Claus dressed in violet. Does that mean we're going back to see those girls? No, there's too much to do here. Besides, how can we tell who or what they might be by now? It wasn't very long ago that we saw them! I put on this violet costume so I could go into the Violet Jungle to track apes. We had come just now in fact to the edge of the Violet Jungle. Everything was colored violet in this jungle. Santa Claus, being dressed in that color, was almost invisible. Come on, everybody, get on your violet costumes, and we'll go and get the apes! Santa Claus laughed. Quite seriously, it just seemed a good day to look like the sky. It had the sun now with a violet glow. Strange, that the prose of daytime should be so much more fantastic than the poetry of night. We flew eastward.

"Why have I come to Australia," Ace said, "the bonded continent,
So-called because of the bonds that have ever united this country
And continent in one to England, and also because
It is one country and one continent, so unlike any other,
With larger and smaller bonded, country and continent
Linked by indissoluble bonds of identity together, Australia,
The 'South-Land,' but why have I come here?" Ace did not know
And he feared he was losing his mental faculties which never
Had been extraordinarily secure, for even during his childhood
He had lapses of memory which were sometimes to him costly.
But Ace had found that in an aircraft he had perfect recall, that
In fact he was aware of, reflected on, and thought of everything
And never did it vanish from his mind. So he had taken to the air.
There was this curious thing, too, which has already been noticed,
That his face reflected the air above the places where he had flown.
And these things were connected, as the country and the continent
Are connected in the one place, Australia, over which children ponder
As Ace did now, wondering "If this then is country how is continent?
If continent how country?" and so on. Ace had gone there
To get some information about koala bears. Soon he would come back.

We landed on Koo-thoo-bah, where we again thought about the girls. There was something very touching about them, Bud said, just in the way we saw them and met them. Our just having had such an accident, I mean and— What? Are you still talking about those girls? said Santa Claus. He was walking toward the group rather unsteadily, as if he might be slightly drunk. He had, in fact, that afternoon been partaking rather heavily of goobah-na-goot, a drink that the Malay imbibe at weddings, election celebrations, and funerals. What happened today, Santa? Jill said. He smiled at her teeteringly. Jush nuffin at all, he said, and ran out into the clearing. There Bob had cleared away everything except the new Australian giraffe-o-plane which the Cold Bachelors had sent to us in tribute. Santa Claus leaped into it, flew up, and came back. The girls are still there and they still all want you to come back, he said. Luc and Bud leaped into the plane but were unable to make it start. Santa Claus laughed. I put cement in the engine! You don't think, do you, that I am really going to help anybody to fly away from the Robins? We'd come back, said Luc. You have no right to meddle in our personal affairs! Since when is it personal to be a deserter? Santa Claus laughed. This isn't the army, said Bud. You're right, said Santa. Go on, go on. You can do as you like. But they never found them.

Ida, the cement that was now lifted out of the plane, had her origin in the Southern Himalayas. Girls meant nothing to her, nor did pilots' groups, such as the Red Robins. She felt glad though to have been a part of something that was going on. As they placed her on the ground, which had grown warm from the all-day shining of the sun, she felt like turning over—again and again and again.

"Ace, you've come back—" "We met some girls in Malaya—" "I found—" Ace was smiling. "We didn't see them—" "Fishbar street-corner. Act—" "But we—" "Australia was the next best thing to air." Another place we'll not get back to—" "The genius of—" "Hello! Ace, Bud, Luc, and— Welcome home!" Jill stumbled against Ida. "What we have always want—" And "Birthday drinks—" We went on to Shu-Fa.

CHAPTER 27
SICKNESS AND RECOVERY

Shu-Fa was built in the Han Dynasty by Chi-Chen, who used the mysterious document of the Tai-Fo Drum, which has since been lost and restored, like beautiful legs, to organize and plan its streets. Of course the city has changed over the past sixteen hundred years, but there remains about it some of the tight and walled-off madness of its founder, Chi-Chen, who had built it in such a strange way. Santa Claus gave him some documents, as Jill uncrossed her legs. The light was dark green. Eddie, wearing his white-dog suit, soon passed into the interior of the town.

Chi-Chen arranged the streets of his city in such a way that one could always find one's way back to the point at which one had started by the following simple method: following the contours of the letter "H." Following the H pattern, you could always return.

And now Bill is lying there suffering in the hotel. The surgeons of China are called to benefit him. Many are lost trying to get to the hotel (they forget the "H"!). Every radio in the hotel is blaring. It is extremely hot. Many wonder what they are doing there, trying to treat someone is such a strange place.

Yes, I think we will take of his left leg—though my . . . The rear dorsal section . . . A hundred pieces . . . If we could fumigate . . . Not always a dial pointed at the sky . . . This evening . . . A section . . . Though we might be able to put him back together if . . . Wonderful spring weath—. . . Can you at the same time . . . Slice . . . Don't know the name of it, if I could remember . . . His hiatus bone? . . . Nonsense . . . That lovely cloudless sky . . . Hard to see today—better not oper— . . . Hold on! Here's a two-faced fly . . . Earlier than comic brassieres . . . Look, how— . . . No, that's a last resort . . . Say . . . American President is . . . But hardly credible . . . Sky . . . Like to get my hands on HIM . . . Who wouldn't . . . Breath cloudy . . . Hers . . . Highway to Tin Fan . . . What? . . . That pink roof . . . Where? . . . In outer . . . Can get lost in this hotel . . . Say crossing legs streets . . . To anaesthetize? . . . Yes. Hand me that knife . . . No, I'm not . . . Just this drifting as . . . What? beginning to be tired though filled with energy? . . . Well, what you recommend I . . . Perfectly obvious . . . Pray he pulls through . . .

And so he did, then on out into the H's of the streets, and back into life.

Quite a few birds here if— Impossible to see it . . . From what has been said, can easily understand . . . Your pocketbook . . . With pills of consolation . . . Thank you for that . . . Every . . . At the intersection of the two long paths in the garden . . . Were you . . . Will . . . From the distance and position . . . Yes, I am and . . . The long holiday . . . Gorilla . . . Now came to an end . . . Naturally his political aspirations . . . Without idle or weak spells . . . Your claimant . . . My birthday . . . As . . . He bowed to the chaperones . . . Tomorrow . . . Yes, tomorrow I will awaken her at nine . . . She has "portions of death" . . . Was the . . .

Excitement. "Let them be attired in violet, and let us declare this a day, a day of days, a day on which it mattered what came into our gentle regard. But St. Louis! calendars! oceans! mansions!" The dreamed quai was absurd. A coatless dinosaur ran through the universe of our nightmares and the next day we went over to our planes. In a sober mood. Their hard wheels scratch against the runway's gravel. And then goodbye.

"Princess Hamika! that's her name!" It's the evening before we are setting out, and Bill has been trying to remember a particular name. She was the character in an old story. The princess held up a mirror. The glass was filled with a total emptiness. And the maimed ranch hand struck out for the seventeenth time in a row. Maybe it would be kinder not to let him play, said Lieutenant Girl. But the sheep were already five miles ahead—it was impossible to stop.

Glitter of banana as Jill removes her shirt to the sounds of trans-Asiatic guitars. Some got too strong to hook them up with. Lyn, down in the city, associating with the demos, learned from them an ancient ceremony. And Mr. Terranfazer leaned against the laundry smiling. The steel bonds, the ocean's vanilla, the lilting aquacita of the street of guitars. The *Baruch Spinoza* lifts anchor at three. Will we be ready? Will it be ready for us? Pack *mes Malheurs de Sophie* with the butterfly vaginas in the old Creole decks. Yes, yes, I shall be back soon. No, not to these H's. I have the Master of Death in my head and A Woman's Fate in my legs. To describe them both would be too long. But I shall return, pirate's bandanna. No, kiss me, yes . . . Don't know what we shall do without you—Alice, we will miss you very much. Sea spray now against the bitter laundry and Santa Claus's luck still holds.

Tell me, Apollo-Buddha, in what week are you fixing to linger in the white-bony church of our feet?

CHAPTER 28
IN THE SKY

In the sky, and this is something that has been noticed before, everything seems to be all right. Cares vanish. Coming back to land, though, can often be a trial. Balzac wanted everything—fame, money, love, power, acceptance—and he was able to get them all. Yet he was tormented. Byron was born an aristocrat; he was wealthy, handsome—and a great genius. Yet Byron led a miserable life. Tennyson, too, was an unhappy man, in love with his landlady's son.

The most remarkable thing about the sky is that there seems to be nothing there, and this probably has something to do with the feeling of happiness (or perhaps it is only euphoria) which is produced in a person by being there. Large, black birds flying around Condor Island seemed to have none of this kind of feeling, but they are not human. For birds, the sky is full of things they are interested in, things they are afraid of, things they want. Other birds, for instance, as well as insect food and dangerous draughts of air. This may take the sheer, pure joy out of flying there for birds.

Most people who are pleasant on earth can be even more wonderful in the air. When Lyn and I have our planes close together up high, that is a moment I love. Conversation is often impossible to hear but sometimes seems to have a celestial quality when one is flying.

I wonder if Napoleon was happy—and Homer. Nobody even knows where Homer was born. There are three "Homeric birthplaces" in Greece. Nobody is even sure that Homer wrote the

Odyssey. Apparently, he was blind. Like Jim, he was an island sailor too, though Jim is a sailor not only of the ocean but of the sky.

Was Mu-Kai-an-Dahk happy? Certainly not. And the man who built all the hotels, full of carpets and plumbing and the white, safe walls to the door? And the lonely engineers of the chimneys— Were they happy? Was the Mexican architect who built the first sky-way happy? Maybe a little happier than those: he was closer to the sky.

It's easy enough to jabber on about why one is happy there. There is a happiness on earth, too, which bears a certain relation. When Lyn looks at me I am happy, if she looks in a kind way, and when she or someone else praises something I've done, or when I think of some idea of my own that I had before I broke my leg. Now it's hard for me to get around.

Is John Bull happy? The question is probably meaningless. A hard, cool wind began to blow from China Northeast. White-grey birds flew down and pecked at the hurried leaves of trees. The palm flags, as Bill said, were waving.

Jesus Christ, perhaps the most influential man who ever lived, was almost certainly extremely unhappy. Socrates was unhappy. Mahatma Gandhi was unhappy. I guess you think Mao Tse-tung is a happy man. He is suffering from gastric ulcers and can scarcely ascend the ancient speaking mound. The fact that we are betrothed to old age and death is enough to make all people unhappy.

In the air, I feel completely occupied. There is the steering, there are the controls, there is that sense of being "above it all" yet par-ticipating in it in the most lively and exhilarating way. I wonder if "escape" is the right word, as someone once suggested when I talked of these things, for something which so wholly absorbs the being and which requires so much skill, and which brings so much of life into one small span. The countries that float by down beneath are like chapters in a book; and I feel them, and what is in the air above them, in my face, and in my heart, and in my mind.

CHAPTER 29
A POEM BY JIM
AND A CONVERSATION

Adamantine and flowery Urkh
Where the divus and the submarine fish
Meet in swimming amity, and above them
The flowering branches case their full density of charitable blos-
    soms,
Can you, emeraldette and rubyized, O charming Urkh,
Retain for one second the burden of my argent song?
Yes! you will! and you will remain unburnished—for others have
    sung,
Surely, travelers and men of letters, wandering bards,
All have chanted your lovely beauty!
Are you but in the eye of us, your beholders?
Do you exist when you are not beheld?
You need not answer us, Urkh, and I need not tell you
That you need not, nor that Burmese Horror Shanghai
Has just succeeded in forming in the Ho Lang Mountains,
But just one district
Because most of it was washed away
By the agora'd brilliance of the summer air,
So, you too Urkh shall form and go on forming
As we shall not, but still may we not ever
Lack you for quietness.

"Our parents, my God, how can you think of them now?" Jill
said. "That seems like another world, one we have left behind us a

long time ago, Bob. I feel as though, sometimes, actually, we are not even human beings any more, but birds."

"We can still go back," said Bob. Down the river, in a raggedy green sailboat, came the Leprosy Man.

"Why don't you go back yourself alone if you're so damned anxious?" said Neal.

"Because I promised your parents I'd bring you too!"

She flaps the shutter closed like a hippopotamus.

"Je veux voir y gorillagze hoy become!"

CHAPTER 30
THINGS THEY SAW

Two murderers meet on an autumn road near the Hon-Sha Sanctuary. Each of the two murderers feel responsible for the other's death. Each believes the other knows nothing of the circumstances. Each murderer suspects his companion of being a ghost. In retribution for the crime each feels he has committed, each commits suicide. Previously, neither murderer had injured the other in the slightest. Their idea had been an illusion. Now, however, they have in fact caused each other's death. Mei-Gontako, the first murderer, reappears bathed in light on top of the Hon-Sha Sanctuary. He explains the error the murderers made and the tragedy of the whole situation. Their punishment for self-destruction is that they must have the same experience again and again, until one of them is able to see the truth. Then both will be released from suffering. The shining figure of Mei-Gontako vanishes and he and the other murderer, Shu-Fan-ta-ri, reappear as travelers meeting on the road. Once again, each believes he has caused the other's death and begins making plans for his own suicide that very night.

"Well," said Father Gantaraku, "you are in luck tonight because the Noh players are going to do seven (six aside from this one) of the most noteworthy and famous plays in all the Japanese theatre!"

South Shanghai Horror Castle was already half filled with torture devices, spiders, and poisoned bees. He held out his hand, which turned out to be a large iron claw, not in the least attractive to her despite the fact of its supposedly having been useful in the construction of the nearby "Cathedral of Salisbury" (see *English Buildings in Japan*, Harold Trotter and Marian Teed, p. 90). The Leprosy Man called to the children, but they did not want to purchase anything that night, so he sailed on. I will be back tomorrow, he said. The street was painted yellow and white, in honor of the Syphilis Parade. Another play is starting!

A priest disguised as a flower girl meets Rei-Nagi on an autumn road. Rei-Nagi rips off his breastplate, revealing that he is actually the Daughter of the Sun and the Moon. The two girls rejoice together until dusk falls, at which time the priest's disguise melts away in the dew, and Rei-Nagi is enraged at the recognition that he has been all this time with a man and not with a girl. He is about to smite the priest on the head, but the night has suddenly become so dark that he can no longer find him. He races about, screaming and hooting, with right fist upraised. After he has gone off, still frenzied and shouting, Mei-Gontako is seen, illuminated by a clear white light, standing on a little bridge. He says "Gon-ta-kō" (his name) and the play is over. It was his spirit which had inhabited, temporarily, for as long as the encounter with Rei-Nagi lasted, the bodily shape of the priest.

We walked thoughtfully down the Tsi-Tsen road, and Don said, "I too have thought of a play. I wonder if we could stay around here if they'd do it. This stuff really inspires me!" Jill gave him a look, full of dark green pencils. Don said, "I'll tell you what it is. Two chickens meet, and neither one knows who the other one is. They begin to peck at each other, and eventually their combat becomes very violent. One of the chickens, Gao-Matsu, dies. At this point the other chicken takes pity on him and tries to help him up. Compelled by the virtuousness of this feeling, the spirit of the first (dead) chicken rises from its body in the shape of Gasen, the Chicken God. Gasen takes the spirit of the second chicken (the living one) to Fowl and Bird Paradise at the same time that his body remains enjoying chicken existence on earth. Blessed with a double existence, the chicken can know neither fear nor envy. He sets off on a pilgrimage to the shrine of Gasen, at which time the actual stage play begins. The chicken with a double existence meets Kai-Fa-No, a chicken farmer, who tries to capture it and kill it. The chicken protests, and, to Kai-Fa-No's great astonishment, speaks to him of the nature of paradise. The farmer falls to his knees and prays to Gasen, who then appears and takes the bodily form of the chicken with him to dwell in paradise uniquely and forever. Kai-Fa-No has not seen this. When he opens his eyes after his prayer he sees that the chicken is gone. Throwing away his knife and renouncing his profession of chicken farmer, he vows himself to monkhood and an ascetic life. He reverses his steps, and sets off for the shrine of Gasen."

It is, or in any case it seems to me, Jim said, a little too intricate. Well I'm going to try to have it done sometime soon anyway even if only by amateurs, Don said. "That's good," said Jill. "And, oh, I have found out something so wonderful. We (Count Bernardo El Apehead and I) are cousins! And I am going back to the United Kingdom to get married. I am Baroness Jill de la Cruz." "Do you mind if we don't stay to see the rest of them?" What? Jill, wake up! She was standing there, breathless, hardly knowing whether she was on her head or her heels. Raindrops sweep in. If you don't let me stay, I'll leave! . . . And her arm, dancing with the bracelet. "Let's head for the interior of China." In their going back and forth, they almost entirely forgot the plays.

CHAPTER 31
UP RIVER

Sailing up the river has been difficult. But Santa Claus and Bob say that within three or four days we should reach Stugh-uch-Pen-Ging-Fan. I guess you heard about our planes. None of them work any more. I don't know what happened. It's getting hard to believe that we ever are going to reach our goal. Bud got into his plane, started to rev her up, and nothing would start. We all went down to the planes. Twenty planes lying there (including that of "Stone," a new Robin) and none of them able to fly. Santa Claus decided we should try to paddle our way upstream to Stugh-uch-Pen-Ging-Fan (instead of giving a party and trying to find a mechanic there, which was Bob's idea), where supposedly there is a native man with a genius for fixing airplanes. I haven't the slightest idea how that could be. Four have stayed behind with the non-functioning planes—"Stone," Arnold, Betsy, and Jean—to guard them in any case and also try to see if they can fix them, since after all there is a chance there's no mechanic in Stugh-uch, or in any place else we travel on this terrible river, no matter how much Bill may like to joke about it's "bein' great" or Santa about how there is always a way out of every situation human beings get into. The river is calmer this morning. Last night there was a terrible blow. It got very cold on the river. Today it is once again very hot. Santa says this is a sign that we are getting near the place (Stugh-uch). And sure enough, there it is in the morning light! Stugh-uch-Pen-Ging-Fan bridge, accounted to be a marvel of the East. It is made of a special kind of wood which tastes delicious to animals of every kind. Yet there are millions of wood-eating beavers in this area who have never been able to eat the slightest part of the bridge. Some strange force (so the story goes) keeps them away. Some attribute to this a religious significance, and Bud says the beaver is worshiped around here. There are shrines on the bridge anyway, in the shape of tiny little beaver hutches. Seeing these hutches, for reasons I don't at all understand, makes me feel almost uncontrollably happy. Still, I am glad our river journey is at an end, if only for a day or so. It's been tiring beyond anything I could have believed. The return should be easier, for we'll be going back downstream. But we are not to Stugh-uch yet, we still have to paddle around Dugh-uch-Fan Monastery, where Bob says there have been Christian Fathers for more than five hundred years (They have probably ruined Stugh-uch-Pen-Ging-Fan!) and then tip our craft in through the celebrated floating gardens of Arunshi, which is famous for its oriental mushrooms as well as its mallows and is said by everyone to be a beautiful sight. (We are swushing through them now and they are truly beautiful.) When we passed the Monastery one of the Christian Fathers, wearing a white and tasseled silk robe, called out to us, and Santa shouted hello and Jill waved, but I refused to acknowledge him in any way because of what those people have done. "But you don't know what it is!" I don't care! I think I have a good idea! And as we float here now, there in the distance we see it! Stugh-uch-Pen-Ging-Fan—a miraculous mist of wavering and silver-capped towers, darkened with purple sunlight and golden cloud. If Santa thinks we are going to find an airplane mechanic in a place that looks like this, he must be out of his mind! But, sure enough, there is such a man. At least, so the boat-docksman reassures us. This man, however, is out of the city for a few days, working somewhere to the north. We will have to wait for him. No hotel rooms are available in Stugh-uch. There is only one hotel, and it is, as it almost always is, filled with government officials and their mistresses—apparently, Stugh-uch is a much favored place for illicit weekends and vacations. Sympathetic with our plight, the man at the dock suggests that since we are Christians we might ask the people at the Dugh-uch

Monastery to put us up. Santa Claus at first feels opposed to this idea (the idea of Christian Fathers seeming to make him as uncomfortable as it does me), but Bud and Jill and a few others prevail, pointing out, correctly I guess, that there is really no place else for us to stay. So we pack up and go back down river to the Monastery of Dugh-uch. Well, they are really very kind. They agree to take us in. But I don't know!

Later. At the Dugh-uch Monastery. Father Pa-Hi told us a story: "I am not, like most of the priests who have come here to prosyletize Stugh-uch—incidentally, an impossible task—a white man. I was not born in the West. My own conversion to Catholicism came from Buddhism. In fact, I was, at the time of my conversion, a Buddhist monk!"

"A Buddhist monk!" Just then there was a big stir outside and inside the monastery. The Vice President of a large country was flying over the Dugh-uch Monastery in a bizarre-looking plane. It was made of white porcelain and dotted all over with blue spots, plus there were streaks of yellow red and green all over the wings. "Jesus! that's a beautiful plane!" someone said, and we all went back into the Monastery. Inside the Monastery everything was quiet and peaceful. The great organ was playing. Suddenly there was a tremendous crash. We ran outside the Monastery walls again. It was the plane of the Vice President; it had crashed on a nearby mountain which was filled with juttings, escarpments, rocky crags. When the plane crashed a whole lot of men wearing only loincloths and with big fuzzy hair ran out and began to search feverishly through the wreckage. "Good God!" the priest said, as though in spite of himself.

Just then some big, blue-coated policemen wearing padded hats like Bobbies came riding up and began to shoot the marauding peasants. Two of the policemen went to the plane and dragged out the body of the Vice President. He seemed to be in a state of rigor mortis, but, when they picked up his rigid body and banged it against the rocky cliff, it began to sing. It sang of the people's wrongs in a bygone time, and how the furry giants came and ravaged the people until they were in a state of total stupor. Then it sang of how some rowboats arrived, carrying white men, who shaved the people and made them believe in the true God. Then the people became strong and began to prosper. After it had sung this song, the body of the Vice President relapsed into its former condition.

The Priest Pa-Hi fell to his knees. "A miracle!" We all waited. Finally Pa-Hi got up again. "There may be terrible international complications," he said. "At least it was not the President of our own country," Jill said—"they would come and bomb the living shit out of you people." "You must remember that it was not we who caused the crash," Pa-Hi said, trying to ignore the extremely vulgar manner in which Jill had spoken to him. But it wasn't something I cared to ignore. "What the f—— is the matter with you?" I said. "You don't talk that way to a priest!" "Well, I do," she said, "and if you don't like it you can just take your bloody hands off me and let me get out of here. I didn't want to come to this motheaten faggot-bin in the first place!"

We all went inside. Pa-Hi urged us to sit down. Jill refuses; she goes to the window and looks out of it. In the sky she sees a large red kite with words on it! "Come to the Stugh-uch amusement park, and bring plenty of money." "Look at that," she says. So we decide to go to the park. "But you haven't heard my story," Pa-Hi said, evidently a little disappointed. "That, that about the crash and everything was upsetting to the Robins. I think we're all going to be able to concentrate better after some relaxation," Santa Claus says. "And we shall hear your tale another time."

"Santa," Jim said to me next day, "when is that mechanic going to come? I am sick and tired of waiting around this piazza day in and day out, with neither the calm to pen my belovèd poems, nor anyone with whom (occasion lacking) to dance La Mexicana." "Have at thee in the boom, Jim my umbrella," I flashed at him. "And you knowing full well we are having to wait."

Oh I'm Santa Claus the Grand
When everything else
Gets insignificant

You've got the biggest villain in the land
That's me!
And the Robins still don't know
They are complacent, not me
For they've got used to me
And something truly truly truly truly
Horrible I've planned
Just wait and taste it
Oh
I'm Santa Claus the Grand
Ah! Horrible!

Lyn and Jill have gone to bed and now I am left alone in the forefront of the hotel. We returned from Stugh-uch last night (the mechanic is still working on the planes) and everyone is exhausted. I must confess I am a little bored. I have saved the Robins' lives a lot, but still—I have, sometimes, this terrible wish to destroy everyone and everything!

Yet I would do them no harm. Ah, me, it's little sleep a deadly old man can be getting, what with the misty white moon, which is always shining down over Burma's Carthusian shores, and causing the mouse to wake, and the sea-frightened rat, and to go on nightly forage where the busty song abounds made by millions of jungle birds . . . It may be my cruelty is only a way of showing me my fear of pain and death. But . . . then . . . WHY am I so afraid? Yawn. Zzzzzzz.

AWAKE!

"Jim!"
"Santa!"
"Jill!"
"Santa!"
"It is the rhubarb of dawn!"
"And the planes are running!"

CHAPTER 32
L'ISOLA NON TROVATA

"Oh fresh wind over Asia, blow on me! and may this day be as much as possible unlike a dog! I mean a large black and white dog, smothering me in hair! May it be rather a gazelle-like day, a very yellowy-white butterfly striping hours. Let it be a football if the football is made of flowers. Let it be a day!"

A goat shambles from one side to the other of the cliff. He sees a boat but he does not know what it is.

At the exit to the monastery an immense crowd of young girls and fakirs. "Ah, Little Madonna, you have so many things to keep you busy!"

Black tires rush past going to the garment district of Dang-To-Fu. There, peppery morsels of "gala beef" are downed by heart patients at the military hospital, and great new supplies of the specially treated octopus meat lie suffocating on the wharfs and along the docks of the harbor. He lighted a cigar and began throwing small wooden rings toward the governor general's house. Four hot-tempered young women came out.

Now that we are here, Bob said, what is it? Terence said, There is an island which is said to be near here, which no one has ever found. It is called the Unfound Island, or L'Isola Non Trovata. Supposedly there is a kind of happiness there which does not exist anyplace else. I can't imagine what it would be, Lyn said, coming in suddenly with her orange skirts whipping around her, it must be said, wholly-Delft-quality legs, the most beautiful any man had ever seen. Bud felt a lump in his throat just looking at her. There had been some understanding between those two at one time, but that seemed over now. Jim was the one Lyn looked at as she said what she said then. Jim thought perhaps Lyn herself was L'Isola Non Trovata, but Santa Claus thought it was Jill. Luc remembered the Malay girls and uncomfortably sighed. Terence went around serving drinks to everyone and trying to talk them into going to the Isola Non Trovata. The man with yellow eyeglasses smiled.

"So you are English," she said, taking a can of baking powder out of the glove compartment of the plane and trying to make it explode by shaking it and then piercing it with an ice pick heated to 465 degrees. Bang! Boom! The beach had never seemed more beautiful.

"Yes, we're from the country of lucky gloves," the Englishman said, "though actually I am Welsh and Sally is Irish; Ben is of Scots descent primarily, and Gillia and Tots are from the Channel Islands. I guess it's the great thing about our Britain, though, is that it's such a melting pot—so many different people from different places coming together to form one easily recognizable linguistic group." "Oh I say," Sally said. And "I really mean—" said Ben—or Tots. We didn't know them well yet, though we hoped to soon. So Shakespeare in his plays did that for the English. They always have a *je ne sais quoi* about them that drives me out of my mind.

"And Boots is Australian," the Englishman added, "Tom is from New Zealand, and the five Chinda sisters are actually half-breeds, half Indian and half English."

What are you all doing over here?

Do you remember the small breasts of Anima Coballa? When she walked along the street, shutters would close. And blue and white sparklers would exterminate the sky.

The English walked off. "Oh!" said Anne.

In the hospital they had been kind, but she was extremely glad to be out. Her window had been near the market, from which she could hear the cries of the hawkers of different types of goods.

"Octopus! Octopus! When shall the sun shine on a fairer day than this? Fair and fresh ones! Octopus! Come and buy!"

"All manner of woolen materials!"

"Osprey egg! Lamb's tail! Golden coat!" (This man had just one thing of each kind.)

"And minerals! Chocolate, braver than a winter sea!"

O glands, America of the body, and forelegs, Holland, and you, black birds over the ocean, where is the webbed rack of my song? And the big flocks came, with their winds like weapons, and the smaller birds, too, who had missed the valiancy of the islands, their early days. "If you look from here," said Mogdah, "there is a clear flute line to the south. You can recognize the South Pole if you can see that far. No land crabs in between!" And Bill noticed there that in truth the ocean stretched before him level and smooth as infinitely gazed-into blue eyes. To be alone there!

The treaties had not begun. The French men were standing on the shore. The *Lumpenproletariat* of Indonesia scanned the Malay coast with cortisone binoculars. Knees had not yet come into fashion. Mycaene gripped the oars. Soon she would be the most beautiful woman on the planet. But today, the struggle. The combat with the waves of the sea. Narfield put down the deck of cards with a sigh. "Do you see that smudge on the window?" she said. "It means that John is getting letters from Lampuna." "Which may mean war?" laughed the old colonel, stripping up his flying gear and replacing the ordinary goggles with high altitude tuppers. "I don't believe they have those over here." The men yelled at the duck but it kept flying away. That still seemed no reason to shoot!

This life of birds, how carefree-stupid it is! How amalgamatingly prosperous! Either it is all there or it isn't. More complicatedly the life process of people rolls on. Terence invited them to the hotel. "I just want to talk you . . ."

Poultry squeaked. In the wind, feathers and dust were blowing away.

CHAPTER 33
QUEEN ANNE

"Here it is, all in the evening's paper," Jill said, handing it to the outstretched chieftain who had finally been trying to get some sleep. It's blue— I wish I knew why no one liked it. By then the temple was deserted. A few hours past it had been filled with promenaders and apes. Each person whose head was picked out for the parade was obliged to promise to stay home for the rest of his life—a crazy tale. Bob walked into Senator Knox's office. He said, "You've got to do something about this."

Senator Knox bent over as if he were going to pull something out of his desk. He did. It was a shotgun with a big blue barrel. "Let's make love," he said. "With whom?" Bob said. "There are some girls in the other room," the Senator said. The two men took off their clothes and went into the other room. Sitting on the bed was a beautiful girl wearing a green nightgown. All around her were tiny purple putti flying through the air. "This is a statue of Queen Anne of Nigeria," the Senator said. The policeman came in and took Senator Knox away. When Bob was alone with Queen Anne of Nigeria, he told her about the Robins' situation and inquired if there was not some way in which she could help them. "Poot on your cloads," she said, "and zan I weel try to halp you." Bob had forgotten that he was completely naked!

Queen Anne of Nigeria got into the airplane with Bob.

After a couple of hours Bob was getting tired, so he said to Queen Anne, "You take over the controls for a while. I am going to take a little nap." Queen Anne took over the controls, although she had never driven a plane before. Bob told her it was easy. "Just watch out for the frozen waterfall," he said. Anne knew what he meant. All the hopes and desires that they had ever had, frozen by terrifying neurosis, by overwhelming fatigue, anxiety past and present. So that, coming there, one might ask, "Why fly the plane?"

Is our day over? The sun shot through the sky. Then, suddenly, it was evening. She had laughed enough. Now, somehow, she grew sober, serious. The smile wrinkles faded from her brow.

The dinner was cooking. Bob was still sleeping. "Bob, apple, Hawaiian," she said.

The plane dotted through the sky. The stars like a million points. Beneath them the jungle. Did everything really come down to one same thing?

Then what was that thing? Bob snapped awake. "Anne!" he said. "Bob, wake up!" He was still asleep. Queen Anne of Nigeria stares at him. She has much time to think. She thinks maybe she will go back to the island of Kos, with Bob, in Greece. But Kos is so far away. They fly over the Island of Crowdveltz, a German-owned island. With great skill, Anne brings the plane down in that simple place.

Bob wakes up. "What's going on?" "I brought the plane down. Do you want some supper?" "Yes," Bob said. Greedily they ate. When they finished, they laid out some dark red fur airplane carpets and went to sleep on them. The soft wind blew a flap of her airplane carpet off the bottom part of Queen Anne's leg. Bob awoke and saw the yielding young flesh. He turns, fitfully, trying to get back to sleep. Queen Anne wakes up suddenly. She has had a nightmare. She dreamed that spring was everywhere but that she herself was encased in winter.

Don took the pile of guns down off the shelf. The pachyderm eyed the lunatic suspiciously. "It will take you one day to dry out your trunk. Then I think we can flow into Asia again." The rivers called each other mothers and fathers in the Wahugi legends. Brothers and sisters were stones. A statue of a rabbit was unloaded in central Arabia. Anne lifted herself up. "That was the nightmare I had. Everywhere spring! But I was encased in winter."

She and Bob got into the plane. It was still dark out. In Shanghai the cash registers were jammed. In Cannes a monkey knocked over a bottle of grapefruit juice. M. Hebdomadaire stretched his enormous, white-haired, pleasure-loving body. "Go and ask Hernandez," he said, "if there is much more rum. We don't want to run out before Freddy——" Mazda interrupted him with a flashing display of lights. Bob took the milkman job seriously. But that was long before he had run away. When the vines grew out, they stuck to everything around them. Skeeter held on to the precious container. "I have a letter from Broadhurst," Anne said. After getting in the plane, they went up in the air and flew about until they were tired. Anne told Bob of the story of her life.

"When I was a young girl in Foun-Ta-Foo . . ." "Isn't that amazing?" "Senator Knox has now become completely insane. He goes around knocking down buildings." "Nonetheless it was because of him that I met you!" "Yes," Anne said, as she kept flying; "now tell me—how can I help the Red Robins?"

CHAPTER 34
LYN CARRIES ON

Here is what Lyn said:

Americans should not play dominoes with other countries as counters. Critics should recognize that the work the artist does is more important than their own. Though it is hard to know what that work is and thus what is its importance.

Lyn said, Peace is good, because it lets the people live and fulfill themselves. Though what that fulfillment is we do not know.

She said, The first twenty-five years of our lives there is nothing that rivals the sexual drive. Although we do not know where that drive is going.

Lyn said, Nature is beautiful and we should let it alone, as much as we can, for it enables us to lead a natural life. Of which we do not know the cause, the kind, or source.

Universe, universe without a mirror, for you are all. The water was a mirror for the clouds, as flies climbed up the table legs to dream on the cloth, the sun mirrored them, it black-spotted to our thumb-stacked eyes. Listen! I want to tell you about the cottage which Ann has for octopus in it! I will. I'll come on down.

Wind hit the Mayan Towers and shivered the monument for a minute. Flies were sweeping around. A bird, caught in the tail of the blue proletariat of the tide, screamed bloody murder to the striking marauders of the page, on which only a few last characters of cloud-sky were written, like great actors who find, deluded into retirement, that they are nothing more than heads and hands and feet. It is evening over that sharply white fluttering coast.

If I could learn from Lyn then she from me in equal force and that would be paradise, Jim said, but on returning from his shoe he saw the complications. The plane would not start, and his shoe was equal. Huts crowding the shore. We are here together, he said, and the party was planned for a soon-to-be-remembered night. Anyone who did not come would be (no doubt) nailed to the dynamo of Lyn's sandy regard.

She is so beautiful! Her breasts are like islands, Jim said. He thought about a book called *Charge Yesterdays*. There would be all poems in the book. It would all be concerned with Lyn, and with Jim himself. He can't separate the two. Nor Jim from Asia, nor what he sees from what he really is. The tiger in devising a way to do this could sometimes borrow the dog's wuff ruff wuff and still be thought a bone of contention in the red-suited acrobat's design for the day. But Jim was a container. Mr. Hammergrand spit on the fly. Was everything lost then for the poor Red Robins? No. It simply shrugged its wings, disgusting as it was, and once again ordered itself to move.

Hurrah!

What are you thinking about?

Nothing . . .

The River Han—

No.

A prostitute . . .

She was once. For five minutes. But time refused her . . .

Lyn, are you ready to finish the packing? For Mr. Irington is here and the sunlight is burning the hotel. I'll be there in a moment!

O green-throat plane! O sandals of the pink bone-riddled morning! Santa Claus eyed the insurance against demagogues form suspiciously. How do I know it will work? said the Bald Eagle. You don't, Shorty, said Tim, and suddenly there was silence. Pink October blossoms shuddered insane messages (Come home! come home!) I think there are so many things, said Jill, that are unable to surface— And, Yes I think so too, said Lyn. They were good friends. Jill was more rounded and more thoughtful, perhaps, but Lyn had a streak of interpretation that was as strong as silence. Jim, who was continually busied with the penicillin of his poetry, often looked around at the nature around him and often looked around at Lyn. He was very "The Nymph Talks to the Fawn" about her in those days; and she has begun to write more and more. The plane lands.

Lyn wrote: The beauty of what cannot be changed by us is everywhere in the music of what we see. Look for someone *fin-tah-ka-joo-bah*—not born under a cloud.

Lyn's preparation began in patent leather shoes when she was tiny and has gone on through many mutations. It is in this sense that we can be said to be "ideal." At first she had flown over trees, now she flew over continents. "My brother is the boxer, Ko Nahk Feen—do you know him?" "No, I don't!"

When Primavera
Hits
I must have someone
To care for. It's
She! O Lyn Dominion!
Forever in my head and heart
Lyn carries on.

CHAPTER 35
IN THE CENTER OF LIFE

There are stories that never get told, no matter how much we've wanted to hear them. Here is one of them.

At the Paris café everyone was happy. It was the beginning of the Surrealist Movement, and Karansky the Aeronaut had just completed his grand tour of the Bon Marché Department Store. I stood studying hardware and various purchases when down I glanced to see an ant trying to lead me some way. I went and thus I came to the toy department where I recognized that greatest international criminal mastermind of them all! "Hey, Santa, you haven't been committing many crimes lately," everyone laughed. The Father of Humanity smiled.

"Eh bien, oui!" he said at last, "je suis le Père Noël! . . . Je suis celui que le monde entier recherche, que nul n'a jamais vu, que nul ne peut reconnaître! Je suis le Crime! Je suis la Nuit! Je n'ai pas de visage, pour personne, parce que la nuit, parce que le crime n'ont pas de visage . . . Je suis la puissance illimitée; je suis celui qui se raille de tous les pouvoirs, de toutes les forces, de tous les efforts. Je suis le maître de tous, de tout, de l'heure, du temps. Je suis la Mort."

•

In Asia against the shore the waves crashed solemnly. It was "Ghost Night" in Tuskegee, Alabama. And one was in love.

All the night long of paradise and agony.

it was not spring. It was not any season.

I felt a guilty rustling in my heart.

Then I came to the atomic mountain. It spit forth flames.
Four Americans were being fed into it, each three months four,
Twelve a year. Twelve a year, no, sixteen a year.
Sixteen a year I razor razor fear. O Tristan
and Isolde! what brings us into the back
yards of peace, where where weariness and
woe? The spring is broken, broken like a place
of happiness paradise kind; the kine of music
are lowly and yet they are the only sound visible here
where all takes another's part, yet cannot take its own
else it will be sacrificed. Music! But not love
or yes, love, which is the reason for and the truth of all this:
and how one fears to lose that which one has not yet discovered
and which is the suffering we cannot lose to fear!
The thing has come backwards, and the heart aches like a cloud.

Santa heard Jim writing in the night, and walked over to him.
". . . grapefruit." "It is very dark out here." "Central silence calling."
"Winchesters for apes . . ."

Oh what is the possibility of human names
sang the cupboard of German sweetwater flames
whose blue pyjamas went skyrocketing upward
and the Bamberger elephant lay down in the cupboard;
then I too hopped on the zeppelin
of dancing restaurant owners' philosophies—
O logarithms and branches! is it really spring outside?
the airplane comes home and dances—young airplanes!
Oh how they love to go home alone at night;
they are spending their summer evenings across the ranches
of Thousand Spellings, Idaho, where the kittycats munch
perfect silver cones, and the lilacs hurry to lunch—
but that's from long ago, a rope, a clatter, and a bell
summoning the merry union suits; and I spell
the word "kiss" to you, all to eternize love once again!

Lyn said, Do you speak German? Yes, he said, *ein bissel bissel*. And so they chatted, all through the jungle night. Dot and Ed are going to bring in some basil. Luc went off and patted the airplane's nose. It's very soft, he said. They really are young airplanes. Jim, your poetry is beautiful. Lyn was like a warm young rose. She smiled nervously now but came over to Jim and said, Yes I think so too. Would you believe I started it years ago, Jim said, before I even met you? No, she said, because I can remember just when you started to write. It was a summer evening. Bob came in with a rosy look on his young flier's face. We've just found out, he said, that Jill's parents are not married. Nancy overheard the excitement from where she was caring for the baboon. "Which shows a tremendous amount of feeling," Don said; "the question is how long can you have it?" "Or how much it hurts you while you do," said Lyn, turning away suddenly, with a look of pain, which no one understood.

"To eternize love once again . . ." Jim walked toward the blue cupboard, the sea. Lyn came up beside him, and holds his hand. Together they walk cupcake. And now it is night time and mist of morning. Though Jim's no less sad, he is happy now too, because of what he and Lyn talked about. In one way it was nothing, but in another it was "all we need of hell." Next day, before the planes took off—

Trust in blue, trust in the mother of Les Anglaises
come home silently like *des flammes dansantes*, be swell
as an egg or the limits of a question
of greenest trust; don't care about my vacation;
usual hat such beautiful hair; some summer
either, O phosphorus be calm! the—

And Santa Claus, just then at first, stood looking at Jim. He pulled us all out of there, though. "By my white beard, I am the death of all monstrous mankind!" Then rabbit tips appeared on the horizon, and we were gone. Was it all a phantom? Had we been frightened by "reality" or by ourselves? It was impossible, then, at that time, to make the decision. Said "We'll be back!" Jim never did finish that poem. Life changed so much. Sometimes he would find a letter, at some Asian hotel. "Dear Master—" She came there, too, most frequently dressed in white.

   It was hardly a question of death. We would fly away . . .

CHAPTER 36
ISOLE BELLE

O Eastern Islands! I believe that if there were nothing else in nature you alone would be enough to make the whole unwieldy presence of sand and onion in the universe worthwhile. If one could but stand on you—! Rushing through the day—! And with time gone—! But even with time here—since that is how it is with us now!

And you, sea!
Leave me alone, leave me alone with the sea!
We have a lot to say to each other, don't we?
She knows about my trips, my adventures, my hopes;
And it's of that she speaks to me as she breaks herself
On the cubes of granite and cement of the jetty;
It's my youth that she declaims in Italian.
For one instant we sing and laugh together
But already it's the story of someone else that she's telling.
So let's throw pebbles and sand at that forgetful bird
And move along!

Condor Island, to be appreciated, actually has to be seen; and to be seen it must be seen entirely, and that takes forty days. No one has ever spent this much time on this particular strip of land, and so no one has ever really completely seen it. So to all eternity in all probability Condor Island will remain at least partly—or wholly—invisible. My cousin was a Customs Officer who lived in the Galeeba

Islands not far from the Condor group. And I suppose he knows as much of the island as any man.

Hawaii's shores, the rouge rainbows that we are calamitously stopping beside inlets wreathed in stone! You triple islands of Kan-i-ga-la! Basketball-court-shaped isles of the Pacific Sea. And basket-ball-court-sized! Tiny British tennis-shoe-sized island named Sir Bernard's Cork! Immense paquebot-shaped-and-sized island named Looda. And you, Admiralties, willing to be addressed yet not supported by the sea! You, Marianas, calamitous clouded ladies, holding quonset huts and semi-furled flowers! Evenings above the clams of love! Nights when one can scarcely see you! Surrounded by ocean you have nothing to offer but yourself.

Were all these islands once actually volcanoes, and are we in danger still of being snuffled by them up to the sky? Or are they rather models of good behavior, that child who having vented his anger now becomes milder and a pleasure to all?

The Philippines! the miracle of the Philippines! nature's most wonderful handiwork! Patchwork vistas leading to blue serene. And the immense puff of the ocean, thrown out behind its arm, of land, as in a great Toulouse!

Beaches! like agates in a dream—when the wild strawberry explodes, and the faces of the Japanese milkmen burn like a million sarongs! In you I dip my sea, for you are a shore. "I'm glad you're up," said Saint Purse—"look in the sky!" And there were the silvery planes—of an enemy dawn.

How hard to leave these parishes where we've had so much joy and sorrow! Even though now they are ashes under our feet!

Gruff voices at day-hem of violent nothing!

Standing on an island, in the light-blue amazement of courts. To be king of an island is to be a bandit of the sea. Zoroastrians! Marquesas and Solomons! Our oceanic eyes do good at telling the distance of an object, so quick to know the nature of an eclipse, so quietly saved by what your remembrance can offer us. Isles!

If silver were an island, would gold be on its promontory of repose? I think your actions are suspect, always. If we lived on an island . . .

If I could choose anyplace on earth in which I could hold my bare-breasted love to me hard and never tire of her and do my work to stay alive and have thousands of children, Jim said, each one named after a different segment of the sky, it would be an island like the shape of your back, when our day's toil is done, and, your blond hair sleeping, you turn from me in anguish and surprise as the bat of evening digs down hard into the Carthaginian hills. There the tiger pauses to regard the seven pilgrims of the Apocalypse; there, too, the close-mouthed summoner stands up to his knees in worms. Rocks are displaced, there is a fresh breeze from the ocean, and the day splits into bloom after bloom.

CHAPTER 37
ON THE WAY

Hans woggled and then felt for Julia's head. "Good night, Jill," he said. Antwerp fell cautiously from the fat man's hand. "It doesn't make any sense, Bob," said Julia. "I don't care if Jim did write it while he was riding an elephant downstream and nearly fell off breaking his neck." Bill took the tubing over into another lettuce. "Certainly if Peter Rabbit were being written nowadays, it would not be done in the same way," Bob said. The golden light of dawn was rising like a scimitar over the face of the entire Far East.

We were steering her this way and that way, and still no sign of the big white bunny of the sea. Insofar as that was so, we were contented, as we wished to find her source not her ending. It was very hot under the forecastle, where, huddled together, two amazing strangers went down to the Chinese office of Beefburger East, arranging a hell silence for evening persimmons inside the sidewalk's mouth. Jill was strange as she stood there, hands to the sea. "Childhood and a serpent's tooth," she recounted to someone amazed.

It was dusk now over the farms and the bars in the city. A little girl child came out, standing on the fuzzy streetcar. She hoots after her old nanny, but the morning's frosty fancy has left her exaggerated daddy on some fantastic shore; he will never return again to the little child with her curls like windswept candy and take her on a little bamboo seat to tell her tales of firing and airplanes and the blue clouds make maps of shame. For he has felt an island weather, spit on island leaves, loved an island girl, golden yellow, for all the days of his life. Bury him gently, for he was happy. He never left her and she was sweet and pelvic, like a cleft peach, golden.

The red octopus lay stricken by their love to the shore. There was no longer any need to wrap them, and Wang King walked cautiously, as if she wished to call to her mother, "Bury the golden island girl!" But she did not. Exceedingly black bugs appeared on Santa Mingo's wrap: it was a red wrapper as they sailed down the Pe-Kung to Kor. The baby native lambs were waiting for him at the shore, they took him into their little tuft houses swept out especially for him, gave him a glass of water in her waiting arms. "All these years—Gai-Tus-Ka!" "Chit chit—bury your little madness in my covering breast. My covered breast—at midnight, no matter how," the soprano sang. We were very late getting back to *The Destruction of the Grapefruit Juice;* and our tiny craft was covered with barbs. In the big boat we headed straight for the delta!

"Thank you, Jim," said Ira. "Your tale's inaccurate, but it pleases me; and now I am going to sleep." "Farewell, tomorrow's porcupine," snapped Jim; "already the sun is violating the tubes of the high Himalayas of my distress, my despair, and a lone pink candle is burning where now there is none, no oxygen. Farewell! Goodbye!"

Jim flipped over the hill like an early leaf. He was like a pale yellow one, and was a very swift one, too. They stood with Santa Claus at the Hai pier and felt the cold chill five hours, sometimes it would seem like ten, before they lay asleep. Good night Jim, said Santa, the yellow swan. Good night Santa, said Bob and Jill, sneaking out of their scarlet bed into the yoga-covered night, and Jim came after— "Here! you have forgotten her arm!" Laughter. "Jim, tell us a story!" "Well, one highway-master, named Chong . . ." "Yes . . . ?"

When we awoke it was Chinese button factory. Everywhere you looked you could see the old cigar butts standing around in their figurative attempt to have a good time with the skating essence of the girls. Winter has seldom seemed so old. But to you, Achilles, everything is beautiful. And the day ended.

Arcturus, like a slavemaster of gasoline, moved up over the golden horizon, and Jim tipped over our little boat. It was too sweet, and wet, and cold, being there in that water, until Violence began to sing a song, that of the eternal starch of empire, how petals of rosedust from ancient times incriminate the present with a white froth of Chinese Ireland—or of two men trying to get the same boat onto different shores at the same time! Chahng-pa-king had never seemed more distant; but Jim began to sing a song. It was quite dark by the time the chimpanzee was able to accompany us to the aerodrome. Continuing our search for human beings, we rose into the sky.

CHAPTER 38
THE DIARY OF A POET

This morning a chimpanzee has brought us a book which purports to be Margève's diary. It was an old book, it would have been written a long time ago. Only a few pages can still be made out. Margève was the French poet who wrote about the octopus market at Ytek. His one short poem about it (see Chapter 9) inspired Jim a lot, made him in fact begin an epic poem called Octoparadise Lost—he hasn't finished it yet. He is very excited now about this journal, or diary. Look, listen! he says, and he walks up and down reading parts of it aloud

Burmese Horror Mexico, May 25. *To be the first French poet in the jungly atmosphere, amidst all these islands, with the long-billed toucan and—Say, Mister, can you carry me up-river? Alone, and yes. She is beautiful, an island girl.*

Feb. 24. *The fever is getting worse. Today another bearer died, in agony. His name was To-Nai.*

March 6. *In the bushes today two tigers. The epidemic of fever is dying down.*
La vie m'est tant agréable quand
La fièvre n'y est pas présente
Que je me chante un air normand
Chaque matin dans la petite tente.

April 16. *The suffering in my right arm has gotten worse. Abalone Gorilla Village is now only fifteen miles distant; and there, presumably, is a doctor, one of the few reliable ones in this part of the Far East. Hope we can make it. Most of the bearers are dead or dying.*

> *Bien que la mort soit parmis nous*
> *Réjouissons-nous d'être là*
> *Dans une sorte de partout*
> *Entre là bas et l'au delà! . . .*

Presumably, tomorrow we will arrive in Northeast Ytek. The octopus market has already convinced me we are nearing it, by its smell.

April 17. *Ytek. And the Octopus Market! The most horrible thing I have ever seen. And the most puzzling. My arm is again worse. I am barely able to write. . . .*

Margève's journal ends here. It's really unclear to us how he ended up in Ytek if he was in Burmese Horror Mexico (you've heard about the Horror Places, no? Well, it's a long story. They were nightmare versions of various world-famous places which were set up in Asia during the Unknown Years—1896–1910—no one knows by whom or why. Lyn slipped out of her blouse. Lake Michigan Horror Castle was the one horror area the Red Robins were trapped in, though only for a short time. The ability to fly made it easier to get out of such places. We were very glad we had it. Anyway, Burmese Horror Mexico is in Burma and nowhere near Ytek. Bud says that either something about the diary is false or else the whole thing is. If it is, Jim says, a deception is being practiced against us, and we ought to know it. At this time, the sun slipped through a cloudbank and killed the first sweet early pink of dawn. The poem that had been seething in Jim's head burst as he sat down and wrote it:

> Oh Margève
> We've read about your travels
> And your suffering
> And I know all your poems
> And I admire them,

Margève, can it be possible that you
Are just a fantasy or trick played on us Robins?
I don't believe it.
We rose up in a plane of white and blue
And Lyn was in it, and I was too
And in my seething mind-frame so were you,
Margève.
So let us know through time and space
Communications Special Inc.
Just what hard things we have to face
And how we ought to feel and think,
Margève.
For Lyn now puts on her bonnet of pink goodbye.

That's beautiful, Jim, said H. E. Tulberson and we went out to
the Tryst (a party in the jungle given by apes) but we were still worried. The Tryst was in marvelous swing that night. Men and girls
were there from all around the area, and the twins had an excep-
tionally wonderful time. As did everyone else—except for one or
two Robins who drank too much and threw up and one young
woman from Ashanka whom the gorillas carried off and covered
with stones.

Mrs. Palmerston, bring me that book, will you? Thank you so
much! Yes—have you read it, too? It's—what?—yes, Ruther-
ford—*Tales of the Far Pacific*—Won't you sit down? It contains the life
story and the diary of Margève. The beautiful white-ruffled young
lady of twenty-five leaned over. "No. I cannot. Mr. Palmerston will
be arriving at eleven. And I have borne him a son." The duck
quacked and walked off and downtown Peking was a hum and a
buzz of traffic. Suddenly a large green and yellow bus opened its
doors to the summer breeze. "I wonder if any of us will ever come
back," Ace said. "It's that, I don't know, the world has become so—
and there—it's encapsulated—Have everything you need—quality of civilization—friendship—" Jim: "My fame is known as far as
Chung-King Province. That's my business." Ruffled young personality that he did have open-necked shirt on very ready words. He

was so speak. He talk very high, lady. Wan-Po, the Nurse, on September evening 9/14/1962 to Jill Broame, A F S C T I L. May I sit down? Broacho! What did you say? Nothing. A perfect evening, isn't it? I killed a man once. What is your name? Louis! you're back from the dead! Being a hillbilly isn't exactly being dead! What a joker! Jill her yellow ruffles dress he open neck they buy many nefarious shirt on 2/24/1960 Shanghai. Do you take cream? The fireworks landed at about six o'clock, this time in the flower market. So long! He walked her past, still thinking of Margève.

CHAPTER 39
THE PARADOX OF BIRTH

My daddy is back—I never was glad when he was gone!
Little baby, you aren't even old enough to talk yet, why are you speaking?

Come, Earth, it is time to go. The lepers are covered with marks; it is five o'clock.

You must come to me in the sea! It is the "Balakta," or "elephant congress."

Such were the things that were said, and such were the fears expressed by those whose good right arms had built the sailing ship *Alacrusha*.

Now it was darkening over the poppy-seed-filled pier where so many green-shelled clams had been, bringing terror to the people of Shanghai.

A young woman in a green fur suit seals bluebells while a child watches. Suddenly the child speaks of her, the toy words mounting to his lips with an uncommon fervor. "Mayannah meetah," the child says, "cownooah gaeeyah flota."

I wanted to have a baby, but he was gone!

You could have pursued him in the branches.

No, it was not he.

Everyone at this time was thinking of having a baby. Lyn had decided she would name her baby George. The President of the Malay Republic was ready to come down and officiate at the christening. But no one as yet was pregnant.

He told me, he tore at my sleeve, at my blouse as well. He said he wanted to make me pregnant, to give me a baby. And I believed him.

Well, did he?

I don't know. It has been so many years.

Did you have the child?

No. There was a plank there. And a weightlifter. A thousand pounds. No, I never was pregnant then.

Come with me.

Why should I come with you so that you can place in my body—what? Am I a garden?

You will bear seed to me.

I will bear what?

You have borne me a son.

No, I have borne you nothing. You have not know me, I have no conceive. I am carrying these clothes on my shoulders and I will never take them off.

The jungle is humming. You should . . .

Join in the life process . . .

Then what is that sound?

It is Mak-Dor the Gorilla in the trees with Pai-Shan-Dor his mate.

And she will bear him a son!

Well, let her bear him a gorilla son! What has that to do with you and me?

I love you as Mak-Dor loves her.

She will bear him a gorilla son!

The baby smiled. And formed an "O" with its lips as if about to talk. But she said nothing.

He had no more to say to her.

Are we to be silent forever?

You must bear me a son.

I shall not.

The gorillaboy came forward and took the father's hand. Ink cha ka moy, da-dek, he said. I shall be your true son.

And he took the log upon his shoulder and carried it for many miles.

Now will you give me my offspring, he said.

She smiled at his shoulder. She was wearing a savage blue.

Listen, she said, come over. And he knelt beside her. He could hear it.

Vell, said the gorillaboy, cham-dek. I vants to be your true son also.

That will be possible. Go look in the cardboard. See what you can find in that palmtree desk over there.

There was an office in the middle of the road. The heat slammed down on it. The gorilla boy went and looked in the top drawer of the desk and came back with some money. You must use it for what you need, she said.

Is this then your love? I want my children!

Oh I don't know, she cried. She was grateful for having been filled up with purposeful humanity.

But suppose it's just an incident? she said.

Oh that, he said, that you never can tell.

She cries a little. Hot weather spills from the trees. Soon there is the yowling of babies. And the true drama now becomes their own.

I have walked into a savage forest.

Yes, Bik-Dek.

Strange, Lyn said, what happens to us when we're asleep.

Waking no less so, said Bob. Hey, were you serious, *chérie*, about having a baby?

Someday, maybe, but not with you, and not now, said Lyn. Jill is the one you say you've always loved. Why in God's name would you want to have a baby by me?

I just would, said Bob. But this didn't take place.

Jim looked at the baby one more time. Jim said, Jill, do you remember that? And she said, Yes, I do. I remember the tall trusts, the evenings. And the baby cried.

Everyone said these things. Are you going to rape me? No, you said, I am inviting all these people to my home. The gorilla's "home" was someplace we had never been. The child resembled me in every particular but his sex and his name. What was his name? Narpa. What is your name? La Lee Ga Na Kee Pah Ti Ah.

CHAPTER 40
THE NEWSPAPERS

RED ROBINS EXPRESS CHOICE
the headline said. And

THEIR CHOICE OF FAR EAST TO BE DISCUSSED AT NEXT SESSION
Every once in a while they'd fall a prey to world publicity, "like
telescopes."
Caruso-Tsik Lost
ELEPHANT BELIEVED LOST AT SEA; PARIS IN ARMS; CHANCE FOR HOSE FEED-
ING STATION IN TUILERIES HELD COMPLETELY LOST
Violence over the Ocean! An Elephant Devoured by an Octopus!
The Human Monster!

ROME BUILT IN A DAY; CLASSICAL ARCHITECTS FINISH TRUE-SCALE MODEL
OF FAMOUS CITY WITHIN 23 HOUR DEADLINE
Elephant Believed Lost at Sea

MUSSOLINI HOSPITAL REOPENS TO CHERRY ICE-CREAM HOLOCAUST
Two Air-and-Sea-Borne Groups Meet Within 40 Seconds
Living Bodies of Group Members Dropped at Sea All Recovered
Save Bair

FILING CABINET BELIEVED HELD LOST AT SEA
Use Disputed

ONE "BACHELOR'S" STORY: "THE ROBINS WERE ENTIRELY AT FAULT."

LOUISIANA PROTECTORATE TO INTERVENE
Sea Lions Amoncelated After Lemon Shortage in Cambodia
Bao Dai Sees Models
One Robin Floats Sadly into Port

STEAM ENGINE DROPPED AT SEA
Electric Button Control Plan Unit Believed Held Sunk Off
Solomon Islands

LOVE NEST REARS OPEN TO TURKESTAN TOURIST DEPARTMENT
Charges Robin Sea Kidnapping

IN THE COLD MAJESTY OF THE DRIFTING WATER
California Acts to Release Housing Act Funds with Aim to Protect
Local Lemon Shortage After Aghast Sea Drops

BAO DAI POSES THE QUESTION: PEOPLE OR TREES?

LIVES OF 147 UNACCOUNTED FOR
A Survivor's Story: "We Were Moving Along Through the
American Summer—" "But—!"

PARTICIPANTS' SENSE OF PLACE THOUGHT EXACERBATED
Dying

ELEPHANT IS DISCOVERED AT LAST
Floating Amid Flowers He Is Greeted by Gay Tahitians

ELEPHANT IDENTIFICATION CEREMONY HELD LOST

ELEPHANT DYING

PLANE IS NO MATCH FOR SEAFARING CRAFT THESE DAYS
Says Grizzled Captain

A DISGUISE?
Notorious Criminal Santa Claus Held Perhaps Found

Shark for Lunch!
"All we could find to Eat . . ."

GRIZZLED SEA CAPTAIN ANNOUNCES WHALE FOOD AS WHOLESOME DIET
SUPPLEMENT

ELEPHANT BELIEVED AND HELD UNHAPPY ON TAHITIAN SOIL
"Starts" at the Sight of a Map of India
Half-Dead Robin Identifies Animal as Indian Temple Supplement

RUMP PARLEY HELD OFF
• • •

You can imagine how glad we all were to get back to the Tibetan
plains. For the first time in fifteen years the hawsers had neither dried
up nor cooled off. Everything was red hot for the takeoff, which we
immediately took, our motors revved up to a point which, if you had
told us about it five years or even three years earlier, we simply would
not have believed. Bob had on a tall high hat and Lyn a wafer-thin
blouse. The plane sides were cool, and the air was clear and shining.
Bob said, "Pull!" and we all rose up, up into the frosty sky. Tibet, as cold
as Alaska, the land below, looked to us like nothing so much as a large
tamed elephant, whose dream of becoming a photograph was now all
but forgotten. After somewhat more than five hours, the doctor
released the pigeons for feed. Gabor Banshawe jogged toward them
slowly. The sight (and even the love) of a beautiful girl like Lyn was
nothing to him. "Good luck, darling, as you work your way toward
the dazzling temple," she now to him said. And he jogged onward,
with his mazy trunk twisting in the air. "Home run, farewell!"

And as the weary and defeated "Bachelors" struggled to shore
on another of the Marshall Islands, a vast number of the local birds,
alerted by one white dove who had come this far to tell them,
seemed to be exchanging what can only be described as joyful and
necrophiliac looks. Poor Bachelors! Will they ever, once again, be
able to learn how to fly?

ANSWER UNKNOWN

CHAPTER 41
INSIDE THE MYSTERIOUS WALL

Peace be with them. This was China. Jill and Lyn had gone down to the Chim Buk Toy Market to buy imported slippers. Jill's silk blouse slipped down around her shoulders. A fly bit her shoulder. Lyn, peering out between tresses of light blond hair, smiles at the people who throng the streets. A large city in the largest country in the world.

Elsewhere in China, orange flowers were in terrifying blossom. Jim and Bob and Don would see them soon, while others in some hospital recuperated. The problem was evading the snakes who were writhing on all the streets.

"Come, I will show you the, how are you, pagodas very fine." Underneath her blouse, Lyn's breasts were throbbing. Bob and Jim and Lum caught up with Jill and Lyn and helped them elbow through the crowd. China is whew! hot! You had to agree. One has taken off his red fur suit and is lying puffing sweating semi-naked by the old Nangking Express. They don't use it any more.

The market is jammed with pushcarts. There were three dozen pairs. The white ozone of Lyn's face seemed like a barrel of honey to Bob as he passed out. "So I am bringing you this rose, Madam. Live with it if you will, or let it die close to your immense and welcoming bosom. I, for one, shall never leave you, since I contain your love. Signed, The Hotel."

When the children woke up the next day, China was filled with sunlight. The bittersweet music sounded sad. But the bear eating stars in the hotel— But the dyeing of the silks in the American print room—!

"Listen! I want to live here for hundreds of days!" "I know you 'thought' this and you 'felt' that, but what did you *know?*"

She was born in France, though both her parents were German. Streaky Meistersen used to hang around the Stuttgart airport motel. "I think he might have news of Mona," Ludwina said. That was the last time we ever saw her. Lyn's blouse slipped off the dresser. Naked, the clouds passed before the reviewing stand of the sun.

Tom the Tiger, whose brother had eaten a tremendous number of Tibetan farmers, came out and stood on a rock overlooking the hotel. Its flag matched the colors which the sunlight showed on his teeth: red, yellow, and blue. We saw him as we marched away from that spot, very far away in fact, so far we became lost in nature. It was a wintry nature we entered now, with Lyn in her furs and Jill in a sealskin gown. Jerry had told us how wonderful the place was to which we seemed to be going, but no one had really told us *what* it was. "I'm tired," said Don. And Joe said, "China is vast!"

CHAPTER 42
SUMMER ROAD TO TIN FAN

The chimpanzees were ready at five o'clock. It was Mr. Robertson's plan to keep bringing them jugs of rainwater until the planes could fly. One of the larger chimpanzees, Bozo, has an itch on his left paw. Ben and Bob were on the Lookout, and Ann was in the Oyster Hut with Mr. Thomson. He had been acting very interested in the planes. "If they won't start," Mr. Thomson said, "I don't see what good are the baboons—" "Chimpanzees," Nurse Thomason said, and she closed his lips with a kiss. The chimpanzees played a game with the rainwater—"Monkey-bath," they threw jugs of water at one another and jumped, jibbered, and screamed— which kept them busy till we needed their help in pulling the planes out of the covert in which they'd been so damned definitively stuck. We had by now given up the boats and come back to try them again. When he awoke, he saw that the whole coastline seemed dotted with ships. However, it was really only the spray on the sea. Lepers began to choke beyond the outer perimeter where the chimpanzees stood, shivering now, in the first blue holocaust of morning.

The joy in Santa's eyes as we went up in her, "I love your pontoons but goodbye!" The Red Robins are looking for the Earthly Paradise. It was last seen in an elephant's tusk in northeast Asia. We watched the ducks fly down. Among them was one duck, Flort, who seemed to be their leader. His wings were the color of sand, and his eyes were like stones in the Yellow River above Han Chang.

While the rest were leaving, one wrote her a letter beneath the elm tree's flowers.

What would happen if we were together I don't know, being unable to think about anything beyond being with you. On the steps in Shanghai once I touched your arm beneath its red flashing silk and I turned to look at you: what I saw was the sky. The merriment of the drinkers' laughter was now largely gone. They had returned to the zoo with dimmed spirits, knowing that tomorrow, as usual, no one was going to be let out. But there was one hippopotamus who didn't cry. For he was in the brimstone of his first youth. The frond was strong in him. He ran in to Tuckie his mother and laughed all night, and next day he was a spectacle there, a dead thing shown. Monto the Hippopotamus was dead. So, Jill, am I when I am not with you.

Lyn pulls down on her light deep-blue dress, the climate has changed, and it is time of the early first snowfall on the River Chang.

May I meet you cousin? Goodbye!

The Tin Fan flowed on, over the rough red valentines.
Bobby Service poked his head up from amid those valentines.
"Where are Lyn and Jill?"
And death covered him. A duck bill suddenly appeared, which
    snatched him up.
No, it was an "octopus horn," I think.
But he was merely hiding under the stones.

He'd had an invitation from Professoressa van Flügel for Valentine's Day for seven long years. A huge valentine heart lay sleeping. Big Cinnamon. The octopus. Forever yours.

Careless clouds drew word portraits in a blue and ivory fishnet sky. In the corpse-littered traces of afternoon, a giant sea gull was being filled with leaves. Lyn backed up holding her white cigarette holder in her hand, which, as she stepped backwards, she waved slightly, cautiously in the air, as if a gesture to Bob to take advantage of his one chance to escape.

"Hymna, would you give me the soap? Yes, that lavender-colored bar over there! For the planes will fly, but so high that we may not see them. I have borne him a child."

The child's name was Sonny and he grew up to be an airplane manufacturer in Duluth, Minnesota. So many men were frightened by the Depression that they were determined always to have money. He was her child but I think he was one of those

Who tried to grow rich from life
In place of enriching it with their love . . .

CHAPTER 43
THE STAIRWAYS OF SHANGHAI

Shanghai is a city famous for its stairways. To amateurs of marble, metal, concrete, or even in one case paper stairs, there is literally no other place in the world to be. Now, I am not much of a stairway man myself, at least I wasn't before my coming to Shanghai, but I have garnered more pleasure from the things than I ever have from chairs, tables, roofs, doorways, smokestacks, and windows put together. All these things are stationary, unitary; but a stairway moves. You go up it, and it goes up itself. Which cannot be said for a window, a chair, or a door. You could say it of a smokestack but it would not be literally true. The smokestack merely is where it is and as it is and tall as it is; it doesn't change and rise the way a staircase does. Or seems to. And I reckon the very most beautiful and elegant stairways in the world are the ones that give that feeling the most. We will begin in Northeast Shanghai.

This is the locale of the famous Chi Chung Escalier. Built in eight hundred and forty-seven by the Emperor Cho Chen, it spans over two city blocks. It is made of transparent Fukinese marble of colors mainly yellow, pink, and red. The stairway is partly circular, partly square, with the square part being that part close to the earth, the circular section being above it. The stairway reputedly was built to be the stairway of a palace, but the palace was apparently never built. A palace, in order to accommodate such enormous stairs, would have to be at least thirty city blocks in area itself. Some say the palace was built and destroyed but there is no evidence of this. The stairs rise about half a mile above the city. From their top one can see the farmland surrounding Shanghai as well as the famous Dang Tuk Railroad Station, which was the first one constructed in China (it was built by an American entrepreneur).

Descending from the Chi Chung one heads northward perhaps two or three hundred feet and already one sees rising before one the vast bulk of the Chang Wa Stairs, built out of iron for the Autumn Festival of eighteen ninety-two. These stairs, originally black, have rusted now to a beautiful shade of green, due to some chemical element in the climate in and surrounding Shanghai. These stairs are five hundred yards tall.

But we must hurry. For this city has innumerable stairways that are worthy of our attention. Northeast Shanghai alone has seventy-five alabaster staircases catalogued in *Stairs of the Earth*, and hundreds which are not but which certainly would be if they were in any other city. We have time to indicate only the chief six or seven major staircases which any traveler must see. To truly know the stairways of Shanghai would take years; the pleasure from even a superficial knowledge of them is so great that many persons have settled here, with nothing in their minds and hearts but to go on seeing them for the rest of their lives.

It is perhaps the central or "southern" portion of Shanghai that houses—the wrong word here, I'm sure—the most fantastic examples of stair architecture anywhere. Here, along Cho Tung Boulevard, at the junction with the Avenue of the Thirteenth of September, is the Ho Ka "Palisade," or Paper Stairway of the Gods. These paper stairs are entirely colored gold and silver, and in the noonday sun they are blinding. They rise thousands of feet in the air. The method by which they have been preserved is a secret guarded jealously in Peking. No foreigner, or no Chinese for that mater that I have ever known, has known what it was. These paper stairs are reputed to be several thousands of years old, but their age, too, is a guarded mystery. Leaning against them, Lyn felt her back edged slightly by something so cold and so exciting, that she knew that she would never see England again. Or Philadelphia or Chicago in America either, for all of that. These paper stairs can be climbed at certain times of the year, but this is only by certain individuals and only at night. No one is allowed to see it happening. It is apparently a kind of test of the stairs, to see if they still merit their name.

Just three hundred yards down the Boulevard (near Wo Kai Street) are the Glass Staircases of Miravolto, a set of gorgeous transparent staircases given to the city of Shanghai in the eighteenth century by the Italian Whirlwinds, a group of wealthy adventurers whose home base was Venice but who lived there (in Shanghai) at that time. These stairs were built so that they would reflect the Ho Ka paper stairs just before sunset. And they still do so. The sight of the silver and gold paper stairs reflected in these pinkish-white glass ones, at this time of day, is, it may be, the greatest pleasure in Shanghai.

The "rubber" stairs and the "Banana" stairs in the market section of the town are well enough known from recent literature to need no description here. There are hundreds of thousands of worthwhile small staircases in Shanghai, as well as the large public ones. To climb them all would take up every week for a year. Lyn and Don, out of breath, walk through the ozone and they are trying, but it is hard to get to even one five-hundredth of them in one day. Bill tried flying over and up to them in his plane, but he crashed against the infamous "Metz" Wall in nearby Shu-Fa. You've read about his recovery. German immigrants built this wall to keep everyone else from coming to China, but it failed. The stairways of Shanghai, for some reason, are by no means as familiar as they should be to those who care about the daring and beautiful things of this world. When you see a person on one of them and you are on another, it is traditional to say "Eng-Ta-Ko" which means "Up-Down" or "Which way are you going?"

CHAPTER 44
ON APLAGANDA'S SHORES

On the shores of Lake Aplaganda, in a small hut, Jim, Lyn and I. In a facing house, Santa Claus and Jill. Between us Leper Lake, as Aplaganda is called.

The octopus surfacing began at eleven o'clock. In a third hut were Don, Bob, Bill, Mona and Bud. In a fourth "floating hut" (actually on the surface of the lake) were Sandy and Ace. Louis and Gabor Banshawe held a fifth hut between the fingers of the lake and the tawny shore. What's for lunch?

You'll have to wait a while! For Cook, dear, isn't ready!

The magnolia grew fifteen feet high.

I never hoped that Jill would understand this, Bob said, but now, behold, she does.

It's really good for our sporting party, said Amos.

Are we allowed to shoot them?

Oh ho ho I wouldn't suggest it no that I really wouldn't, Bud, in his flimsiest German accent, said. They would come up in force to these cafés and mangle us and till we were dead.

Ann used to take individual octopuses into her "house" and "tan the fragrance" with them, but Bill said the overshoes should not be permitted back to Cleveland until Uncle Harry could weld a successful statue called Passion by the Sea.

On the shores of Lake Aplaganda, in a small hut, Jim, Lyn and I. And the word *redundant*. And the word *sharp*. The words *taking a casual roll*.

Bob found himself getting a little tired after watching the octopuses rolling around for six hours, so he went off on a little path into the jungle to find someplace to take a nap. He didn't know about the "octopus mosquitoes," which exist only in two parts of the world and that's one of them. These mosquitoes are particularly deadly to white people. Fortunately, the mosquitoes were "off-campus" that day.

Amalgam Octopus, one of the head and oldest octopuses, was the first we could see coming to the surface. They did it every year. It was called "taking a roll." First you could see their backs—colored yellow, white, and off-green—then they would flip over and go back down. They did this about thirty at a time and each octopus did it until it was tired, which sometimes would take three days. There was so much frothing and churning, so many candles and butterflies in the hotel! It was accounted one of the great sights in the Far East.

Fruit trees were blossoming all around. Santa Claus did a daring "ducking" act in the lake, in the midst of all those octopuses. I think the man is mad! No, I'm not, smiles he, but maybe immune to some of the kinds of fear that you others are after having. For I am Santa Claus the Grand. He winked at Jill and dived in the lake again, this time staying there for several minutes and this time he came up uninjured but covered with weeds and slime. That's enough for me! he cried. I'm heading back for Vermont! He vanished then and reappeared as a king. He wore gold robes trimmed with white ermine. Lyn fell in love with him but Jill quickly knocked her off the truck. The octopuses were still surfacing.

It's time for lunch! called Helga, and we went into the middle of the cool albergo arena which the "Mutants of Asians Tuscany" had set up especially to accommodate travelers who came to the lake. We were the first ones!

Déjeuner (Collazione) Lunzh (sic)
Peppery Octopus Soup
Tiny octopods à la russe (with "red" mayonnaise, peas, and little slivers of pepper)
Whole Broiled Octopus
Seaweed Salad, Vinaigrette
House Cheese
Fried Bananas with Octocaramel
Lake Aplaganda Coffee

The chef, Wing To Fung, comes out to chat with us after the collation. I hop you like, he says. Oh yes, we say, it's very very good. Sex was not permitted to anyone, rape or not, before the age of sixteen, for girls, and forty-seven, for men. The whole land area is filled with the carcasses of octopuses which people have dragged on shore for purposes of eating and sex. But Wing To Fung assures us the octopus that is served at the arena is absolutely fresh. Oh yes, he says, nothing you have here mo than fife hour old. Thus reassured, we plunged back to the watching huts to see the octopuses surfacing until the end of the day.

The octopuses stop surfacing when it gets dark and don't begin until the water is fairly luminescent, so we had a good long night to relax in before we started watching the second "tournament," as Bob calls it. He sees it as some sort of contest between the octopuses, but we don't know what the rules are. Don says it has something to do with the oxygen content of the water. At certain times of the year, this being one, the water becomes "heavy" and contains not enough oxygen to nourish the octopus's rather curiously constructed inhalation system as a result of which they all have to put on red skirts and stroll about the harbor—i.e. come to the surface again. Without this, there would be nothing in this part of the world at all. Some say, even as it is, there is very little, but I have never been able to feel much, aside from slight annoyance, but pity for skeptics. My last (and this really is the last) quotation is from *The Boyhood of Octopus Champions:*

... When a young octopus is taken from his mother, he ... atomize ... dut ...

Then, who are you? asked an astonished Tony, as reddish-pink clouds began to scud over the darkening early morning sky, predicting a desperate thoroughfare for those who would rise into those cloudy spaces. Lyn begged Santa to go, and to leave Jill alone. I don't know why.

CHAPTER 45
SUNDAY

How quiet the water was! Here a frog leaped up; and, there, a "parade" fish. The Noh players had already spread out their equipment on the grass. Lyn began to undress. Her chest always had a surprising effect. Rivers would begin to run in Russia when she laid it bare, there in the evening air. A big derby scow, all lighted up, would be floating down the river so created, and Gorky would be aboard it, reading Stevenson and Rilke. A horrible strawberry milky shine would gloze the eastern sky. Camels would refuse to accompany their masters to the dawn manufactory. At Lake Michigan Horror Castle the waters would freeze. Nothing else would be impossible for the undressed model speeding in a red Impossible through Shanghai. Ireland's hand would be lighted up. The picnickers would desert the old Greek theatre and wander as far as Biarritz. Lyn! "It isn't natural to stand before you so." "Yes, it is! it is! Why, we are not born with clothing pulled over our heads." The standard light began to shine through the seraphic plum trees. Jesus took down the George Washington split-pea valentine from the top of the Folkestone meadow. Hawsers began to splash and shine in every direction. Lyn started to put her skirt back on. "Bring that brilliance closer to us," they pleaded. "Why, has there ever been a city as beautiful as you are?" Jill pleaded, too, that Lyn be let go, and at last they acceded to her desire.

Amid the downtown dingy streets the forest of Shanghai the life of your limbs continues to be as a jigsaw of my first imagining the town.

And as for "Tin Fan" . . . The old ranger smiled as he remembered how long he had been in China—"always searching for the same thing," he said. "I don't know," he said. "I wish I had come here when I was a child. Then I could have known this country as one knows a woman's body—as a violinist knows his instrument, as a cartographer knows his world." Jim spit out the straws of wheat and began to think about canceling appointments. Nothing could give so much pleasure as listening to this old man. His tone, too, suggested he could tell a story which would help him so much to comprehend the world—uniting sex with knowledge. Sometimes sex seemed to him the main thing. A quick rat picked up the wheat straws in his teeth and ran off with them. Stones were flipped into the harbor by a twelve-year-old boy. Everyone on earth aimed for simplicity, and no one had found it. Lyn's bosom radiantly suggested it. Young old man, tell me who you are.

"Yes, I am Doctor Lunch," dixit, passing now his terrifying glance from one to another young Robin. His ears were loaves of bread. His eye—a pineapple. His other eye a smoking yellow dove. Thanksgiving morning dawned beautiful as the Hebron, and we crowded into the little tiny orange-and-green-painted Chinese junk en route to Bong-Kai. I was on the foredeck, throwing sandals in the bay. Bob put his hand on his heart, or where he thought the heart of the tiger might be. Good God! I am sorry to be so talky and so vague, she said. He said, Yes you are a little unclear. She said then, her wide eyes widening and her beautiful large bosom appearing to him radiantly now in its airgirl flotilla of orange and light-yellow fluff, she said, Don't you know what that means when someone is unclear? No. That is saying something very clear, she said; it is saying I can't be clear. I love you, he said, and they went to the Mahorga Islands.

The sea gull's complexity, she said, differs from the complexity of a fish. And then he began to court her again. Sometimes they'd be mythologized, symbolic, I don't know what, sometimes like part of a dream. To the camera it makes no difference. You know that, though.

I am an old man, said Dr. Lunch, who seems completely composed of food. As Ace's face seemed composed of the way the sky seems over various places. Lyn stood up. It was beautiful. Tell us a story. Of what? Oh, of Gruenhelt Island. Where Ni-Shu went crazy once? That's what they said, but it wasn't really true. For me, she was the everlasting embodiment of youth, kindness, spontaneity and joy. That's where we could have lunch. Could have had. Now it was too late.

CHAPTER 46
THE RESTAURANT IN THE SEA

Gruenhelt Island was the only member of the Marquesas to have remained in German hands throughout world-wide wars consistently lost by the German people. Very few people knew that Germany owned Gruenhelt Island, and about the same number (perhaps three to six) even knew that it existed. Constantly washed by a slimy green and blowfish-filled tide, the island was so slippery that no one could stand on it without special equipment. A man named "Blazes," who was a Chilean, a South American, and who was a friend of "Tubber," whom we had encountered at a much earlier time, was determined to make a million out of the island. He was building a restaurant there out of something he called "sea cement" which he claimed could withstand the tide. Mrs. Parker had let him have three million dollars in letters of credit which the Agence Havas had consigned to its maritime fund in lieu of replacing the larger amount with a certificate for the amount in bullion not due until the second quarter and thus negotiable for only a limited period. "Blazes'" men had been worked harder than men had ever been worked before. Many died and would be instantly replaced. "Blazes" himself contracted a fatal case of sea-mold fever the day before the completion of the restaurant, to whose opening the sea's most notorious personalities had been invited: Afternoon, Catatonia, and the Moon. Even the Tides had considered attending this irresistible gala, but they had at the last minute refused. Sea gulls had brought them word of "Blazes'" fatal illness.

When the restaurant opened, the Chilean entrepreneur was still alive but he knew he was dying. His face was a sickly yellowish hue, and his arms, chest, legs, and body were like sticks. He welcomed everybody as best he could—dressed in a white, blue, green, and yellow costume (to represent the Sea!)—but every few minutes he would have to retire into the restaurant's back room to grapple with a coughing fit which would make him even yellower and further reduce him in size. By the time Oceanic Porpoise reached the restaurant, "Blazes" was no larger than an atabrine tablet lying on a windy windowsill. He blew off and was seen no more on Gruenhelt—or, more properly, it being largely known by its English name, Congers Island.

So the restaurant continued without him and became one of the favorite gathering spots in the Far East. It is all ruins now, ever since the time of the Giant Porpoises, but in its day there was no surer way a flyman could please his blushing airgirl's heart than to take her to "Blazes"' restaurant and eat the food and hear the tragic story. Was it so tragic, though? "Blazes" was a cruel man. Then the long walk along the jetty, dreaming of the East. And thinking about the rights and wrongs of living. Making plans for the future, too, when, maybe, marriage and baby would come—and this all seem like some crazy dream. Oh Domberg, take me to your cousin! "I cannot! For he is the greatest traitor in the harbor!"

One morning bright and early the baby porpoises swam to Conger (Gruenhelt) Island and began to beat their tails against the paddles of the approaching customers. Men feared the porpoises and soon the island was abandoned. The classical arcades of the ruins are a source of joy and wonderment to all. A man with a moustache once set down his impressions of these arcades and was raised high above the other artists in his native land. Then complaints began that his art was not "local," that it was subject to "exoticism," and he was banned and starved in exile, ironically enough on this island, surrounded by the storming sea.

CHAPTER 47
SIC TRANSIT

 These girls,

whose breasts gave them the right
to glare like lions

came out into the clearing dressed in dop! an airplane costume and pop! a helmet, of goddess-like design. Lyn held them for a while in a girlish parley, and then they all adjourned to the whorehouse dining room, in which a game of Australian backgammon was in full swing. Ace, Bob and Bud, meanwhile, were carrying the rattan and ogilvie in from the jungle, with which to build the boat that would carry us to O-Chu-So-Chu, from where a clear view could be had of the whole wide country adjoining Pin Lan. The River Hing, which we were going to follow, mysteriously ended at the summit of a high, abrupt plateau. Once there, his helmet-bonnet encased in sunshine, Santa Claus explained what he hoped we were going to do.

Lyn and Fan, unfortunately, had become embroiled with the Fairweather Daypools of Hong Kong. Dressed entirely in feathers, Kee-Fa tried to enjoy as much as possible her hacienda on the little hump of camel which Chai-Gah had given to us, while noting down the emblem "Do not undo your mothers as you would have them do unto you, for that way lies madness." Listen, said Uncle Mutt, the Pekinese Trojan Horseway leads straight out of here to Mee-Jee-Kow-San, from where we can be horseless and boatless and—Lyn interrupted him with the comb book which Lee-Fee had given him. Nile River, said Cha-Ki housemother, and downtown Honolulu was deserted. Only in the yellow leaves of the tree could the map of her misfortunes be dissevered, and long before that time the party had winched Marion's knee. Oh good night, fortune! Dalberson said; and he went into the Orient House where the girls were and brought them, like a planet, out.

On the blue water we flew as through the waterblue sky. And John played a song.

Oh Mary, Mary,
Where are those broken hearts once mine
To glance beyond
This fabled blue . . .

Suddenly a horse was donkey, and the monkey-man came to an end. Lyn lent Domberg the hundred and five dollars which Luc had given the urban Siamese Santa Claus for penitence-in-October's-birthday. Here come the traders. They insist on various clauses and venisons and artifacts but finally Luke the Gorilla fools them. We are left dumbfounded standing on deck, with the sadness like a halo around us. Says Ogilvie, No I cannot help but build you that boat. When she did so, the under-linen was shining. A plough appeared under Chou-Ka's raincoat. Now the Stutterers could go home.

With what blue shutters they tabloid-plated the sheet-music temples of the inaudible. Oh those were the raincoats! Lyn was crying a little bit, so Bud went up and gave the young gorilla a bucket of sand. Distribute this, Lee said, to everyone you see who is all wet. And it will make him dry. Lee passed right by Lyn.

And indeed the Japanese Noh players were there. They camped down on Lemon Suda and would come up and tell us how the bugle blows. Like this, said Tanagawa, "bloodle de bloop bloop bloo." The air, castirons-man of the weather, took a cattleboat out of autumn's sleeve, and strove to be a bear with it, but nothing happened more than a lint light as tamarind seeds on Lyn's gloves. I wanted to be a vibrance, she said, and here I am trapped in famous walls. Bumblebee, happy that nothing happens, flies over. Autumn leaves fly with him.

The Han Dynasty Symmetries went floating beyond their clear original home.

Look at this, everyone look, said Santa. I have a program here showing every son of a bitch in the Far East. Tear it up, Bud said; we don't want to cause any trouble. The autumn leaves were falling, and the chimpanzee. The chimpanzee came into the aerodrome. Jill had on her pockets and gloves. Kong wiss me, said the cinnamon. We didn't know what that means. But I have "gone with you" a number of times, a startingly lovelier but in every way wiser Lyn said, and we went only to the Doughnuts of Oblivion. Well, this time, said Dr. Fast, I am going to show you the Tin Market. Oh I don't believe it, Jill said. So, happy birthday, Map! Dr. Pinkwater walked along the thin line separating Tin Fan Province from O-Fo-Cha-See. It was Mary's way of keeping fit. Santa said, All right I am going to tear up the list. But not before we see who some of these are.

And down they went, they walked under the embankment, it was miles away. Nine years before, the island parliament had voted by a majority of nine to one to totally bar Westerners from the island. But then when the king had been seized by a fit of ague, a white doctor had come and cured him. From that time forward, whites were welcomed and automatically given the status of kings. Now they were blowing the horns and fishing her out of the bay. Her name was Alice Loveless and she had breasts the size of Ebeneezer Finch's home in Simple, Arizona. He learned to read by following her directions. The necklace slipped from his hands and he saw the sky. Octopus giving a cocktail under the sea, shine on this Fourth Republic of my bosom! So she ranted, and so the doctor said, Give her peace, thy most precious gift. Kabloona thanked me and drank some more of the weird lemonade. "The Protestant butterflies decided to kill the octopus." Bill, hold her down, I think she is raving!

A young human named Hannah Bluebell enters the Beautiful Wrist Contest in Jumpahead, California, quarrels with her lover, Tom Shantworth, over her flirting with a judge to gain the victory, and, her heart determined, sets off with the lucky judge for the shambles of the Pacific Sea. After breakfast, the morning after that, she suddenly becomes ill. If you and I could live on an island . . . But think of the slimy plans. Think of the horror. "I thought of the horror when I read the magazines. Disease is everywhere."

But people had tried to kill Santa Claus before. It didn't help them later on, when they had to adjust. A two-piece orchestra were poisoned by mistake in Chuckee, Nevada. We never heard of it out here.

CHAPTER 48
LAKE HOO-MO: THE RENEGADE

Luc helped pass the time with this story, on our long trip over the Wa-Chi-Gi Range:

Henry Rand, whom birds' wingtips had never touched, was the son of an American career diplomat in Outer Mongolia. He shipped out on a Norwegian freighter when a child of five, and from that time forward until God had brought him to his thirty-fifth year he had spent but a few weeks of every twelvemonth on the dry parts of the surface of the earth. After learning the ways of the freighter, he had become the ship's boy, then deck-spot, then, within ten years, captain of a fleeter of his own. Within three years of this time he had transferred his allegiance from freighters to ships of war and his nationality from Norwegian to English. No one ever knew until much later, and when it no longer mattered, that he was an American by birth, a natural son of the country of Betsy Ross and of Lincoln, that has been so much corrupted in our own day.

The bright, hot colors of the red white and blue, what is more, stirred very little loyal fervor in Henry Rand's breast. His parents, as has been said, lived in Outer Mongolia, and he had left them forever at the age of five. English had but rarely been spoken in Henry Rand's house, the language spoken most often there was Chinese, though he had also begun to learn French from a Russian governess, and such English as was spoken was not that which one would hear at the exit to a bar in Milwaukee, Wisconsin, or on a street near the Bay, where the shore-encrusted barnacles break their black backs to the silvers of morning, in San Francisco, or on Downes Street, in

Georgiatown, or at the Significant Spoon in the gulf port of Hellas. No, it was an English as is spoken by those born to the English tongue, British English, not your common tobacco-y American, which idles along through the dirt-dustied morning like clear waterglasses at a much-used counter, and now, Sway your backs, porpoises, for young Mr. Henry has gone! And the house in tears at the departure of the babe. But soon a new dust settling, and the diplomat ensconced with a new mistress, hazel lilac rose, and birds in the houseparty garden, while the great grey wings of the trees make unforgettable screens overhead. "Henry! what news is there of Henry?" His father did not forget, but man is mortal, and his father died, and there were none left to mourn the loss of the barely undiapered son. So Rand had known little American and almost nothing of his native land. By the time he was eight he could barter for glasses and beadware in Gok-tu and could share enough of what the men said to him in Norwegian to feel himself a natural-born Scandinavian son of the sea. When he was twenty-two it happened—he met the girl. From that day forward he knew he was no Norwegian, and he knew that the remainder of his days could not be passed upon the bosom of the deep. Her breasts were like lilac dials, through which a brilliant haze of foliage and sunlight could be seen, and they felt like the first robin of each morning, on a twiggy stick, shaking off the dew. "Good morning, sir, will you have your tea now?" "I must go back!"

Wah-ta-Lee-Ka. He knew that first he must become a war-ship commander, then become British rather than Norwegian. A foul country enslaved her isle—only England, he felt, could set it free. Himself there, commander and free-er of the island, what more fitting than that she like plum drop into his arms. Red sunlight above the Admiralties showed him the wounds that he might and must inflict, and perhaps even suffer himself. He armed himself in showers of reflection that night, and in the first glimmers of dawn, when Britain freed the isle, he could already feel her in his arms. And soon she was actually there.

The ecstasy Rand felt at the possession of his island girl was to be, however, of short duration. International war, which has a way of breaking out in despite of human passions, called Henry Rand to

Saipan, where he was instantly declared chief of operations of the British Eighteenth Fleet. Wah-ta-Lee-Ka, covered with tiny bruises and cuts, and more beautiful than a laundry of the moon and sun, followed her maniac lover to the jungle cottage where he proposed to bind her with gu-jap leaves and so force her to remain till he came back. Since the war was long, however, she soon died of thirst and starvation, and there is a Chinese landscape scroll, believed to be lost, which was said to give some indication of the gradually lengthening despair and madness that she felt, as the days rolled by, and life's activities went on but her lover did not return. Rand had left instructions for Ga-fee-Fa, a cabin boy, to nourish her, which the boy had done for a few days but then had gone wild. Found roaming through the jungle foaming at the mouth and roaring, he was shot by a Siamese trapper. No one ever found the girl.

No one, that is, but Henry Rand, but by that time of course she was already dead. After the war's successful completion, Rand had come back to claim his prize. Seeing her there, starved and lifeless, he lifted her somehow miraculously preserved body into his arms (the gu-jap leaf bonds had long ago rotted away) and carried her to Lake Hoo-Mo, which was reputed to have waters which could heal any malady, even death. Standing upon the bank of the lake, and dipping her head, then her shoulders and waist into the water, Captain Henry Rand lost his balance and fell, and, caught inextricably in the long twining hair of the beloved whose life he had taken and tried to reprieve, he was forthwith strangled and drowned. Two months later, however, according to my story, the miraculous lakewaters sent the two bobbing to their surface, loving, healthy, and alive. At this point, Rand renounced his connection with the Navy but as soon as the Admiralty found that he was still living, they insisted he return to service. Wah-ta-Lee-Ka, they said, as a special privilege, would be able to accompany him. During the first voyage after his return, somewhere between the Solomons and Tahiti he and the island beauty mysteriously vanished from the decks of The *Royal Traveler* and were never seen again.

CHAPTER 49
OLD AND NEW WINGS

Fidelity is a thing unknown to the lovebirds in the Admiralty Islands. However, they continue to come over in vast, white-winged flocks every so often. Oh these days full of waving and wind! And it feels to us as though our group now is a little larger. But what's the evidence?

It is quite an interesting problem how one becomes a Red Robin, how new members are found, and so on. Does any member ever deliquesce, i.e., does anyone ever leave the organization? It seems to remain the same size, although it gets bigger. I don't know. Louis left us for the monastery once. He road on Gabor Banshawe through the Hindu wilderness. But then he returned and defeated the lepers. "Stone," the new Robin, was with us and then after that seemed more or less not to be. Was he a relation to "Roughie"? Do you remember "Roughie?" That I don't know. "Stone" it was at the time of the Christian monastery and the Vice President and the unfixed airplane gears and so on—or was it the starters? The goldenrod was heavy with the breeze over Sha-Tu Point. Jill picked at the rabbit skin eagerly. At last she was about to find the clue of how someone could become a new Red Robin. It was by being—Exactly! Pleasing to Lyn and to Bob. And to Santa Claus. Me too, thought Jill. Those were the main spirits around in those times of early to middle Asia. Yes, Lyn said, you will be mine! And she took off her duffel dress, her stockings and her shoes and she lay with him all through the jungle night. In the morning the cow octopus were standing on the limbs of the sea. Hello, I said, tipping, as an overcoat of pincushions began to slam, yellow, through the day. She had her eyes on me all along but I managed to get out of there, fast. I've never wanted, really, to join anything. But I love these islands. Would you like another drink?

So they gestured and so they talked, and they knew it was the best time for them, then, of always, and some others would come and bother them—rich or professionals—and then they would go away. Flying above the Marianas one sunny March afternoon, Bob spotted a whole tribe of lepers down below. I have completely forgotten it! she cried to Louis when he at last came home. Now it is incomprehensible. Then what will he make of it? I— The birds at this moment were chased away bitterly by wasps. Hens gathered around to listen to the Story of Dad. (A yearly occurrence.)

LA STORIA DI BABBO

Dad always had a lot of stories, anecdotes, jokes, and tales. Technically, he could do anything. Tell them in rhyme, tell them in prose—exact, accurate, and critical or wild stream of consciousness, Dad could do the lot. He had a sweetheart, I had a sweetheart once, named Mona, he said. But kissed her I—she was only fourteen. When she was brought in covered with spots, I didn't know what to do. Ei Babbo, squeaked the Robins. And that day we spoke no more.

Luc had for a long time now been a Red Robin. Luc stayed a little bit in the background. He was of French descent. Jim sang this song:

> When I meet with that she
> Whose eternally fresh raspberry beauty
>   Will show me that she is to be mine alone
> I pray my heart will not be heavy as a
>   Do I dare to say it? stone! and that I may be
>   Praiseful of her beauty
>   As we glide along, alone, alone
> At the bottom of a barrel of dreams!

Jill joined in, and we all went up into the sky, with our young legs forming, for all who cared to watch from underneath, the words

One thing is sure: we needed enough Robins to do that. In this fashion we pelted through the sky. Stoneland, Asia, was our first destination after that time. Where would you like to go next? Just before dying, Gabor Banshawe recovered his name. He was known as Caruso-Tsik. Cohen couldn't keep his eyes off the newspaper, in spite of the fact that most of his best friends were there, in the freshly painted war canoe, as well as the young woman whom, no matter what happened, he knew he would always love. Really love, not just touch happily and share things with and care about. Love. And he thought he could never have her. The lion hunt was scheduled for nine o'clock. Shanghai was breasts and combs. At the last moment Lyn says she has "something else to do" and can't go. Once left alone, she thought of Caruso-Tsik, and began to cry.

GHOSTLY ELEPHANT HELD BELIEVED LOST ON ASIAN SHORE
Israeli Cabinet in Surprise Move to Condemn the "Index"

DAYS AND NIGHTS BELIEVED HELD LOST
"Clouds" over the Western Pacific
Lovebirds Show Human Beings in Disgrace

Lyn wrote:
Dear Mr. President,
Robins are not all red. Factories are not all smoky. It's not always so that no news is good news. Robins, reputed to have red breasts, often have vermilion, orange, or brownish orange ones. A man stood among hawsers, trading news. On the red agate pier, a girl, dressed like a Lydian king, gives a salesman a porch on the sea, and the almanach-maker the roof. A little bit of sky turns blue on the slopes of our nails. How are you, dear President? When secret things happen to me, I want to tell them to you.
Love,
Lyn

CHAPTER 50
MOUNTAINS, VALLEYS,
AND RIVERS

One of the greatest twentieth-century scholarly artistic exploits was the discovery, somewhat after the middle of the century, of the Chinese landscape scroll collection, Chan-Tung F, which had been thought to be destroyed by invading Tatar armies in about 1256. The scrolls are of immense historical as well as artistic importance, since they give a clearer idea of the earthly paradise at the time and place when human beings seemed closest to it than any other documents verbal or pictorial in existence. For an insight into Chinese and universal life, they are of a value more than the plays of Shakespeare, the Bayeux Tapestry, and the Cathedral of Chartres put together.

After Lyn had rejoined us (our patents were all right), she and Bud left with the rest of us after a day to go to Chi-Chen-Fi-A, where the scrolls were kept. Once the scrolls had been seen, they could never be forgotten. A radiance shone out of them which said, over and over, "I am the exact combination which the humans have been seeking for a million years of art and reality. Look at me that way and I am one, look at me this way and I am two. I am not what you are every day. I am what you always are. I disresemble you entirely." But most of all it said, "When you are with me, you are looking at everything."

Most of the subject matter of the scrolls was landscape. Most of the landscape was mountains, valleys, and rivers. In many cases the landscapes were snowy; at other times, burgeoning with greenery in spring. Men and women appeared, in a variety of positions, pursuing various occupations, many just sitting around, seemingly doing nothing at all. Their clothing was sometimes extremely and even extravagantly beautiful, sometimes they were barefoot and in rags. One immensely long scroll showed many different phases of battle: the invasion of the land and palace of the Tchou Emperor by an army of wild dogs, seven million of them, the most savage and ferocious creatures (you could say so to look at them) who had ever lived. The dogs tore up the sentries and snagged with their bloody streaming teeth the long dresses of the palace ladies. For two months the Emperor's troops kept them at bay, but finally, inexorably, at last, the Imperial Palace yielded. As it did so, and as the dogs tore into it under the pale pink necklaces of oriental dawn, you could see the Emperor Wang-Ti standing above them, the top part of him dissolving into the air. The lower part did also, and the dogs consequently ran right through him, without doing him any harm. Also they did not see him and so they continued their ravaging attack far beyond the palace, searching for the Emperor. Finally they went ravaging so far that they reached the end of the Tchou World, the banks of the River Kai-Boon-Ka (our closest meaning to it is "Time," though it is more than that) and still looking for the Emperor leaped into it and perished. Meanwhile the Emperor retook possession of his form and forth-with built up and fortified his kingdom. Dogs were allowed to enter it only if they would abstain from speaking the imperial lan-guage (Chinese) so they could never organize and threaten him again. These new regulations about dogs are shown toward the end of the scroll. Its eastern border however is composed of pictures of the ghosts of the ravaging dogs in the Kingdoms beyond Time, planning a bloody, insane, but obviously hopeless revenge. Like the other scrolls, this one is drawn and painted with a delicacy and lightness unmatched in any other achievement of human hands. Other scrolls were mainly notable for their treatment of snow, landscape, fir trees, bamboo, feathery birds, and animals (above all, horses), but this, though absolutely flawless in that respect as well, was incurably, inexhaustibly interesting for the story it told, one in which sages in China, Burma, Japan, and other countries of the Far East saw one of the four essential mysteries of human existence—

transposition and detail: the mystery of how the changing of physical detail can effect a spiritual transposition of the most significant kind. Two of the other three mysteries were suggested, though not entirely shown forth, by the other scrolls.

Bud found out about the scrolls during our stay at Ai-Ga-Fay-Ta where we all had gone because Jim had been invited there to be honored for his poetry, which had come to the attention of an adjunct of the Pong Choy emperor, Yu Fu VII, who had been taken by some of the poems (two, to be exact: "Tchou Morning" and "Sitting in Shanghai and Loving You") to such a degree that he had shown them to the "Snowy Red Eminence" (so Yu Fu was called) himself, who had shared his adjunct's enthusiasm. Every five years Yu Fu gave a festival in his dark palaces and amazingly sun-filled gardens, to which the most famous, gay, happy, dreamy, savage, civilized, melodious, and in every way far-reaching citizens of his domain were invited; some, like Jim, were invited from the outside, though never anyone who had not within that five years set foot on the empire's soil—there, in any case, there Bud chanced to meet with an old man who told him about the paintings, which have been not at all advertised in the West.

The discovery of these paintings was important to the Red Robins in various ways. To Jim, the scrolls suggested a great new poem, which he wanted to make, he said, somewhat mysteriously, in the first bitterness of evening, "as long as the landscape scrolls themselves," whether he meant one or all of them together not being entirely clear. And in what sense his poem could be "long as a scroll" was not sure either. In any case, at once he started out and that is what he has been working on ever since. Little white spiders covered Lyn's hand as she began to think what the scrolls' discovery meant to her. Perhaps in some way these old, strange manuscripts made her see that there was indeed no way that she could ever see the President again. I do know that after we saw them she stopped writing to him. And something else about her seemed indefinably changed. She was a little bit happier mornings and evenings, more agreeable to what others suggested, yet at the same time more deeply committed to what was especially important to herself. She has been wearing a cream top lately and a swift yellow bottom which has been of great interest to Max the Spider. The evergreens mixed their indescribable smell with the stenches of gas from the planes. Topics of heaven: that's how Bud referred to our flights. For him the discovery of the scrolls was one more in an endless series of adventures in which he played a central part. That's how life seemed to him then, before, and since. He is a reassuring person to have around. Bill found the scrolls "slightly unpleasant." "In terms of the culture I'm working in, they don't make really any sense," he said, drawing on the large cigar of productive evening with a wink at the picture of Ni Shu which Lyn was carrying in her goggles case. And the beautiful night settled down, with cloudlets for cushions, which were as white as thighs, and through them, in the dreams of some, that night and other nights too, raced the dogs of Kai-Boon-Ka. Then all woke up to the mystery of morning.

CHAPTER 51
AFTER ALL

Ah me, cried The Bluebirds and ay mi, shouted the crowds. And Lyn is with me now, sang Bud, as he rose into the heavy Canton air. "Rose the Loop" Sonderson has been lost over Near East Pai-Kuht, and Dirt Ratville has gone to find him. Jill looked around the compound for the picture of Nar Ga Shu Aki which Akvhan had given her. Louis, believing in devils from his earliest years, now imagined that he saw them, his silver airplanes, glozing through the darkness. It was Wallaby Tuesday in Melbourne, Australia, and all of the Cold Bachelors' parents had come out to watch. "Drip" Aquabogue was holding a two-handed mock-frog in his octopus catches. The purple moon went down into the cup which Taniakban was holding. When the landscape cleared we saw it was what we had always, so hopefully, dreamed of: the thin white line of a dirtway to magic Tin Fan.

Jill leaped into her skirt, Lyn pulled on her britches. We were ready to go! Bob fastened his helmet, Jim carefully strapped his writing equipment to his waist. Ace looped the loop above us already, that early morning. Queen Anne of Nigeria was gone.

Dutler, whom the kids hadn't seen for a month of Sundays, was now about again, saying Hi there and Have a little catch and he would throw them across the sward. I am only a yellow belt or a green Dutler would say but when he was good at it he was very very fast and the apes watched him. No one of the apes wanted Dutler to get better than he was. Meanwhile we were piling into our planes, "lillies without" and "roses within."

Oh, Lady, you whose eyes shall light upon this booklet
And for whom the sweet violet nods its head
Have mercy on its author, who in Brooklyn
Once an old wrinkling folded paper read—

"Malcolm" Tuesday, now on his pallet in Melbourne, Aust., writes this to Lyn Presle, chargée d'affaires de l'amour de Reddishest Robinska, M.U.L.E.A.:

"Dear Fabricants—"

Floating in the clouds, there, who would not wish a harmonica, a handcar and a heavy chain? When Jill's parents came back to America they lacked for nothing, but still they were sad about their girl. She, of the white handarms, and the glorious lover Red Muff, went winging over the Ping-Chuk Mountains, with Comparisons and Nestles for her guide. O Jill, my darling! I shall never have enough of you in life! Nor in death, either. Here above China, I'll have my will! Jill laughed at us and kept on flying. She could have been a captain in any army.

"Mammary capacities have I none," said the flat-chested weeds along the magic road to Tin Fan; it was spring on the Char-Ko River. It looked a little like Paris. Here a fragment of Champs Elysées, there a hill-misted suggestion of the Bon Marché. And now here is the bubbling and silvery water, like a sumptuousness of new Paris girls.

CHAPTER 52
THE LIST OF ORGANIZATIONS

GROUPS AT ONE TIME ASSOCIATED WITH OR OPPOSED TO THE RED ROBINS
A List Put Out by the International Ministry of Control

The Rabbit pulled down a hanging scroll and indicated the different items. He said, We have no word now from any of these groups.

The Cold Bachelors. At one time confused with The Marooned Bachelors, a wholly different group, see ci-dessous. Commanded by an Irish teetotaler named John Patrick Shenahan, this group is now entirely dead. They were lost on the Solomons.

The Shards. The Easter Rabbit's own group, now disbanded, with some of its former members in America, some in Europe, but most in small businesses somewhere in Asia.

The Marooned Bachelors. Eaten by birds in the Marshall Islands.

The Demented Acrobats. A group now forming in the Admiralties, its members mainly from British possessions in the Far East. The purpose of their group is to move from one end to the other of the Entire Far East, including all Pacific islands, by the sole means of acrobatic leaping and hanging.

The Bluebirds. A group still active though now working in total secrecy. The aims of the Bluebirds are not known. It seems possible that they are a shadow organization of the Red Robins, that what the Robins do is imaged, somewhat less plainly, in them. Bluebirds have sometimes been known, in complete disguise, to act in favor of various good causes in different areas of the Far East.

The Crowds. A group of people of different nationalities, ages, and sizes, who are loosely organized around the central theme of cities. The Crowds are not the same as the ordinary groups of people one finds in cities, but they are hard to distinguish from such. The Crowds all gather together for two annual feasts, one at Po-Ch'in, in early springtime, the other at Hangkow in early fall.

The Tuscan Traders. These people formed the restaurant at Aplaganda Lake, attempted to take over the management of La Compagnie de Restauration de l'Ile de Congers (but were unsuccessful) and are otherwise active in establishing, owning and frequenting food-dispensing establishments in the Eastern Pacific area. Their planes resemble sea gulls, with which the members of this group are often, from a distance, confused.

The Noh Players. Not in fact a group of the kind being considered.

The Thundering Octopus. Still in formation.

Gorilla-flames. Disbanded.

Now, of all these groups it is only the Red Robins who seem to have a consistent record of success. That is, they are still alive and they need for nothing. Each morning finds them bending above steel table with hacking alloy, and the smile of a mariner in their heart. It is a pretty thing to float through the sky there every morning, and to have all of the earth's history within. They must be destroyed. Don't ever ask me why. Simply every time I think of them, I—Here Doctor Poach-Eye was interrupted by a disturbance in the brush, and he hopped down and went away. Then who should we see coming out of there, honestly, but Don Juan Spinzermeier, who had warned us not to talk to the Rabbit. And he was followed by a whole lot of really damned good-looking flyers who, I suppose, were the Red Robins. In fact, they were the Lovely Bluebirds, and they soon flew away.

CHAPTER 53
FOUNDING CHAFT

If I used up my share of the fire . . .
Here, have a drink!

Ape was talking to us seriously. Jill, you phony, that's Ace not Ape! well, he's Ape to me!

A certain highwaymaster named Chong . . .

. . . Had the idea, isn't it, that birds hadn't developed a very high intelligence because they were always able to . . .

. . . Fly away from their problems—precisely!

But then—

Yes, why haven't ants developed high intelligence, and moles, for example, and cockroaches . . .

Maybe they all have, Jill says. What creamy thighs . . .

The world was dead that morning but we were alive.

Thank you, Bud. The radio goes off and on.

Getting ready for the Air Show . . .

Trying to find this yellow pathway to the dawn . . .

. . . Of Old Tin Fan.

Is Ni Shu . . .

The . . .

Jill had gotten into her bathing suit at six o'clock. By nine she was winging well over the most distant Karetic Islands. In the distance the Admiralties, pink as a smock when dawn's hue just touches it, lay asleep.

•

Good God, cried Jill as she read the enclosed missive. Hand me a snowball, Santa, for I am going to cry. I want to "freeze up" my tear ducts the way the Urts do, a people as you all know we found out about on our last voyage to a Northern clime. But no, seriously, I am going to break down and start weeping; I knew that Bob loved me, but not with all his heart. Why, read this letter; it drips with valentine sentiments but also with true fears and loves.

Please do not leave us here on Desert Kurt. Santa says I am very sorry I am going to have to do just that. I must get back to the hotel at Pai-Kuht I really am overtime now. The great plangent-mouthed chimpanzee of evening is descending over the rooftops, and, biding, he awaits me there.

Goodbye, Jim. And then, holding out his hand to Jill: Goodbye, Jill. I have always loved you. You know that. And no matter what the red mountain, or green stupid nagging train, what hard hillocks of evening may come between us, know that I love thee still. He vanished, and the sweet May breezes fanned our brows; we sat down, weeping a little, but in the presence of those fresh white apple blossoms and cherry blossoms as well, it was impossible to be sad for long. There was a softness in the air as if caused by a sigh, from the sweetest lips in the world. Santa Claus laid down his paddock. I cannot leave here, he said; we must build a city. Of the every kind of weather we Robins had had, none of it had been spring, none this unusual kind and blessed May. The weather of course on which we thrive the most. And that evening who among us was strong enough to resist crying?

The city was called "Chaft," and it sprung up on the banks of the Urlk (no, it was the Ho-Kai) as if by magic. Santa Claus was happy there. He ruled as a kind of Oriental King. The city, Bob said (for now he was back with us), reminded him most among other cities of Naples, which he called Queen of the Sea and told us about in great detail on those delicious evenings. Here it was always spring. We lived on custard root and baitch. To think, said Bob, that there has been at some time in the world a promise of happiness! Overwhelming as these simple experiences were, we could not resist the sprig hard Chinese detection comedians for long. They kept calling us off, to their smoky city, where the black land met the tough wooden boards of unreason. It cannot be May forever, Santa said; and we folded our bags like the leaves. "Chaft" can now only be found in certain abandoned picture books, viewed there its sketchiest of foundations seem pink and white, like the gentlest blossoms a human hand has ever known.

The gorilla was waiting for Santa Claus at the hotel. Immediately we knew that there was going to be trouble. Even the Noh players skirting about the lobby seemed to be aware, in their own inscrutable fashion, of our imminent danger. For they came to warn us with pink pennants and orange leaves. And Santa Claus stands there, talking to the manager of the hotel . . .

Five years ago all this talk about danger and the truth would have seemed pretty meaningless to us. But now we have the ledger rather heavily balanced in the other direction. Bob and Louis are still walking, on guard, up and down outside, and we have as yet, of course, no word. But Lyn has returned from her freezing shellfish trip to the island—we had thought her lost—which is certainly a great cause of relief to all concerned there. Hell with her and her making a God-Damned flat boat out of shellfish shells, sea shells, and driving out on that freezing rough sea when we have so many obvious concerns, and in so many directions. But now the first peach blossoms are beginning to show full on the hotel tree, and it is thought that the great drinking party on the porch tonight will solve all of our problems. I honestly don't know why we have such a crazy idea, but I can assure you that we really do. No solutions of course are permanent, but the preparations for this party have been truly massive, impressive: forty-five bamboo walls brought in from the jungle! and natives having fabricated ninety-seven bamboo chairs! I, Jill, am going crazy with dish-carrying and napkin-mending; and now it is the full moon and a jungle night.

CHAPTER 54
LOOSE ENDS

Senator Knox, Mr. Broadhurst, Jill's father, and the Easter Bunny met with the President of the United States in the Oval Room of the White House to discuss the problems which those assembled felt were presented to the United States and to the world by the activities of the Red Robins. It was Senator Knox who had brought the matter to the President's attention—but the President of course knew of it, due to his correspondence with Lyn. "As citizens of the United States," Senator Knox began, "they had no right to do the harm they did to Dr. Pep, who is a Yugoslavian national. I think they can get us into pretty deep trouble on this one, sir." "Yes, but they were helpful to Marian," the President said. "And what choice, really, did Santa Claus have—Pep attacked him. As for Pep's slipping into a poisoned sweater, that seems to me his own responsibility. The sweater was not his to take." The Easter Bunny, disguised on this occasion as an illustrious French banker, the Count N. de N——, was seized by panic on realizing that the President knew far too much about the Robins' situation to be a perfectly disinterested witness. I suggest we adjourn this discussion till another time, he said, gazing with apparently innocent pleasure at the blurred Monet-like landscape of the White House lawn, covered today with different-colored protesters. This morning seems too lovely to spend in a discussion which is bound to be painful to us all.

And yet, the President said, here we are, and such busy men all of us, it is not easy for us to find the time to get together. I agree, said Senator Knox. And Mr. Broadhurst nodded and Jill's father did too. I think Santa Claus is a fine man, but I want my daughter to come home.

If you are all so worried about the Robins, I do have a surprise guest today whose testimony will doubtless interest you. He rang a bell. Mona, would you please show her highness in?

The supposed Count N. de N—— began visibly to perspire, and tiny white hairs began to appear through his make-up. Senator Knox shifted uneasily in his chair. But it was too late for either of them to move.

Hello everyone, said Queen Anne of Nigeria. I believe I know all of you except for this gentleman (she pointed to Jill's father). I am Queen Anne of Nigeria, a good friend and trusted confidante of the Red Robins. I can see white hairs showing through this man's face—he is the Easter Rabbit, who hates the Red Robins without cause. He even went so far as to unite with Dracula. The President placed the Rabbit under arrest. And this man, Queen Anne said, pointing to Senator Knox, is insane. He may be good-hearted enough but he is a sexual and otherwise maniac. He raped seventy-two women in Shanghai. They all gave their permission, said Senator Knox. Yes, when you threatened them with your gun. Go on, get out of here, you miserable trash! she said. And the President had him arrested. Now, as for you, Albert Broadhurst, you're just a lustful old skunk. You want to take your revenge on Lyn and Jill because neither of them would sleep with you. Jill's father started up in his chair— Why, you old skun—! Easy there, fellow, the President said. Sit down and listen to what Queen Anne of Nigeria has to say. I don't think you're evil at heart. You're just a damned fool. I've said nothing, said Broadhurst. I just came in good faith to this meeting. Yes, well, you must have come here for a reason, said Queen Anne, and I am sure it was to do no good to the Robins. Mr. Brule, she said to Jill's father, you have been sitting with people who do not have your daughter's group's best interests at heart, I am sorry to say. But, said he, I do want my baby to come home.

She is not a baby anymore, said Queen Anne. She is a beautiful and mature young woman. Besides, said the Chief Executive of the United States, you were over there, at the Coluhdson as a matter of fact, and spoke to her, and met with Santa Claus, and according to my information you gave them your blessing. Now it was Jill's father's turn to be surprised at how much the President knew. Well, yes I did, he said. In a way. No, not in a way, said the President. You really did do it. Yes I did, he answered, but it is very hard for Mother and me now. We want our daughter to be near us.

I'll tell you what I'll do for you, the President said. You are in the restaurant business, are you not? Yes, sir, I am, said Bud, who had been sitting there disguised as Jill's father. He had wanted to see (as did all the Red Robins) just how far the President would go. Well, I will give you one of our islands there, a small one, you can open up a place on it. Oh Excellency you are so generous! Wait a minute, the President said. Didn't I hear the slight trace there of a German accent? I didn't know Jill's lineage was German. Only a little bit, sir, Bud said, terrified that now he'd been completely exposed and perhaps punished by—what? he didn't know—perhaps even death. Only one tenth of one percent. Well, then, said the Chief Executive, what do you say?

I think that would be a great honor, sir, said Bud. And I would like to come to the restaurant on opening day, said the President. Already his entire body was boiling with lust at the thought of actually placing his hands on Lyn. Oh my God in Heaven, he sighed to himself, what will ever happen to my poor country? For I am totally obsessed by that one girl! Yes, yes, the President cried. I will come to it. As a matter of fact, I may yes I will have to come over there right now to help you find the right island. Hold on for a minute, while I go and pack!

Bud was frightened. He didn't know the President would be so brusque, so impulsive. He didn't want the President hanging around the Robins. They none of them did. Lyn not at all. She was very happy with Jim. Oh my god, Queen Anne of Nigeria, do help us now! he impulsively cried. I am not Jill's father but Bud and we do not want the President being part of the Robins!

Wow some disguise, cried Queen Anne. Okay don't worry, I'll take care of it. When the President came back in, Queen Anne told him straight out that Lyn was happy with somebody else. The

President sighed in agony. How can she be? etc. Queen Anne said, Well she is. God damn you all get out of here! the President said. Go on, get out of here. Go. And he put his head on his huge red desk and cried. He cried at all the deprivation he had gone through to get where he was now and at all the disappointment he felt at the fact that now that he had gotten there he could not have what he wanted. Damn! he finally cried. I shall find a way to have it in spite of all! With the help of the Easter Bunny! he said. And he bade that evil and powerful person to be brought before him. But so vile and so powerful indeed was he that he had already escaped, by simply breaking down the prison's walls. The President repented right away for what he had intended to do.

Dear Lyn:

Our motion obscures the stillness which was its aim. And so . . . blue snow flurries, endlessness of methods. I want to build a city, Miss Accident, to prune your name. The excitements of sensibility will never be mined to the fullest extent by that juvescence of which the air doctor formerly spoke. And then, he said, the knot of doctor-air will be ultimately solved. But I wonder. Her underpinnings became an island in the East. I've never gone there.

If this seems unctuous, don't worry . . . I have already forgotten you. I am writing to a peach, in a foreign hemisphere, I seem to be begging this peach to come and like me. I pass over other peaches, oranges, and pears. You, peach, are the one I want! Missed you! Now what will become of my life?

I am worrying because there are tremendous weights to be tossed. To be sure, I have great faith in my lady. Smiling under a shell of blue, she graces me with a pyramid of cosmetics in which I can somewhat less rudely face the anger of the bells. But there is so much more to be lost. Is history really only the roots of trees? You slip there and break you arm, or even your neck. Railings had been constructed around the airfield. He was frozen. Like the other octopus, he had been brought to this country by mistake. The plane took off. Inside it, Buck was writing a letter to Madeleine. The phrases he used were all from other books.

Ten-Koo! The sunlight was asleep. Only one canary, Mah-Tah-Kah-Fah-G-nah, stayed awake to guard the Red Robins from their horrible enemy of the capital letter E.

Octoparadise lost! . . .

they sang from the ocean, or so the seabreakers seemed to sing, and

You are my non-pin cushion—sleep with me!

and

Mak-too-gah-pleen-ak-lam,

which is octopus language for Where can there be room for anything in your heart if there is not love? Toward what black ink of oblivion would these young aviators go? They soon flew away from this place.

Robinas, addios!

sang the octopuses. Gold filtered into every single corner of the sky.

The President walked up and down. "A mere child, compared to my years. And what have we been saying in our letters? The most beautiful child there is. Do I dare to go to her? As men went off to be monks in earlier times? (He must have been thinking of the Emperor Don Carlos.) She will not come here. But I would not be going to save my soul, but to lose it, perhaps,

In the frail body of a human girl . . .

No! I must keep my country strong. Oh Lyn, Lyn, Lyn . . ."

CHAPTER 55
DEPARTURE AND RETURN

The plane circling over

Chick recognized it immediately as the Aureng-Zebe

Bob got out of the cabin and shouted with happiness: "Irene, Irene! the snow has stopped, and we're going home!"

The young mistress smoking with a man in a red jacket in the hotel garden. "For so many millions of years now the earth has behaved itself like a good child . . ."

Believing in rivers

Chick immediately recognized it as the *Toe-Nail.* At last Bob was on the right field. He leaped out. "To-Nai!" he shouted, "To-Nai!"

In a silver dress, with the shell-white of her chest showing through, she was the model of all he had ever wanted. Lyn came out. She was wearing a white, dusted "Dorothy" dress. She touched Jim's shoulder. "All right, I think we can go."

And a man in a yellow coat, a tall man holding in his hand an excellent green tobacco cigar, was standing in the boat-house doorway. Was saying, "I do not think the gulls will fly this year." Or was saying, "I do think they will fly, will fly very high, so high above our sights, our heads, and heavens, that we shall never see them." And the blue dregs from his cigar like the ashes of the sea. "Shall fly high, and we shall never see them, so that to us it shall be as if they had never flown at all."

And so all the Red Robins began a senseless voyage that would never end. We all know perfectly well that we are not really going to go home. White octopuses have been sighted at Mao-Ting Point, and girls in short low-cut white dresses have been dancing the "dance of density" on Pabla-Awwannah's shores.

I know I know. She kissed the periods on the heads and then tore up and burned the manuscript, leaving only enough of it in her hand with which to make a white paper rose, which she did make, and after she made it, she threw it in the fire.

And that, said the littlest tortoise, is how robins became red. Now, good night.

Bud, whose Rhodes Scholarship ended the next morning, decided to give them all a party. "Come on, shape up!" everyone walked around and said. And "How nice to see you again!" and "Good Robin!"

"What's happened here?" The party was in full swing. A blue-bird, just out of the nest! Would you like me to show you another? No thanks, said Bob. It is enough to know that there is one like that on earth—then every feeling, each perception, every heartthrob and nervethrob will be preserved for us, in its own sweet impor-tance, until the Day of Consciousness, which should, I think, be just about now!

Men and girl pilots brushed shoulders easily as the tan and pink sunset conquered the sky. Soon it would be dark and they would hear the cry of the *chee-tah*. I am so happy to be here again. Yes, isn't it fine! What has become of Santa Claus? I don't know. I haven't been seeing him around! Look—I think that's he! For now, the sim-ple carved lemon blossom leaf delighted every palate. And that cold hooker the Malay call the moon ran shining through the mid-November sky.

"Dahlatta" ("The Worm") Domberg stands drinking a glass of water on the far side of the porch of the hotel. Ve fill neffer giff Congers up, he says to the gorilla lord, but that island, as Domberg well knew, was already gone.

CHAPTER 56
THE CLOSING OF THE RING

The snowy landscape becomes even more convoluted and yet at the same time brisk as one continues up the coast and especially if one adventures inland, as we did, in a small boat, of which Lyn had set the ring, and with the body designed by Bob, the engine designed by Louis, and all of us, really, having strange thoughts, and grateful for having, insofar as we had, "escaped" from Fu-Kien. Bob began to play the lute. Then the fog became intense. And the next thing we came on were islands of people, and water that, strangely enough, had not frozen.

Many are the commercial but few the personal uses of the River Chang. Supplies daily pursue their laden path down the great so-called "Hong-Ching Highway," and fishermen, too, though few pleasure boats are seen—ours were the exception. Bedecked with an awful gaudery of green and blossom, with raspberry umbrellas aloft, we must have seemed . . . But Bill was calling, "Help me! Save me!" so we did put the river to a personal use: we leaped into its freezing stream. As we tried to swim to shore, however, we found the path obstructed by an enormous sandbank which we were obliged to walk around. In the vicinity of this bank of sand, the water and the air were extremely warm.

Bill was ecstatic at seeing us. He had been afraid, he told us, of being "lost for good," since he had not seen anyone he knew for thirteen days. He had been mistaken in his choice of a trail, two weeks previous to that time. We shook hands all round. Then, after a hot, steaming meal of ricocheted octopus, we began to work at the construction of a new boat with which to continue our journey through the convoluted fairy-tale loveliness of Tin Fan.

"After the mule's deliberations were over, someone was going to be kicked. I hope it isn't selfish not to want it to be me." And now it is morning. The bird calls, which formerly were silent, have now begun to be like tablets, which, sprinkled with a certain kind of rosewater, begin to rush upstairs and scream. "Canton! Wake up! For it's dew-flash of East Continental morning!" Notations of summer and sun. Mike waves goodbye (in his mind he does—actually a tiger cannot, or will not, make that gesture), feeling, "Now that they are going, it seems that they can love us tigers." He looks back. And Bob stood there. He seemed a single notch in the hotel. Suddenly behind him were sea birds. And palm trees. To think, Bud said to Lyn— And that's not all, she said. And that's not all. Her grandfather had been Jed Brush, who invented the hunting basket. In this, when there is enough light you can catch a tiger! What would I want to do that for, when I so very nearly have one of my own? Oh, that again! The Dream of Rei-Nagi came to the mirror and barked. Let me in!

The Easter Rabbit never did appear to them for forty moons. Then, one August afternoon, in the precinct of Hai-Kar, he vanished, leaving the Melody Muffets without a truly serious enemy. Albert Broadhurst opened up a charity hospital in China. Here, on August 14th of the fifth year of its existence, he was poisoned by the youngest laundress there whom he had tried to rape in the steam room when it was much too hot. His body was placed in the Mound of Wisdom, about sixty-five versts from Shanghai; and many pilgrims have gone there to look at it, including a curiously beak-shaped-faced man whom many of our readers would be able to identify as Dr. Anastasius Pep. In his hand he carried a leafy quince which, from time to time, he addressed in these words: "Marian, Marian, flower and star of the sea." Many thought the Spirit of Marian inhabited the quince, but others claim to have seen that young beauty on the dusty roadways of Tin Fan. Good night, Algernon. Good night, Porky. Soon the entire contingent was asleep, and melodiously curving leaves could not once more begin their ascent into human vales. I do not know in what part of China the Promenading Plum Tree Blossoms are now, but I hope it is Tin Fan and I hope that young Marian is with them there. "I will be glad dance," she said, and she was swept up. Soon the Glittering Glee-birds were no more, and their places had been taken by the Angry Aviators, who were intent on tearing everything down. These, in turn, gave way to the Monoliths of Northern Siberia and they in turn gave way to the Non-Serious Burns.

Jill looks at the old clam shell moodily. "If we could actually get these people on our side . . ." Mutt reappeared, like an old shop. She has tattoos all over her northern shoulder. "I am determined to stay out here until old why not!" shouted Evelyn and ran over and planted a kiss on the tiger who was so inspired by this that he ran off and started to kill all the apes, and Santa could only stop him by yelling and running after him himself and Lyn ran after him and the tiger clawed her my god it was horrible said Red I can't think of it without but she is all right now thank God thank God.

And everyone helped until finally there was darkness and the lepers came and carried some of them off but more kept blossoming and Bill and Santa Claus and Bob and Ed and Jim kept saying Oh my god thank God. Meanwhile the Radiant Raspberries have started dashing through the Burmese clouds. Goodbye! chorused one Orangeade Oriole. And goodbye! chorused some sheep. Jill, wake up! It's time to burn down the hotel. Why? What is——? The snow keeps falling, heavily. Jill said, Lyn, are you all right now? And Lyn said, Yes. One chicken was slightly plumper than the others, and Mamma Ti King bought him first. When I had grown to maturity I was unable to leave the monastery, he said.

What shall you do, then, with the flares?

God speed you, cried the Madonna as we rode off into the skies. And Good Rust to you! nailed the planes. Pow wow koo tang chan, sang Uncle Windy. And the Birds lifted their curious eyes into the atmosphere. Kow tow lan! Shanghai was freezing. Jill placed her left hand on the banister. Come on, he said. It seems a long time ago, she said.

So long!

Goodbye, Cheepy! Good sign to you of the ferns! The turbine turned over easily, and the bad crops were garnered up into good ones, as the old yellow and white steam mow was seen no more, and the tinkle of girlish voices was being drowned out by the wind.

"Come, everyone! Tomorrow is not here yet. There are still a whole lot of splinters on the floor of this hotel!" "You may not have that many admirers, but the ones you do will really be worth having." Jim looked at her. "This whole celebration is really for you. You 'gave me back to myself' in the best possible way. And even though we couldn't be together

> Because
> It was too soon for my
> Finest page
> Of thought—"

"I think we've all gotten a little sleepy," Domberg said. It had started to be extremely cold. Quietly, Lyn bent down and picked up the ring.

HOTEL LAMBOSA

1993

To Karen

CONTENTS

ANTONELLOS

Janice and I decided to look for every Antonello da Messina in Sicily. Mostly portraits, they had a noble clarity and the suggestion of a quick intimacy that was obviously more than one could hope for with persons so grand. There weren't very many of them and Sicily wasn't very large; but there were twenty of them and Sicily, if you subdivide its size by its means of transportation, is five times as big as the United States. We were looking at inaccessibility, and no doubt about it. There was one supposed Antonello hung in a chapel on the side of a cliff, I couldn't imagine how anyone but a goat would manage to get there. Four of the paintings were in cities that were easy to reach. The rest were really, it seemed, randomly scattered all over that savage island, which was not exactly organized to assist one in the task of seeing them.

We had to content ourselves with seeing six, which wasn't bad, given our limited means, of money, transportation, and time. My father was propositioned by a young Sicilian man, who offered him sex in exchange for money, but my father refused. My mother encouraged the local "artists-for-tourists" by purchasing samples of their work. Janice's and my daughter, Melissa, was only a tiny girl then (two years old) and she was featured in many, many photographs, most of them shot on the elegant grounds of a large hotel built into or inspired by a monastery—I forget its name. What do you think about this situation, Stuart? my mother said. What situation? said my father. The fact that Kenny and Janice pay so little attention to us? Melissa! Melissa! she called the tiny girl. Come back from the edge of the garden. She might fall off. My father went and picked up Melissa. He was wearing a white suit and smoking a Lucky Strike. At home he had a Buick but here he had a rented Peugeot. I don't know why he didn't have a Fiat but he had a Peugot. Stuart! What, Lillian? My father was holding Melissa now by the hand and he was smiling as she was attempting to lead him around. This way! This way, Dumpa! she said. Well, you haven't answered my question, said my mother. Well, Lillian. My father smoked. At this moment Janice and I appeared around the hotel bend. We found a new Antonello, I said. And some peaches, cried Janice. Here, look! I've never tasted anything so delicious in my life, said my mother. Janice picked up Melissa and gave her a big kiss. Hello, Baby! Mamam, mama, Melissa said, agitating and pointing. There was something she wanted Janice to see. Two rabbits were holding completely still in the garden. A blue-and-red-feathered bird—what was it? it couldn't be a parrot—landed near them and still they didn't move. Oh, how wonderful! Janice said. Then she hesitated, and my mother changed her facial expression. We shouldn't go any closer or they'll be frightened. How was your morning, Lillian, Janice said, holding tight to one hand of Melissa and approaching my mother's chair. At this, my mother got up, raising herself as if it were difficult and saying something like "Oooohf!" You don't know what it's like to get old, she said.

Janice and I looked beyond the family's doings to the exquisite tone, pathos, dramatic poses, and coloring of Antonello's paintings. As often as not, we were walking about with some form of the following sentence in our heads: "Antonello introduced easel painting into Italy." He found it in Holland. That meant that, before him, everything that was painted in Italy had been frescos or paintings on wood. Antonello ruined painting—frescoes were better! Antonello saved painting! Where could it have gone, that wall-dependent art? These ideas were nourishment to us. A wide-brimmed hat above her and with my father standing at her side, my mother in the hotel garden breathed the Sicilian air.

WIND

The wind was blowing very hard. Don't, she said. I can't stand here. Someone will pinch my derriére. Well all right let's keep walking, the young man said. They were standing in front of an art gallery in Florence. The works inside it were hysterically bad. They were comprised of button shapes of all colors arranged as if the canvases were coats. There were twenty-four of them. At the back of the gallery in a smaller room there was a smaller show of someone who painted apparently only squiggles. On a white background you'd find squiggles of gold, green, and navy blue. Usually it was just one color to each work. The two walked along but they had little more to say to each other. He had shown her his interest in the physical side of her, and she had shown him her toughness and her know-how and her at this moment not wanting what he wants. So they are even. Each has shown an attractive quality, desire and refusal, and there is not much more for them to do. In six or seven years perhaps or maybe eight, some equally windy day, she herself will have her paintings in a gallery, and she will say, when some man says the way she looks, the way she is, drives him crazy, she will say, Does it, do I really? Well, it's nice to know one is pleasing. Have you seen the work? When the young man who turns out to be the same one says yes that he has and he likes it but that he doesn't wish to talk about that, she says Oh! and he then Do you remember me, from seven or eight years ago in Florence? It was an example of bad behavior on my part, liking you, but I did nonetheless—I don't know. She said, What are you saying?

EM PORTUGUÊS

They were listening to the fados, sung one after another. Each fado sang of the scorched terrible unsatisfiable lost wretchedness of love. There is no happy side, except for intensity of feeling, to a fado song. They felt the excessively narrow reality of the fados shoving into and bumping them, like a drunk. The man's hand untightened itself from the woman's after the momentous finale of the song. As they got up to go back to the Hotel of Ionia and of Camoëns, they were accosted by a waiter at the exit, saying You forgot your coats. We didn't wear any coats. My love is gone, my heart is like a smashed mask of glass. If my shoeprints are steeped in your blood, woman, you will know that I have come back. Those coats belong to somebody else.

THE VILLINO

My wife and I were waiting for the train to come that would take us from Rome to Florence. She had on a bright pink dress and a white straw hat with a yellow bow around it. I was wearing some old khaki army trousers and a dark green canvassy sort of shirt. I didn't wear a hat, so, as soon as any evidence of the train came by, I could see it. It was some leaves, swirling in an arc lamp over our heads. Look, Janice, I said. The train is coming. And she said Oh then looked down the tracks the train came and we got on it.

The train stopped at Viterbo, Orvieto, Chianciano Terme, and Siena. It wasn't an express, that is, not what in Italy is called a Rapido, so it gave us a lot of time to enjoy the trip. The ride was bumpy and sometimes, even in between towns, the train would stop and we'd spend five minutes just waiting. At the stations I always looked around for a man or woman with a cart with drinks and things to eat on it but I never saw one.

Between Siena and Florence, my wife said, Well, what are we going to do when we get to Florence? I said, Find a pensione, first a place for tonight, then after a few days we can start to look for a regular place to stay. I'd like to do that as soon as we get there, she said. Oh no, not tonight, you know, but tomorrow if that's all right with you.

Well, it might be nice to look at a few things in the city, I said. More practically, I said, it might be good to get a sense of the city before we decide where we want to settle down. Yes, I guess that's right, Janice said, although I think her heart was more in getting settled as soon as we could.

Actually, by the end of the first day, it seemed to me amusing to start looking for a place. It was a change from regular touring to go into an office where there was a man in a coat tie and shirt who acted interested in helping us do something we wanted. Ah, I think I have just the thing, one such man said. But this was on the fourth day.

This man invited us into his car and drove us out to inspect the villino, where he proposed that we might like to live. He said, Here you may be very happy. And it is an advantageous price. We rented that house.

Now, thirty years later, I think I can still see that house very clearly. I can see the kitchen window through which she or I would sometimes (just idly) stare, because it was mostly from right there that we seemed nearest to the Italian song-singing by the house-maid next door. I most emphatically recall the gate, though what was its color—green? white?—where an "old man" (he may have been sixty, sixty-five, or seventy, but he was bent over) came, saying, when I walked down to open it, I am Ottavino, the peasant.

Janice's room and mine had in its center a fairly big bed. I wrote over here against this wall. In the living room of this villino there's a fireplace and it's truly needed, expensive as the wood may be, because the Italians think in Italy it never gets cold.

In this house some extraordinary things took place. One night we were leaving the house to go to the Florence Opera, to hear *Un Ballo in Màschera*, with Gianni Poggi. Janice adored and was fascinated by and was also somewhat amused by this tenor, Gianni Poggi. He had a beautiful lyrical tenor voice, and he sang in the new bel canto style with considerable sweetness and gusto. He was also short and plump. The skill and sweetness of this fat young man's singing was a reminder of the consuming and infinitely soothing unreality of art. Whenever, wherever we traveled, we seemed to run into operatic performances with Gianni Poggi. Who's singing tonight? I asked Janice. Who do you think? she said. Gianni Poggi! I remember a little moonlight circling her head, as she said that, and as we walked out, into that tender night, where later Gianni Poggi, all pudgy five feet of him, would sing, to a slightly taller soprano,

"M'ami? m'ami? m'ami?" in such a way that it turned our hearts to stone, if stones could feel, could retain that warm night and that moonlight in their mass, and be as heavy ("M'ami?") as they are and as light as we were, when, without nervous impulses or headaches we would head back "home"—to the villino, which not three weeks before had been hung out on the road past the Ortopèdico a little sadly and emptily "for rent."

We probably paid about a hundred dollars more a month for that place than we should have. An agent told us this, the friend of a friend. John Fardras was renting some rooms in the Palazzo Gambolini and once on an exquisite warm and airy late spring evening, we broke our general pattern of behavior (mostly, if there was no opera, we stayed home) and went to his place. These rooms were very beautiful, at this old palace, and I thought it would have been a different destiny for us, maybe, if we had lived there. But there was no avoiding our house.

VENICE

I dreamed last night that Marcello told me it was too complicated. I had this dream last night. I wrote the libretto this past summer, in July.

Everything is a dream, said his friend. What's the difference if Marcello sets the libretto or not?

None, he said. But *you* write a libretto and then let's just see if you'd prefer to have it set or not. I'd like Marcello to set it, and Ronconi to direct it, and for there to be simultaneous performances outdoors above the Canal in Venice and at the Metropolitan Opera. That's what I want.

When I heard my wife's voice on the telephone, calling me in Venice from New York City, I knew that someone must have died. We didn't phone each other now about ordinary things.

Venice. The cemetery. Walking around. Arm in arm, sometimes. Occasionally, hand in hand. Her eyes look up. His look down. They look down together. A grave.

Evening. Later. The shine of plates. The smile of knives and of forks.

Hotel. Stone balcony. Opposite church. Great big faces. Almost in the room. Stone they stare at them with their own face. And yet since it is Carnival he and she put on masks. One red mask his. One black mask hers. This is happiness. There is no other. Cold water faucet. A slight pain in the chest.

She takes. Opposite church. To miss what massive. Increasing silence. Man at the desk. Woman at the desk.

Dream band. Marchers off the street. Canal-side restaurant. No more eels! Isthmuses of islands.

I have. I have a reason. I have a reason to be sad. Here is a reason to be joyful. A grass turf. A striped day. But, most of all, this girl.

It became what it began to be: a cemetery. An island dedicated to the dead.

Black were the gondolas in the canals, and black the clothing that the gondoliers wore. Black were the buttons on the coat that he did not put on, to go out, because it was spring. Black were the steps on the stairway when he first came to them, blinded by the sun. And then his body went off.

Again said Marcello, I said I won't set it and I won't. It's too complicated. A librettist in writing should seek only to inspire the writing of music. You haven't done that.

I have more friends than you, Marcello, I said.

Ah, but they don't set libretti, Marcello said. But if I don't set it, of course you are free to give it to someone else. But here. Let me look at it one last time.

At this point I woke up. The complicated dream was at an end. Actually, Morton had died, and I was walking around thinking, thinking, whether I wanted to or not. Thinking neither of Morton nor of the opera but of you.

NEGATIVE BLOOD

The car was long and blue, an Italian car, rather surprising that the young doctor should have such a nice one. But why shouldn't the young doctor have a blue car? It was an Alfa nineteen fifty-four. In the car there were two young persons as it drove across the Arno—a doctor and a young man, about thirty. They were driving to a Catholic hospital on the side of Florence toward Fiesole. On a stretcher on a bed in the civic hospital in Florence was the young man's wife, who needed the blood. There was said to be some in the hospital on the other side of the Arno. The baby had miscarried and was born dead in a violent hemorrhage. It wasn't, as they thought, placenta previa. They didn't know what it was. She was losing a lot of blood and needed more and there was a shortage of it. The nun walked up and past them, swinging her censer, and against her blue slightly bloused-out uniform he could see the big batch of keys that would be needed to get them into the room where the blood was stored. Forgive me, the doctor said. It's all right, the sister said. She interrupted the little service to save the young woman's life. It was a lucky chance that a container of A-RH-negative blood was there and had not been sent to Hungary along with all the other containers of blood for people in the failed rebellion against the Russians. It was nineteen fifty-six. His wife lived for twenty-five more years. For her, the experience of this night, while she was experiencing it, had nothing to do with driving, with nuns, with Hungary, but with one wild wish, that the baby not be dead, that she be herself again, and that she and the baby be together, as they had never been, but as she had imagined, for so many months now, that they would be.

AN ORACLE

Evan said, Don't ask me. About love. I'm not the one to know. Evan had flying folds of love like pennants and flags forever flying from his person. On the Greek island of Hydra girls flooded toward the piers in a parade, all of them loving Evan, begging him not to go away but happy to be begging, happy to be in Evanid procession, glad to be living in that moment, in Greece, in a twentieth-century peaceful day. This is one of your lobotomy perkings, said Evan. It isn't a "story," but it's not the truth. In a story was the development of character. Minna was very shy, bony, awkward. As her body grew to fullness, self-confidence came, and behold, she was a changed character. God, it's boring! Evan said. He looked at two rabbits who were holding stock-still after darting around. I'll tell you what you should do if you want to write a story. Just write down what you told me about Ellen. How you tried to find her. And then did. It makes a perfect story just that way. I suppose so, Herndon said. But he wasn't going to write it. He was dying to question Evan about love. No, said Evan. Yes. Listen. I am leaving this island. Never in my whole life will I come back to this island. I just know it, don't ask me why, I feel it in my bones. My *bones*, he emphasized, grinning and gritting his jaws. My bee-hee-ho-ho-ho-ho-hones. My bonezeezee. What is love, Evan? Stay away from women, Evan said. And certainly from men. Then at least you'll have some chance of finding out. Good-bye. They went on suspecting, as Evan got into the boat, and away, that like everybody else, he knew more about it than he had told.

Don't expect anything, said Evan. And, You'll get the payback soon. Be *careful*. Just forget it. Get over. He was a major general in the wars of love. I'm just kidding but seriously, he said. Get out of it what you can. He went into the toilet. It was hard to hear him through the door. I was afraid I'd missed something. I said, What did you say? Nothing! said Evan. It doesn't matter what you say or what anybody says. But probably the less you say the better off you'll be. They remember *everything*. He likes the harem effect, he said about one. Oh, they're absolutely wonderful, Evan said. Don't get me wrong. He said, Good. Enjoy it. You know, there's not so much time. Hello, Angel, Evan said. The true history of Evan can never be told—because he is always telling it himself, as advice and proverbs. He knows it, too. I have become my admirers, said Evan, quoting Auden (about Yeats). Or rather, not exactly—s-zzz-miling: I have become my *conferees!*

What else did Evan know? With determination one can get to the bottom of a thing. He wanted to be close but not too close.

After each encounter he wanted still to be completely himself. I don't blame him.

Still, what would be wrong with his being slightly influenced? No one has ever seen him slightly influenced.

On the island what he had was like a dog, a very large happiness-creating dog. This dog was his wild, warm, positive personality.

He spoke some Greek. He could read and recite Ancient Greek. He was in some ways like a god, not a Greek but a big mild wild American god.

You could study Evan as a part of a study of American divinity. His divine energy and gladness were not qualities that turned women off.

In addition to his real qualities, Evan, like some of the Greek gods, was a great bullshitter. He tried to make girls think he was even more vital (and important) than he was. "I was saying to xxx," he said. Actually Evan was as good as, or better than, all the world-class people he so much mentioned and admired.

That they didn't mention him so often may or may not have been at least partly due to the fact that they were all so busy working that they couldn't be gods.

Evan gave his time to life, which is the reason we all wanted his knowledge about women—it wasn't quite what you'd call know-how.

Because Evan's information wasn't calculated to make you succeed—more to help you understand and to avoid the worst pain.

Evan is lighting a woman's cigarette. He wants her to be completely understanding of and completely generous to him. Then he will reward her with the food of the gods: silence, talk, no children, love, a bemused and vague infidelity.

I want something more!

Most of what Evan says can be understood in light of this situation.

They remember *everything*. And so on. There was something right about Evan's views of women, but there was something definitely wrong about them, too. Don't let them get to you, Evan says. Herndon can take Evan's advice when he is on the outside but not once he is starting to be on the inside of feeling in love. Then there is something so sweet that Evan's voice can't enter. Always, though, at such times, happy times, Evan goes along. Aren't they, isn't it, marvelous? he says. Dig it! When Herndon is thrown out, he needs Evan's advice. What can I tell you? Evan says. I am obviously the *wrong man* to tell you about *anything!*

LE JEU DE L'AMOUR ET DU HASARD

On the porch of the hotel they sat and looked out at things they could see. They played a game. The father said, It is red but stippled, and they had to guess what it was. No that could not have been the game. He was sitting in an automobile four years later thinking about that game. Perhaps it was this: the mother said: I see three things beginning with an *L*. She meant of course in English not in Greek. Maybe that was possible. The child, a little girl, was at a certain disadvantage in being only five years old. She played along though, and of course the mother and father made it easy. It was best when she would win. After they played the game for about half an hour, the mother took the child inside. Their rooms were on long corridors. Bathrooms were at the far, non-porch end. After a while the father got up and went into his room. The mother (she was thirty-one) was lying in the bed. The father was thirty-six. He looked fondly at her and said, Did you like the game? She lied, Yes. Then she said, I'm asleep.

STEPS

The baby was walking up and down the steps in Herakleion. These were some stone steps, part of a royal or it may have been just a slaves' stairway, now mostly destroyed, and most probably entirely destroyed and now just partly reconstructed, of the Palace of Knossos. The palace was dedicated to the Cretan version of the Olympian gods—Apollo in the guise of Helios was a prominent one. Here had lived the king, the court, and all the utter craziness of Crete. King Minos, with his Labyrinth! His annual sacrifices of beautiful boys and girls! King Crazy, if you ask me, said Mollie, in the bright sunshine, who was helping the baby walk. Up down, down, down, down, down, now, now, here, down up up up. The baby walks crazily, she is like King Minos. She does what she does to make sure she can do what she is doing. She, though, does no one any harm. Still, if she had the power . . . ! No, her father thinks, as he walks about trying to look at the palace and thinking of his baby daughter at the same time. No, if she had the power, she would be kind. But how can one be sure? A hot breeze slapped him, then, dust in his face. From a stair his daughter fell and she was screaming. Rapidly he turned around to get her, and then he was like a god.

IN CRETE

I love you! the girl called up the slope of the small hill on which I stood gazing after remnants of a few stones of Crete. Well, I love you, too, I cried, touched and excited, though she seemed only about twelve years old, dressed shabbily, smiling very happily, there right next to her sheep. But, why do you say such a thing? where does this feeling come from? you've just seen me for an instant, since I got to the top of this hill. The beautiful sun shone down, and there was a breeze to which all shirt parts in response fluttered, and did, too, in its way, my smile, that was not so much fixed on my face as by the slight breeze being held in place there smiling yes tell me. The world is at peace, I thought I heard coming from the cliff. She then kept smiling, happiness-looking lips and teeth. She gave me a little wave. I know now she hasn't understood more than one word (maybe "love") of what I've said. Did some American, tourist or soldier, teach you to say that? I said. She picked up a little lamb and held it so I could see all over its fleece. Smiling, waving I was. She put it down, turned then turned back to me, giggled, waved, again turned and walked away. The world had been at peace for about ten years. Greece, though, was still full of (new) ruins and the terrible just about undealable-with feelings left over from the civil war. I stood there not in love but, I thought, aware of something in love that love had never brought to me. There didn't seem any reason why it should, although it was a possibility of life.

AGOROKORITSO

Agorokoritso, a rather badly made movie about a Greek tomboy who finally finds love, is showing at the one local movie theatre. Three persons are in this theatre, it is an outdoor theatre, though with the construction of an indoor one. That is to say, it is like a "regular" theatre, though very small, without a roof. One doesn't drive into it but sits in a row. The little girl went to sleep after five minutes. When she woke up she saw her father's hand on her mother's shoulder, his arm around her back. The movie had just ended.

The house they go back to has no running water. Water is pumped into a cistern by the water boat once a week and may be taken in bucketsful from there. How dry the climate is! though not too dry for ants. There are, what, maybe thousands of them in the white-baked-clay-wall-bordered courtyard.

After watching them one day, moving around, the husband wrote a story, called "The Storm of Ants." In the story, he stressed the need for enduring suffering and going on with one's work, since suffering was bound to come anyway and work was all to the good. The main character was a young man who after successfully completing his course of study at the University of Athens, was caught in, defaced by, and shortly killed by a storm of ants— whence the story's title. He showed it to his wife, who said she didn't like it much, it seemed needlessly horrible.

Later, feeling restless, he found himself walking down near the theatre again. *Agorokoritso* was still showing. This time (he looked in and saw) there was no one in the theatre at all. The film and his story had no audience.

IMPENETRABLE LIFE

Two rabbits looked out from behind a rock. Robin saw them and looked away. He was waiting for Patrizia. He kicked a little stone. It skittered about ten feet away. The rabbits were startled and began to disappear. Disappear is not usually qualifiable, but what the rabbits did was to dart then freeze, which gesture they, like certain tribes of Indians, believed made them invisible. Then they started to run the rest of the way. Patrizia came up the walk. Robin ran down to meet her, and the rabbits, re-startled at what seemed this new direction of danger, began another sequence of disappearance, a sequence that actually brought them more into the view of anyone who might have wanted to harm them than they had been before. They darted here and there, and their day was full of disappearing. Big-eyed and excited, they ran around as if other beings existed only as avoidable dangers to themselves. That is why one could find them lovemaking, or eating some grass, later on in the same day, with the greatest calm, as if they were without any doubt at the center and the earth were theirs. Family organization was loose, and it had no social or political extensions. Each rabbit was on his or her own, like a stranger at a party, though a stranger who looks basically like everyone else. Robin and Patrizia's return, their walk back up from the rocks by the water, alarmed the rabbits again and brought on another sequence of disappearance.

WITHOUT A DICTATOR

The girl too felt sunlight on her shoulders as she stood among the stones of the "Altar of the Nymphs." The boy had gone there first, and now she was standing there. After he had been there a few, maybe five, ten, minutes, the boy had run down the steep hill from it like a sheep. A little lamb, maybe, or perhaps a goat. The girl kept standing there, though, and putting her hand on one after another fragment of stone.

Mussolini was happy that the Rhodes "ruins" had been rebuilt. Now the trains run on time, now man knows it is better to be a short-lived lion than a long-lived sheep, and now there are ruins standing again on Rhodes. The people say that under Mussolini, too, things were "cleaner." That they were nicer, as well as things being on time. On Rhodes, in fact, so far as Professor Shoates could see, there wasn't much that could either be or not be on time. It was hard, too, to figure out "nicer" and "cleaner." It was nineteen years after Rhodes had been liberated from Italy, and everything appeared to be both nice and clean.

His son has vanished. He's worried about that. The boy has a little history of being unbalanced. In the time of Mussolini, Sergeant Kanakatos says, you could be certain that you would have your son back with you before dark. But now there is a different kind of person, and less discipline, and we don't know. Katie wasn't frightened, just sort of in a vague mood of concern. Buddy's disappearance makes this island less clear to her in one way and in another more vivid than it was before. It was now a part of their own lives' legacy. Could Mussolini, if he could be brought back, really help, have helped?

Shortly after dark Buddy is back all by himself. Seeming a little perplexed, and also annoyed, at his family's concern, he said simply, as if that accounted for everything, "I met a girl." Katie knew it was not the one he had been at the "Nymphs" with, for that was she: so it must have been someone else.

ARTEMIS

 I got out of the car. So did Delia. The wonderful, white Artemis statue was on our left.

Artemis served such a variety of roles in different phases of Greek religion that if you were to come up behind an Ancient Greek and suddenly shout Artemis! he would not know what to expect.

He might think he was going to die (Artemis was a goddess of death), that his wife was about to have a baby (she presided over birth, was a sort of goddess-midwife), that the moon was up, that he should look to his virginity—or to someone else's—that it was time for the hunt. These were just a few possibilities. She was beautiful, there with her deer or her dog. And shining quiver!

In her dress, with its stiff folds hanging down in straight lines from her shoulders, unbelted Diana! Later, she leans partway off a small vase that the Ceramics Museum was selling a three-dimensional copy of for so many thousands of drachmas that was the equivalent of four dollars. Can we get it? Delia asked.

Of course, I said, though I felt a pain in my left shoulder from saying it. Four dollars seemed a lot to spend on a little jar. Delia was my wife, and it was nineteen fifty-five and I had, but she had not, changed any money. While the young woman at the counter was wrapping it in newspaper, I felt weak. I-I can't buy it, Delia, I said. It-it costs too much.

Oh, Gilbert, Delia said. I like it.

But I don't have—   (She): Well, all right.

I bought four little vases—gray, pink, and white—for 8000 dr. (about five cents) each, in part because I liked them and loved their being so cheap, and in part to make up for not getting her the other one.

From time to time I felt bad about being so cheap. Sometimes I tried to make up for it.

My desk faced a window, and on its wide sill stood one of the five-cent vases I'd bought in Greece. When I stood up, the desk bumped, and the vase fell off, down into the courtyard. We heard a tiny sound, "Ptootph." Delia was standing there, wearing her old faded pink dress. She looked wonderful in it. I should, I thought, buy her a new one.

What was that? Delia said. A little vase. Oh go and get it, she said. I probably can fix it. So I did. It was only broken in half. When I got back upstairs Delia was smiling. Listen, she said. I'm going to have a baby. Are you glad? We can afford it, yes? I hugged her and gave her a kiss. Of course we can afford it, I said.

Delia looked particularly beautiful when she was pregnant. She was the only one who really cared for our baby, modestly and increasingly carrying her around. And after they were two separate persons, too. She almost died when the baby was born.

Artemis, in sculptural representations, was smiling, either because it was easier to sculpt mouths that way, or because a tradition of divine (including Artemis's) facial expression was begun by its originally having been easier to carve mouths that way, or—and this is the part that for us had all the interest—because she is full of some secret happiness that we can never know. Why is she so happy? Delia and I discussed it. Artemis certainly wasn't cheap. She spent everything she had at every second, living, as she did, in the midst of an infinite supply—not of money but of power—like all the other gods. Could that, along with sweeping self-confidence, be what made her smile? Delia thought not.

We were drinking ouzo. Delia had on a pleated white dress, and when she stood up, she picked up her light raincoat as if it were a bow and arrow. A Hellenist we knew, who I think was in love with Delia, said that sometimes she made him afraid. Delia thought this absurd. Bob would look better without a beard, she said, about him. He had a brown one.

He came calling. In some ways he was better than I was, but Delia didn't love him. He would certainly have bought her the vase without hesitation. I was glad she didn't love him. I was afraid that without her I might be dead.

The problems with this story are several. One is that it is set in the nineteen fifties, when (1) Artemis was no longer a real force in the world, certainly not recognized as one except possibly by an Artemis Cult somewhere, and (2) the marital customs, the relationship between Delia and me, have acquired a distracting "period" effect that threatens to be more interesting than what I mean the story to be about: my finding of Artemis/Diana—with her powers of death, childbirth, chastity, the moon, the hunt—in my modest, shy, intelligent, midwestern, upright, cool, blonde American wife. Reading the story up to here elicits comment on the "fifties relationship" the two of us had—I changed money and Delia didn't, I made the decisions, she cleaned up the house. We had to live sometime. It might as well have been in the fifties. There—look! It's fifties! Fifties wine. Still, you drink it and it makes you drunk. Whatever the epoch, I was drunk on and mystified by my wife.

Hello, I said, when I met her. She was standing in the same big office I was in, at the University of California, in Berkeley. The hills were foggy in the distance. Bees, and other less useful insects, jumped up and down and around in them. Oh, Delia, I said. What an inter—what a beautiful name. My glance traveled around her. A man came into this office, and a woman left. The desks stayed there. A goddess, I said, rather foolishly, in the Berkeley T.A. office (Delia was another of the names of Artemis/Diana). Well, she said. A few days after that, we went out together. We drove into the hills and parked and kissed. Later Delia was willing to make love.

young
We loved each other and were ignorant.

    Gradually the Dianahood of my wife-to-be possessed me. Delia gave me all the things I didn't know I wanted.

    She wanted something, too, she told me, from our making love. "I want to experience evil," she said. "I've never done this before."

THE MUSIC OF LIVES IN BED

In the middle of the night (it was about five a.m., their middle of their night) he asked her to turn over and reassure him that she was not gay. She thought that was ridiculous. She had been his mistress, then they were married, and now they were divorced. Why would they still be sleeping together if she was homosexual? She thought, I won't even bother to ask him that. Why use logic to dignify this idiotic conversation? It was this sort of misunderstanding, of unwillingness to talk, that had broken up their marriage. That, and his foolish, over-anxious, unself-confident questions. Now, it seemed, though they were back together, they were starting to be detached from each other in the same way. I hate her, he thought as he shaved on his way to making her breakfast. I detest him, she hummed as she pulled the top sheet up to the top of the bed. She is loathsome, he whispered inaudibly as he set down the coffee. He is a horror, she barely murmured as she lifted the cup to her lips. I want to go to the movies today, he said. Let's go then, she said. And feeling various ways about each other, they went outside. The day is chilly, there is a little rain. She takes his pleasant, reassuring, reassured arm and very silently says Phhhhtff!

A SENSE OF THE TRAGIC

The Dutch have no sense of the tragic, Charlemuth said, as he and Georges and I gazed at the seemingly happy folk of Delft riding on bicycles, sometimes even wooden-shoed, garbed in blue and red, hilarious. No sense of the Tragic at all. My days then were wonderfully untragic as were my nights. The nights were clear and as if blown away, or at least blown clear by every passing day. June was wonderful. June was the woman I was with. June combined beauty and kindness with an incomprehensible fondness for me. In the great industrial suburb of life we had found each other. Each of us looked for a sense of the tragic. Soon the Chinese may become just like us, Michel said (some months later). I said I doubted it. Under the stars everything was clear, like Byron's clubfoot. If only they had named it something else, Byron said; but the English were unsparing: they called them as they saw them. You wouldn't find them eating herring, wearing blue white and red, and wooden shoes, and riding about on bicycles. Not the French, Charlemuth said, either. His poetry was always so sad. Clouds vied with azure and stone to accomplish miracles of solitude and darkness. Willows wept. And night broke clear of them all. June decided, after a while, that we should be married. She wanted to have children. She wasn't tired of ramping around but she also wanted that something else. I was hesitant. I talked about it to Mack. Don't have children, he said. You're right. It's completely unnatural! Don't you think you're going too far? I said. No! he said. For emphasis, he stopped the car. Holland was far behind, far away. No, I mean it! Eventually I lost June. Mack, Charlemuth, and Georges were still around.

RELATIONS

At twenty-six, one night in Paris, I dreamed that my parents came to visit me. The dream had the vividness of an hallucination. There was shuddering and shaking it seemed throughout the hotel. My mother said, "Kenneth!" Her voice was loud and intimate at the same time. Then my father shouted my name, too. They both appeared at my door. A little snow was falling on the rue de Fleurus. Busses had stopped running hours earlier. An occasional car was still able to move easily through the beginning snowfall. I sat up with terror at the sound of my parents' voices. The snow kept falling, though it didn't fall more heavily; and, after sitting up and staring, getting over the dream, then walking around the room for ten or fifteen minutes, I lay back down to try to sleep. I would have left my room and walked a little ways through Paris but for a peculiarity of my hotel, the Hotel de Fleurus. Once ten p.m. had come, you could open the hotel door from the outside but not from the inside. If you were in the hotel you were in for the night. In this respect, being there was like being a child.

I wrote a poem in this hotel room. I wrote several poems, but none worked out. The one that I liked was really only part of a poem. The four lines I wrote were written three years before I had ever seen Ekaterina. I was not even a graduate student at this time. At this time I courted Sonia and Gilberte and Anna of the dark smiles and eyes, Anna of "I don't know how to kiss." All this and all these were far far from the "I do know how to kiss" of Ekaterina, and the "I know what follows after" and "be careful, you are playing with fire" to which I replied, stupidly, "what else is worth playing with?" Ekaterina was a moderately tall blonde woman in a candy-striped green-and-white dress in an undergraduate class at Rutgers, the same age I was, twenty-nine. And, soon after meeting her, I finished the poem, with my subject now having appeared, after so long, starting with the lines I wrote before—

Oh what a physical effect it has on me
To dive forever into the light blue sea
Of your acquaintance! Ah, but dearest friends,
Like forms, are finished, as life has ends!

AN ADVENTURE
OF THE FIFTH SENSE

Tommy grabbed hold of his hand as they walked out of the school's little auditorium, where they'd seen, along with Tommy's sister Annie and his mother Chloe, who lived with Mike, the film in which Mike played an important part. It was secure to hold on to Mike. His image had been on the screen like a true image. Much mysterious affect was to come after this, but this was that. The city (Paris) lay stretched out before them like a huge laundered but unironed shirt. So many fluffily white passages and uneven trails. But Mike was Mike, this was safety in one big number, and Tommy holds his hand. He has very small fingers, but for Tommy it's hardly a question of a small hand (his) and a large hand (Mike's). They are, the two hands, completely different, so then how can each be a hand? About fingers, nails, palms you don't make a judgment. You hang on. Chloe is far from being jealous. She has Annie's little hand in hers. And so the City of Lights is navigated today. People who would have been of no importance in the time of Louis the Fourteenth are now the object of attention. Even their slightest feelings are the objects of attention, of the most intense and serious kind.

PLANNING LIFE

They'd made an agreement (his idea, poor goof) not to make love. Each understood that this was just for a while. After this time they would devise something, neither knew what. Fond of him, she took her blouse off but this was before the agreement. He went to adjust the stereo, through which Bach was coming penetratingly clear. Blue white cloud on azure green photograph sky. Vienna and Rome. Places. The arch of your left foot. So forgive me. Oh silly, he said. He'd found it terrible not ever seeing her. But now what was he going to do with his collection of desires, the desires for her, that he wasn't going to fulfill? When they made love for the first time again, she fainted. She felt the excitement of a walk of which she didn't know the end—adventure, wandering. In America, a nineteenth-century French writer said, *tout est chemin,* everything is a path. How could she not go everywhere she could? How could he not, too?

LIBRETTO

A friend is coming to dinner, the friend he would like to set this text of his to music. Henry, a middle-aged man, who had lost his daughter when she was a baby, owns and operates a gas station somewhere in the American West. To this gas station comes a young married couple, Bert and Matilda. Their car has broken down, and there is no place but this one where it can be repaired. The mechanical problem is serious and takes Henry several days. Henry and Matilda fall violently in love. At the moment they are realizing that this is so, a car drives up for gas. In the car are a man and woman and a small child. The young parents sing a duet that begins:

> Fill up our gas tank with Texaco
> We all are driving to Mexico

Their revelatory conversation interrupted, Henry and Matilda now look at each other in a startled way. The sight of the young family in the car has brought them what seems to be a memory—of intimacy, of a voyage, of a loss. Aren't you—no—could you be—Henry stammers. And Matilda, Oh no! My daughter! Lost, in time long past! No, cries Matilda (Louisa), no! But yes seems certain. The lovers' union cannot take place. Arias are sung, cried, whispered. The fear of incest prohibits them. There is no consummation. Bert and Matilda (Louisa?) leave, she full of the ravages of a forbidden love. Henry, as the automobile's sounds fade, sings, whispers really, just one word: "Louisa!" Two: for then: "Matilda!" It may, after all, have been a mistake.

He finished the libretto around five o'clock. At seven-thirty, Alfred arrived. This young composer is American and has been living in Paris. He read the libretto. Ellen said, Here is dinner! It's beautiful, of course, Alfred said. But I don't think it would go over in France. The French would find it incredible that they didn't even make love once, since they don't really *know* if they're related. Oh you've been staying over here too long! Sean said. He was offended. He wanted the breakup to seem a necessary thing.

The year before, before marrying Ellen, Sean had fallen in love with Louisa, who had a husband much older than herself. In the libretto the older man was the lover and the younger one (Sean's age) the husband. In reality it was the other way around. She also fell in love with Sean. She said to him, they were on a bus together, I can't leave my husband and my son (he was five years old) in any organized way. I don't have the heart. But if you will take me, I will go with you right now. Sean said, Wait. A while later it ended. Sean despised himself for what seemed to him his cowardice in not having taken Louisa for his wife.

The libretto wasn't set to music. Composing, for Alfred, was more a wished-for than an actual pastime. What he really loved to spend all his time doing was playing the piano. He went on becoming famous at doing that. Sean died young. The apartment where Sean wrote the libretto was torn down and replaced by a condominium. Alfred has a carbon-paper copy of *Louisa*—or *Matilda*, the only copy of it left—but it's missing the last page. A composer who long ago heard of the libretto now wanted to make it into an opera. With no copy of the end of the libretto in existence, it is now possible that the story could turn out in a different way.

Three persons are eating oysters in the Café du Dôme. One of them, twenty-eight, the youngest, is smiling, and it's not only the wine that is making him high. He is full of the pleasure of a libretto that he is "taking over," getting into someone else's skin to write. His new contribution to it is to take the events that have happened since, and the secret details he has found out concerning its composition, and to make that all a part of the libretto. The new text delighted the composer, who wrote a beautiful score.

Louisa! Matilda! Applause, applause! Ellen comes to Paris for the world premiere. She is wholly carried away by this opera. Like several others in the audience, she is part of the story. In Bayonne, New Jersey, sat Louisa, who didn't know about the opera and who wasn't there.

HOTEL LANCER

An angel flew in the window, of fine fresh sunsplit air, so rare in London, and they both turned around. They had been quarreling by the open French window, from which you could see the river. The quarrel began in a discussion of the plan for the day. The mother wanted to go someplace and sit (and write postcards); the father wanted to do some vigorous touring. He had a list. The quarrel now was about what each of them wanted to get out of life. The little girl sat crying on the edge of the bed. When she was born, the father sent a telegram to his parents: Charlotte fine and Baby Helena into the bargain. We send you love. He telegraphed, at Charlotte's request, to her mother too: Both girls brave and beautiful your baby and ours. They decided to take a boat ride on the Thames.

GILBERTE

I

Gilberte, restless in her limited modernity, came from the provinces to Paris and was rather silent there. She came to the crémerie in the evenings, after her restless afternoons. Je suis étudiante en droit, she said in her fairly low voice. Gilberte was unhappy, or, as she put it, she had "les idées noires." This was the fate of almost every aristocrat in Heian Japan. Despite the just-about-continuous sexual activity and the most refined aesthetic behavior ever seen on earth, the Heian were pervaded by their fateful knowledge of the Buddhist philosophy of history, which placed them in a hopeless age. There was no way out. Gilberte tried to drown herself but stopped. One evening she turned on the gas in her apartment, but a window was open. At twenty-five she finished her studies and became a law clerk. She went back to the provinces to see her parents. She remembered, as it happened to her again, how helplessly she started to stammer when they were around.

2

I was immediately interested in this particular girl because her name was Gilberte. This was because of Proust. We both ate in the little crémerie, I suppose there has never been a really big crémerie, on the rue de Fleurus, in the block between the Luxembourg Gardens and the rue Madame. Gilberte and I joked around. I was happy to know enough French to be able to talk to her. She seemed glad of my acquaintance, as odd as I must have seemed to her—a tall, skinny rather clumsy American (this is 1950), and always joking, in a language I didn't entirely understand. She wasn't exactly pretty. She had the trace of a moustache and rather dark skin. She wasn't especially happy either, nor joyous, nor what is called full of life. Sometimes she seemed very sad. If I asked about it, Gilberte would tell me that she had "les idées noires," the black ideas, dark unhappy thoughts. But what did I know? Gilberte's reality ended for me with the wall of the large building that held her tiny room (I never saw it, she never invited me, or permitted me, in), there to be succeeded by her irresistibly seductive reality in the pages of Proust. So I was puzzled by the actual Gilberte time after time.

Reading her letter, saying she was sorry but she no longer wanted to see me, I was, as I had often been with Gilberte, on the corner of the rue de Fleurus and the rue d'Assas. The afternoon shadows hanging from the corners of the buildings were as dark as my first image, before I knew what she meant by them, of Gilberte's "idées noires." I felt a sharp pain in my abdomen and in my chest. I might really never see Gilberte again. I was twenty-six years old, Gilberte was not my first love, and, actually, not my love at all. Though I was reading *Remembrance of Things Past*, I did not at that time understand how horrible the life in it was. I felt its great variety, its nobility, its sensuousness, and its heroism, and I wanted it to be mine.

WAGON-LIT

The wagon-lit was rumbling. Trick tracks climbed up through snow-mountainous light. His hand is on her thigh but someone else is speaking. She just felt sexy. Later on she would rebuild an important museum, and then when she thought of this night she would think, That was not me really. I was not myself. Meanwhile back in the Unreally somebody if not herself is essaying to lie partway down so her new acquaintance here can be inside her to make love. The train lurches, it's not easy. Soon the bright dark light of Paris is staggering over them all. Swaggering. The Gare de Lyon collects them and flings them out into Paris while it is snowing and neither one can find a cab. A taxicab strike, which is not really itself, has just about immobilized a great portion of France's capital. Whoever thought we'd breathe this fresh spring night again? he asked his friend. She smiled and said, I have to phone Marie. Tonight she was scheduled to arrive in Paris. What happened on the train? In Italy the coffee tasted good. At every moment, as he drank it, he was thinking of what would happen later on. She didn't mind him, but that's the way he was.

THE ALLEGORY OF SPRING

The blossoming cherry trees were quarreling. She thought this when she was fifty yards away and when she was closer, right in amongst them, she imagined she heard them. One tree said to another: I am prettier than you. And the other said: It is impossible for you to see yourself. But I see you. And I tell you you're wrong. The first tree disputed the illogic of this remark. And so on. She went on walking, and when she came out of the cherry grove, she had been through a lot. She hated quarreling. Dietrich was standing by his boat. Come, can you go out with me? he said. I don't want to quarrel, she said. He didn't understand. Well, will you or not? he said. Yes, she said. Then she said, No.

BORDER

At the border the French customs person, a woman, seeing the baby, Charlotte, two months old, swathed in white, smiling, and transported in a basket, commented "Quelle Calvaire!" What a Calvary to have to travel with a baby. Whereas moments before, far from confiscating anything or delaying them at the border, the Italian customs crew, two men, had untiringly chucked the baby under the chin and exclaimed about how beautiful she was. The baby grew up and liked Italy better than France but not for this reason. Deeper and underneath this and all similar reasons was the passivity these Americans showed—you could call it, if you wished, receptivity—in regard to the voiced opinions of the Mediterranean working class. Deeper than this, even, was the instinctive—or old-civilization-induced-become-almost-instinctive—wisdom and grace they assumed these Mediterranean people had. Deeper than this were the groundwaters of which the Mediterranean itself would be formed, one fine morning when the chill wind blew over from the Atlantic and the hot from the Sahara, until the rocks and bitter thyme and pollen said, "Here we have a sea." Boats slavishly crossed it, for millennia. Charlotte was born. She who one day standing on the jetty felt the terrifying shocks in her, like cannonfire and not too distant, of motherhood and love. Whereupon another tiny infant could become the subject of the Solomon-like decisions of the sun-tan-faced people who kept working all the same. Che àngelo! Tesòro! said one. And Ah M'sieu Madame quel cauchemar! (What had the Mediterranean to do with this?) said another. Butterflies, yellow and blue, groped up the white cliffs almost never reaching the top. We have to ask you to open your bags, said the man in Italian customs. All right. She held onto his arm because she was always frightened of customs. You may close it, please. The baby was screaming like a car accident. Bon dieu, Good god, said the French customs, can't you get that little monster to be still? The baby also was named Charlotte, and she grew up.

WHITE NIGHT

Moon shining on Dan. Who said, He likes you almost as much as I do. Therefore. A party again. Scotch and soda, orange juice, marc de champagne. In a garden of tilleuls were broken. They sat around, raspberry juice. A few of the lives were in a state of being broken. Tears would follow, and shaken heads. Chins would be raised in sad determination. Those who were lucky would love again. Some craziness would be dissolved. It was too bad for this one and not so bad for that one. Have a glass. In the glass was something. It changed the way you felt and were. Alcohol, that simple hand, pushing you to this and to that. But it will never find her. The man needs the woman he will have to fight. One is a slob, aloft and away from his feeling. He wants to be a doll. She wishes to be a dog. It has to be gotten through. If it is not love, is it convenience? If it is not convenience, is it Dan dreaming really? This happened very fast to be happening again so soon. He has gotten a bit closer. He reaches for her hand. She showers him as with moonlight with a smile. But this smile is to please her and is the last he will get, for a while. Later, there will be other smiles, in other places. How did they get in this position that so encumbers and burdens their hearts?

One night in Barcelona, he said something. And then she felt something and she said something. But what had happened before that? Back and back and back it goes to their attraction the first time. He has something that she needs. She wears a slow white dress. Close up, they are finding the most of reality in satisfaction of an infantile wish. This thread led him to this party. The minute hand was turning. The second hand was broken. After a long while, there was the sun.

A DOUBLE STANDARD

A man walked into the public baths, and after a few minutes a woman walked out. Inside the Baths the man was asking about the price of a towel. The woman at the steamy little desk told him what he wanted to know and pointed to a hallway of tubs each protected by a door. On the doors were steamy edges, vapor drops, little squiggles of water that leaped and stood up. He opened one and he hung his towel inside. In moments he was naked. A moment more and he was filling up the tub. The water boils, it manifests a mighty gurgle. He turns the knob and stops its flow, puts in one foot and then he sinks into the tub entirely. The woman walked out into a sunny day. An automobile was standing in the street. Like all women, like all men, she wanted to be loved. For some months now she has felt that this is not happening. She is young, she has no humor about it, she needs to be reassured. The man who is taking the bath has no idea. She is wearing a dark green blouse. He is not her man. And she is not his woman. But he might as well and she might as well be. For this bathing man's woman is thinking the same things of him, and she has no humor about it either. The two women, one in a light yellow dress and the other now running across a park, dressed in green and whose eyes are dark blue, will decide this matter. The gray statue in the park has a curve of rock to its hair. When the man gets out of his tub he seems larger than usual, because he is in such a small room. Later that night he is diminished. He breaks a window, he even tries to break the bed. She will never come back. That god-damned bathtub, that god-damned fool that I was! The second man's wife, on the other hand, relents; he remains temporarily—maybe even permanently—ignorant of the way things are.

ON HAPPINESS

It was distressing to think that Kawabata had committed suicide. It wasn't distressing, however, to find out that he had defined happiness as drinking a scotch and soda at the Tokyo Hilton Hotel. An acquaintance of mine thought this was a terrible thing to say, to such an extent that for him it seemed almost to destroy the value of Kawabata's work.

Sitting on the terrace of the Hilton!

What's wrong with that?

A friend of mine, a woman, once explained happiness to me.

We were sitting in the Place de la République in Paris, an unlikely spot for happiness. We were tired, had walked a lot, had sat down at a large, generic big-square café. Dear though it may be to its proprietors and its habitués, it seemed ordinary enough to us. So we sat there and she ordered a Beaujolais and I, a beer. After two swallows of beer, I was overcome by a feeling of happiness. I told her and I told her again about it later.

She had a theory about a "happiness base." Once, she said, you had this base, at odd times, moments of true happiness could occur.

Without the base, however, they would not.

The base was made of good health, good work, good friendship, good love. Of course, you can have all these and not be "happy."

You have to have the base, and then be lucky, she said. That's why you were happy at the café.

Kawabata asked my acquaintance in turn: How would you define happiness? He told me his answer: "I said 'How can anyone answer a question like that?'"

THE LOCKETS

It's just the worst kind of weather, he wrote to his fellow poet and friend, for writing poetry. But when he came home, he had a marvelous long poem. He had been telling the truth about the weather. It was cold clear and still and it didn't inspire him. One day, though, he started to write *The Lockets*. He felt good because he had been patient enough to wait for a true poem to arrive. Usually he wrote a poem all at once, but this one occupied his time for day after day. By the time he finished revising it, it had been almost a month. This seemed to him a very long time but also a very short time, since if the poem was as good as he thought, it was a lifetime possession, a place, as it were, like a country house, in which he could live whenever he wanted, a place full of sunshine and clutter, comfort and surprise. The weather he hadn't liked was in it, but transformed by words. There was also a certain irony in it that sometimes he thinks he would have liked to leave out, but that is the kind of person he was at the time. Most of it was like a big, cold, frilly place by the water, decorated by someone else (Poetic Tradition?) in a more elegant and fancy style than he could have found for himself. He wanted to show it to his friends. He was sitting now in a room on West Eleventh Street looking at one friend reading it who seemed almost shaken by terror because it was so good. It might have been, in fact, since the friend had a cold and a slight fever, that he was shaken momentarily by a chill. But the sunlight filled the room, and what did it matter? He knew that his poem was good, and that his friend, whether he thought so or not, would tell him that it was, and that he would believe him.

NOTRE DAME AND CHARTRES

Of the three young women standing in front of the cathedral, one was worried about her sexuality, another was in the midst of a probably destructive love affair, and the third, who was so far a virgin, was blind. Nora did not use a dog to help her move about. Today, she was with her friends, and in any case, she had been blind for a long time and had developed a sure sense of place. She carried a cane. For Catherine, sex was good and sex was bad—of course, in different ways. In a way it was the summum bonum and the happiest thing in her life. Leaves swirled—taken up by the autumn wind as a waitress takes up her apron—across the parvis, the forecourt, of Notre Dame. Women, in her secret belief (this region of her secret belief was in some respects like a small-town library containing random books in different sections, some in Religion, others in Mechanics, Physiology, Politics, Literature), women did not feel overt sexual desire. When she felt such desire, she felt she was less a woman. Never admitting to her sexual feelings, even when they were very strong, she would allow herself to be surprised by them, and give in sexually to the most inappropriate men. She was unable to talk about this situation with her two friends. Denise standing next to her was intent on pursuing a sexual passion to its end. The man, object of her desire, was rich, married, arrogant, much older than she, and unfaithful (even to her). He had a pleasant voice and dark blue eyes that, each time she saw him, seemed to pass like a long needle or a hat-pin straight to her heart. He had a certain way of touching her, carried over from his profession (he was a doctor, an internist). To patients it was reassuring; to her it gave an impression of sureness and strength. These two were describing the right front doorway of Notre Dame Cathedral to Nora. Three days earlier, they had gone to Chartres, and there both Catherine and Denise (to their surprise) felt jealous of Nora's enjoying it so much. Clearly much more than they. Only human relations cause that much joy. Nora's was from the kindness of her friends—as attentive to her as lovers, and two of them at that! She was fascinated, at both churches, by every detail.

LIFE AND ITS UTENSILS

"Life and Its Utensils" is at the museum. A song runs toward us with its poster. It is the sun! At the museum, the utensils are arranged according to use: here a knife and fork and platter and chopping bowl and a neon sign saying KITCHEN, another saying MANGER. Here are some dark blue paintings—the utensils, it appears of Waking up. Here are the seams, the pins, the pink roses and yellow cellophane thread that are the utensils of Summer. The weakness of the show is its disorder, its incompleteness, the evident fact that the user of all these utensils is not here.

The use for things I find (I think) when I am with you, O perspicacious heavenliness. That's you, over here, with me, now over there, whiskey, a summer flatness, a winter's snow, oh you're the one, who is saying, Green crayon, green crayon, green crayon, who knows what coils are in your heart?

When we came out of the museum, nothing was the same. That is, for a couple of seconds. Everything looked like a utensil: the hill, for supporting the sky; the sea, an electric knife for slicing the sunset's cake, etc., etc. In another museum, there is a show entitled "Objects: Lost, and Found." A very large blue mirror is just inside the entrance door. Looking at it, one sees into it, as is the case with mirrors, and there is nothing in it at all. That is the Objects-Lost. The rest of the museum is filled, I mean really genuinely filled, with objects found—everything, gloves, engines, canisters, barrels, flowering plants, love manuals, she-goats, backgammon boards, coffins, fat people, seeds, everything that could possibly, ever, in a lifetime or two, be found. The trouble is there is no room to walk in this museum, no way to see, except from a distance, most of these exhibits, and going into and among them, a person becomes one of them him- or herself.

Space travel is gone, Leaves of Grass is gone, Bonington is gone, Delft is gone. All that is left on this highway is a couple of trees. Under them a car, that is, it turns out, a little museum. "Life and Its Dashboards" inside. If you're not distracted by this, I am. The life of anyone shows how happy one can be. And how unhappy.

We found in the Museum of Words, a man who had never taken a wash. He was all alphabet, from head to foot. From foot to head laying him sideways he spelled DEUS RERUM AQUEO (God is the water of things?) and reading him head down it was A NEW SILENCE. We couldn't speak to the man, so we went away. Prose and her handmaid, Poetry, followed us. The Words Museum had many other shows. I was alone. I sang a song I had known from other cultures:

> When man alone
> Suffers enticement
> Greece overthrown
> Rome's no replacement
> A railroad terminal scudded with snow
> A lovable scene designer's elbow
> These will all fall under the knife
> Of the Utensils exhibit of life!

After I had locked my song in a neighboring window, I walked out onto the museum promontory to smoke a glass of blue air, when suddenly, you (the woman in question) come back in sight. Where've you been? Gerard Manley Hopkins is gone and filigree is gone, filigree effects are gone. Here's the Summer Wind Museum, with its technology of throats.

And the Museum of Being Permanently Closed. It isn't a museum, it's a mortuary, a coat for old friends. You were startled by being in your coat. You startled me.

The Power Museum is gone, and the Hooks Museum is gone, and the Life Itself Museum is drifting away. The French have hysterical blindness, the Italians depressive moods, the Spanish what? Hesitation about being around.

You'll admit that it's been quite a day for going to museums! A medium-sized amphitheatre now, filled with car wrecks, would, for this twenty-four-hour period, be sufficient to round things off. A young schoolteacher (Andy?) who lives in these parts is tagging along with us, asking questions: Do you like our country? Which show did you like best? What, according to you, is the most significant for our time? Oh, all of them, Andy, all! But it would be great to go swimming! The Museum of Occanography is right here. Great sharks pasted to the pinewood, corals hiding beneath the timbers of the floors, mermaids and mermen dancing attendance, and everywhere the mysterious artifice of salt. After this, finally, we go home, to the non-museum of sleep.

THE RESTAURANT ON THE BEACH

In the Trattorìa della Toscana e del Mare, clamshells and the "sounds of the sea." Shellfish—clams—by the dozens were being devoured. Pick up slip slap slurp clack jangle back onto the plate. A woman had a pain in her jaw. A man, a lover or her husband, placed his two hands gently on her jaws and eased them a few times open and closed. A mother and daughter had hardly spoken to each other for a year. A year in such circumstances is a long time. Napkins flew in and out of the diners' hands. The girl finally found it in her possible feelings to forgive her mother. At the table their hands crossed. The mother seized the girl's two fingers and held them. A bare-looking beach, flat, not generous, with its sand, though furnishing a base of hard sand for whatever sand might be added, though it would be sturdy sand that could resist the breeze but above all the waves that, small and low as they were, periodically came all the way up, just about to the edge of the Trattorìa della Toscana e del Mare, this beach was brightened by sun and by the sun's reflection. Automobile horns honked, but just a few, on the half-kilometer-away road. The restaurant from the outside seemed only a shack, but it was comfortably set up inside. The mother let the daughter drive, a relief to them both.

JULIAN AND MADDALO

The young Englishman and the equally young Italian nobleman were riding in the latter's carriage on the outskirts of
Venice. They continued their trip in a gondola, from which at a certain point a little island could be seen, with a building on it with a
belfry. The Italian told the Englishman the building was a madhouse. Somehow from this began a conversation about the
Christian faith, about whether it was possible to believe in it or not.
The Englishman said it was not; the Italian said he found it amusing how passionate (and persistent, he had known him before) the
Englishman's feelings on the subject were. More momentous than
what they said or did seemed the beauty of the end-of-the-day
Veneto sky, a pale bright splendor of pinks, oranges, and golds.
Having been tired but with their tiredness now turned to tenderness by this visionary loveliness, the two friends descended from
the dark gondola at their respective homes. The next day the
Englishman went to call on the Italian nobleman. The latter had
not yet risen, so the Englishman took advantage of the time to play
with the nobleman's daughter, a beautiful, sensitive, intelligent
child. Her eyes, he thought, were like twin mirrors of the Italian
sky. They gleamed, however, with the luminosity and intelligence
that one found only in the human gaze. He was sitting with her,
rolling balls about, on the floor. When his friend was ready, the two
men set out in a gondola once again. They continued their conversation, now bolstered by the passage of time, and by the events of
the night and the morning, about the viability of the Christian
faith. Their plan was to go to the madhouse on the island they had

noted before and, once there, to talk to the "madman," who turns out to be not at all mad, though a man who was, years before, temporarily driven out of his senses by the reverses of love. Voluntarily he had confined himself to an old tower amid the isolation of the Adriatic isle, and then his strange ways, which consisted chiefly in his unusual wish for solitude, caused people to think of him as eccentric, even mad, and to begin to call his tower the madhouse. The two friends hear all of his story. It enchants them. Christianity and its problems are forgotten. Each of them—they are both profound lovers—feels close to the madman; with a common desire they ask him to return to the mainland; they will help him, financially and otherwise, to set up a new life. No, thank you, the madman said. No, I cannot. And in this perhaps, only, but perhaps not, he was mad. Finally, their kind offer kindly refused, and the dark night coming down, Julian and Maddalo go home. The eight-year-old girl is called to dinner. The "madman" waves to them. Later he falls, stricken— by some malady of the heart—his painful life at an end.

A MOMENT IN THE LIFE
OF ANNA TAGLIAVANI

Windows slammed, doors opened, and she walked into a place where there were banks of drawers. A note left out on a filing cabinet fluttered to the floor. Bending to pick it up, she saw a white folded dinner napkin hanging on a very low railing. First she picked that up in her hand and then went after the note. When the entire area was clean, even spic-and-span, she closed the doors, opened the windows to let in some fresh air, looked out at the canals—there were two of them converging where she could see—took off her dusting cap, dried off her hands against her apron, smiled, and twirled around. She did a little dance, a sort of tarantella, then opened one door and, going out through it, resumed her place in society once again. This "cleaning lady" was a talented dancer.

Anna, there is an opening at the theatre. Gerolama is ill.

A little more cleaning work, then, for money. And hours and hours of exercises. She had done them all along.

She even did some housework the last possible day.

Off slipped the apron and down threw the cap, and the broom is replaced by a wood post on which she leans, breathless, about to take her first longed-for (tanto) leap onto that stage. In midflight she imagined herself cleaning, and, for an instant, she looked about, to see what was there. But by the time she landed, that phase of her life was done. She might clean, a little, now and then, in secret, but she would dance (it seemed decided) for the world.

ELBA

 They lay on the beach.
While they lay there, the sun came up.

This means that they had been lying on the beach all night.

The beach they were on was not anonymous.

It was the beach Napoleon had landed on when he was imprisoned on Elba.

It was a beach that was a moment in history.

Napoleon, landing there, was unaware of this beach as "beach." This is not so now.

Now it is Napoleon's beach. How can it be anything else?

However, this endless life of tourism, of conquest, of idealization, of adventure, of going "out of oneself," to what can it lead but murderous disappointment and depression? You only think that way sometimes.

At other times, you love life, you love this beach.

Lying on it, you may be covering with your body the sandy places where once Napoleon put his feet.

If nothing else were happening in the world, this would be a little something. I admit that it's not much. However . . . what do you say to a night on Napoleon's Beach?

All right, I will!

AT LAMBARÉNÉ

From the ocean came a light and salty breeze. It made a delicate light film around everything it touched. Sick persons were arriving, sick persons were getting better, some sick persons were dying. The sea rose with a sort of wail at Lambaréné, and after a very hot, close "taxi" ride through the bush, on jagged bumpy roads, Lopan got out, stretching his limbs and straightening his sleeves, he was wet, from the heat, and went walking in, expecting, almost, to see Dr. Schweitzer himself. Schweitzer said, The death of an insect is a significant death to me. It had been hard all Lopan's life to live in the shadow of Dr. Schweitzer. Miracles, he thought, might still happen in the world, but probably not here. Schweitzer had done whatever could be done, and in its turn this initial inspired miracle was now the scene of the humdrum of accustomed failure and success. An old woman, maybe eighty?, attracted his attention. She was sitting in a low chair in a room with a poured cement floor and with half-opened curtains of brush grass between her and the view of the sea. She was softly singing (there were interruptions for coughing and sometimes what seemed like gasping) a traditional Fang song that Lopan knew. The old woman reminded him of his mother, who, he thought, might have been offended at being compared to an old sick black woman in a hospital in Gabon. On the other hand, maybe not. It was something to him that there was no relationship—he could, at whatever time it pleased him, move on. He left the old woman and walked about—looking, asking questions, saying polite things. He too, of course, was a doctor. After about forty minutes, he walked outside to the cab and told the driver, who was surprised that he had come at all and that once there he hadn't stayed longer, that he wanted to go back. The driver was a Mpongwe. Like the Fang, the Mpongwe were a tribe that inhabited Gabon, though far fewer in numbers than the Fang, and who, unlike the Fang, so far as Lopan knew, had never been cannibals.

ON THE SAVANNA

The zebras, like the wildebeests, are always on their toes, so to speak—alert, anxious, sensitive, worried-looking. Some distance away reclines a lion. These elephants, though, seem relatively at ease. They have an air about them that they are the only ones there. I don't think they're worrying about lions. The elephants are vegetarians, and like vegetarians everywhere they know what's right. What's right for them: trees—Wham Gark Thank You Bark, Heave Sleeves Thank You Leaves. The elephants are going at it, an independent centrally-willed group that feels its identity so strongly as to make it feel safe. The elephants are not only centered and living by rules, but they are *big*, too, and have tusks and a trunk to go along. An adult elephant can handle a lion. A baby elephant cannot. The babies, being possibly edible, are connected to the rest of the savanna. A little older, they are too strong and too tough. The mothers close off the appetitive connection as much as they can. At first sight of a lion, a baby is surrounded, and the lion goes off, its mind already on other prey. The elephants' isolation goes on as before.

THE CLIMATE OF GABON

In the brush nearby there were only small animals. At the Hotel Rampinadanda, Madame Oubala is writing a message down. The stamp is too big to go on the card! What a laughter from the back of the lobby and some students were staying in the hotel— students in France, dans la métropole, though teachers here. Among these, Hervé Blanc. Mme Oubala lifts up her pen. The message is written down. The blazing white-pink sunlight fills the lobby air with a tuneless sort of illogic, as if it were the eyes of a great animal, whose hide and claws and horns were the trunks and suitcases that are beginning to be dragged down the stairs. Hervé, though he would have liked to stay in this what-could-seem-for-an-instant paradise of early hotel morning, has decided not to stay. The young women who work in the "casino" are still in bed, mostly sleeping. There is one whose hair in disarray she is staring down at the distant swimming pool. And shaking her beautiful head and hair, she says (to Jean-Simon), Hervé is leaving today. Did you know? Jean-Simon rises from a pile of white linen and stares into the hotel room sky. Could you give me my glasses, please? he said. She did and also took up hers in her hand, and thinking of Hervé's going they both put their glasses on. He has a large property in France, he told me, Sylvia says. That's nonsense, Jean-Simon said. Jean-Simon was right. Hervé does not. The sunlight is getting very hot. Hervé was thinking: I have to go back because my life isn't going anywhere here. Could I take Millie with me to France? "Hervé is leaving, as I always knew he would." The sun is very high now, blazing, though it is cool in Sylvia's room. For a while, there, she and Jean-Simon go back to sleep.

HOTEL LAMBOSA

He closed the university down, she said.

There is nothing like being in the middle of a seduction in a strange country in an unfamiliar hotel.

Especially when one has known the person who is its object for only about forty-five minutes.

Being "inside" this person was a kind of enchantment.

Each instantly had the feeling that the other would be lovely to be with in a bed.

This feeling turned out to be true, and the strong, swift sunlight cluttered and clouded their room with pennies of the future and nickels dimes and quarters of the past.

When he got up to pick up this money, he saw that she was there.

She was lying on her side, gazing at him.

She said, So now no classes for a while!

ACHILLE DOGOS

I

The African (a Zairian man) spoke, sang, recited, wept, laughed, talked with amazing rapidity. He was performing, for a large audience, but specially in honor of me and a few other visitors to Zaire, a work he had created about the politics, excitements, anguishes, and ironies of World War Two and the years just after. He took all the roles himself. At one moment he was Churchill, at another Eisenhower, at another de Gaulle, and so on. He was Hitler, Mussolini, Stalin, Konrad Adenauer, John F. Kennedy, and all the other leaders of the wartime and postwar world. At the same time he was speaking, crying, and singing, he darted around the room, turned his face, adopted different poses, lowered his head, threw his hands in the air, fell flat on his rear, scuttled across the room on all fours.

A good many of the connections of the act were made by puns—Hey ha ha, where you build a church? It's up on a hill, that's why we call it Church Hill! (Enter Winston Churchill) Did I hear my name? Going to strike the animal, strike it where it sleeps. We have to Hit Lair! Ho ho, speak. (Enter Adolf Hitler) Well I am Hit-lair. Who now says my name. If then when my friend feels not so strong, he'll lean on me. He must lean on me! (Enter Benito Mussolini) Ho, I am Benito Must-lean-on-me . . . Once introduced, all these characters acted out the wartime and postwar doings of their respective nations. This included the lead-up to the war, the invasions of Poland and of the Low Countries, the Blitz, Dunkirk,

America's entry into the war, the Russian front, Rommel versus Montgomery in North Africa, and so on and so on. The conclusion was an impassioned plea for peace by John F. Kennedy. At the end of it, the performer fell down as if shot—many spectators screamed—then got up as himself, Dogos, and bowed.

This performance lasted about an hour. I applauded with all the strength I had left. The others on the podium applauded as well—enthusiastically, for a long time. I was weak from what he had done. I was also frightened, given the applause, that he might do it all again. He didn't, though. Instead, he bowed, graciously (the applause continuing), then walked over into a corner to talk to a friend.

2

The Churchill part was hard to figure out, but at last he got something that resembled (in Luba) an upper-class British accent. Adenauer was easy, the German accent was. American was hard, French was hard. Italian he thought he could fake. It was fun to figure out what the people would say. It was more than fun, however, his act. It was complete involvement for him and total exhilaration. It gave him the feeling that in his body—in his temples, his shoulders, his neck, his strong thighs, in his abdomen, and in his vocal cords and mouth and throat—he had the entire true history of World War Two and the period after—this period so important for Africa. Period of independence and struggle. And of good leaders so hard to find.

When ready, he went to present himself, with held-in feeling, at the Nomakin granary door. He had once or twice been in a real theatre but it was usually a place like this, made into a theatre for the occasion. There was one he now thought of, outdoors, on the Esplanade by the river, a rough place, dangerous to act on, littered with sticks and pieces of stone. His performance there was one of his first; after that, usually, he asked for a place indoors. The granary was crowded with spectators. He took a long breath, concentrating on imagining himself to be Churchill, and walked in—to board-thumping, screaming, and thunderous applause.

3

Achille Dogos is walking by the River and he is listening to its sounds—Agounaboupaboumba. Here is the idea for a play all in one phrase. A goon named Boup invents a kind of music he calls Boumba. He plays it and thousands come to hear it by the River every night. In *français* the *Fleuve* says *un-con-aboup-aboumba*, more or less the same. Well, is a goon a *con?* Achille has yet another idea. Of course. And this idea is the River itself . . . Congo. Or else, modified by the sound he had heard it make, *Con*Goon. The idea for the play is now clear: *The Con*Goon: a collection of foolish actions performed by one French and American character, both of course acted by Achille. The Congoon. All the sounds in it will be the actions of the two fools.

4

Achille Dogos was puzzled when he received a copy of Edward Paunaman's long poem *The Lockets*. An American passing through Kinshasa had met and liked Achille Dogos, had thought he might like and profit from a little avant-garde American poetry, and sent him the book. Achille read it with great difficulty (it took him almost a month), and when he finished it he immediately began to work on ways to act it out. With the first ten pages he did pretty well. He liked what he was acting, he thought he was feeling in his body the freshness and violent activity of the text. The long set of stanzas about the different kinds (some fantastic) and colors of sub-way cars stymied Achille for a time, but not for too long, for he found a way to get down on all fours and slide back and forth while shouting them out. The slight narrative thread of the long poem—it was a parody of a nineteenth-century British girls-cum-aviators-book kind of romance—delighted him and gave him ideas for many things to do. That, and the grand, very grand, climactic whirl of the conclusion, which left him sprawling and exhausted, spread-eagled on the ground, or, when it was indoors, on the makeshift stage.

The piece, for the wild energy of its performance—and given Achille Dogos's already-great reputation, the love and esteem of which he had for a while now been the object of in Zaire—this enactment of *The Lockets* became a "hit," and a standard part of Achille Dogos's repertory, wherever in his large country he went. Almost every educated person in Kinshasa had seen it, and many rather simple and uneducated persons, too. Still, when Edward Paunaman won the Nobel Prize, Achille Dogos didn't hear of it. Nor did Paunaman know anything about Dogos's performances.

Persons crippled by polio are permitted by the government of the Congo to go with free passage on the ferry boat across to Zaire and to bring back a certain amount of merchandise without paying customs duty on it. Many things not available in Brazzaville may be found in Kinshasa, and the helpless persons (mostly men) have great trouble making any money and satisfying their needs at home. Thus, this is a compassionate law. The boat, almost every day (it crosses the Congo once in each direction every twenty-four hours) carries a surprising percentage of passengers in wheelchairs with crippled limbs. One of these, to his delight, has found someone to wheel him to a rare daytime performance by Achille Dogos. Forget, he thinks, the duty-free merchandise. He has to—the performance lasts all day. And he must be back in the Congo by dark (the ferry leaves at six). Today's show is a special one—a gala performance to celebrate the election of the new Premier. Or, rather, of the same Premier but from a new election.

The sun shines on Achille Dogos's body, as for the middle section he hurls himself to the floor and begins the passage of the "underground trains." This passage, to the cripple, Mouno Agoba, seems the very image of his sad and twisted life. For the first time since childhood, he bursts into tears. Paunaman, could he have seen this, might have struck at his heart with his hand and not known why it was there.

THE HEART ATTACK

I had a, well, a thing with a very important man, she said. An industrialist. Lived in Zaire. We were. It was a man of fifty-eight years. That would have made her at the time sixteen. We were happy. Last year he had a massive heart attack. Not quite dead but the affair was over. He was enfeebled, weak to the point of bed rid. He lies on a couch, exhausted. He cannot move his arm. Frédérique. But his servant does not hear and does not come because. He is living. Oh but for me it is as if he is dead. Tales from Africa. This man was the bridge from her sixteenth to her eighteenth year. It had, too, to be in the "colonies." That kind of power and isolation in the Métropole does not quite exist. The chief confidence everyone had who had the strength and the leisure to think was that the situation in regard to money and power would stay in place. An ornament, a decoration of this status quo was she who came like a gilded butterfly to pose on the stark dark arm of the man with two billion francs three years before he was going to die. His wife is in an elegant room taking care of him. The French are the cleverest people in Europe. This continent is dark but its sun is bright. The man, dying in Africa, very frequently thinks about the girl. Her father was a friend, in the Ministry of African Affairs. "If you make her happy—" He put his hand on the girl's father's shoulder, who without being able to help it, slightly recoiled. His heart attack finished it really. I had to leave Africa. At that point, everything was impossible.

AMBROSE BIERCE

When I reached my hotel room, which was on the twenty-second floor of the Hotel Rapontchombo, from the windows of which I could look down, in the daytime, at the tiny naked breasts of the wives and daughters of French residents of Gabon lying sunbaking at the pool—they excited me, perhaps even more than such a pleasant sight ordinarily would, because they were just at a distance to make them resemble in size, and thus for me in remembered splendor, the tiny photographed breasts of the Folies-Bergère girls on the rough ivory-colored and sepia brochures my mother forty-five years earlier had brought back from France—in any case this time, this night, when I got to my room, I saw something horrible: lying on my bed, a torn-off arm spattered with blood. It held down a piece of paper on which was printed, in large letters, *To Professor Koch, from his most appreciative students at the University of Gabon.*

There was a story behind this kindness: it had to do with the American writer Ambrose Bierce.

"Their favorite," the coopérant Jean-Pierre said to me while we walked along in the heat and even a hot breeze, ouf, and the lizards, I telling myself every half hour at least whoever it is was crazy telling me that Libreville was wonderful, beautiful, "Paris by the sea." The best thing I've done here, I thought, is get a second kind of malaria pill to take in addition to the other one. Favorite—Jean-Pierre was teaching American literature at the University—American writer is Ambrose Bierce. Why? Well, his stories of the supernatural, of magic and horror, seem like just the plain truth to my students. It corresponds to their view of life.

I was in Gabon to read my poems to the American and English literature students, and to discuss poetry in general with them. Several times in their questions they brought up Bierce.

Bierce's stories are filled with ghosts, disappearances, mutilations, acts of magic, all varieties of weird events. One poem of mine I read was "The Magic of Numbers"; this poem interested the students far more than anything else I read aloud or said. In it I used the word *magic* somewhat ironically and fancifully as one might in a phrase such as "the magic of Italy" or "the magic of a kiss." They, however, taking me at my word (magic) hoped they might, in penetrating the poem's secret, find out something of use.

Thus the arm, the bloody severed arm in my room. It wasn't really a human arm, but something that looked an awful lot like one, a pretend arm that some gifted craftsman among the students had made out of papier-mâché, bamboo, and paint. The arm was to show their opinion that I was of the high order of American writers that included Ambrose Bierce. I knew the world of spirits.

At least this is what one of them—Kabamu—told me the next day. We were standing on the Rapontchombo Hotel "breezeway," where the air was completely still. What he told me made me eager to see my students again, to talk and think about all this—I liked being regarded as one who knew the spirits—but there wasn't time.

Oh well, I had the arm! I would take it with me and read more Bierce. When I got to my room, though, in the last hour, ready to pack and to leave, the arm was gone. Of course, it would be! On the bureau in its place was a note, signed by the whole class: "Professeur, bon voyage!"

STREET THEATRE

What's bad about Italia, Maria Teresa said, is that you do something buona nobody notices it. But you steal the rear window from a car, eh, if you steal that, eh, quello è bravo!

My wife and I were startled. Yes, of course. *Bravo* meant, and it had been years that we had been using the word at theatre at concerts and at the opera, *bravo* meant "good."

"That had never occurred to me before," I said.

"Well, yes," Maria Teresa said. "It's evident. That is what is wrong with this place."

She came to live in America (in New York). Nobody said bravo about anything except in a theatre.

Ten days afterward I went out in the morning and looked at the car. Its rear window was gone.

It had been perfectly, meticulously lifted from its rubberized frame; not a fragment, not a scratch. Niente. Nothing. The May wind came in.

Quello é bravo, Janice said. In America there'd be glass all over the place!

SEA

The sound of the sea is:
   1) illusory
   2) not noticed
   3) noticed but not cared about
   4) cared about for a practical reason
   5) cared about for a general, poetic, artistic, or life-center reason
   6) ?

No matter whether perceived or not, or how it is perceived, the sound has the same reason: the boom thrut thrum of the impell-ment of strong ocean against bashed tides by leavings trials and leanings of wind. So a child becomes a poet and is impractical. He never learns how to use the sea. So a child becomes scientific and eludes its suggestions. Together they both live however in a world that includes (and importantly) the sea.

How do you like the ocean this a.m.? Beautiful, isn't it?

Ranging from a velocity of forty miles an hour . . .

R-R-R-R-R-R-Roar *rush* rush . . . . . . Sfooroom . . . .

I found a quarter this morning lying in the sand at White Peach Beach.

Show it to me show it to me show it . . .

Taking it she touched his hand and that day, affectively, was over.

The next day there were still a lot of battered-looking barques on ocean surface.

Life does nothing to change it. Does it change us? It is, we obviously are, different from it. Proof:

> possession of ears, a mouth, a nose

Insofar then as we can talk about it, everything (except the real problem) is solved.

She is excited to be spending so much time in the salt water and in the sun. If only he had known how little time he was, comparatively, putting into his (psychological and emotional) investigations of her salt-slaked body. The ocean was making a noise that was in no way a reminder, and was completely unpolitical, too.

A political movement resembling the ocean should be thought about only on a page.

It keeps reminding them of health, and in a way, too, of love and delicious sex.

The sea is neither masculine nor feminine but a great gross encourager of both.

By the time she had the ideal view of it, for her it was too late. And that was true of him, too. Nonetheless in the absence and in the ill of it, in the near-missing and in the concussion that was in reality too the confusion, they went on hearing it and being approached by it, from time to time, as if they were in such control of it that they could stroke it and make it roll, contented, away.

The resort closes. One more season! Or one less! A note is pinned to the door:

> NO CATS
>
> NO HELMETS
>
> NO BILLBOARDS
>
> NO SOUND OF THE WINTER Z
>
> PROHIBITED!

And not even in the evening do they or any come back.

END OF THE DAY
AT ALABIALAVALA

The French always made us wear these "colonial" hats, said Mrs. Ribaviabala. She smiled, almost laughed. We were sitting down to lunch, white tablecloth. For some rice water? Oh thank you yes. Mrs. Ribaviabala a rather elegant lady. Rose white dress. Dusty two of us Americans are from the road. Nice you to have us. Oh yes, Mrs. Ribaviabala said. Pleasure our. Drank we and ate we very nice. To I have made a translation, Mrs. Ribaviabala said, these for you some of our Malagasy verse. I then thank you, she me them handed. White sheets of paper clouds in sky clear above Alabialavala. The poems do not say much. Nor to judge by these translations are they very advanced in technique. But the ambiance nostalgic of that Ribaviabala! It's her giving me the poems translations harmonies! I will read them in the speeding car. Dear Mrs. Ribaviabala, Thank you for lunch. And thank you for the poems (translations), which were good to read. He did read them or he does not, says Mrs. Ribaviabala. It seemed a polite man. So often though Madagascar Europe American people do not what we want. Even when it is promised. Mr. Ribaviabala walks up from the garden with a cricket in his hand. Saying, in Malagasy, "Look at this!"

SAINT-JOHN PERSE AND THE SCULPTOR

The sculptor worked.

The jungle—bush, really—was around him, and the sculptor worked. He said, Dis-moi, Chef, to the tourist there. He said, Dis-moi, Chef, why are you come here to Gabon?

The tourist had come there to see a woman he loved. His love was composed of several factions. One faction wished to see him dead. Another wished to raise him, victorious, above the sea.

I don't understand.

Dis-moi, Chef, qu'est-ce que tu fais ici?

Now you are beginning to sound like Saint-John Perse.

I met him once at a party.

What did he say?

Oh he was very much like this sculptor.

Covered with dust? half-naked? twenty-two years old? and working on a false folkloric head?

No, of course not.

Dis-moi, encore une fois.

The dirt, the dust was swirling.

Henri had to find Catherine by eight that night. Vingt heures. After dark it wouldn't, probably, be possible; and the next morning he had to return. Oh well, why did he have to return? His job, his law practice, his living. But wasn't this the living that really mattered? He turned to the sculptor. What? Perse said, What is it that brings you to this gathering? And the young sculptor—"Chef, qu'est-ce que tu fais, donc, ici?"

The answer to both was love—incurable, unsatisfiable love, rephrased as (to Perse) I wanted to meet you, and (to the sculptor) I wanted to see the country. At the reception for the famous writer there had been Jeanne, the attaché's young wife. Now Catherine was in Gabon. Both answers were true and false, as both questions were genuine and insincere.

THE LIFE OF THE CITY

The whole city could be seen reflected in the surface of the rectangular flash bulb of his Canon AF35M II. Or at any rate, that of it which seemed to him significant. There were the old city wall and the first line of buildings. And there was the sky with, piercing it a good ways to the left, the white spire of the Cathedral. City, church, and nature were represented there. His wife had an automobile accident and broke her arm. His daughter was once again mended, after falling off a horse. His own health was excellent. Of the city there were both the political, governmental aspect, represented by the wall, and the private, familial aspect, represented by the buildings, which were houses. His daughter had been arrested for dealing drugs. His wife was under the care of a doctor, for alcoholism. He himself was dying of merely having been alive—for eighty-five years. The camera was gone. The city wall was still there, but many of the houses were gone. They were replaced by enormous "high-rises." These buildings were colored a darkish yellow, mainly, or a dark pink. That was nice, he thought. He wasn't really very old at all. He was going to meet his wife for the first time, at a dance in the Old City. Inside the city walls a few old buildings were, apparently, crumbling, but he was young enough not to even take care as he walked past and around them. The young woman was lovely. The spot where he met her was covered by a large shiny pump.

A BUS

The Muslims would not eat seafood and did not eat pork or drink wine. A seaside bar-restaurant in the middle of pig country would have had, here, little success. Yet this was not such a place, but rather merely a place in which to drink tea. The tea was sweet and had sprigs of mint in it. On these sprigs, as often as not, there were bugs. Ira looked at the bugs but drank the tea. The word *assassin* comes from the word *hashish*. Groups of men were given hashish and verbally inspired with wild dreams, then sent out to kill the victim someone wished to be dead. Hashish was differently esteemed in a culture where no one could drink alcohol. It could be regarded as the only "out." The "in" was to drink the tea, which Ferrabonzo found "molto forte," very strong. He looked at Ira, considering him as someone he might speak to, but rejected the idea. Ira had fallen asleep. He was very tired. Ferrabonzo slapped a few coins on the table, stood up and went out into the street. There a camel brushed against his shoulder, leaving traces of straw mixed with dust. Ira woke up. He didn't want to order more tea. Several of the bugs had crawled up out of his glass and moved lazily across the table. The bugs looked more repulsive out of the glass. He was sorry now he'd drunk any tea. He thought if he drank a bug it would give him a disease.

His wife smiled at him. She had stayed awake. Their daughter, who had been asleep on her lap for a long time, was very small. Don't worry about the bugs, she said. They won't hurt us. Beepie, Beepie, wake up, she said to the baby, who, however, continued to sleep. Come, sweetest. Daddy has to pay and then we'll get on the bus. The large, filthy, dark yellow, wheezing bus had just started breathing harsh breaths in the street. The driver came out of it into the relative cool of the café. Ferrabonzo was already on the bus. He had decided to go on to Elizir. The driver called out, in Arabic, Anybody for the Elizir bus? Ira was nervous and the baby had just started to cry. A brisk whiff of hashish seemed coming from where the bus driver stood and a largish man was pushing his way off the bus. This was Ferrabonzo. It all smells of hash in there, he said half to himself and half to them. To ride on it doesn't seem safe. Although each carefully guarded his or her individuality, in such a situation as this, thrown together by a portentous circumstance, they couldn't help talking together. The driver hesitated at the door and on the first step of his bus, noticing that now he had one fewer passenger than when he got off, and that two (three including the baby) very likely passengers were making no move to get aboard. They were, instead, indeed, all walking away. So be it. He went up the stairs and into the driver's seat, conducted his foot to the accelerator at the same time as one hand to the wheel, with the other on the starter. Then the bus smelling of hashish smoked by a previous passenger sped away. This possibility—regarding the hashish—occurred to Ferrabonzo, to Ira and Helena, at the same time. Now they had seven hours to wait, with no prospect of much that was agreeable except sitting around and dozing and drinking tea. To their pleasant surprise, however, the bus came back. The driver had forgotten his purseful of change, which he'd put down on the counter in the café. Unsurprised, ungratified, uncurious, and truthfully, a little dazed, he watched the three (plus the baby) formerly-supposed-secure then supposed-lost passengers laughing and excitedly getting on the bus.

IN THE LOBBY

When she came down she found him talking to the manager of the hotel. They had, it seemed to her, developed, for such a very short period, an extraordinary intimacy. Each man in fact had this "intimacy" close to the surface all the time. It wasn't exactly "intimacy" but a volatile personality substance that could turn into it on contact, by means of speech, with the air. From this intimacy she felt somewhat excluded. Too bad. He had a far finer substance ready for her, made up of all that he had ever felt, secretly felt, and thought and seen, and which, on contact with her person, with her talking, her mere aspect, turned into love. It did this when he saw her now, and his closeness to the manager faded. It faded quickly. The woman, seeing him so engaged there, had walked outside. He followed, and there on the porch were three women, between medium height and tall. One was the woman he felt love for, but for a fragment of a second he couldn't tell which one she was. Understandably. In fact it was three shining images created by the blindingly blazing sun. She was all three. As, shielding his eyes, he walked toward her, she laughed and said, How did you get so close to that man—in such a short time? I was surprised when I came down. Did you get the bill? He had paid it, and they put their bags in the car and drove off. He would always forget that moment and always remember the one of her telling him she was surprised. She said things about him that seemed to be praising in him some virtue, but later he felt she had possibly been ascertaining a fault.

LES ONZE MILLE VIERGES

Saint Ursula made sure that every one of the eleven thousand girls she took with her on the expedition was a virgin. A non-virgin would have ruined the perfect symmetry of the population of the expedition, have made the titles of paintings or verbal accounts of it complex and difficult, and could, too, have exercised some kind of bad influence on the other girls. Why are thoughts like these in my head? Eleven years ago, after learning that a friend of mine had unexpectedly died, I went out and walked through the city "inhabited by buildings." This phrase is Pasternak's, for Venice. I went (it was nearby) to the Accadèmia to look at Carpaccio's Saint Ursula paintings. At the harbor, in the boat, again on land, silvery, yellow, orange, blue, were all the Virgins, alive at first, then massacred, laid out flat. On each slain one was a speck of red. The most stirring pictures were those of the Virgins in the boat. Heading, heading for somewhere, for a Good Destination, they all stood facing in the same direction. My friend didn't paint subjects like Saint Ursula and the Virgins. He was far from doing so. He painted friends and family members, though the way he painted them they seemed to have a kind of innocence, even a blank and optimistic spirituality that might be associated with the looks on the faces of the Carpaccio girls. That is, if anyone had ever wanted to make that connection. I can see eleven thousand of them—Jimmys, Johns, Annes, Lizzies, Katies—all shining with blankness and enthusiasm in a boat. Not on their way to martyrdom, but there, posing, on their way somewhere, even if only into paint.

CITIZENS

One cloud had gone away, and then another. Pretty soon the sky was a clear light blue. No, there is still one tiny cloud left there, toward the horizon. Dominick was sitting down staring at his shoes. They were big army shoes with dried mud on them. He was trying to remember the words to a song he had sung when he was fourteen. No use, though. The words wouldn't come. Dominick was eighteen and had nothing to do today. He stood up, feeling the ache in the back of his knees, and walked toward the Siracusa town line. In ancient times, Siracusa like other Greek cities had not been a closed-in place. You could be a citizen of Siracusa, a Siracusan, if you lived twenty miles from the center of the city. Whoever came into Siracusa to vote was a citizen of Siracusa. Walled cities were a later invention or the invention of different civilizations. Like Athens, like Sparta, like Corinth, Siracusa as a political unit was not geographically confined. It hardly remembered being Greek now. It remembered and it did not. There were fragments of walls and a fountain, the Fountain of Arethusa, which was actually Greek water with around it an Italian low wall. And there was a tablet made and incised in twentieth-century Sicily to explain what the "Fountain" was. By now, Dominick was pretty close to the fountain. When he got there he again sat down. He traced figures in the dust with his right forefinger. This good-looking tall indolent boy was the favorite of his mother, among her eleven children. Dominick threw a pebble at a bird but he egregiously missed. The pebble hit a wall and the bird went rapidly off. West of there, about five streets away, was a balcony surrounded by fence wire on which an idiot or at least someone out of control of her life was moving back and forth, able to take the air in safety because of the wire. This unfortunate, fenced-in girl was Dominick's second cousin, Lucìa Caranotti. Her condition, in Siracusa, was believed to be untreatable, without cure.

POLENTA

He really loved the polenta, and so did his friend. Next to it, on each plate, was rabbit. Wild boar sauce was on the large flat noodles three-fourths of the way up the hill in a smaller town. It was also on the broad flat noodles in a small tabaccherìa-contrattorìa seemingly hung between two peaks of mountains, farther south. When the four terrible-looking men walked in, another friend of his had said (and how the wind was blowing—you'd think the whole place was going to come unattached and blow off), I hope we're in an Italian movie and not in an American one. If we're in an American one, we're really in trouble. The first polenta preceded an opera, and the female singer was a wonderful new star. She was going to be a star. Now she was first being recognized as a potentially great singer. She too ate polenta and was indifferent most of the time to her own eyes, mouth, and breasts. The first friend didn't meet her, and it would have been nothing if he had. In her career she was too busy. Well, it might have been something. You never can tell one hundred percent. The cold wind blows and the people want polenta. She moves among the chairs onstage, almost breaking them, waving her arms, head thrown back, she is singing. Afterward she is alone and in tears. That would have been his moment to come there. But he was in a restaurant, having some polenta in order to taste a certain wine. Heavy, a little heavy, but good. They went to see the opera the next evening. And they talked, they were so delighted with it, in the car, all the way home, and ever further on into the night.

THE TANGO PALACES

I am going with my wife tonight to the Tango Palace! There were five "tango palaces" in Beijing. These were large roomy spaces in the enormous underground network of air-raid shelters built to protect the populace from nuclear war. Abandoned now, they constituted, burrowed under the crowded city of Beijing, a good deal of almost livable space. There was, however, a limited supply of air. And it was cold and damp, inconvenient for shopping and for other aspects of normal community life. It was true that certain things could be stored down there, and certain things were. There were problems, though, of rust and rot. It was no place for a zoo! Unappetizing for restaurants, as well. The dampness, the lack of air and, too, the lack of light made the shelters a problem to use. For dancing, however, they were all right. The snapping sultry sounds of a tango poured out into the dusty Beijing air. The government had come to a decision that was rather amusing, if sometimes hard to understand. Might not there be the risk of being questioned, or even arrested, while trapped there underground? This didn't happen though. Hao Guang and Ming Pei and the others there with them simply danced. There was enough air, with a nearby entrance left open, for two hundred couples to dance for several hours. After that, they had to leave.

It should be explained that in China, "tango" is a more or less generic name for a relatively slow and in-each-others-arms (up to a point) dance. Some of the music played in the palaces was actually tango, but most not. The word "palace" is also used oddly, to designate a special place of instruction. Special after-school arts schools for children, for example, are called "children's palaces." For a reason known only to some part of the government, after twelve months the tango palaces were closed. The "ten entrances," as the passageways down into the shelters were called, were sealed up. For a while on Saturday nights guards stood at them, guiding people away. No more dancing. It's finished; the air-raid shelters are closed. Hao Guang came past with his wife, dressed and ready, after their one-hour bicycle trip, to dance, only to find such a guard. News of the closing had been in the paper, but in a note on the back page they hadn't seen.

Eight years later, the inhabitants of Beijing were told to get rid of their dogs. This, for most, meant killing them, since very few had relatives or friends in the countryside to whom a dog could be sent. The dogs, the government held, had to be eliminated because there was a shortage of food. With the people on strict rations, it was ridiculous for the dogs to be consuming meat or even rice. So every dog in Beijing, except for a lucky few was killed. The most humane method of killing the dogs was by injection but for many the serum was difficult to get, so dogs were drowned or shot. Some had their throats cut.

This might have been a good time to revive the tango palaces. Though the practical-minded Beijingese are not sentimental about pets as many Western people are, still there was sorrow in many houses. Dancing could have been a pleasant distraction.

The reopening of the palaces was possible. The gas emanations that had been detected in them were a problem that could be solved. Bringing the dogs back to life, of course, was not possible, though starting a new dog population was. Neither policy, however, changed.

PLACEBO

There is a pharmacy in downtown Beijing that sells, among other products, deer-horn powder, promoter of longevity. The government leaves this establishment alone. The people who work there can sell, and the customers can buy, all the ground-up deer-horn powder they want. As for the efficacy of this remedy, no one knows. A pharmacist says, Well, a lot of people use it, and they keep coming in for it, that's a sign it's doing something, they are still active enough to walk, and they're still alive. It's true that it's hard to know if they would be also if they didn't take it. No one has tested it against a placebo. Bright blue yellow and white original-painting advertisements for products were shining on the pharmacy's walls. A customer came in for the powder—the old man, who had taught physics at Beijing University, was white-haired and just vaguely bent over. He paid for it with crumpled bills from a worn-out pocket. That night, the pharmacist assumed, he would be riding high. Much better than with a placebo! he thought. The bent old man walked home. He lived in a dark low small nineteenth-century Beijing one-storey building in the midst of many others much the same—this was good housing for Beijing—about fifteen minutes away. Once home he put the package on a table, hung up coat and cap, and pulled the shade of his one window all the way down. He went to a corner of the room and what seemed to be a box, but was actually a cage, in which a tiny toy Chihuahua was trembling. He took it out and stroked it for a while. Then, holding it gently with one hand, with the other he showed it what he had brought. The tiny creature wagged its tail. He put the dog down, got a spoon from his kitchen cabinet and put one spoonful of the powder, with some water, in a little dish. This concoction the very old, completely illegal dog lapped up, then went to sleep on the old science professor's lap.

PING-PONG

Ding Wei slaps the ball hard and it falls on the far left edge of Song Jia's side of the table. Song Jia returns it with a slice so that it lands, then spins, then scarcely rises from the table on Ding Wei's side. Ding Wei lunges for it and just manages to lift it up so that it goes above the tiny low green net, but Song Jia is there to smash it, into sports oblivion this time, and the point is his. What you want to happen may happen but may not happen often enough. If you win, you will go to America. If you lose, you will stay right here. Life will be hard, but you will live. There are the pleasures of family. But for excitement, for travel, and for your country, it will be far superior for you to win. Ding Wei and Song Jia know this but only one of them can win. This is the last day of the Shanghai Divisional O Yun Dong Hui. Ding Wei holds the ball in his left hand. He is ready to serve. After the game, Song Jia goes out to walk along the Huangpu River. The night air is soft. In the river's surface the shining lights are like his shots—that white light there traveling to a black water wall, and this light, light white one, hung in the middle of a wave. He plays the last game over in his mind. Ding Wei also thinks of it. The difference from their last match, which he had lost, was so slight. As if physically moved by this thinking, he gets on the plane.

A SONG OF PARTING,
OR ZHAO FAN AND I
IN THE CAPITAL (BEIJING)

The furniture parts of the market were hard to go around—you had to face right into them like furniture yourself. No one here but fur/Niture allowed! their song seemed to be. Later, after a narrow ride, there are very cheap dumplings on the Forbidden City outside. It is astounding how little there is to do, so Zhao Fan and I decide we'll go visit some old house or houses in an unknown-to-us quarter in fact maybe doesn't exist. Get this, we're sitting in this box on wheels and a bicyclist is pedaling us around. This's called a bikeshaw or something like that it's passing

> Extremely quickly
> If it is still
> Here/there at all
> Whoomf! it's vanished
> And now a bird call
> And it comes back
> Such is fate

I remember when I used to think I had fate. Now two chances in ten of dying, one and one-third of going insane, one tenth of one percent of going blind, and so on. It no longer seems like fate. My destiny is done. Here's what happened: I wanted to be a ball player. I wanted to be a cartoonist, like the person who drew Maggie and Jiggs or Skeezix. I wanted to be a Poet. Then why my homodiecidigithrop are yez now writing the prose? I can't help it. I am a poet and something in me cried out: Prose. Write fiction! Go to China! Eat sleep! How can one eat sleep? Zhao Fan is wearing a thick brocaded dress. Snow falls on the Forbidden City, as on the market. No one expected that.

THE LONG MARCH

On the long march, Wang Chuli said, during our rest periods, we read Whitman to each other. Which passages? I asked. Oh, I don't remember. Some of them are very grand. I tried to imagine exhausted impassioned aching goal-driven soldiers reading (or listening to) "I am he that walks with the tender and growing night," etc. Well, possibly. But I would like some verification. As to my getting on the plane and thus out of Kunming, "It depends on the weather," the agent said. "If it is over sixty-seven degrees we cannot accommodate you. If it is under that degree, we possibly can." I don't comprehendo. In the plane there is an expansion when it is hot, and it can take on fewer pounds.

In the few days before the plane would leave, I was with Xiao (Young) Li and the American girl, in the southwestern Chinese weather. The Green Lake Hotel lay all about me like a novella by Henry James but with one important exception—as far as my glance might reach, I could see no aristocrats. The Minority Nationality Girl, quite attractive, was no exception. Like the panda, even when at home— here my thoughts were interrupted by an arrival of Chinese friends.

They came, in an organized way, as a group. I myself had always cultivated a gift for aimless lonely wandering that gave no more pleasure than it gave pain, it gave a little of both; for aimless lonely wandering one had no one to blame but oneself. One couldn't say, If only it weren't for this damned delegation! Or Long March. I like the name Long March, as I should have liked, I thought, the name Big Breakfast or Endless Bath. But already my friends were in the lobby, looking for me. I was right there. Hello! What's up? I looked at my watch.

We've been sent to take you to the airport, Wo Lo said. Climb on the truck.

The American girl was turning into a subject for a novella—or perhaps for a poem by Gerard Manley Hopkins. Why not forget the general public altogether?

This American girl was one who, if things went right for her, would have a good influence on the world. She is passionately attached to the "environment." Not the theatre nor cosmetics nor the world of medicine or law had anything to say to her as fascinating as what was said to her by the environment.

The environment, after all, is just the place we are; it's what's around us, I said. What's so important about that?

Knowing that I was joking, she bared her teeth. You'll see, she said. You'll see. Meanwhile Xiao Li was buying, as he later described it, his first "Western" coat, a suit jacket, thready, gray, for about four dollars, on the street, in a stall. An enormous sum, really, for him, but still, a new wardrobe, at least the beginning of one.

Do you think the marchers really could have been interested in Walt Whitman? I asked the girl (Louise Farnham). Louise was nineteen years old and Xiao Li was surprised we weren't married since we spent so much time together talking. It is not Chinese but strange, he said. I would have thought it stranger for us to be married. I was fifty-nine years old, living with someone else, and didn't find Louise attractive enough to make me want to change my life so as to spend it with her. She was pleasant enough to talk to, but there was not, I thought, any prospect, even, of the "admiring excitement of union" (Auden's phrase). I seemed to get more of that from wandering around and being alone.

What a joy, though, sometimes, to talk to somebody! As Ruetta said to Bodge in Paris, At last! somebody from New York! Or one panda sees another one on the beach (improbable). Could the Chinese marchers have seen Whitman that way? How should company be cultivated? Good-bye! (to the group) I am on the plane. The true subject of the novella: people being together and being alone amidst the "environment." The plane starts moving. We're in the air.

THE GUIDE

My husband wants me to take the veil. No, I don't think it would interfere with my work. There are some women guides who do it. However, I don't feel ready for it yet. Maybe someday I will. Probably I will. She spent all the day or most of the day talking about Horus and Hathor and Anubis. The lotus is the symbol of the South and the papyrus of the North. Nervousness is nothing to her. She seemed a complete stranger to embarrassment. Her lips were quite red and her mouth invitingly pursed up into a shape suggesting readiness for a kiss. This was not inviting, though, to Trakl. He simply regarded her in a theoretical sort of fashion as "attractive." Her manner of speaking he compared to the clucking of a chicken. In her English, everything had the same intonation. Because of this lack of, or mistaken, emphasis, no one learned anything at all from her about Egypt's past. How deep do her thoughts go on the subject of taking the veil, of becoming a more devout and traditional Muslim? Trakl was thinking this while the young woman guide Aneha was looking at him sideways and at all the rest of the group. They seemed to her no better than animals. She didn't like animals. These people lacked Egyptian good humor and other attractive qualities. I am longing not for my children and not for my Egyptian husband but so much simply to be walking by the sea. Anyway, away from this river, this fateful long river that goes through the sand. She wanted some rest. She did not want to wake up in bed with Trakl, and she never did. Life was not long enough for that.

STUCK

Downstairs the children were very busy on the machines, looms they were, they were six and seven and eight to ten years old, boys and girls, weaving; their results were placemats dresses and rugs. Mostly rugs. Their little fingers popped around the looms with considerable skill. Their faces and eyes were nervous as they turned around. The money was stuck to the pockets of the American crowd, as if velcroed to their thighs' clothed walls. To give was to condone the enterprise. This enterprise seemed in no way laudable. It was announced, very improbably, that doing this work, the children made money that would enable them to go to school. Abdullah Ragui was one of these children, nine years old. Across the river (the Nile—there weren't many others) small figures of men, women, and animals were performing tasks necessary for survival. None had—or could be seen to have—a skill like Abdullah Ragui's. Ptit ptit ptit ptat ptatt! her fingers raced across the loom. There were no answers to the questions the tourists had. Some bought rugs, to bridge the gap. The act left responsibility for being kind to the children to the men who sold the rugs. They would give the children money or they would not. Certainly, Doctor Peterson thought, if they gave it, they wouldn't share it but only give them a little bit. If I, though, give this child (Abdullah) a lot—he imagined a man taking it from her forcibly, hurting her little hand. He thought, We are stuck, and these children are stuck. Even the awful (probably) men who sell the rugs are stuck, and there is no good my trying to get out of it by not giving money to a child. He gave a few dollars to Abdullah. Thank you, she said, and went back feverishly, going faster than ever, to her task, as if such violent energy were what had brought the gift about.

LUXOR

I burst into tears when I saw the Temple of Luxor. My woman friend and I had been quarreling; throughout this brief but difficult trip we had a very hard time. We were to break up within a month. More precisely, she would leave me. I would alternately love her and detest her. I would fall down on the floor and cry. These would be hard cries. But now I was in Luxor, on a trip to Egypt, and I had no idea that any of this would happen. Then why did I cry? Why, when I looked the first time at those soaring columns, and then quickly looked again, as if to verify that the cause was there, did I burst, collapse, into bitter and almost uncontrollable tears? Something weighed down on me. Don't boss me around, she said. I had said, too many times, on the boat, Don't drink the water. As this kind of problem shows, I was too old for her. I was probably too old for her. Luxor, not too old for me, was electrifying in its presence. The temple was just old, and just repaired, enough. I certainly didn't identify myself with the temple. Nor was it like my friend, though in a way it reminded me of her legs. I admired the simultaneous shapeliness and solidity of those legs. Sometimes, she put one over me in the morning to help me to sleep when I would wake up too early. It made my anxiety go away. So did Luxor—by being so grand, so beautiful, and such a relief from the waste of the rest of that trip.

DEAD

 Tet, Hathor, and Osiris were getting ready to welcome a newcomer to the Land of the Dead.

Big temple was there but it was useless. No one lived in it. It was still there for the purpose of what was left of the Dead.

After three thousand years can you feel sorry for the dead? You feel perhaps a little shiver, and that's that. But they have been dead for such a long time that you think, well, after all they are really genuinely dead. One doesn't have to worry about them so much.

Docrow stubbed his toe on an unseen step hidden by sand at the Temple of Osiris-Pik. Ouch ouch! he lay down bending his right ankle, the one with the painful toe, in his hand. Oooh, damn it!

He wasn't dead. One doesn't die from a stubbed toe. Maybe, though, a scorpion had bitten him.

He dreamed he was walking along a dusty white road with a bird-headed individual. He dreamed of being ferried across a river on a boat as he lay flat on his back and wrapped up in cloth. He dreamed of being welcomed by animal-headed people, being gestured to, being handed an ivory staff.

Hathor was dressed in blue silks to receive him. She had the shoulders and the body of a woman but the head of a cow. She was beautiful.

She was Marie-Christine, the woman he had seen on the tourist boat earlier in the day, crossing from the West (Land of the Dead) bank of the Nile to the East (Land of the Living).

The pilot of that boat was Tet. The man who went about taking people's tickets was Osiris.

He himself, Docrow, wore a wrinkled white shirt. It was barely presentable. Now, however, he was dressed in gold. He solemnly received the gods' greetings and never for the rest of time did anything else.

ON FOUR CONTINENTS
(SIX STORIES)

IN WEED

The shutters were open, so you could see out of the dance hall
There was mountain outside. Also the door was open. There was
an almost chilly breeze.

The name of this place was Weed, California. That was actually
its name, Weed.

She looked very beautiful. He looked wrinkled but fit. He was a
soldier. She lived near there.

Of course, they never saw each other again.

Her hand held his as if each hand were a small animal, when
they walked across the floor.

Goodnight!

LOSING

Of course! he thought, dissatisfied with Alice. I'd love to have this
evening. I'd be much happier alone. And forever, too. Not just now.
Eventually I'll find someone better for me than she is. In fact, once
cut Alice loose from him and he is desolate, despairing, off the
walls. No wallpaper, no net, no ring of fire can hold him. He must
have Alice back. All modern technology (telephone, etc.) was at his
service but he would never get her back. He had made his characteristic mistake. Alice was totally unaware of this kind of error. She

put on her black coat and was crying, crying bitterly at being unloved. In her calm way, then, eventually, she found someone else. Let humanity beware!

PHOTOGRAPHERS NEAR THE RAIN FOREST

Snap! He took her picture standing in a doorway. Snap! near a car parked by the curb.

Snap beneath a plane tree. Snap snap two in the place where they stopped to have a drink.

I'd like one cappuccino, she said. And he said, Just a Brazilian coffee.

IN AFRICA

After the market the sunlight hit their faces as they gradually worked their way inside the shadowing garden doors of the hotel.

His foot was in the door-turn when she went in.

Can you spend the night?

What would we do all night?

Who built this hotel?

UNAWARE OF THE DROUGHT
(after some lines by Wallace Stevens)

During this great hot spell it's impossible to get coffee, it makes the café too hot. Cold drinks are almost impossible to find. People hoard beer, soda, bottled water. Only here and there, an old sailor, drunk and asleep in his boots, wakes up with a terrible thirst and takes it for granted.

A LIFE OF ROSSINI

Rossini woke from a deep slumber and began to play the piano. I've got it! he cried. Bravo! Bravo! The wheat withers in the fields. A baby is crying. Of what use to us, after the opera is over, is Rossini? They heard scraps of Rossini's music everywhere. Springtime had come into its own. Despite everything, the child cried a little less. At the Teatro San Carlo they had the impression, known to be false, that time had just begun.

TO THE RED CROSS

Sitting by the Willimantic River, his idea and hers, she shows him her Notebook which is full of "sayings," quotations Betty's copied down from poetry, about nature and even more about love. How corny is it, he thinks—how much I love her! He didn't exactly love her. High in the hills of Saipan, she let him take the jeep, he took her hand. Betty if we were— Yes, I know, she said, someplace else. He was an enlisted man and she of an order (the Red Cross) that was reserved, so far as socializing went, for officers. A mere private, such as he was, had no right to place his hand on her arm. She had a romantic sentimental however you want to call it maybe even melodramatic philosophizing attitude about life, which was one of the things that led her to join the Red Cross. He felt adventurous and ambitious at the same time. I have to leave tomorrow. Can you come to New York? I hope so—I don't know. The Red Cross was lucky to have had her for a few years, though the same could not be said of the army's having had him. She, two years older than he, was in a way of forever being a mother. A woman of twenty-four. Summer's coolness, her phrase book, and the light-reflecting trees!

OVER

Every day, near lunchtime, the small planes flew over and dropped explosives. No sooner had the men of the Third Platoon, Second Company, Third Regiment, of the Ninety-Sixth Infantry Division started opening their cans of food—carrotflake and beefcake—that was keeping them alive, than the zooming would be heard and soon, overhead, there were planes. Mouths anticipating eating, or already begun, the men dived into trenches. It was, luckily for the infantry, without fatality or even injury that these raids took place. One beautiful cloudless day, the planes didn't come. Not the next day, either, nor the day after that. After a while, the men got used to a quiet lunch. Then the company moved on; they had occupied this first position for fifteen days. Later, the planes came back to drop not bombs but pamphlets telling Americans to end the war. Like their other missions, this one was without result—in this case, the company wasn't there. Thirty years later, a man from this company and one of the pilots sat facing each other across a large oak table. They were drinking, looking around, and talking about electronic chips, as were the others at the table. Just as lunch began to be served, a violent noise came from the ceiling. On the floor above, someone, or something, had knocked over a pile of stacked-up chairs. "My God! A lunchraid!" Hirschenson cried, and Kanamaka, astonished, knew what he meant.

SURRENDER

His heart beat furiously as he walked back and forth, trying to work out a scheme to keep his wife from going out. He wanted to keep her in the house.

He had been a colonel in the tank corps. He was frightening and stern. Orders from Supreme Command, his orderly said. He went to the military field phone. Mmmmmmm.

That was when Ivan surrendered his regiment. It snowed. He couldn't follow the order to go around and attack from the side because he knew that his entire regiment would be killed. He didn't surrender to save himself but to save his men. There was a principle. He felt he was right. Yet surrendering is always dubious, giving bad feelings because it gives you good feelings about those you hate. They put him to work in a factory in Germany and there he met her, his wife—she had been captured on the Russian front—and married her. After the war, they came to America. He was only twenty years older than she was, but sometimes it seemed like much more. He had some very old ideas about how a man and a woman should behave.

Ivan didn't learn English, he wanted things to be the same. Ekaterina had a dream that she was rescued from a blazing building and she walked forth from it into a field full of tall green grass and blue and red flowers. Ivan said, Mmmmhmmm; and she said, No, not tonight. He would have surrendered, he thought, his regiment to her, again and again. But it was too late.

From the porch where he was walking back and forth, he saw the bus. There was Ekaterina! His heart almost stopped, though he was a strong man. The bus stopped. He was running, but he couldn't reach it. The young woman, about twenty-nine, got in. Beautiful New Jersey spring day of yellows and lilacs, with stone-and-muddy streets. Hard breathing. He saw, as he reached the bus, which was leaving, and she gazed out the window, that it wasn't his wife at all, but a young American woman, who was shorter and had a slightly different chin.

AFTERWARDS

Did I ever really think of Ekaterina? he thought. Of her happiness in and for herself? Meeting again after thirteen years, they went to a baseball game. She had gained not much but a little weight, and her face no longer had quite that angle of beauty that had cut him like a knife. Never in his life had he been so happy, nor so bloody. He walked through New York like a wound. She had entered into his system (bones, nerves, blood vessels, arteries, brain) like a necessity, and death and time were the only necessities that could drive her out. He felt now a touch of that old electricity, a spring day after many cold nights, and he stared at the stone seatway beneath him and at the yellow railings above it and at the backs and the hair and the caps of the persons seated in front of him and thought he understood what it had all been about. "You may visit, like Turgenev, on our porch, and see her, or you can stop seeing her entirely," her husband said. "You may choose either of these ways. But you may not make love to my wife, or else you'll die." Fair enough!

A FLORIDA BREEZE

Well, Lennie, he said. He felt awkward and cool. She felt, as she did often in these early days of her pregnancy, nauseated. She did not say, "I feel nauseous." Lennie had learned English as a child, learned it just about perfectly. Her native tongue was Yiddish.

Hobhouse was Jewish on his mother's side and half-Jewish on his father's. The non-Jewish half of his father's was where the name Hobhouse came from.

Hobhouse admired Lennie's intelligence and her petite qualities.

They were, however, in the midst of a crisis now. Lennie's parents were urgently pressing her to name the child Schnerdel if it was a boy, and Schnerdelin if it was a girl.

Hobhouse thought these names absurd and said so.

Then I won't have a baby, Lennie said.

What? said Hobhouse. He couldn't believe it. This was a totally exaggerated and ridiculous threat.

Don't you figure they'll be upset if you don't have the baby?

No, not really, Lennie said. Not having a baby may be disguised as a quirk of fate, but not giving it the name my parents want can hardly be masked as an accident.

If you don't have the baby, you'll never see me again.

It will be a boy, said Lennie, and it will be like you and I will have it and hold it and know that you are never gone from me entirely.

You mean if I leave you'd go ahead and have the son?

Yes, and I'll name it Schnerdel.

But I only said I'd leave if you didn't have the child!

I won't have it if I can't name it Schnerdel, she said.

Then, he said, you'll be alone.

When will you leave? she asked.

Well, obviously not until you make it impossible for the child to be born.

You're in as much of a hurry as that? she cried. To murder your son?

No, not that at all, he said, not knowing and by this time not really caring if he was winning or losing, I want you to *have* the child. Agh! Name it Schnerdel if you want to. But what a terrible name! How would you like to be sitting in a classroom and have the teacher call out your name Schnerdel.

Mine would be Schnerdelin, Lennie said.

Hobhouse thought he might be going crazy. But aren't you glad it's not? he said.

Listen, Lennie, he said. Isn't this *our* baby. Don't we have the right to name it what we want?

She said, I want to name it Schnerdel (or Schnerdelin).

Lennie, he said, don't you think you and I should *agree* on the name of our child?

Yes, of course I do, and I don't know why you won't, she said.

Lennie and Hobhouse were in the "Florida room" of their recently purchased home in Coral Gables. A child named Schnerdel or Schnerdelin in Coral Gables would have a severe handicap. Actually, almost any place English was spoken, but especially in the United States, Schnerdel or Schnerdelin would be a disadvantageous name. To help parents realize this, the Schnerdelin truck will go around. Each Coral Gables (and then other cities) neighborhood will be visited by a sound truck that blasts out various children's names: Kenneth, Anthony, Bruce, Edgar, Samuel, Emily, Ruth, Channukah, and Elizabeth, for example. Then the voice will say, Compare these relatively "normal" names to such a name as Schnerdel, or Schnerdelin. Why would any parent be so cruel as to give a child a name like that?

Lennie looked concerned. Hob was behaving oddly. What, what did you say? she said. She had heard him mumble something, but it didn't seem to be to her.

For a moment, he'd been asleep—oh!

I'm sorry, Hobhouse said. I guess I went to sleep. Listen, he said, Lennie, do what you want, but the truck was right—Schnerdel or Schnerdelin would be a mistake!

Wait! Lennie said. What truck?

I saw it, Hobhouse said, standing up. His white linen trousers, his white shoes, his white cotton shirt. He was wavering. Lennie felt concerned.

I guess, he said, Hobhouse is a funny name, too. Lennie is not so great, Lennie said. Maybe, though, Hobhouse said, we can do better for our child.

On what? Lennie said.

Sneddle, Hobhouse said—he was starting to drift off into a dream again, he could feel it, it made him a little afraid. Lennie, I have to get some rest.

We'll talk about it tomorrow, Lennie said.

No, Hobhouse said. Or well yes all right. But about this one thing I'm clear. Sneddle. How would that be as a compromise? You can pronounce it however you want when your parents are around.

And for the girl? Lennie said.

Sneddelin, said Hob.

Do you really think that's better? Lennie asked. Sneddle, Schnerdel, what's the difference?

There's a difference to me, Hobhouse said. He felt his lack of complete Jewishness was making him clear—or unclear.

Lennie was smiling. Of course we can give it (girl or boy) a middle name too—maybe even (she hesitated as if she might be violating a sacrament) even John, or Jane. He reached out his arms to her but she was against him before that. Oh Hobhouse, I thought we were really going to lose it! What? he exclaimed. "Sneddle John Weismuller," she said.

LIVING IN THE SUN

Terence was a painter. He said he wanted to be a black iris—whatever that meant. By sunset he was often drunk. He threw a glass of beer at me, that's how I met him. He was sitting in the Aga Rheion Café with a beer beside him, and drawing. He said he threw it because I looked pretentious. He also must have known I wouldn't retaliate, and that if I had, he could have gone into an act, of being drunken, helpless, insane. I was, on the contrary, interested and pleased that a beer was heading for me: I felt lonely. My wife and daughter were there, but we had, up till that moment, made no connection with anyone else. This drunkenness of Terence (to which I owed our friendship), if it started in the afternoon, usually lasted till ten or eleven, when those who can stand the thought of getting into it are beginning to think of bed. At this time of night Terence slightly perked up. He talked and talked, sometimes at his very best, making it harder for anyone to leave him—which may have been an unconscious (?) purpose of his being, at this hour, so entertaining, so loquacious. For those who knew him and liked him, Terence's drunkenness was as essential a part of life there as the sea, the tar, the broken glass, the tiny white chapel built to the Virgin by a sailor, the cliffs, the dry fig trees, the idea of going to Mandraki to drink ouzo and eat fish. "Let's Rilk," Terence said. That's fine with me. To "Rilk" was to respond in an exaggeratedly oversensitive way, as Terence believed Rilke did, to everything. Oh the unerring orchidism of the waves! Terence cried. Oh, help, hic! Terence said. I'm Rilking again! He also had considerable disdain for the French. Oh, vraiment, Terence said. Quel snobisme per-pét-u-el!

Tant pis! he groaned. And Je suis désolé. The French language he considered an affront and everyone who spoke it was a fink. Blooulp! Terence said. Let me introduce you to Margaret. She is a real black iris, aren't you Margaret? Ah, what? Margaret said. She was a nice young woman. When Terence was sober (I more often saw him this way years later, in New York, before he died), he was a little bit dry and wistful, brittle almost, like paper that has gotten wet and then was very vigorously dried out by too much heat. Underneath this dry plainness, though, Terence was crazy. With alcohol he was able to leap over the dry phase into the exalted, funny one. The island, Hydra, was sort of a hospital, at least for a while. Life there was relatively undangerous and had simple, regular lines. Finally, though, it simply didn't have the necessary equipment. Booze, boys, friends, octo-bits, Monsieur Oui-Oui's Restaurant, the non-electricity, the art school on the cliff, the non-doctors, the water shortage, Leonard, Arnold, the woman who came down to the harbor after seventy years, these weren't enough. Terence went back to New York. He was in the hospital and he painted. After six months he left, but they still have some of his paintings hanging up there. Apparently, by law, they belong to the hospital. When Terence was young, in his twenties, he was, I had heard, very beautiful. You could see it in him still, his beauty, and it was probably one of the reasons that certain people (the ones I knew about were women) became so unswervingly attached to him. He was very talented, too, and very smart. All of this he was always giving—if not throwing—away. In the heat of Hydra, in July, the sun was like a mallet and there was no way to work between lunch and the cool of late afternoon. Terence, though, sitting at a table in front of Monsieur Oui-Oui's, is working, with ink and pastels. A Pierrot head and a broad neck lead down to a rectangle in which are the names of three Ohio towns: Toledo, Akron, and Dayton. To the left of and somewhat below this, little pastel-colored balls (of chalk and smoke) emerge from the top of a head with a smudged green face. And to the right an ink-and-white ballerina points one toe down to his printed (I arrive just in time to see him sign it, or maybe he signs it because now I'm there) name, TERENCE.

SONGS OF THE AEGEAN

Black is the cover of my true love's hair. Stoffard sang as he went out in the boat. The black was a yarmulke. Stoffard was a comedian. This was his idea of a joke, a Jewish version of an English folk song. For him his warm wit blotted out all his troubles and even the sky. It was in Greece—it may have been only the deep imagined complications of the Greek past that made the simple silly joke have a purity and a clarity that it couldn't have had any place else. A big ship went by, far enough away not to be a danger. A dog was curled up on the shore. Helen smiled but didn't laugh as Stoffard sang the song. She had heard it just an hour before, when Stoffard invented it. Black is the cover. The salt water leaped up as Helen looked over. And Stoffard was standing up, she's afraid it may turn over, and he is singing a song. He places his one hand on the boat's side nervously, feeling a little splinter stick and says, God this is a terrific day. Helen, Helen, don't you like it. Smile! Tell me you do! Helen smiled as the sun hit her face. Now he is rowing, and the boat leaps away. "Black is the cover." "And so we'll go no more a-roving" had been sung there before. And "Kale Khios," by the Greek sailors. And, long before that, "Kore" and "Rododaktolos Eos—O Oinops Pontos."

CHRISTINE AND THE DOCTOR

Christine was fifteen going on sixteen, and, distressed that she had a little wart on her hand, she had a tendency to keep it out of handclasps with those to whom she was attracted. Her mother had married a second time; her stepfather was Robert Lindt, of San Clemente, California. Her mother, now Mrs. Lindt, was the former Barbara McLennon. Christine had brownish-blonde hair, which she wore long, and an alluring sideways look of her eyes. Dr. Motson asked Christine where she was going, and she said, "Over there." Over there was a place where you could hear the drums. Christine is walking along happily, when suddenly in her path there is a snake. A snake can go anywhere it wants. It is like a whole chess set in itself. It can go sideways, forward, backward, curving, and up; it can spiral, it can slip down like a sleeve; and it can strike like a hand-grenade and a clock. Christine was frightened. She ran back the white dusty road to the café where the doctor was drinking a cup of tea. What, Christine, what's wrong? said Dr. Motson. Oh well, there's a snake that's after me, Christine said. Motson went out on the road, leaving his teacup in its saucer on the tabletop beside which Christine stood, and looked around. He looked up then down the road. Down it he saw a smallish disappearing splat! as if a wire being pulled by an electrical contractor. Put that circuit over there! It was the snake. The snake was now going somewhere else. It did not, or perhaps, could not, distinguish Christine from anyone else, although there was a chance that it knew she was a human. Motson came back to find Christine had sat down. She was smoking a cigarette. The doctor wiped off his brow. Do your parents allow you to do that? he asked. He said, I did see the snake and he's gone. No, Christine said; and Well thank you I was scared, but now I think I'm going to walk a different way. That night in the restaurant Christine told her parents that she had seen Dr. Motson. Dr. Motson? Where were you walking that you saw him? her stepfather said. Oh, out that way, said Christine, pointing, she didn't know the names of the streets in this town. He saved me from a snake. Her mother also still had rather long hair. She had a shrimp on a fork, and a white silk blouse. Tell us the story, she said.

AFTER THE ELISIR

Complimenti, the tall good-looking young man said. Maestro, complimenti. Thanks, grazie, answered the maestro. Followed a brief conversation in Italian. The young man turned to his friend. Est-ce que vous parlez italien? No, only English and français said the lumplike but equally tall young man in a black suit standing there also. He says (the maestro, that is) you look Italian. I take that as a great compliment, the lumplike young man said. He was making lots of money. The tall, good-looking one seems a little weak, something of a toady. Meanwhile, quickly, the two tall young men had gone. My daughter, Graziana and I were alone with the maestro. This was the moment that no one had been waiting for. The maestro's mother just before had been whisked off to see the Star, in his dressing room above. The maestro was permanently married. When we went out into the corridor, Graziana, I noticed, was looking, but aside from a long radiator, there was nothing much to see. She is puzzled by opera. She doesn't know exactly what its great appeal for her is. But it is certainly appealing; it is sometimes overwhelming, like a fireworks display in the heart. Directing it, the maestro said, was *divertente*, full of adventures. The Star, who is over fifty, had considerable fear of losing his voice. The maestro's mother is eighty-two. She has a somewhat frail presence but a very commanding voice, especially on the telephone. The maestro is unable to prevent her from following him to his performances all over the world. The Lump and the Goodlook (Toady) have the American rights to the work. Many of the artists, including the Star, whom the maestro's mother had just gone up to meet, are under long-time contract to their firm.

THE INTERPRETATION OF DREAMS

The small bird's wings on the bare tree had in the uneven sunlight the look of wood chips. This brought back a memory. He was standing in a park. In his hand he held a long thin bean. Inside it there were kernel-like or pea-like things encased in goo and stickiness. He knew they were not meant to eat. He had a dream about this park, in which he found the beans, that reminded him of Marina. She had been gone for twenty years. In the dream she was someone else. She was also a boy, named Keekle. He ran to his house, it was really a collection of little houses around a court but the buildings were connected. He ran very very fast. I'm lost, he thought. The collie was big and fluffy. The dog's name was Stizzy, pronounced Stitzy. His hair was always coming off on the furniture. He found time to look at the collie but Marina did not. Proposed they go to the opera or the theatre. Our life is dramatic enough, said Marina. I don't see how it could be any more dramatic than it is. Who needs the theatre? In Paris the snow is falling outside his rue de Fleurus hotel. He has never seen Marina, and won't for another four years. The apartment is dark and there is snow out. A friend calls him on the phone. When will we see you? Life is going by so fast. Stizzy has not come home. He phoned Marina. The operator said there was no such number. Marina, he thought, is crossing her slim legs now in Boston or in Los Angeles or wherever she has gone to live. Her thin dress. The earrings I bought for her at the fruit store that spread out its goods on the sidewalk. Wearing a nightgown, she came to his bedside and said, "Why?" There were long corridors open and latticed to the night air. There were dredgings, upheavals, transportings, roarings of the sea. Curtains flew. He was unable to answer, because he didn't know why. Why things had to be the way they were. Why his life with Marina remained only a possibility, a set, or a foreground. Why he had never imagined it as anything else. Why? Why? Marina (the dream image of Marina) said. Keekle ran in and Marina wasn't there any more. He knew a foolish mistake was thinking that Keekle was as important as Marina, that his dreams were as important as what really happened. What knowing Marina excited in him, most deeply of all, was his childhood. A new wave of freshness, of absolute springtime, broke over his eyelashes like hail. He stood in the park with the bean. It was reddish black and had more or less the shape of a wisteria seedpod. It had an acrid smell. He knew that there were certain things in nature that you were never supposed to eat, even to raise to your lips. Tucking it under its wing, his love relationship with Marina had soared off, like the swan that it wasn't, with his childhood as it was only once, or maybe five thousand times, he could no longer tell, since it was really gone.

THE LAW

 Are we allowed to do this? he said.

She was tied up almost in a knot on their bed.

She was smiling. No, she said. I don't think so.

He said, Why are we allowed to do this? Why isn't it against the law?

He spoke about the law as if he expected someone, or some force, to be vigilant at all times, at every second of his life.

If he was looking for this, the Conscience was available, or its more dreaded unreasonable compatriot, the Superego.

Of course he enjoyed the lawlessness, the violence and the humorousness of what he was doing.

Her wrists were tied to her ankles. That was enough.

She sighed. She moaned. She said Oh! Oh! She laughed, I think it is against the law.

How could people be allowed to have so much pleasure in such a funny way?

Vavoom! She had a pleasure that almost knocked him down.

He started to untie the ropes but she: "Let's do that again!"

He said. All right. Then, Just a minute.

He walked to the wall and looked out the window at the car. It was green in the chalky October light.

"All right," he said. And she: Ymm. Hummmm.

This second time it was slower, and sweeter than, and not so violent as, the first.

Afterward, she stood up, stretched, leaning her back against the wall. "My goodness!"

IN BETWEEN

About every other day, it was an impulse she found it hard to resist, she called him up. As soon as she heard his voice answer, hello high or hello low or hello medium or sometimes a somewhat joke fake theatrical or accent hello, she hung up. She wanted to be sure he was all right and she felt that the sound of his voice could give her this information. She had left him while he was ill, she felt she had to, but her guilty feelings seemed unending. These feelings, in extreme and then more modified form, would last for years. When someone dies, there are similar feelings, and in those feelings, of guilty grief, there is no one to call. Instead, a person prays, speaks to the lost one in imagination, weeps and suddenly stops (this in some ways is like the hang-up call), may even write something down. But how can the person hope that the one who is gone will read it? Brrr-ring! It is she again, he said. Wishing. For him, this communication, that was also noncommunication, was nourishing. Actually, he didn't know if it was she or not. He couldn't, as he sat, this time silently, with the instrument in his hand, hear even a breath.

THE BABY

I can't tell you any more than that. I'm going to have a baby. Who is the father?

Well—I don't want to say. I don't think you'd get a fair idea of him from what I could say.

What does he do?

Nothing, now. I don't want to say.

Do you like all this? Do you love him?

Yes. I like having a baby. I'm very excited . . . I dreamed about it last night.

I *dreamed* about it. It talked to me, even though it was just a baby (she says *bay*-bee). It was a little girl. And she talked to me. She said something funny and made me laugh.

What did she say? Do you remember?

No. I'm trying. I wish I could. I *loved* it. Listen, I have to go. This person is here, the father, I mean, and I can't really talk now.

Write me. Please?

Six years ago she said to him, Oh, something is terrible. He asked what. She said, I have to tell you. What. I'm pregnant. Oh, he said. He was elated. He thought there had been something wrong. He'd been afraid she would go back to someone else. That's wonderful! he said. What? she said. He said, Wonderful. I love you. Do you want to have the baby and get married? What? she said. No, I can't. Listen, but I love you, too.

Six years went by, with separations, reunions, and finally some fear and some indifference—not indifference but forgetting.

This second conversation (it was between two cities) was both unbearable and bearable. Now they are both waiting for the baby to be born.

THE DRUMMER:
A OAXACA LEGEND

The Corpse was walking slowly through the fields of central Mexico. This Corpse wore a gray hat, and a black dot-dot-dot-dot smile, black dot eyes, and cotton stuck against its head sides for hair. As it walked, it was swinging its arms. It also kept turning its head. The Corpse was looking for something, that was pretty sure.

The Corpse had been walking for almost three hundred miles, from Mexico City to where it was now, this side of Oaxaca. Its walk had taken it ten and a half days. Some people say Corpses walk fast, and some say they walk slow. One thing this Corpse did, whether fast or slow, was to keep walking. It didn't slow down through towns or go to sleep at night.

The Corpse was headed for the town of Oaxaca. It had a sister who was there, who was still alive. And it wanted her to do something for it. Him, I suppose we might as well call it, since from the build of it, it seemed to be a man.

When the Corpse found his sister, she was at first very scared but then when she calmed down she agreed to do what it said. He asked her to go to the Church of the Soledad, which had a whole little part of the town that was built up into and around it, and ask the Bishop there (the priest there was a bishop) for a set of drums that the Corpse used to play on when he was a boy and he was alive, before he'd left Oaxaca to go to the center. Now, once dead, he wanted to play the drums again and he thought he would like to play those.

His sister went there and asked. Those drums had been broken for some years. The priest said, though, that he had a boy there, whom he would tell to make the Corpse a new but similar set of drums.

The boy, Paco, worked on the drums, and the days sped past. When the drums were finally ready, not the sister but the Corpse himself came to get them. It was just before the time of a service, and when the people saw him, they fainted away. The Corpse took up the drums and placed them on the altar, beside the place where the Bishop usually stood. Then the Corpse played, putting into the music all he had learned of what it was like to be dead. It made extraordinary music, and the people woke up and felt happy. The Bishop came up to the altar and stood beside the Corpse. On its other side, the people all at once noticed, there was a beautiful young woman, in white, attired and also winged like an angel, and who was also a bride. It was the Corpse's dead girlfriend, Ramona, whom he had left behind when he went to Mexico City to work in a plant.

The people listening to the amazing music realized that it was a privileged moment. When it ended, chances were, the Corpse and Ramona would return to the world of death. Even while the Corpse still drummed—it did so for ten hours—people began to beg the Bishop to find some way to save the Corpses. The Bishop himself had been hoping for the same thing, praying that it be the Lord's will. Upon being thought about so intensely, the Lord snapped into action and looked down at Oaxaca. The Lord was, after a millennia of isolation, only in the vaguest way sensitive to earthly music. But he saw that the people listening to the Corpse were happy. So he said, Yes, the Corpse—and I guess along with him Ramona—may return to life for seven years, if he so wishes. After which time I would like him to come up into heaven, to play the drums for me. It's a long time that I've been without the blessing of that kind of sound. Thank you, Lord, the Bishop said. And then, daring, But Lord, be patient. What are years to you? Let this man live twenty-eight years and the woman with him. Then take him to your breast. To my bandstand, the Lord said. Then, Yes, all right. Twenty-eight years it shall be. Whereat the Bishop turned to offer the Corpse life. But the Corpse was no longer there. A serious-faced young man of thirty-nine stood nervously at his side. Well, what? Play, the Bishop said. You have been granted life. I guess I've played enough, the former Corpse said. He embraced Ramona, and came down. The great stamina of the dead was no longer his. He grew old peacefully in Oaxaca, as did Ramona. And when twenty-eight years were up, the Lord did not take him—he was living still. Indeed the Bishop had calculated that within twenty-eight years the Lord might forget his interest in hearing Mexican drums.

The Corpse then, when by ordinary standards he was over sixty, was living beyond his appointed time. However, in the sixty years that were counted as his normal span, four of those had been spent dead. Thus there were four years that were still due him, which the Lord, being the Lord, did not forget. So that, when he was sixty-four, Javier happily died, and Ramona died with him, and at the graveyard, they being poor, there was no tombstone, but the Lord at the last minute sent one down that was in the shape of a large drum.

This story is still told in the streets and in the bodegas of Oaxaca and in the surrounding towns. In Acuitlán the Corpse is changed to the corpse of a lion, which performs acrobatic feats. And in Cuzuno, it is the corpse only of a huge pair of feet, which dance. Ramona does not figure in these two versions, but in others she is the more prominent figure. In the tiny village of Suninos, Ramona is the traveling Corpse; she comes to the almost-larger-than-the-village church of Suninos, mounts the altar, and sings. No one has ever heard such songs. The Lord is so moved by her singing that he thinks of reviving the heavenly angelic choir. Her lover, Javier, appears in this version as a minor character, as Ramona does in the first.

A MIRACLE OF SAINT BRASOS

The number of Corpses living in Oaxaca was growing. When it reached three hundred, a meeting of the Town Council was called. Something had to be done. So great a number of Corpses might change life in the town for the worse. Jobs and living space were limited. The Corpses might deprive people of both. In fact (it was persuasively argued by a prominent citizen who lived with one of the Corpses, his brother, and knew their ways) there was nothing to fear. As far as jobs went, the Corpses did kinds of work that were all their own and were in no competition with the Living. As for lodging, Corpses who didn't stay with relatives lived in ramshackle places outside town that they had built on otherwise unvalued property. Nor did the living dead encroach on Oaxaca's supply of food—they ate special dishes, composed of leftovers; and in fact one of the Corpses' main activities was gathering leftover food and repreparing it in special "Corpse" restaurants, to which other Corpses flocked every day—to Las Momias, Su Muerte, and El Skeletòn. Other Corpse occupations were playing drums, sifting through heaps of rubble, and repairing lost, wrecked, and abandoned cars. In these cars, the Corpses sometimes drove, on Sunday afternoons, in the surrounding country, large numbers of them— eight or nine—in each car; they drove slowly, said little, and looked around, grateful for their presence in the midst of life.

The Town Council meeting ended in a spirit of good feeling, but the Corpses were nervous all the same and soon after called a meeting of their own. They wished to find a way to contribute something useful to Oaxacan life. A Corpse Used-Car Lot was proposed, at which the cars that they put back together would be sold, at cost, to the Living. In this way, the citizens of Oaxaca would have an almost endless supply of inexpensive used cars, and good ones at that—the Corpses were expert mechanics. We run the risk of seeming useless, said one Corpse, Alonso Betraens; there are so many useful things that we cannot do. Corpses couldn't plant or harvest crops, couldn't serve as guides to the nearby ruins, couldn't practice medicine (who would go to a dead person to be protected from death?) or law—the dead, though not exempt from the law, were regarded as in some way outside it. We can certainly make cars, though, he said (and here all applauded); and driving in them, Oaxacans will be grateful and will sense our utility to their lives. I think it is a great proposal. The proposal was approved.

The car-sale facility was quickly set up. The Living thronged to the lot, and it seemed the Corpses couldn't make cars fast enough to satisfy the needs of Oaxacans. Esteem for the Corpses grew, and there began to be a kind of sunny happiness in their lives that had not been there before. Only a little—they were still very much second-class citizens—but something positive, nonetheless.

In April, about four months after the car sales began, the criminal saint, Brasos de Guadalajara, was in Oaxaca. He bought from the Corpses a high-roofed white De Soto from a very long time past, which had room for his robes and his halo, and spent a part of every day driving it around. Every day he did so, every day he stayed in Oaxaca, there were two or three more persons dead. It seemed evident to the people of Oaxaca that this strange Being in a corpse-car was related to, and probably the cause of, all these deaths. It should be said that Brasos's robes and halo were invisible to mortal eyes. Feeling began to turn against the Corpses. This murderer, in one of their cars, was one with them. Wasn't it most likely that he had been brought there to kill the Living and to thereby increase the number of Corpses and bring them closer to being a majority in Oaxaca? The "Cemetery Springtime" mood the selling of the cars had brought at first was now at an end, replaced by suspicion and fear, even hatred. Seated in the De los Muertes Mole Restaurant, four eminent Corpses of Oaxaca convened, urgently, to seek a solution to the problems that the man in the De Soto had caused. Reluctantly, they determined that they would have to kill him. His actions seemed not only destructive but also incomprehensible, without reason. In fact, he was there to carry out a revenge on twenty prominent Oaxacans who had behaved fraudulently in the reconstruction of Santa Maria de la Soledad, the great church that was the dearest to Saint Brasos in all Mexico. It was here he had been baptized, and here he had, at only two months old, first attempted (and miraculously, successfully!) to climb up the great stone cross on the central altar and to sing to the assembled citizens. His family moved to Guadalajara but Brasos did not forget the Soledad. Every year he had made a pilgrimage to it. Usually it was only for a day, but this time it was for longer, for as long as it took to eliminate those who had cheated on materials and labor, so that, if nothing were done, in ten or fifteen years the great sad church would collapse. Now, by the morning of the de los Muertos Mole meeting, Brasos had killed the first nineteen. The last, Homeró Gómez, Brasos did not kill immediately, but with his Saint-sense informing him that something was wrong, he instead bound him and placed him in his car, which he drove to the building of the Town Council. The four eminent Corpses, having come out of the hill-top restaurant, which was located just above the Council building, recognized the De Soto and immediately bringing automatic weapons to their shoulders began to fire on the man who came out of it. They fired two hundred rounds. The man they destroyed was not whom they suspected, but Homeró Gómez. Saint Brasos had sent him out as a decoy. With the twenty malefactors now dead, the saint was ready to enact the last part of his plan: to explain his actions to the Town Council, and to give them the money to rebuild the church. The Council were frightened, but they were convinced. By a powerful act of his will, Saint Brasos enabled them to see his halo and his robes. He gave them the money he had taken from those guilty of fraud: it was thirty-five billion pesos. Leaving the room, he once turned back. Mind you spend every peso on the church, Saint Brasos said. And mind you build it well. If you do not, I guarantee you (here he let them see his halo again) that every single one of you, and everyone else in this town, except for the women and children, will be most definitively dead. Then he left, the mission he had set for himself being accomplished. The members of the Council, believing that Brasos, along with whatever else he might be, was also an emissary of, and perhaps even a King or Divinity of the Dead, resolved not only to repair the great church but also to do everything possible to improve the status of Corpses. This meant granting them rights they hadn't had: the right to own property, and to attend school; Corpses could serve as guides to archeological sites, and if they were qualified, could even practice law. So life improved for the living dead in ways they could not have dreamed of when they made their modest decision to sell used cars. Brasos, who had himself been dead for hundreds of years, did not plan this change, though it was his miraculous behavior that brought it about.

A MAN OF THE CLOTH

 "It's odd to be dead and making cars."

"It's kind of a confusion!"

"Explain it to me."

Mrs. Wallabee is standing talking to the Corpses working in the used-car yard. "Why don't you people just enjoy your life, er, uh, death?" she stumblingly said.

"We like to make a contribution," an old Corpse said.

"It's a job," said a younger one.

"'Tis fun," said another. And then one other, "It is good to be occupied, Señora. To do the Lord's work."

This last one who spoke was a dead priest.

He still bore the uniform: high collar, etc.

"Why don't you do priest's work 'mong the dead?" quavered Miss Halberstrom, Mrs. Wallabee's "companion." Were these two lovers? the priest wondered, but it was, he knew, none of his business.

So far from him they were, norteamericanas, gringas—and the living as well. True, some day they might be dead, even among the living dead. But they would probably not be down there, down here, in Mexico.

He felt a stab of lust for Miss Halberstrom. But that, too, was inappropriate. What beautiful young woman would want a dead lover? and a priest, or ex-priest, at that?

"Well, Miss Halberstrom," he began. How did you know my name? she said. "The dead know everything." He laughed. "I saw it on your button," he said. In fact, Miss Halberstrom was wearing a large off-white plastic button that said HALBERSTROM, MISS on it. It was a badge given her to permit her entry into a soft-drink plant outside Oaxaca.

This priest was an interesting man. He was dead but seemed more full of life than anyone she had ever met.

Violet Halberstrom did not have lesbian longings and was not the companion in that sense of Mrs. Wallabee. They were merely *compagnons de route.* They had met when Mrs. Wallabee's car broke down in Albuquerque and had decided to drive down here together.

The ex-priest had scored a kind of hit with Miss Violet Halberstrom. Her live eyes exchanged with his dead ones some incantatory gleams.

"I could settle down here," she thought. "And work for the dead. I think that I could love this priest."

The summer was very hot. Father Jimenez said, "The reason I do not do priest's work is that my fellows here, the dead, have no need for it. Above all, that work is to prepare people for death."

How interesting! Mrs. Wallabee had grown silent. She sensed that there was something going on between her traveling companion and the dead priest. She, too, lusted for Violet Halberstrom, although Violet did not know it. The priest's suspicion had been based on something real.

It was difficult not to desire Violet Halberstom. This young woman was truly a beautiful ripe peach, nectarine, whatever.

Time buzzed around her. One wanted to join in with time.

"Violet! Tell me that you care for me!"

"Of course I care for you! But I also care for other things."

That is what is so attractive about you, the priest thought.

Then he seemed of a sudden to remember what he was supposed to be doing.

"Are you ladies interested in a car? We can make you different kinds, either one based on one model or combining several. Take a look around."

Miss Halberstrom, looking, wandered, and the priest gazed at her. It had been like this, he remembered, too, when he was alive and had taken death on him, to become a priest.

IN CHINA

He got in his car and asked the chauffeur to drive him to the office where he was going to work that day. It was very early in the morning but already there were thousands of people in the streets. Almost all of them were riding bicycles. As the morning grew warmer and the pink sun lifted itself above the silvery coverlets of the clouds, the streets were even more filled with working-day life. Hurry, the official said. Hurry! But the chauffeur could not hurry because of the immense crowds in the streets. Tomorrow we will start earlier, the official said. Meanwhile, please, go quickly. Do the very best you can. The magician, who was waiting for the arrival of this official who was scheduled to rehire him for another six-month stint on the Huangpu River Cruise boat, lackadaisically did a few tricks—palming objects, taking things out of his sleeves, cutting and then restoring to its wholeness a length of rope. The official meanwhile was working with a little computer, which kept catching brighter and brighter yellow rays of the early morning sun. According to what I've calculated, he thought, it will be simpler to give him a contract for the whole year. That will lessen my responsibilities and will also spare him the unpleasant suspense of waiting once again to see if his work is approved. His work seems to me very satisfactory. And there is no reason to suspect that a magician of his calibre and of his rank will suddenly become an unreliable or unpatriotic performer. So let it be! Xu Zhang won't object. I'll have the final permission later today. This work and these thoughts done, the car has arrived and here is the magician, he sees him, entering his office. By now the sun is quite bright yellow white. Ah, Bo Hong, the official says, this morning I have good news for you. I really do!

MAN WOMAN AND DOG

The dog stayed in the car. She went into the café. Auguste was sitting at a little round table right next to the big glass movable walls through which you could see what was happening on the street. Althea felt discomfort in the front seat so she jumped into the back. He turned around and started then continued to get up to help her sit down in her chair. On light front feet, for a moment, the dog bounced. She had a bouncy sensation. Once she had her body collected in the back, she turned, rearranged herself and sat down, or rather, sat up. Her nose now was lightly touching the window. Her slender legs ran down from her throat to the seat. Hello, doggie! a passerby noted. What will you have, he ordered. She stayed coffee. Two bills, all right. The waiter crescendoed, beckoned. A five-o'clock laugh. It's quite early. She rearranged themselves. We spoke. We went to bed too early, she said. Made love. At first he didn't argue with her theory. The dog was not accustomed to being in Paris at this hour. Usually it was later or earlier. There was something in the light that made her keep turning her head about. He said, If we hadn't made love too soon we probably wouldn't have made love at all. A big dark man was walking determinedly down the street. I think this man must have resembled a man who once accidentally kicked her. When he passed, she whined. He looked, she whined. He smiled hand-gesture, she kept whining. Eh, chien, he said and he walked along. Jean-Christophe said: Why are women always ecstatic when they make love, whereas for us men such ecstasy is fairly rare? The woman, Robert said, because the woman is always in love when she makes love.

Otherwise she doesn't do it. Well, possibly. Althea barked and barked and barked. Who was there to save her? The car's windows were closed. Ruhwahff, ruhruhrrwahwahfff, Althea cried. Hélène couldn't hear her, however. She had gone to the restroom to calm herself because she was crying. To readjust her face, too. When she came back upstairs Auguste was holding Althea, panting, hairily, on his lap. Who leaped at Hélène but Auguste didn't wholly let her go. Stop stay stop, he said. Althea'd been so upset in the car. She found it also rather nervous-making here. She smelled, so hot. A clean dog but an excited one. Hardly hold you on my lap. We can make love again, he said, around the neck of the dog. And this time may be just on time. This was clever but didn't approach the real subject: Are men, or men and women, incapable of love? And, beneath that: what. Mild anxiety moved the waiter the people in the street and the sunny haze. It filled them. It was the tone of the day, shared by Althea. Are you feeling better? he said. Yes. Maybe we should give her something to drink.

GENF

The working class Italian man unbundled an Italian loaf of bread with a large hollow in it filled with some kind of pungent meat. I have to get off at Geneva because, while talking flirtatiously to Sandra, I neglected to go back to my compartment when the train crossed the border, and my bags, as a result, are in Austria. The Swiss promise to get them back to me sometime tomorrow. Sandra is a dancer and she has been dancing in Trieste. Now she lives in Geneva. She bends over slightly in the corridor. It attracts my attention. Her breasts are rather large and pretty, and this fact, at the thought of speaking to her, fills my body with a sort of heat—I find it a little too much actually—like steam heat in a hotel between seasons when, legally, it must be on but the weather doesn't necessitate it. Sandra, well, I say, after I have found out, I have to get off the train. Can I see you tonight? Yes, she says, but remember you can't expect too much of me. I am involved with someone else. Involved—did Sandra say *involved* or did she say *engaged?* She didn't say *married.* Out on the lake in a boat the next late morning: Sandra, should I stay? In fact, may I stay? No, she says, nicely, and the wind blows. The Swiss find my bags. You've found them, so fast! I said. (The end of romance!) Yes, said the brisk fat fellow at the railroad counter—he is pleased—Dot's Svitzerland!

PETER AND CASSANDRA

Ronsard and his friend and fellow poet Valdeluzes were walking in the valley of the Var. Each was eighteen years old. Pierre had not yet laid eyes on Cassandre (Salviati), of whom his idealizations were to form the substance of his great collection, *Amours*. Marc (Valdeluzes) was somewhat in advance of Ronsard in this respect: he had already seen the girl about whom he was to write his best poems. Her name was Anne Desmoulins and she was the daughter of a lawyer in Boule-sur-Var. Ronsard was envious of his young friend's precocity in love. What will my love be like? Ronsard wondered. Ronsard knew he was a better poet than Valdeluzes, and in the field of poetry being worse or better was just about all that counted. What you actually wrote, how much, and on what subjects, were substantially less important than how good you were. In regard to his status in this department Ronsard felt quite at ease. Still, his life wasn't helping. And he did need some help. Perhaps, after all, he wasn't meant to be a great poet—where was his subject? In such a state of dreariness of mind, Ronsard reached, with his friend, the line of plane trees that signaled the southernmost extremity of the town of Blois. There, two years later, Ronsard met Cassandre Salviati for the first and only time. To her, and to his memory of their brief meeting, he wrote a startling number of sonnets in the succeeding years.

Cassandre Salviati is there, in her gray-white silks, her rosy cheek, her ivory hand, a fan, green, in her left hand, oh she is dancing. Ronsard, clutch your heart! You can't reach it. No way to get to it. Your blood is beating. Something is. A violence, deep inside, caused by the outside. What a miracle! Quickly, go home and write!

Years later, shaken, distressed, Ronsard signed off writing about love in the following sonnet:

> That Love which tried to place me in the tomb,
> With weeping trees around Himself now lies
> In so dark place not even that Her Eyes
> Can enter there nor her Fair Limbs find room.
> Love that did lead me on and promised Soon
> Shall you find haven surer than the skies'
> Then left me piercèd and away He flies
> Now is Himself as dead in Time's cocoon.
>
> Midway to love and death I turned aside
> Said I shall love no more, no more compose
> Poems to what in death may solely end.
> Whereupon Love grew suddenly my friend,
> Implored me, begged me, promised her as bride,
> But I affixed a funerary rose.[1]

---

[1] *Ce dieu qu'au tombeau me mettre tentait* (Sonnet M)

UNKNOWN

The desire came back to him, but the girl was gone. Girl! She was a woman now, and had been for years. She had married six years after he'd met her, and that was in nineteen seventy-three. Now it was nineteen eighty-six. She was fifteen (was that right?) when he saw her for the first time in her sister's house; her room was next to his. That means she is twenty-eight now. That is not very old! He, on the other hand, is nearly sixty. That is not very young! She thought of him with pleasure, too, but not with desire. For her his identity had been subsumed into the drama of her own life, of her being alive and fifteen. In an ancient culture they might have been monarchs together, she continuing on the throne after his death. She would weep for him, but he was gone. In her floods, her actual torrents and storms of tears, she would imagine he was back, and he would be, in a way, given watery body by what she felt. Now if he dies she probably won't know it. Her laundry is hung on the line. It's an old-fashioned way to do it but that is what she likes—clothes dried inside aren't the same. He imagines her with the three children, the husband, their quarrels, their making up. He sees this: in bed with Bernard, her husband, she turns over on one side, away from him, and with her right shoulder at an angle of somewhat more than ninety degrees. The sheet is large, is not stretched, its percale accommodates her motion. She is a large woman. She was a big young girl. She had a mixture of depth of sensuality and of innocence that intrigued him, almost irresistibly, even when he was afraid he might be doing something wrong. But all they did together, the most intimate thing, was to run off under the low, overhanging branches of some trees and kiss. The sheet, as she turns now to the right, makes the sound of the leaves of those trees.

THE MOOR OF VENICE

Othello was a Black American painter living in Venice. He had a studio in the Dòrsoduro and very often in the daytime he sat in his favorite café on the Guidecca, looking at everything and everybody, talking, and drinking wine. His Desdemona was an aristocratic girl. She was not very pretty but she was very Venetian, which is not precisely the same thing as being very Italian. She lived with her family in a gigantic and pleasing palace, near (two palaces away) the one in which Byron had lived. If you rode down the Grand Canal, you could see the chandeliers glittering through windows into the night.

The Duca Di Duro liked Othello's paintings, and bought some. That is how the painter met Isabella Di Duro. She was his *belle laide* and he her *mécontent*. Her father, a gentle and rather effeminate man, was sleepily troubled and wryly twisted by this relationship. Isabella's mother, the duchess, was scandalized, but knew the love affair would end. Tolavon painted a large yellow and orchid portrait of Isabella.

Her father bought the painting. It was not only for his black skin that Tolavon was called Othello. He was also violently jealous. After three months of knowing Isabella, he came one afternoon to the Palazzo Duro, and saw her with her arms around another man's neck and her body against his. The white handkerchief pinched in her fingers looked like a rose; the stem was Augusto Del Tavo's spine. Othello walked past them, took a knife, and slashed at his canvas. He could as easily have slashed them. Instead he walked past violently to the door.

The man was Isabella's cousin, just back from his travels in the United States. Seeing the Tolavon canvas, he cried, Ah a Tolavon, a great one, the best I've ever seen! Isabella, moved by his enthusiasm, had thrown her arms around his neck. Isabella bravely went after Tolavon and found him—after three days. At first he wouldn't believe her. Then he did. Afterward, he was milder.

He repainted the painting. It was better in some ways and less good in others than the first one, and on the whole it was quite a different work. The duke liked it less but took it and hung it in his palazzo. It pleased him and troubled him; he was worried about his daughter. The sunlight blazed into the palazzo windows. His ancestor Andrea Di Duro had been right to construct a palace on the afternoon-sun side of the canal. Tolavon was pleased to have his big painting hung there. He even thought of changing his café, since from the one where he now sat, facing the Guidecca, the duke's palace couldn't be seen. He didn't do that, however. He did put some lire down and stood up and left his table and walked. Tolavon was beginning to be known and to sell his work. An independent life, and freedom, unrolled like flat waves at his feet.

Now, though, he stood out in the Dòrsoduro air, waiting for Isabella to come along. He felt the sea in the canal air on his skin, Putting a finger to his cheek, he found it came away cool, and damp—condensation!

Keep up your bright swords, for the dew will rust them, Shakespeare's Othello said. This one, Tolavon-Othello, had an idea for a painting: Isabella standing, with the dew-wet, misty Palladio, San Giorgio Maggiore, on the island just across from him, at her back.

THE WISH TO BE PREGNANT

A bird just sat on a tree branch outside my living room window and when it opened its beak, bubbles came out. They looked like soap bubbles. I have no idea what they actually were.

Serenity was not a main subject or even concern of the New York painters. A big bully of a guy, named Haggis Coptics, was strutting around the bars.

It was spring, and the alloys in the earth were melting. I saw my wife with the pot in which a chestnut soup was cooking. Right after our marriage she began to cook exotic and flavorful foods. I half-expected quickly to grow fat in this marriage, as L. Tagenquist had in his, but I did not. It was only a few years after this that mildly excessive eating began to cause me to put on some weight. One morning I looked in the mirror—"You are much too fat!"

A valentine was exchanged for a handclasp then a kiss and then finally another valentine from the shop. Held hands veered down-street together. For one the holiday had not replaced feeling at all. But this one was a dog.

Hello, said Jerry, coming up from behind me with a blindfold in his hand that, he said, he had just tied around the eyes of a girl. I fucked her in the basement, he said. Well, that's better than doing nothing, huh?

My wife came in from the kitchen. Lunch is ready, she said. Then, Oh, how I want to have a child!

THE NEW ORLEANS STORIES

1993–2000

CONTENTS

NEW ORLEANS SATURDAY AND
NEW ORLEANS SUNDAY

New Orleans boys
New Orleans girls
New Orleans men
And wives with pearls
All go fishing
Weekend days
In the junk
Where treasure stays
New Orleans Saturday Sunday

The weekend in New Orleans we spend most of our time collecting junk. It's a tradition in our family.

Saturday morning Pop gets up first and starts yelling at everybody else to get up. Mom gets up right away then but I roll over in bed and try to sleep a little longer but I never can.

We always have a big breakfast. Along with coffee and bread and butter there is usually some kind of fish. Today it's Mako shark. Mom fries it up and it tastes really crispy and good and not greasy or anything and makes a better breakfast food than you would think.

After we all finish the shark, Pop stands up.

Off your butt, everybody, Pop yells. It's time to go collect us some junk.

We all get on old clothes and we go out in the street then and start to look for junk.

We never have far to look. There is always a lot of junk on the street in New Orleans. There is more on the weekends than at other times because people are home from work and they have time to go through their things and sort things out and then throw away what they don't want which is what is the junk.

Everybody's different though and likes and wants different things and we find plenty of stuff that WE want in what other people don't. That's the beauty of collecting junk.

We do the bulk of our collecting on Saturday and then by Saturday late afternoon we have it all home and maybe even have a little time to start going through it.

Sunday bright and early we get up and go through the junk usually until early afternoon say one thirty two p.m. then we've got sorted out the stuff we want, we fix the rest of the (unused and unneeded) junk in piles and so that nobody will notice it too much we take out one of these piles every day.

So every day there is one pile of junk going out and it doesn't seem too strange.

Pop thinks it would be okay to take it all back out on Sunday but Mom is embarrassed because everybody is going to church and besides with that much junk outside the garbage man wouldn't collect it, not Monday or any day.

There would be an extra "carting charge" and maybe even questions and all stuff like that which our family doesn't need.

Anyway today Sunday's a very good day with a bright shining even if a little rusted toaster almost as good as new (Pop is fixing it) and a kind of grey cap for me and for Mom a real stiff plasticky kind of apron that has red hearts strewn all on the front of it and it says Happy Valentines Day.

Pop finishes getting the toaster fixed.

Here Mom Pop said. Now it needs getting washed.

Mom did it and dried it off and I put on my cape and she put on her apron and we sat down and made and ate some toast to celebrate.

It is always worth looking Pop said because you never know what you will find. He and Mom looked approvingly at the junk. I looked at it too.

Just think—from right out on the streets Pop said, eating some toast. And we were, too.

New Orleans Sunday
Saturday too
It's a big weekend
Just for you
Find that junk
Take it back
Not one thing
Shall you lack
New Orleans Sunday
Saturday too . . .

NEW ORLEANS MONDAY

New Orleans Monday
Mom and Pop
Feelin Fine
Nothing but rouble
In policeman's mind
You may see
Strange Victory
Some time
New Oh Monday Monday

 You would never believe the story of how we ended up hav-
ing a pet octopus.
I came home.
Mom was there.
She was sitting in about the middle of the steps.
Hi Mom I said.
Hi Sonny she said.
Mom looked unhappy. What's wrong Mom I said.
It's your father she said. Your dad, Pop.
Pop can do no wrong I said. That was a family maxim. Another
one was New Orleans is the best place to live. Another, not really a
maxim but more like just a saying, was Tell it to the fishes in Lake
Pontchartrain.
What's the matter Mom I said. Is Pop sick or something.
I secretly thought maybe they had taken Pop back to jail.

I thought about the fat man. He didn't do it I said.

Sonny you are growing up. It's time I have to tell you a few things.

Things like what Mom I said.

Things like about me and Pop.

What's wrong with Pop I said.

It's wrong with Pop and me Mom said.

Just then before we knew it a policeman was at the foot of the stairs.

Mrs. Henreid, the policeman said, I have got to inform you that your husband, Pierre-Louis Henreid, is presently in police custody.

Oh no Mom said. He didn't kill that man. About what?

I am not at liberty to disclose the reason for his incarceration at this time. But you and your son—it is a little boy isn't it?—are urged to accompany me down to the precinct station at this time.

Okay Mom said. Just wait till I go put on my clothes.

Mom had been sitting outside there in just a bathing suit.

All right take your time. But hurry. Do you want to change your clothes too the policeman said to me.

No in the summer I always just go around like this I said. I had one of Pop's big shirts on and it hung down over me I guess like a dress which is what made the policeman ask if I was a boy or a girl I suppose.

If he doesn't approve of these clothes he can lump it I thought. I didn't like policemen. They were always interfering in what we did.

Mom came out all dressed up, she really looked spiffy. She had put on a fluffy purple dress and purple shoes.

Just where do you think you're going lady the policeman said. This aint a party I am inviting you to but to a police station.

I am going to see my husband Mom shot back, and to see him I always want to look my best.

The policeman shook his head and said Okay lady and then we got in his squad car and went a long ways down to one of the furthest police precincts in New Orleans it was the one over near Lake Pontchartrain in fact right on its banks just a few yards of sidewalk away.

Pop was brought out all wet and a little dirty too and he was moving a little funny like maybe he had been a little beat up.

Here is your wife and your child—son the policeman said.

Hi Mom Hi Sonny Pop said.

What is the charge Mom said. She knew how to talk up to policemen.

There were some big squishy weird noises coming from the back room.

What's that I said.

That's an octopus little boy the police matron said. Did you ever see one and I said no so she took me back to see it. It sure was a big slimy scary purple-podded looking thing. I wouldn't want one of those in my house but that's just where we ended up with it.

All right, officer, Mom was saying to the police when I came out. I promise by my own head and by that of my son.

And you, sir, the police said. Yes of course I agree Pop said. I will do anything you want. And I will certainly abide by my wife in this instance.

So they let us go.

What happened was Pop had been illegally fishing with a big net in Lake Pontchartrain and had come up by accident with an octopus and the police boat had spotted him and brought him and the octopus both into the station though they'd had to fish for Pop he had jumped out of the boat and tried to swim away. There was a struggle when they got him and that's why he looked a little beaten up.

What he'd done was illegal but actually he'd ridded the Lake Pontchartrain and the people of New Orleans of a big pest because there weren't supposed to be any octopus there. So they said he was guilty but they would suspend the punishment and instead he would be obliged to keep the octopus he had caught as a pet for at least one year and under no circumstances dump it back into the lake under penalty of forty-five years in prison. (That was what they had asked Mom about while I was in looking at the octopus with the Matron.)

Well Mom you saved my life Pop said. And as for that other thing, about the woman—

Don't Mom said, in front of Junior.

I won't Pop said and about that I won't ever again. And you will see—

SQUUUSH! that thing was making a noise—it made me scared but I couldn't help laughing at the same time it and the noise were so funny—you'll see Pop said talking louder over the squush that things are going to be better than they ever have been.

Mom said I hope so. The sun was hot and Pop had dried out.

How are we going to carry this thing Pop said. The police said they would see to that and they piled us, Octo and all, in their truck and brought us home. First seeing Octo here was really really strange. It went squush!

Let it be a reminder to you Mom said, and Pop punched her lightly, jokelike, on the jaw, and then they hugged and kissed.

Octo went squush! again, and I went out to buy it some food.

New Orleans Monday
Pontchartrain
Hides its treasures
Every one
You may find
In your mind
Monstrous thing
Of every kind
New Orleans Monday

NEW ORLEANS TUESDAY

Doin' nothing
Sittin on the stairs
You Mom and Pop there
Nothin compares
To New Orleans Tuesday . . .

"I walked up the stairs one by one. I didn't expect to see Pop.
Pop was sitting at the top of the stairs.
Hi Pop, I said.
Hi, son.
Where's Mom, Pop?
She's inside.
I went inside. I saw Mom.
Hi, Mom.
Hi, son. Then, Where's Pop?
I said He's sitting on the stairs.
Yeah? Tell him to come in.
I went outside. Come on in Pop, I said.
Okay, yes, sure.
Pop came inside.
Hi Pop said Mom.
Hi, Mom he said.
Then we were all together, Mom Pop and I.
A faucet broke.
Pop went out to get somebody to fix it.

He came back. He had a young man with him, in overalls, about twenty-two. Fix this, said Pop.

The boy couldn't fix it. I told you I wasn't a regular plumber, he said.

Yeah, but you were cheap, joked Pop.

The young man said I'm not cheap if I can't fix the faucet and you have to pay me something anyway, for my time.

I'll pay you, Pop said, and I'll fix the faucet. It's worth having you here so now I have somebody who's supposed to be able to do this and I can show him how to fix it.

All right the young man said, how do you fix it.

Pop got under it. He said First you got to get under it.

To make a long story short Pop finally fixed the faucet. That had more or less shot the afternoon. All Mom and I and the young man had done was watch.

Well, how much'll that be? asked Pop.

Oh 'bout fifty dollars, joked the young man. It took all afternoon.

Okay said Pop here's the money. And he gave him some Mickey Mouse bills totaling fifty dollars. Each bill had on it instead of the face of a President the face of a character from Disney.

Thanks, said the young man, but, since I am not a mouse who lives in mouseland, I don't think I'm going to be able to spend this money. To everyone's surprise, he pulled out a gun.

Pop had really pulled a bad egg out of the basket this time.

Don't shoot! Pop said. There are women and children present. I'll give you the money.

Hand it over, the gunman said.

All right, said Pop. Mom, I'm just going to leave you and Junior here as a hostage while I go into the bedroom and get a fifty-dollar bill.

Pop came out of the bedroom disguised as a gigantic red bird. It was covered with lots of red feathers; it was a Mardi Gras costume. The boy was startled. Pop, as the bird, grabbed his gun away from him and shot him in the head. That stupid kid was finished.

White bright air flashed through the apartment. Mom had left a curtain ajar; and that was the sun.

At last our ordeal was over. Pop picked the dead body up and put it with the junk.

Every day we had a load of junk that went out.

Mom expressed concern.

In this junk they will never find him, Pop said. And if they do, we will just say the truth, that he tried to shoot us.

He added, We have witnesses.

Mom said, I didn't think blood relatives and your wife were allowed to testify for or against you.

Pop by now had completely taken off his big-red-bird outfit.

Well, they can't, he said. But this is a special case, since you were the only ones around.

Well, I guess so, said Mom. The sun was really shining, though it was late in the day. A spilled egg started cooking by itself in the kitchen it was so hot.

Well, Mom said, reminded I guess by smelling that egg, I guess I'd better go and make us some LATE lunch.

Yes, it really is late, said Pop. I think, if you don't mind, we should just call it dinner, and let it go at that.

Okay, Mom said. Come on, Buddy (to me).

Pop said meanwhile I'll just go and take out this junk.

Mom said, Be careful. She was afraid the stupid kid would fall out. But he didn't. And that was that.

Just a stairway
Plain and empty
Summer city
Crime a-plenty
New Orleans Tuesday . . .

NEW ORLEANS WEDNESDAY

New Orleans Wednesday
Sittin' here
The cops come 'round
And when they're done
They may be floatin' in
Lake Pontchartrain!

Well, the cops came anyway. It turned out they went through the junk and found the kid. Only Mom and me were home. Where is your husband they said. I didn't kill him, Mom said. We know that, said the policeman but where is your husband. Your father, he said to me. Where is your husband, they said. Pop come in then, wearing his rubber I-go-down-to-get-it-for-you-in-the-sewer suit. Hi Pop, I said. Hi Pop, Mom said. She said, Here are these two policemen. Oh, Whoops! Pop said. Do they think I did something bad? Well, I didn't. I am a peace—Phee-yew! Yelled one of the policemen. Can't you get out of those stinking clothes. I CAN'T STAND IT! I thought in police work you had to get used to stuff like that, Pop joked. Sure if they bother you I'll get out of it and just put on something else. Pop had seen them from downstairs and he had gotten out of his ordinary clothes and put on this stinky sewer suit that he kept for an emergency. Most people aside from Mom and me couldn't take the smell. Okay so I'll just change this, officer, Pop said, and WENT INTO THE OTHER ROOM. I was jumping with excitement but I didn't show it. I knew what Pop was going to do. I'll be right out! Pop said. Whew. 'Stink.'

No funny business! the policeman said. Oh don't worry, Pop called out, I know all too well what side I'm on, it's the police. This calmed them down a little bit, the two policemen, and they just stood there. Then Pop came out, don't you know it, dressed up like that big red bird. Death to all traitors! he cried, and, Protect all women and kids! And he gave them a bash, really hard, with the wings, they're filled with steel or lead or something but Pop can really move them, and these two policemen then were lying there dead, or at least not moving. Mom was scared. Pop said, Don't worry. Just let me get out of this funnyman outfit and get that sewer suit back downstairs. It stinks and even I can't stand to be around it. So he did and when we next see him Pop has on his regular clothes. We wrap the cops up in sheets and blankets and carry them down to the street. Pop knows some poor old guy with a truck that he talks into letting him use it and we pack up those policemen and dump them in Lake Pontchartrain after it's gotten dark. It is a hot and muggy night, with these mosquitoes you can hear but you can't see biting you all over your arms and neck and face. I hope this is the end of it, Mom said. And Pop put his hand on her shoulder. Don't worry, Eveline, I promise you, it is.

New Orleans Wednesday
Come along
And see
What life can be
In New Orleans Town . . .

NEW ORLEANS THURSDAY,
AND AFTER

Lazy days
Lazy mornings
Lazy afternoons
Lazy nights
New Orleans
Thursday . . .

Thursday five hundred policemen came and surrounded our house. Pop couldn't do anything. They led him out in handcuffs into the street and then into a big wagon and drove him off.

Mom and me went to see him in jail.

There's not a thing to worry about, Pop said. They don't have a shred of evidence. They've just absolutely trumped this whole thing up. It's a phony rap and I guarantee you, with my lawyers, I'm going to beat it, you can bet your bottom dollar on that.

Pop's lawyers were a couple of funny looking guys, both of them short and fat. Their names were Perkins and Perkins. I guess they were brothers. They had the same name and looked alike.

I asked Pop if they were twins. He said he thought so, but he wasn't sure.

I'm afraid they've cooked up some phony evidence, Pop said.

Here is what was the evidence. Both of the policemen were still alive, they had only been stunned by the bird wings, and by some miracle they had been able to swim their way out of the lake.

Even with these cops, though, the State didn't have much evidence. All the cops could say was that they went to such and such a residence, having such and such a suspicion, and that while they were there they were beaten to a pulp by a gigantic red bird. The next thing was they woke up in the lake.

Pop said he was terribly sorry, he would pay gladly all their expenses, that his neighborhood of New Orleans had been troubled of late by an immense red bird, no one knew if it was a real bird or a human-in-the-disguise-of-a-bird killer. He said the bird had attacked Mom and me, too, and the twin lawyers (I guess) had us come up to the jury and show the bruises and gashes and scratches on our arms and face. This was really places where we had been violently scratching at those mosquito bites, but the jury didn't know.

When I am released from bondage I will devote my every waking minute to seeing that this monster is eliminated or at least captured, Pop said.

For a long time there was a hung jury and then finally it was permanently hung, and Pop got off.

He came home in pretty good spirits. He was mad at first that Mom had burned the bird costume: it was Pop's favorite and he loved to use it at Mardi Gras. But pretty fast he saw the smartness of what she'd done and cried Honey! and gave her a big hug and kiss. Mom fried us up a big New Orleans style dinner of gumbo, shrimps, oysters, red snapper, and sting ray.

Pop said the great thing after all is to have such a good family.

On that we all pretty much agreed.

Comin' round
Seems like the worst day
Ever found
But stick with me
And you will see
What life can be . . .
New Orleans Thursday . . .

NEW ORLEANS FRIDAY

New Orleans Friday
Comin down
Into that old
New Orleans town
Watch your head
And watch your hair
New Orleans Friday
You beware.

Pop had a barber chair he used only on Fridays, morning and afternoon. He'd move it out on the street in front of our house and put up a sign he has that said Barber. Expert Elegant Barbering. Haircutting Outdoor Salon. Shampoo and Cut, $7. Shampoo only, $3. Cut only, $5. You saved one dollar if you got the cut and the shampoo together. There was other stuff he would give you, too, for another dollar or two, like hair lotion and some stuff that dyed your hair. Pop stood up behind the chair with a towel over one arm and a scissors in his other hand and smiled and the people traveling in the neighborhood sometimes came to him for a shampoo and cut but mainly it was the people in our neighborhood, who liked the way Pop cut their hair. Mom usually did the shampooing. Mom also did manicuring by special request ($4.50). If anybody wanted their shoes shined, I did that ($0.35).

When word about Pop's trouble with the Law got out, more people came and less people came. More came out of curiosity and less came to have their hair cut, some being afraid to sit down in front of a man with a big scissors in his hand when he might be a murderer. Pop took this change in business philosophically, saying to Mom and me, Well a good thing is we got more time on our hands to be a family together and talk over things.

Pop and me talked about the chance of New Orleans getting a major league baseball team, which we both and a lot of other folks thought it should have because it was always right up there when people talked about American cities it was one of the major names and Pop thought it certainly deserved a major league team. We talked it should be called the Royals and we were pretty mad at Kansas City that they already had that. One Friday, it was really sunny and hot, we were talking about this, and Mom piped up that maybe the New Orleans team could be called the Bayous and me and Pop thought that was funny but maybe a pretty good idea after all, so we were talking when this man came up he was pretty big and fat and had a white shirt on that seemed starched on to him and black pants that were too hot for wearing there then and black shoes and a bowler hat but no tie. He had what looked like pearly buttons on his shirt. He gave Pop a ten dollar bill and said Give me a complete treatment.

Well, Pop went at it as thorough as he could and this man didn't seem to be in any big hurry, so Pop really gave him the business, Mom shampooing and then did his nails, Pop said Do you want the nails that will be an extra four dollars and the man reached into his pocket and gave him a five-dollar bill, that made fifteen dollars in all, and Mom was buffing the nails and Pop was clipping away at this guy's hair and even clipping hairs out of his nose and ears and eyebrows and all that stuff and put slicker on his hair and some black dye and boy when that guy came out of that barber chair he might still have been too dressed up and too hot but he looked great, I bet like he never before looked in his whole life. Pop held up a mirror so he could see what a beauty he'd become and the man smiled and said thank you to Pop and Mom and even to me and he gave each of us another dollar bill.

After he left Pop was feeling a little worn out from all the work he'd done and said Boy I feel like going jumping into Lake Pontchartrain like them policemen and not working any more today seeing as how we already got eighteen dollars and we all laughed knowing Pop was going to stay there and hope to get a couple other clients like that. Usually he would make maybe twenty twenty-five dollars, the most ever was forty-five or fifty or something on a Friday but today he already had eighteen dollars and it was only nine thirty A.M. Of course three dollars of that was tip but we always put all the tips in the general slush fund and then Pop would dole out to us the amount he thought we needed afterwards. Well, Pop had just sat back in his barber chair for a minute to rest when we heard a big BANG! like somebody firing off a gun. Some men in suspenders and shirtsleeves come running from the corner of our street yelling help! help! murder! stuff like that. Pop said Whooa there! and got Mom and me to help him strip down the barber chair and roll it back inside. He told Mom and me to stay inside and that he would go out and see what was the trouble.

Well, wouldn't you know it, this fat guy we had spent so much time on had gone and gotten himself killed. It seems he had come to New Orleans to shake down a pimp or something I didn't know what they were talking about but only knew that this guy had walked into some kind of trap that was too big for him and he had gotten himself rubbed out. Pop was telling us the story that night, when we were having stingray again. Mom said isn't that a tragedy because he seemed like such a nice man and he was very generous to us, too. We certainly, mainly you Pop of course Mom said, made him look good. I bet he never looked that good in his life, and I am glad we gave him the chance to look that way, like his whole best self, the way his mother would have wanted and the way the Lord God meant him to be, just that once anyway, before his death. And Pop said yes he was glad too and that if you could do a service to mankind, no matter how small or menial it was, and no matter when or how it happened, even if it was right before the person was going to get murdered, that you had done something to make the world a better place to live in. We felt sad about the fat man all the same, and we held a little vigil for him, trying to remember him and exactly what he'd said and done while he was in Pop's chair and even the little bit before and after too. Mom lighted a couple of candles and we just sat there with the lights off and pictured him coming up to the chair, asking for the "complete treatment," agreeing to the manicure, shelling out the extra money for it, then looking pleased and giving us all tips at the end. It really is a shame he got killed Pop said, after it was over. And he said You never know what you are going to run into in New Orleans. That is the truth.

New Orleans Friday
Rolls around
Big new fat man
Comes to town
Watch out watch out
They'll cut him down
Cut . . . him . . . down
New Orleans Friday . . .

NEW ORLEANS CHRISTMAS

Watch your step cause
Santa Claus
Goin to come
And set new laws
Got to get
Self in step
In time because
New Orleans Christmas

I came home Christmas morning and Pop was sitting on the steps.

Merry Christmas Pop I said. Hi Pop I said.

Merry Christmas hi son Pop said.

He was eating what looked like a pot of glue.

What're you eating Pop I said.

That's for me to know and for you to find out Pop said. He laughed then and went inside.

I had been gone down to the gas station to get some oil but I couldn't find anyplace open on Christmas Day.

Mom and Pop didn't care. What it really was was a surprise.

It was a surprise for me that they had to have me out of the house so they could set it up to be ready when I got back.

The sun was shining like fury in the old living room window.

I went in there after Pop said No not now wait then come on in Son.

I figured there was some sort of surprise.

And sure enough it was. It was a real big red and blue bicycle. I'd never seen anything so wonderful in my life.

Oh shit I said that's

Watch your mouth Junior Mom said. She's right said Pop

Beautiful I'm sorry I said but wow hey really thanks Mom and Pop you both shih—well oh that's just too much I mean it is for me isn't it.

It's for you and it's also for Mom and you Pop said.

I felt weak. Mom and me? How come?

It's you can use it just about most of the time Pop said and also it's a house bike that you and Mom can use for family errands, shopping and emergencies and the like. Well really it's yours but for emergencies say it's for the whole family as well.

Gee that's just fine Pop I said. I was aching to get my hands on it. I wanted to twist those handlebars in my palms.

Oh Pop I said oh Mom I love this bike. Can I take a ride on it.

I don't see no harm in that Pop said. Do you Mom?

And Mom said No, so I bumped this old pumper down the steps and got her out onto the street and rode on her far and wide all over New Orleans and didn't see a durned gas station open I wasn't really looking but just noticing and by the time I got back home it was dark and Mom and Dad were already asleep.

They'd left a big note for me on the door: Merry Christmas, Son. Hope you enjoyed your bike. Unfortunately soon you may have to give it up because it's stolen merchandise. But we are glad you got through this day without being stopped, which we thought you probably would because it was Christmas.

Tomorrow we're going to use it for some "family purposes" and then within a day or so after that I should probably put it back where I took it from so I don't end up in jail. Love Pop (and also signed "Mom").

So that was my Christmas bike.

I was sad to be going to lose it but hell I got stuff of one kind or the other almost every day, like my cap and all, so I wasn't too sad.

She really was a beauty though and she rode like you wouldn't have to be pumping her at all unless you wanted to go fast which I did and who cares if it made me ache it was one of the best days of my life.

New Orleans Christmas
Strolls around
Lookin for children
In New Orleans town
Gives them presents
If they're good
Just like any
Christmas should
New Orleans Christmas

THE SOVIET ROOM
2000

Every house—and apartment large enough—used to have what was called a Soviet room, where, if they liked, people could sit around and talk about Communism. The Soviet room in our apartment was about ten feet wide by thirty feet long. It was possible to feel a little crowded in it; it was like a corridor. Like "a corridor of history through which we, with the rest of mankind, are passing" as one of our visitors said.

I remember many lively discussions there, though I was just a child. My main interest at the time (when I was nine or ten years old) was acting in school plays. I liked being in Shaw and Ibsen plays particularly. "You shouldn't let yourself be put into those bourgeois plays," said Mr. Barrelson, one of our frequent guests. I said Okay okay though I didn't know what he meant, but those are the only plays around, the only ones my school is doing, so I want to be in those.

At least they're not doing Noel Coward and Arthur Wing Pinero and other such trash, said Linda Lillienhauser, who was another regular. Shaw and Ibsen, you know really aren't so bad. Sunshine blazed into the Soviet room's two windows and hot tea was served, with cookies or sometimes with buttered bread. One time Ashkenazy spoke to us, of some aspect of Soviet mining, and we were enthralled.

Later we heard that Ashkenazy had gone off with a married American woman and also that he had renounced his Soviet ties. Most of us didn't believe that. However, after a while, it was evident that it was really true. Others deserted the cause as well. And soon there were so few left that we didn't actually know any of them and the Soviet room was closed.

My mother had it converted into a closet. After my father died, she began collecting old clothes, which then she would give away. The clothes were stored in the old Soviet room.

One day a heavy Russian ermine coat hung mysteriously turned up in the room which my mother had no memory of buying or of being given. She stared at it in wonderment, almost in fear, and then called me to come and look at it, too.

It is the spirit of the Old Soviet room, come back to remind us of what once was, my mother said. I laughed, when she said it, because it sounded so much like something in a play. Well, we'll see, my mother smiled and said, what happens next. At least she wasn't frightened any more.

However, she locked up the closet and kept it closed for sixty days. When she opened it and looked around for it, the Soviet fur coat was gone. Lev Ashkenazy pressed the buzzer at our front door, wearing it, two weeks after that. My mother expressed her surprise. Lev revealed to her that in fact the coat was his. He had left it by mistake in the room and then picked it up the next time he was there. But how did you get into the room?

Lev said there was a passage, which led to the old Soviet room from the outside of the building. It had formerly been an air shaft, now no longer used.

My mother trembled. You, you have been coming and going from the room? she asked. Lev nodded his furry head, tipped up his glasses to his forehead from the bridge of his nose, smiled, and said, Of course! A small cell of six of us has been using the room for the past three months. We didn't tell you because we didn't want to expose you to unnecessary risk. What we've been doing has been potentially very dangerous. But now no longer. Gorbachev has succeeded in revamping the Russian state. We are his American team, doing what we can. You have been doing this in our room? My mother said. She was almost fainting from excitement. Then, our room has helped! Because of it you have done good for the communist cause! Well, not exactly but in a way, yes, said Lev. He took my mother in his arms. I want you to be my wife, Olya, he said. His voice was husky but not dark. I can go back to the motherland now and I want you to come with me. But what about the woman you ran off with? My mother said. Simple. She never existed. That story was a cover for what was really going on. Well? he said. He was still holding onto her. Will you be mine? I didn't know you cared for me Lev, she said. But now you do, he rejoined as she said yes yes yes: I will go with you and be your bride. But what about Samantha and the room? Oh I'll be all right mother, I cried, as happy as I could be in her happiness. You needn't worry about me! Right now I'm being offered lots of parts. As for the room, I'll fill it with my costumes. And maybe, if there is ever need for more discussions, I'll use it again! We all smiled and shook hands on that.

Colophon

The Collected Fiction of Kenneth Koch was designed at Coffee House Press in the historic warehouse district of downtown Minneapolis. The text is set in Spectrum with Officina Sans titles.

Funder Acknowledgment

Coffee House Press is an independent nonprofit literary publisher. Our books are made possible through the generous support of grants and gifts from many foundations, corporate giving programs, individuals, and through state and federal support. This book received special project support from the National Endowment for the Arts, a federal agency. Coffee House Press receives general operating support from the Minnesota State Arts Board, through an appropriation by the Minnesota State Legislature and from the National Endowment for the Arts, a federal agency. Coffee House receives major funding from the McKnight Foundation, and from Target. Coffee House also receives significant support from an anonymous donor; the Buuck Family Foundation; the Bush Foundation; the Patrick and Aimee Butler Family Foundation; Consortium Book Sales and Distribution; the Foundation for Contemporary Performance Arts; Stephen and Isabel Keating; the Lerner Family Foundation; the Outagamie Foundation; the Pacific Foundation; the law firm of Schwegman, Lundberg, Woessner & Kluth, P.A.; the James R. Thorpe Foundation; the Archie D. and Bertha H. Walker Foundation; West Group; the Woessner Freeman Family Foundation; and many other generous individual donors.

This activity is made possible in part by a grant from the Minnesota State Arts Board, through an appropriation by the Minnesota State Legislature and a grant from the National Endowment for the Arts.

MINNESOTA
STATE ARTS BOARD

NATIONAL
ENDOWMENT
FOR THE ARTS

TARGET.

To you and our many readers across the country,
we send our thanks for your continuing support.

Good books are brewing at coffeehousepress.org

KENNETH KOCH (1925–2002) was born in Cincinnati and served in the South Pacific during WWII. A poet, playwright, novelist, and Columbia University professor, Koch also published five books about reading and writing poetry, including the groundbreaking *Wishes, Lies, and Dreams*. He was the recipient of the Bollingen Prize, the Bobbitt Library of Congress Prize, and the Phi Beta Kappa Award for Poetry, and was a finalist for the National Book Award and the Pulitzer Prize for Poetry. In addition to *The Collected Fiction of Kenneth Koch*, posthumous publications include *The Art of the Possible: Comics Mainly Without Pictures* (Soft Skull) and *The Collected Poems of Kenneth Koch* (Knopf).